Praise for *A*

"From Jewish synagogues and rites to the foundations of faith and love, S.W. Leicher deftly crafts a landscape in which kindness and forgiveness too often only emerge after violence and loss.... Replete with images of these transformation moments and the challenges which overlay them, Acts of Atonement is filled with powerful insights and revelations... highly recommended." ~ D. Donovan, Senior Reviewer, Midwest Book Review

"The core beauty of Ms. Leicher's brilliantly written Acts of Atonement *lies in how deftly it draws us into the pain, irrationality, and joy of family, captures the nuances of love between two women, and tests our personal capacity for tolerance, acceptance, and empathy."* ~ Michael J. Coffino, author of the multi-award-winning novel *Truth Is in the House*

Praise for *Acts of Assumption*

". . . The people and worlds in Acts Of Assumption are singular and universal at once, and vividly drawn. Leicher is a novelist to watch." ~ SJ Rozan, award-winning author of *Ghost Hero*

"In her debut novel, Leicher presents a sweeping tale of faith and family that explores the abiding love between two independent women. . . Readers will find joy in the passion and depth of their commitment.". ~ Susan Gregg Gilmore, author of *Looking for Salvation at the Dairy Queen*

"[Acts of Assumption] is a rare book that can be read by everyone who wants to understand the richness of diversity in contemporary America. . . . Compulsively readable. I highly recommend this book." ~ Dr. Rosa Gil, author of *The Maria Paradox: How Latinas Can Merge Old World Traditions With New World Self-Esteem*

"Serach's and Paloma's voices are so eminently engaging and alive that ...despite the toll of living against expectation...the novel assumes their right to a happy ending—together." ~ *Foreword Review*, January/February 2019

ACTS OF ATONEMENT

a novel

S.W. Leicher

ISBN #978-1-940189-30-7

Twisted Road Publications

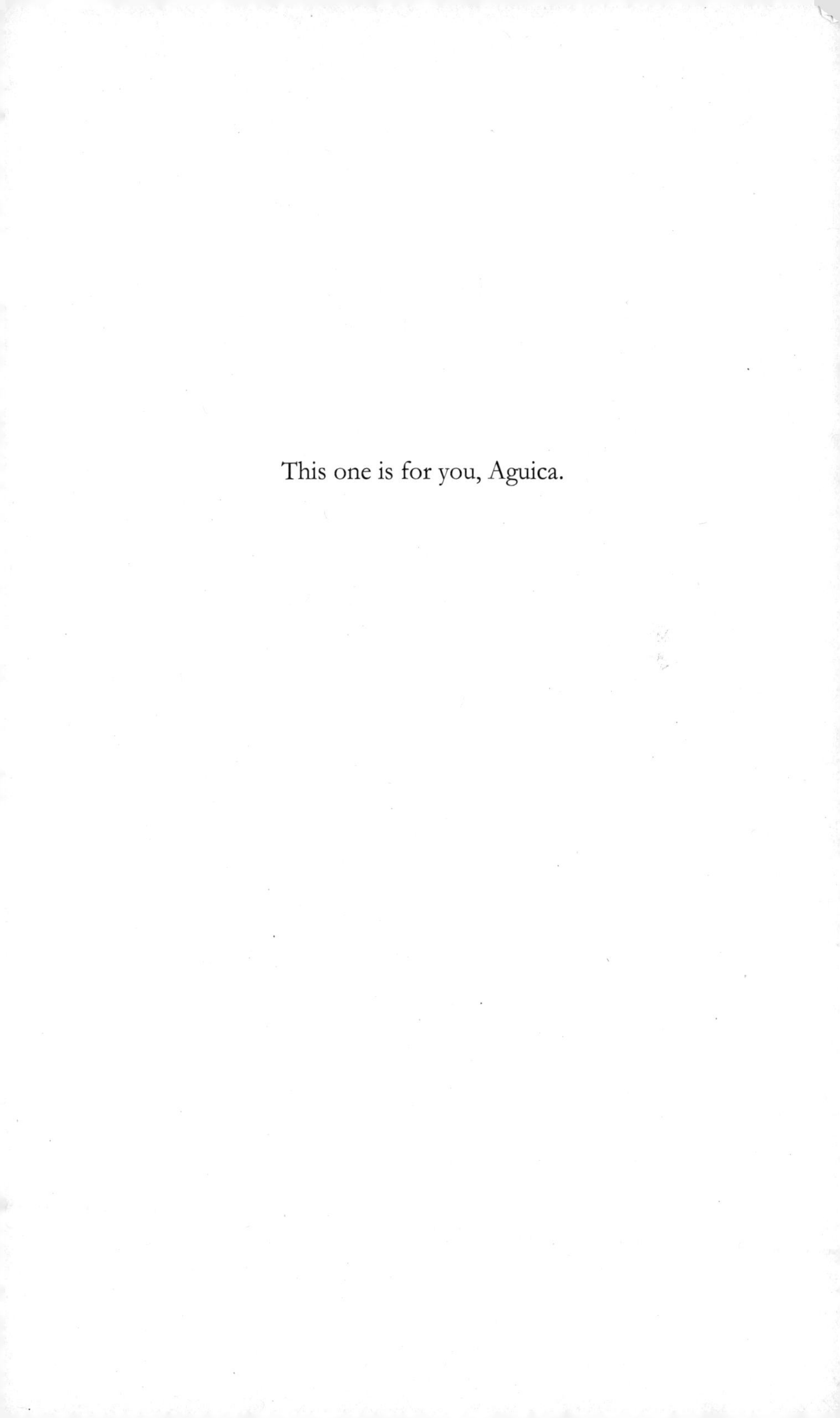

This one is for you, Aguica.

CONTENTS

Definition of Atonement:

1. *Satisfaction or reparation for a wrong or injury; amends.*
2. *Reconciliation (archaic).*
3. *"At-one-ment"—unity (from the Medieval Latin; compare Middle English "onement"—unity).*

From Merriam-Webster Dictionary

"The only thing worth writing about is the human heart in conflict with itself."

William Faulkner

CAST OF CHARACTERS

GOTTESMAN FAMILY

Serach Gottesman—the eldest daughter of a Haredi family from Boro Park, Brooklyn. She lives in Prospect Park South with her partner, Paloma Rodriguez, and works as an accountant.

Rav Shmuel Gottesman, AKA Shmuely—Serach's brother, the youngest child and only son of the family. He is a teacher at Jerusalem's *Yeshiva Derekh ha-Emet* and is married to Ruchel Seligson.

Beile, Mierle, Chava and Shayna—Serach's younger sisters.

Ya-akov Rapaport—Mierle's husband.

Reuven Gottesman—Shmuely's first cousin.

Batya Gottesman—Reuven's wife.

Reuven and Batya's son, Nussen Gottesman, and three other (unnamed) sons.

RODRIGUEZ FAMILY

Paloma Rodriguez—The Bronx-born only daughter of a Colombian immigrant mother. She lives with Serach in the house that she inherited from her first employer. She works as a nurse.

Manny Rodriguez (m. Beatriz)—Paloma's older brother. Co-owner of the *Los Milagros* Auto Repair Shop

Oscar, Roberto, and Ramon Rodriguez, AKA *Negrito*, *Gordito* and *Anteojitos* ("Little Blackie," "Little Fatty," and "Little Eyeglasses")—Manny's three sons.

SELIGSON FAMILY

Ruchel Seligson Gottesman—Shmuely's wife and the youngest member of the Seligson family.

Yehuda and Binkel Seligson—Ruchel's parents.

OTHER FIGURES OF NOTE

Various other teachers at *Yeshiva Derekh ha-Emet.*

Frank Davis—Paloma and Serach's part-time housemate and good friend. He is a concert pianist.

Fernando Reyes—the son of the founder and co-owner of the *Los Milagros* Auto Repair Shop.

Kae-Dang Jeung—Frank's concert clarinetist boyfriend.

Frayda Goldblatt—Serach's good friend from her old Boro Park neighborhood.

Etha Burnett—Paloma's good friend and former colleague from Maimonides Hospital.

Carlota Quiñonez Regalado de Bianchi, AKA: *La Piranha Salvadoreña* ("The Salvadoran Piranha")—Co-founder and President of *¡Adelantamos—El Bronx!* (Onward—The Bronx!).

Victor Bianchi—Carlota's Argentinian businessman husband.

Ricardo Peña and Anatolie Balescu—doormen in the Bianchi apartment house.

Consuelo Acosta Muñoz—the Bianchis' housekeeper.

Marta Figueroa—Bronx-born co-founder and Executive Director of *¡Adelantamos-El Bronx!*

Magdalena Torres and other participants at *¡Adelantamos-El Bronx!*

Evelyn Porter and Edna Gallagher—teachers at St. Gertrude's School for Girls in the Bronx.

Assorted students at St. Gertrude's School.

Bernardo Suarez—Bronx Borough President.

Mendel Schacter, Esq.—civil lawyer and Serach's client.

Shulamit Robinson, AKA: *La Hormiga Colorada* ("The Red Ant")—Mendel's niece and a criminal defense lawyer.

Dalisay Hipolito—Ruchel and Shmuely's Filipina housekeeper.

André Johnston—House Parent at The Excelsior School.

PROLOGUE: The First Yahrzeit

"He who conceals his sins does not prosper."

Proverbs 28:13

May 2018: Jerusalem

Rav Shmuel Gottesman ("Shmuely" to his familiars), youngest teacher at Jerusalem's *Yeshiva Derekh ha-Emet*, was a man of entrenched habits. On Sundays, Mondays, Tuesdays and Thursdays, he worked late and then joined the end-of-day prayer services in the school's Assembly Hall. On Wednesdays and Fridays, he left campus at 1:00 and stopped in at his house for a bit of lunch and some further study before attending the services at his local *shul.*

On the Wednesday in early May when everything began to shift, however, he had a task to perform that required different arrangements. He remained on campus long past his last class, prayed with his colleagues, and then slipped back upstairs while everyone else headed off to dinner.

He reached the now-empty second-floor corridor, traversed its length to his office, unlocked the door and—without bothering to switch on the light—sat down at his desk.

"We honor the anniversaries of our loved ones' deaths by remembering them in the flame of a *yahrzeit* candle," he sighed, as he reached forward to turn on his computer. "I will mark the first anniversary of losing Serach by recalling our Skype visits by the glow of this electronic device."

If anyone who mattered were to learn what he was doing, what might they think? That it was foolish—blasphemous, even—for him to take part in such a *meshugge* observance? Yes. That it was sinful for him to be pining away for his renegade sister in the first place? That, too.

And what would Serach herself say?

She'd say: "Why you've invented a whole new religious practice, Tatteleh! How very enterprising of you!"

His half-smile at the memory of her teasing voice faded almost as quickly as it had arrived however, as his computer burst into life. For the collection of icons that materialized on his monitor did not, of course, include the Skype symbol that—for the five long years of his own yeshiva training—had broadcast Serach's presence. Had let him know that she was poised at her desk back in Brooklyn, as eager as he was to take part in one of the monthly virtual family visits that the school allowed its students.

He stared for a few seconds at the spot into which that bright little shape had reliably popped. He acknowledged his role in erasing it for good.

Then he shut his eyes tightly and allowed himself to mourn. Sitting in the dark—arms wrapped tightly around his chest—*Yeshiva Derekh ha-Emeth*'s most rapidly-ascendant scholar began bobbing back and forth in front of his monitor as if he were parsing a sacred text.

It was several minutes before the approaching ruckus brought him abruptly back to his senses. And just in time, too! For there were Rav Goldshteyn, Rav Adelson and Rav Zekind, unexpectedly barreling down the hall, arguing at top volume as they always did.

Chas v'cholileh they should peek in and catch him in that secret, embarrassing act.

Shmuely stood up and bolted out of his office—slamming the door behind him and waving peremptorily back at them over his shoulder.

Rav Zekind, glancing through the window at the top of Shmuely's door to note that the computer was still on, called out to his colleague to come back and attend to it. But it was too late. Shmuely had already rounded the corner and was speeding down the stairs.

And thus it was that Shmuely's monitor—with its screensaver of a Jaffa orange grove and its unequivocally missing Skype icon—continued casting its implacable rectangle of light into the dimness of the office, deep into the night.

PART ONE: Curtain Calls

"A joyful heart makes for good health; despondency dries up the bones."

Proverbs, 17:22

"The Lord is close to the brokenhearted; those crushed in spirit He delivers."

Psalm 34:19

May 2018: Brooklyn

1.

It was the tenth time that morning that Frank had launched into Prokofiev's Second Piano Sonata. He never got beyond the first page and at times seemed to be simply banging and re-banging through the same five measures.

Paloma's head hurt. She was already panic-stricken about the speech she had to write, and Frank's cacophony was further splintering her concentration. She leaned over to rest her forehead on the cool marble of the kitchen counter. The pounding in her temples continued.

She slipped quietly into the living room to stand right behind her erstwhile housemate. She watched his thin frame flex convulsively over the keyboard and forcibly prevented herself from yanking those sinewy arms away from their gyrations. She then tipped slightly forward and gently (almost imperceptibly) stroked the back of his neck with one fingertip.

Frank stiffened immediately and stopped playing.

"Frank, for the love of God," she said in a voice that was sultry even under the most trying of circumstances. "For the love of our beloved Blessed Virgin Mary. Please give it a rest."

Frank paused with his fingers held half an inch above the keys.

"It sounds perfect. You will be brilliant. Please, Frank! I've gotten nowhere on my draft, and it makes it twice as hard when you keep playing that… passage… over and over."

Frank shut his eyes.

"It does not in any way sound perfect," he said, without turning around. "And may I remind you that I am performing it in front of twenty-five hundred people in less than two weeks?"

Still, he relented, closing the piano lid over the keys, deliberately and primly.

"I'll grant you one hour of silence, Paloma."

"Well… actually… I was hoping you could also… maybe help me think through what I need to say? And how I should say it?"

"You don't ask for very much, do you?"

"I ask for everything, Frank. You're my best friend and I totally count on you."

"I am not your best friend. Serach is."

"Serach is my partner, Frank."

"Well, then… Etha is."

"Etha is my pal and colleague. But you are my oldest and dearest friend. As well as someone who understands the art of performance better than anyone else."

Frank sniffed.

"All right," he said, after a pause. "We'll make it an hour of… tips and enlightenment."

"It won't take longer than that, I promise. I'm going to ask Serach for help, too. And with the two of you contributing your brilliance, it will just… write itself."

"Well, let's hope so, dear. For everyone's sake. Meanwhile, go fetch Serach while I calm myself down from this rude interruption."

Paloma paused briefly in the ground floor bathroom to down two painkillers with a palmful of tap water before zooming up the two flights of stairs to Serach's study. Typically, she would stand at the half-open door for a moment to take in Serach's fierce concentration—and the singularly graceful tapering of her back. Today, however, there was no time to spend on that small reliable pleasure, so she just knocked briskly and walked in.

"How's it going?"

"Not as smoothly as I'd like," Serach murmured, her gaze fixed on the monitor. "This tax return is so complicated. This client is so demanding…"

"Well… maybe you should take a little break? Help me out with something?"

"Paloma! Don't do this to me. I need to keep going. I have only four days left to complete this thing. My every waking moment is accounted for."

"Serach, I'm under the gun too! The first draft of this speech is due Monday, and I haven't written a single word. I'm completely blocked. And tomorrow, my brother and his boys will be here for brunch, so that day is shot. I mean, I guess I could call him and cancel…"

"No, Paloma. Don't. I've factored their visit into my schedule and am very much looking forward to it. But if I'm going to enjoy it, I need to keep going now. I'm at my sharpest first thing in the morning. As you know."

Paloma walked up to Serach's desk chair, placed her hands on Serach's shoulders and bent to give her short-cropped, golden-curled head a kiss.

"That's the whole point. I need a dose of that miraculous early morning brainpower of yours. Can't you spare me just one little bit of inspiration? And then I'll leave you in peace till every decimal point on that ghastly tax return is firmly in place. Promise."

Serach shook off Paloma's hands and spun around slowly on the big green ball that she used as a desk chair. ("I read that it would help me improve my posture," she'd explained on the day that she'd first hauled it home from the store, hoisted it up the stairs and rolled it up to her desk.) She massaged her forehead once or twice before raising cool grey eyes to meet Paloma's wide-open black ones.

"Paloma…" she began, very deliberately, so as not to say something she might later regret.

"Serach! Even Frank is going to help me. And he has a big deadline, too. Super big."

"I was wondering why he'd stopped playing."

"And I've been wondering how you can work with all that racket."

"I like Prokofiev."

"Please, Serach! Please help me!"

Serach glanced up to register the fear that was dimming Paloma's typically mega-watt smile. It was disconcerting.

"Okay," she said, carefully shutting down her computer and standing up. "I'll do what I can."

They slipped down the two flights of stairs—Serach in front and Paloma behind—and entered the living room to find Frank tipping precariously backward in one of the Louis XV chairs, his legs stretched out long and his hands tented in front of his face.

"Sit up, Frank, we've arrived," said Paloma, taking a seat in the chair right across from him.

He slowly lowered his hands and brought the chair legs a half-inch closer to the ground.

"So, Paloma," said Serach, settling neatly onto the couch, "tell us all about it. What's this speech for? What's it supposed to achieve?"

"It's for a luncheon honoring our $100,000-plus donors. We'll be updating them on the sheer fabulousness of Manhattan East's Cancer Care and Research Unit. And trying to persuade them to increase what they give so we can become… even more fabulous."

"Will they be serving pheasant under glass?"

"No, Frank. The Development Director likes to show that it's… 'all about the patients.' That we don't waste a single cent on anything else. We'll be serving them rubber chicken, for sure. But we'll be dazzling them in other ways."

"Such as?"

"Well, the first speaker will be our Lab Director, who'll talk about using what he calls 'a pair of molecular scissors' to 'snip away' at cancerous genes. He'll be followed by the Director of Research. She'll describe all the miracles we're seeing with Car-T-Cell Therapy. I've never heard either of them speak, but they're both known to hold their audiences spellbound."

She paused.

"And then," she sighed, "little Paloma Rodriguez—who's been at the hospital for barely six months and has never given a speech in her life—is supposed to stand up and talk about the Nursing Department. The Nursing Department! What on earth were they thinking? What can I say after all that impressive stuff?"

"They were thinking that you are the most dazzlingly attractive nurse that anyone has ever laid eyes on. And that beauty can be … very persuasive."

"Frank! Be serious."

"I *am* being serious, Paloma."

"If I were you," said Serach, narrowing her eyes, "I wouldn't even dream of trying to out-do the molecular-scissors man or the Car-T-Cell lady. I'd steer away from describing the exemplary training that you receive or the cutting-edge equipment that you get to use. I'd go right to the heart of what you do. *You.* Paloma Rodriguez."

"Serach, that's not helpful! What do you mean 'the heart of what I do'? What am I supposed to say about it? How do I even begin?"

"You begin with a question," said Serach. "All good speeches do. And all good sermons. And all good prayers. 'Why wasn't Moses allowed to enter the Holy Land?' for example. Or: 'Who is like unto thee, oh Lord?'"

"I'm not leading a prayer session, Serach!"

"Of course you are," said Frank. "May all the $100,000 donors become $200,000 donors and let us say: 'Amen!'"

"Frank!"

"Shush, both of you," said Serach. "Here's your script. You ask: 'How do you help people to heal?' And you answer: 'You provide them with the best medical care on earth. And you deliver it with… lovingkindness.' Don't you always say how you like to buy flowers for the patients who receive no visitors? And find time to sit quietly with them for a while when they seem inconsolable? Remind your audience of how terrifying it can be to face a disease as wily as cancer. To be pumped up with toxic chemicals. To fight sleep because you fear you won't wake up again. Tell them how nurses' small, kind gestures help bridge the divide between despair and hope. How their lovingkindness helps clear the path for healing."

She paused.

"Along with their medical expertise, of course."

"Serach, you're a genius."

"No, Paloma," Serach replied softly. "But I was once in that place of despair myself. And your kindness helped."

She smiled shyly at Paloma before glancing away again.

"And one last thing," she added—all business again. "Keep it short. My father used to say that six minutes into our rabbi's sermons, Mr. Birnbaum would start dozing. And at the seven-minute mark, Mr. Lesser would start whispering to his neighbor. So, make your points, bat your eyelashes once or twice and sit down. Leave them hungering for more—not hoping that you'll finally wrap up. And now, I absolutely must get back to that tax return!"

And she zipped out of the room.

"Well, I think I've got it," said Paloma, nodding to herself. "Frank—do you see why I love Serach so much? I'm going to lock myself up with my laptop and write down everything she said before I forget it. Leaving you to get back to your Prokofiev. Bang away as much as you want. It won't bother me now. I'm set."

Frank put up one beautifully elongated finger. "Not so fast, Paloma."

"No, Frank. I've got everything. Really."

"No, darling, you haven't. We have one more crucial matter to settle. How are you planning to show up to this event? In your headache-green scrubs? Or in one of your boho-chic, midi-length pleated skirts and a neckline-plunging tee-shirt topped by three unmatched necklaces and a jean jacket? Listen, I'll meet you at Saks Fifth Avenue on Tuesday evening—after your speech draft is approved and I'm done with my run-through—and we'll outfit you."

He paused.

"And never mind what it's going to cost. It will be a lot, but you can afford it. And—more to the point—you can't afford not to."

2.

Sunday morning at Paloma's house began as it always did when her brother Manny and his three sons—Negrito, Gordito and Anteojitos—were due to arrive for brunch.

Frank's alarm went off at 8:00 and he bathed, dressed and bolted out the door without bothering with breakfast. On this particular Sunday, he had the excuse of his trio rehearsal on the Upper West Side. But even when there was nothing else scheduled, he made it his business to flee the premises well before 9:00 on those Sunday brunch days—and to stay away till he was sure the rowdy crew of Rodriguezes would be long gone.

"Manny is okay, I suppose, but those boys give me hives," he'd once explained. "That oldest one—he's a nasty little thing, isn't he? And that youngest one—so strange. And that middle one—so awkward, fat and ungainly. Sorry, Paloma. You know it's all true."

Serach woke before 6:00 a.m. as she always did, did her morning exercises, and then sped upstairs to her office to sneak in a bit more work.

And Paloma—finally finished with her speech—allowed herself to loll in bed for an extra fifteen minutes before heading off to the kitchen to make the red beans, yellow rice, eggs, and sausages (a pound of those for Gordito alone) that her clan would expect.

She emptied two full pots of Bustelo coffee (extra-strong) into the big stainless-steel thermos from which she could replenish Manny's cup as often as he motioned for it.

She gathered up the midnight blue and gold Limoges china that she'd inherited (along with the house, the furnishings—and Frank) from her first major employer, the opera diva Judith Skollar.

She then headed off into the dining room.

She could easily have accommodated the whole crew at the big oak table in her oversized kitchen, but she loved the chance to indulge in the aesthetic pageantry that she'd learned under Judith's exigent tutelage. And part of that pageantry involved leading them all off to a table laden with fine china and crystal and real linen napkins.

She knew it didn't matter to them so long as the sausages were spicy and the coffee hot.

But it mattered to her.

She had barely finished her preparations when the front doorbell rang and Serach logged off her computer and sped downstairs to answer it. Paloma wiped her hands on a kitchen towel, glanced at the clock, and walked into the front hall, smiling at Manny's impeccable timing.

When her brother said he would arrive at 10:00 a.m., he arrived at 10:00 a.m. When he said a set of repairs would be ready by midday, the customer knew he could pick up his car at noon. It was one of the secrets of the *Los Milagros* Auto Repair Shop's success.

Negrito, Manny's oldest son, was the first to strut through the door, a small tight smile on his handsome face. He gave Paloma and Serach a brief nod before heading for the dining room. Gordito and his father entered next, shoulder to shoulder—each one nearly as wide as the doorway—so their joint entrance took some negotiation. And Anteojitos, the youngest son, straggled in last, head bent forward on his long neck, thick glasses sliding down his nose and the navy-blue canvas bag that he carried with him everywhere swinging back and forth in his hand.

Once inside, Manny drew his sister and her partner into a hug that lasted until Serach gently extricated herself so she could dash over to Anteojitos and give him a small kiss on the cheek. Gordito saw his chance and rushed forward to re-gather the two women into his own embrace, but before he could give a good tight squeeze his father grabbed him by the arm.

"Time to eat, *Mijos*," Manny said, casting a wary eye toward Negrito's back. He placed a hand heavily on each of his two younger sons' shoulders and steered them into the dining room.

Once everyone was seated and all the plates filled to capacity, no one said a word for a good long time. Eventually however, Manny scraped up the last of his eggs, leaned back in his chair and gave the contented sigh that signaled that conversation and movement could resume.

Paloma picked up the coffee thermos and looked to see whether Manny needed a third cup. Gordito reached past his father for another spoonful of sausages. Negrito stood up, slid away from the table and swiped a big silver bowl from one of the breakfront's shelves to place it on the floor behind his youngest brother with a loud bang. He tapped

Anteojitos on the shoulder and Anteojitos nodded back to him—up and down, up and down—and began fumbling in his blue canvas bag.

"So, Hermano," said Paloma, refilling Manny's cup and pointedly ignoring Negrito's antics. "What's up at *Los Milagros* these days? How's the repair business going? How are those two new mechanics working out?"

"Business is great," Manny replied. "And the mechanics—Negrito, cut out the *locura*—are doing great. They know what they're doing, and they've agreed to teach the boys the basics when they come to work with me next month."

"What exactly are Oscar and Ramon doing?" asked Serach, turning around in her chair to observe them. She had never fully understood the Latin passion for nicknames and persisted in calling the boys by the names with which they had been christened.

"I'm helping Anteojitos practice his aim," said Negrito—who never seemed to be listening but always was. "Watch!" And, in fact, Anteojitos—following his brother's movements like a cat—had begun pitching what seemed to be a bottomless collection of crumpled tin-foil balls from his navy-blue bag into the bowl as fast as Negrito could switch its location.

Manny reached behind him for his oldest son's arm as he sped around the table. "Cut it out, Negrito."

"Nothing doing, Papito," Negrito said, ducking away, but carefully avoiding the extra edge in tone that would have lifted his father out of his seat to deliver a fast swipe to his head. "Don't you see how I'm helping you? How I'm keeping Anteojitos nice and quiet so you and your sister and her girlfriend can talk?"

Manny found himself nodding, despite his better judgment. But then he caught himself, took a swig of coffee to mask his movement and muttered: "*¡Basta, Mijo!*" under his breath.

Paloma, meanwhile, continued to ignore the entire interplay.

"So," she said, piling Gordito's plate with more rice and beans. "Negrito and Gordito will be spending the summer with you at the auto repair shop?"

"Yes, Tía," said Gordito, between bites. "We're going to be learning the auto repair business."

"Though I don't know why we're bothering," added Negrito, as he continued to move the bowl from one spot to another behind his youngest brother. "Seeing as we're both going to be computer programmers and have no reason to learn to fix a car."

"You're doing it so you can contribute a little something toward your college tuition," said Manny in a voice with a potent trace of menace. "Sending you two through Lehman is no joke. And you're doing it because cars are becoming computerized. If you know something about *both* cars *and* computers, you may actually get jobs someday."

"And does Fernando's father still keep showing up at the shop, trying to run things?" asked Paloma after a pause. "Or did that stroke finally put an end to all that?"

Neither Manny nor Paloma ever referred to the auto repair shop's founder and co-owner by name. He was always just: "Fernando's father". The father of Manny's childhood best friend.

"For a while he would barge in every so often with his walker, make a mess of something and then leave," said Manny, reaching for more sausages. "But when Fernando's mother died a few months back—did I tell you about that? No? Heart trouble. Well, when she died, that all slowed down. And then he had a second stroke and that was that. I call him once a week. Ask how he is. Tell him about the shop. He can still speak a bit."

Paloma nodded. Then casually—almost coyly—she asked the question within her question.

"And Fernando himself?" she asked. "Is he finally back from his time in the military?"

Manny shook his head almost imperceptibly, then gestured for more coffee and watched with an unreadable expression as she poured.

"I had no idea you still thought about my old friend so much," he replied after a pause.

"Not so much," she said, glancing away. "And not usually. But sometimes … I find myself revisiting the old days. Don't you?"

"No, Hermana. I only move forward. Like a shark."

He gazed pointedly around the room—from fancy table to ornate breakfront to Persian rug.

"And like you," he added. "Usually."

"So will you also be working at the shop, Ramon?" Serach asked, breaking the silence. She smiled benevolently at Manny's youngest son.

"Anteojitos already *is* working there," said Manny.

"I'm the one who sweeps up, Tía," said Anteojitos, pausing for a moment with a tin foil ball in his hand. Like Negrito, he paid more attention than anyone generally gave him credit for—particularly when Serach was speaking. "Every day at 5:00, I go to Papito's shop and sweep up."

"Oh, for God's sake, don't get him started on how he goes to Papito's shop every day at 5:00 to sweep up," said Negrito, placing the bowl down with a thud and gesticulating to Anteojitos to return to their game. "Or we'll never get him to shut up. Hey, Anteojitos! Try to sink a shot when the bowl is way over here."

"He's certainly very good at it," said Paloma, as her nephew neatly made the slam-dunk. "Who knew that his aim was so true? Maybe you should get him into basketball, Manny? Or golf? Isn't there a golf range near Orchard Beach?"

"Yeah, Papito," said Negrito, moving the bowl even farther away. "Maybe you should teach him to play golf so he can ride around in one of those cute little carts all day. Or maybe get him onto a basketball court with a bunch of seven-foot-tall Black boys and see how well he does. Or… maybe you should tell Paloma what you actually *have* been doing with my brother."

"That's enough, Negrito." Manny clenched his fist, but Negrito sped swiftly out of reach to place the bowl at such a difficult angle that Paloma was sure her nephew would miss.

He didn't.

Serach contemplated Anteojitos' swift, flawless ability to calculate the precise angle and force required to land those tin foil balls right in the bowl, time after time, and sighed at how much of him was being wasted. She walked over to Negrito, took the bowl out of his hand and offered it to his younger brother.

"Here, Ramon," she said. "Re-arm yourself."

"I go to Papito's shop every day at 5:00 to sweep up, Tía Serach," he repeated, shoving the balls back into his bag. He looked up for a moment and then quickly looked away. "I sweep up the shop every day at 5:00."

"I think that's wonderful, Ramon," Serach responded. "And your aim is terrific, too."

She returned the bowl to Negrito and began scraping and stacking the empty plates.

"Are you all ready for dessert?" asked Paloma. "Serach bought you your favorite *rugelach*, Anteojitos. And I notice you brought some *cannoli* as well, Manny. Good call."

She ruffled her brother's crewcut—savoring the brief bristly friction against the palm of her hand for a moment before gathering up the remaining plates and turning toward the kitchen.

"What I've been doing with Anteojitos and his perfect aim," said Manny, in a voice that stopped both women in their tracks, "is taking him to the shooting range that is also right near Orchard Beach and teaching him to use a gun."

Paloma knew enough not to tangle with her brother when he took on that tone, so she didn't respond. But her brisk stride out of the room let him know exactly how she felt.

"What am I going to do with those idiots?" she asked when Serach arrived to place the plates down beside the sink and begin laying out the pastries on Paloma's largest Limoges oval platter. "What the hell is Manny thinking, teaching Anteojitos to shoot? He's barely sixteen years old. Doesn't he know that as soon as the *Crips* or the *Bloods*—or whichever gang is in charge of Fordham Road these days—get wind of that overgrown baby's skills they'll reach out to recruit him? Jesus! What can we do to stop him?"

"I'm afraid that your brother has his own ideas about what it means to be a man, Paloma," said Serach. "And part of that is learning to handle a gun. Plus, it's clear he wants to connect with Ramon any way he can. We can't stop him. Any more than we could stop him from pulling Ramon out of school. Though I haven't given up on that front yet. As you know."

"I do."

"So I suggest that we just focus on getting Ramon back into school and ignore the rest. Manny adores his sons, despite all his bluster. He won't let Ramon come to any harm."

"Oh, I know. And, by the way, I hope you appreciate how much he loves *you*. In fact, I hope you appreciate how much all four of them love you. Gordito would trail you all day like a puppy if you only let him. Anteojitos, of course, simply worships you. Even Negrito shows more respect to you than to anyone else."

"And I love them all back. They're my family. The only family I've got."

"Besides me and Frank, my darling," said Paloma, walking behind her partner and putting her arms around her. "I'm your forever-wife, despite our never having said 'I do's' in front of one of your rabbis. And Frank is everything to you that your idiot brother Shmuely is not."

She leaned in an inch more and began kissing Serach on the back of her neck.

"Paloma, stop it," said Serach, slipping away with something that was a little more than annoyance and a little less than anger. "Right now. Look: Manny is lurking in the doorway. He doesn't want to see you doing all that stuff with me, open-minded as you think he is. And he seems to have something important on his mind."

"He's wondering where the *cannoli* and *rugelach* are. Here, Manny, do me a favor and take this dessert platter out to your sons while I finish washing the plates."

Manny took the platter from her but didn't go anywhere with it. He planted himself right next to his sister, platter in hand, rocking back and forth on his feet.

"Paloma, I need to talk to you."

"Well, you're right as always, Serach. So, Manny. What did I do now?"

Manny said nothing but gave her a hard look.

"I'll take those in," said Serach, reaching for the pastries.

"No, that's okay," said Manny. "I'll do it. This won't take long. But meantime, maybe you should go sit with the boys, so they don't kill each other."

"Sure, Manny. Of course."

Once Serach exited, Manny stopped rocking and stood solidly in place.

"I have to teach him to shoot, Hermana, don't you see?" he said, his voice suddenly very hoarse. "He needs to learn to defend himself. He couldn't even finish eighth grade because the other kids all…" He looked down. "Because they bullied him so much. Christ, even his own older brother bullies him. If he learns to use a gun, at least I'll know that...."

"Manny, for Christ's sake. It's a totally fucked-up idea and you know it as well as I do. But it's clear that I'm not going to be able to budge you on it."

"Paloma—what am I supposed to do with him? He's a total…"

"Innocent. He's a total innocent."

"'Innocent' *es poco.* He's a walking target in that hellhole of a neighborhood we live in. Paloma—who the fuck *is* my youngest son? *What* is he?"

"No one has ever been able to determine that because—instead of taking him to the specialists who might give you some guidance—you and Beatriz simply stick your heads in the sand. 'It's just how he is, leave him be!' You let him drop out of school and basically condemned him to a life of sweeping out your shop and pitching tinfoil balls into a bowl."

Paloma put the plate she was holding into the sink and then turned to look back at her brother.

"Search is the only one who's ever given him any constructive attention," she said in a quieter tone. "But now—instead of building on what she's achieved—you've decided to teach him to shoot. Jesus, Manny."

"I have to, Paloma."

"You do not have to, Manny. You could find him a program that would help him with his problems, give him some skills, set him on the road to feeling better about himself. Teaching him to use a gun is only going to—"

Manny looked at her for a long moment with more pain than Paloma could remember seeing in her tough brother's eyes. Her first impulse was to run right up to him and hold him tightly, but before she could do that, he hurled the platter that he was holding—*cannoli*, *rugelach* and all—forcefully onto the ground.

"You have no right to tell me how to raise my sons, Paloma!" he said into the shivery silence that followed. "What the hell do you know about it—you who've never even wanted children?"

She swallowed.

"I'll tell you what you know about it," he concluded. "Nothing. *Nada*."

But before Paloma could fully register all the emotions that Manny's remarks raised for her, Serach came running in with Gordito close behind her.

"Go back to your brothers, Gordito. We're getting out of here," Manny said in a voice that was all-the-more-deadly for its sudden softness. He moved Serach gently aside before placing his hands firmly on Gordito's back to shove him out of the room. There was a brief commotion from within the dining room and then the front door slammed.

Serach edged toward Paloma and tried to embrace her, but Paloma just shut her eyes, shook her head and waved her partner away.

"What on earth happened? Did you keep harassing him about the gun?"

"No. Well, yes. I guess. Leave me be for a moment, won't you, while I sort out how I feel?"

"Okay," said Serach. She bent down and began picking up the largest fragments of the platter from the floor.

For several minutes there was no sound in the room but the clink of the china shards and the splat of the *cannoli* as Serach picked up the mess from the floor and tossed it into the garbage.

"He's a lot more broken up about Anteojitos than I'd ever suspected," Paloma finally ventured, as Serach took out a dustpan and broom and began sweeping up the smaller crumbs of china and pastry. "He can't figure him out and he can't help him and it's making him crazy."

"Well, what can we…?"

"Serach, that's the whole point. We can't do anything. You just said as much yourself."

"But perhaps we could—"

"Please, Serach. I've just been forced to accept that I can't make things any better. Which means that I'm done with all of that, okay? Please give me some space here."

Serach looked down to see that her thumb was bleeding from one of the shards. She put it in her mouth and sucked on it thoughtfully. It tasted of rust and powdered sugar.

She nodded to herself, slowly and unwillingly, and left Paloma to finish cleaning up.

Manhattan and Brooklyn

3.

Frank had totally outdone himself.

After two long hours cruising the length of Saks Fifth Avenue's third and sixth floors, he'd located the perfect gun-metal-grey MaxMara suit, creamy white silk shell and red kitten-heeled pumps for Paloma's debut. He'd stood sentry while she'd tried everything on and while she'd (reluctantly) paid for it. He'd then hustled her off to the jewelry department, picked out a pair of subtly glistening pearl earrings and matching necklace, and put them on his own credit card.

"You've already had several heart attacks over the cost of today's outing," he'd asserted over her protestations. "Besides, I'm being very well paid for this Carnegie Hall gig."

"But…"

"But nothing. The pearls are essential to the look. And an absolute necessity in every woman's jewelry box. Normally, it's the woman's paramour who takes care of that. But since Serach—much as I worship her—remains tone deaf in such matters, the task clearly falls to me."

"But it's all too much, Frank... For me *and* for you... There was no need..."

"Shut up, darling. Thanks to my efforts, we have achieved the impossible. We have packaged your rampant sexual allure within an ensemble of impeccable taste. Gravitas and seduction—an unbeatable combination. Your audience will take your speech seriously while every straight male in the room will also feel the inexplicable, irresistible compulsion to increase his annual contribution by far more than he'd planned."

"Okay, Frank," Paloma leaned in to give him a small, precise kiss. "You're probably right and I'm grateful. But can we please go home now? I'm—like—totally wiped. Who knew shopping could be so exhausting?"

In line with the Development Director's determination to avoid any sign of ostentation, the fundraising luncheon was held in the hospital cafeteria, complete with bare rectangular folding tables and paper tablecloths. The effect was completely undone however, the moment the donors sat down. The sheer force of their presence transformed those pedestrian surroundings into the stage set for a glamorous power lunch.

"How do rich people manage it?" Paloma asked Frank when she found a moment to report back on the day's events. "How do they take total command of a space like that? Is it their clothes? Their jewelry? Their hair-cuts?"

"It's their expressions, dear," Frank replied. "But really, Paloma—never mind all that. How did it go? How did you do?"

"Well, Frank…" she said, relishing the last few moments of his suspense, "I don't know how I knew it… but within two sentences, that room totally belonged to me. Those fancy donors were all mine. It was… palpable."

"It's a delicious feeling, isn't it?"

"It's the most magical feeling in the world. And when I wrapped up—and yes, I did it fast, just like Serach advised—I could tell they actually wanted more."

"That's what encores are for, dear."

"Well, there's no place for an encore at a fundraising lunch. But there was no need for one, either. It all worked out wonderfully."

"And so… I was right about the suit? The shoes? The pearls?"

"Worth every penny. I felt good. Hell, I felt great. I love you, Frank."

It was only with Serach, however, that Paloma felt comfortable enough to discuss the disturbing conclusion to that otherwise exhilarating event. And even so, it took some doing on Serach's part. Paloma was standing to clear the table of the remnants of the celebratory dinner she'd prepared when suddenly her face became serious.

"What?" said Serach, peering up at her.

"Nothing."

"Paloma—who do you think you're talking to? What's wrong?"

Paloma tightened her lips.

"Come on. The dishes can wait."

"Okay," Paloma said, slowly sitting back down.

"I'm listening."

"Okay. So, once the luncheon was over, a whole bunch of donors came up to me to say how much they liked my speech."

"But that's wonderful!"

"Yes, yes. But then one of those donors did something that totally spooked me. He was this tiny little man—very trim, very blond. He somehow pushed past everyone else to stand right on top of me—so close I could hear him breathe. And then he didn't say a word."

"Yes?"

"A moment later this woman comes to join him. And she doesn't say a thing, either. The two of them just hover over me like vultures till everyone else clears out, when the man finally starts to speak. He's got this accent I can't decipher and this really soft voice."

"People who speak too softly generally do it to make you pay attention."

"Yeah. Well, this guy clearly thought I should listen up. He says his name is Victor Bianchi, and this is his wife, Carlota. That they moved to New York City from Buenos Aires nine years ago for his 'business deals.' And that just after they arrived, he developed testicular cancer."

Paloma shook her head.

"I always marvel when a man can say that sort of thing to a woman without embarrassment, but he seemed perfectly at ease."

"Well, he knew you're a nurse."

"Well, maybe. Or maybe he just thought that every word he said—from 'business deal' to 'testicular'—was a jewel of wisdom. Anyway, it seems he was treated for that cancer at Manhattan East. 'The Cancer Care unit was nothing like what it is now,' he says. 'Still, the treatment I received was superb.' And then he explains that—while it was clearly the surgery and radiation that cured him—what he remembers best about what he kept calling his 'sojourn' was the nurse who cleaned his wounds and managed his catheter. 'No one else has ever touched me with such exquisite gentleness,' he croons in that whispery little voice. And then he nods at his wife and adds: 'Present company excluded, of course.'

"He waits a half-minute for me to take that all in. Then he says that while he's been making annual contributions of $100,000 to Manhattan East's cancer work for the past eight years, my speech convinced him to raise his donation to $300,000. In honor of that nurse. And of me. Then he grabs my wrist, brings my palm to his mouth and kisses it. Yuk."

"But Paloma—unctuous kiss aside—that's wonderful! What made you so upset?"

"I don't know. He made me feel like… he was expecting something back from me. Besides, he looked just like a little blond Ken doll."

Serach had no idea what a Ken doll was but knew better than to send Paloma off on one of her long tangents and said nothing.

"But what actually bothered me most was what happened next. With his wife."

"Yes?"

"I didn't pay much attention to her at first, except to take in how much taller she was than him. But suddenly she steps right in front of me, and I get a good look. She's wearing this perfectly fitted little white-on-white knit suit. Fringes on the pockets? Fancy brass and enamel buttons? Chanel, for sure. Maybe even custom-made."

"Frank has taught you well."

"Trust me. That suit cost more than this house. She says to me—with this bright little smile and her own mysterious accent: 'So, *Paloma Rodriguez*, what country do *you* come from?'"

Serach grinned. "And you answered: 'I was born in New York, thank you very much.'"

"Yes, well, not quite. Her husband had just promised to give us $300,000 a year, after all. Even I can show some restraint at a moment like that. What I said was: 'I'm from the Bronx but my mother was born in Colombia.' 'Oh,' she gushes in that syrupy voice. 'How marvelous. I'm originally from El Salvador myself, but I've lived many places.' I look even closer and, yeah, it all fits. Her eyes are dark, and her skin is olive and it's clear she's not a real blonde—her eyebrows and roots are jet black. I know some people think that it's fashionable to do that, but I've never understood it. I say: 'If you're going to be blonde, go for broke. Think Marilyn Monroe.' Of course, what do I know? I used to date women with purple hair."

"Yes, Paloma. I know that. Go on."

"Sorry. And then she says: 'So how do you honor your Latinx heritage, Paloma Rodriguez?' What is it with that 'Latinx' thing? And with that repeating someone's full name nonsense?"

"The full-name part is to impress you with their sincerity. And the 'Latinx' part is—as far as I understand it—a way to get around gender labeling."

"Well, hell—I'm a *Latina*. I'm a *woman*. What else would I be?"

"Indeed. But please go on. What did you say? About the whole heritage issue?"

"'I said: 'I don't know what you mean.' And she retorts: 'What I mean, Paloma, is: How do you give back to your community?'"

Paloma snorted.

"So I just stare back at her and don't say a thing. But it's like she doesn't care. 'Okay,' she says—and suddenly she's speaking like a normal person: 'Let me get to the point. I am the Co-Founder and President of the Board of the *¡Adelantamos-El Bronx!* organization in Hunts Point. We work with Latinx girls in the foster care and juvenile justice systems. Get them into music and culinary arts. Provide them with leadership training. Give them a future. They could use someone like you as a role model. And we could use someone like you as a fundraiser. And what a wonderful chance for you to help disadvantaged Latinx girls like yourself in your own home borough!'"

Serach looked at her partner with her head tilted to the side. "And you answer?"

"Nothing. I still say nothing. And it makes no difference. She reaches into her bag and pulls out a card and gives it to me and says: 'Give me a call.' Like, who cares what I think? Like, she knows that I'm going to call her just because she told me to."

"Well, you don't have to, you know," said Serach, gently. "You can just throw away the card. So why does what she did bother you so much?"

"Well, dammit, I don't like her implying that I don't do enough for the world already. I'm a nurse, for God's sake. I heal people. And shit! I left the Bronx long ago. And who has the time?"

"Well, Paloma." Serach regarded her partner with interest. She knew Paloma could almost never resist a dare. Or an opportunity. "I get it that you didn't like how pompous she acted. But she could be right. You might enjoy giving back to your community."

"Serach, I give back to my community every time I help my idiot brother with something. I don't need to go messing around with some nonprofit in Hunts Point. And what could I do for them, anyway? What could I offer to a bunch of delinquents?"

Serach looked away.

"What, Serach? What are you thinking?"

"I'm thinking that you have a lot more to offer than you sometimes give yourself credit for. That you might just enjoy doing something for girls who… haven't had the same advantages as you have. I'm sure that there are lots of girls in Boro Park struggling with the kinds of things that I did. I often wish there were a way I could help them."

"Jesus, Serach! You're impossible."

"Well, give it some thought."

4.

The Friday of Frank's Carnegie Hall performance began in an unnatural miasma of mid-May heat, but with the forecast of drenching rain by mid-afternoon. By 2:00 the sky had turned a muddy green and by 3:00 the downpour was so ferocious that Paloma couldn't see two feet in front of her as she peered through the kitchen window.

Frank was pacing grimly back and forth from one end of the room to the other as she wrapped his Brooks Brothers garment carrier in the additional protective covering of a big black garbage bag and draped it over one of the wooden chairs. She was beginning to regret using up one of her personal days to help her friend through this pre-concert crisis.

"Frank, calm down already. You're making me nuts. The rain is not a problem. New Yorkers don't let the weather stop them. The car service will get you to your final run-through just fine. And you'll be utterly on your game from the moment you walk onto that stage. You have that monster of a Prokofiev piece completely mastered. And when you played the Ravel *Pavane* and the Brahms *Trio* for us last night… oh, Frank, it was heavenly."

"And you weren't even getting the full effect of the *Trio*!" Frank stopped his pacing, whirled around and beamed. "My part is glorious in and of itself, of course—but it's even better when the other two instruments are playing along with me. Sometimes it's the cello intertwining with me and sometimes it's the clarinet. And sometimes both at once. It's absolutely thrilling."

Paloma snorted. "Yes, I'm sure the intertwining between you and the clarinetist is, uh…."

"Shut up, darling. Kae-Dang and I are total professionals. And Alyosha is a master cellist, so our passages together are fantastic as well. By the way, do pay special attention to his opening line in the Brahms. Beyond superb."

He closed his eyes.

"The second half of the concert is a … different story. The *Bolero* is wonderful, of course, but the *Third Icelandic Symphony*… well, you'll have to judge for yourself. Still, Kae Dang has a big solo in that too, so all is not lost. By the way, did you know he's the first non-Icelandic musician who's ever played with Maestra Magnúsdóttir? They're incredibly chauvinistic, those Icelanders, though I guess they need to be, or no one would even *notice* them, would they? But Paloma—look how late it is! Why are you letting me dither on and on like this?"

He ran to the window.

"Where's my car? Call them up and—oh, thank God. They're here. Hand me my tux! Hand me my umbrella! Dear sweet Jesus, I hope I don't get soaked through and begin sneezing uncontrollably during my performance!"

By 6:45, the rain still hadn't let up. Serach stood in the front hall in her black velvet jacket, spiffy white shirt and black silk pants. She sat down to spray her little leather ankle boots with waterproofing while Paloma wrapped up her silver stilettos, crammed them into the depths of her purse and donned her running shoes.

Normally the two women took the subway into town, no matter the hour. They never tired of observing the other passengers and wondering who they were and where they were going. Nor of experiencing that enchanted moment when the train bursts onto the Manhattan Bridge to cross into the glittering city. This was not, however, a normal night. It was pouring rain. They were all dressed up. They called for their own car service and awaited its arrival.

"I'm truly looking forward to Frank's triumph," remarked Paloma as they sped across 57th Street with the rain beating relentlessly on the car windows. "But I'm also looking forward to his going home with Kae-Dang tonight. And then to their taking off together on their six-month European tour. He's been absolutely unbearable this last week."

"Why do you think he's been so worked up about this particular concert? It's hardly his first big performance on an international stage, after all. He's played all over the world."

"There is 'all over the world,'" observed Paloma, as she generously tipped the driver, scooted out of the cab, unfurled their big black umbrella, offered Serach her arm and escorted her into the crowded front lobby. "And then there is Carnegie Hall."

They mounted the stairs to their first-tier box seats in time to push their chairs as far forward as possible.

"Frank said he'd kill me if we didn't sit right up at the edge," Paloma explained as they settled in. "He's going to look up as soon as he enters, and we need to give him our best little royal hand waves. He won't acknowledge us, of course. But he swears he won't be able to perform if he doesn't see us do it."

By 8:12 when the lights dimmed and the buzz of the crowd abated, the two women were securely positioned at the very front of their box. And just as he'd promised, Frank glanced up for a millisecond before striding to the gleaming black Steinway and taking his seat.

Paloma took Serach's hand, looked down at her lap and smiled deeply.

"I thought you were counting the hours till he departs," whispered Serach as she caught the brief gleam of tears in her partner's eyes. "You know you're going to miss him like crazy."

They remained still and silent till the last note of the Brahms *Trio* had faded away and then sprang to their feet to applaud madly through both of Frank's curtain calls. Paloma swore that he caught her eye again just before he bowed. Serach wasn't sure.

When he had left the stage for the final time, Paloma darted out of their box to spend the intermission on the line for the ladies' room while Serach waited so long at the bar for her Pellegrino and lime that she almost didn't make it back to her seat before the lights dimmed. Then neither one moved or spoke until the concert ended, the final applause died down and the lights came back on.

"I really could have done without that whole second half," sniffed Paloma as she stood up and stretched. "Frank warned me about the Pörirsson *Third Symphony*—awful, wasn't it? The *Bolero*… well of course I loved it, it's the original crowd pleaser. But all I really wanted was for the whole thing to be over so we could rush backstage and hug our star."

"I didn't like the Pörirsson so much either," replied Serach. "Maybe it takes a few hearings."

She smiled.

"Or maybe nothing would make a difference. But really, how could the marvelous Maestra Magnúsdóttir come all the way to New York City and not do something Icelandic?"

Paloma shrugged.

"Paloma, you have to admit she's terrific," Serach was continuing. "So tall and blond and strong. And such clean, efficient motions. Did you catch how she managed to cue in the brass section by just flicking her right elbow at them?"

Paloma stuffed the concert Playbill in her bag, pulled at the hem of her silvery dress, adjusted her spaghetti straps and motioned for Serach to precede her out of the box.

"Yes, yes," she said. "As you say. Frank seems to truly admire her. But none of that really matters, does it? What matters was that first half. Frank's half. It took me a while to fall in love with the Prokofiev, as you know, but the way he performed that piece tonight was a revelation. I'd never noticed how jazzy it was. And the *Pavane*… I truly felt that he was playing it just for me. And the Brahms! Did you see how Kae-Dang kept swooping toward Frank and Frank kept swooping right back at him as they played together? Oh, Serach—wouldn't you give just about anything to be a fly on the wall of their bedroom tonight?"

"Paloma!"

"Come on, you know you would. Frank has been having ecstatic fits over Kae-Dang's *embouchure* for weeks. He thinks I don't know what that is—but I do. And I can only imagine..."

"Well, what is it?"

"It's the way… that wind-players hold their instruments in their mouths."

Paloma was still giggling as they negotiated their way through the departing crowds, crossed the Parquet and entered the Café for the post-concert reception. Frank was already at the bar as they walked in, drinking Pellegrino. And Kae-Dang was right by his side, sipping champagne.

"Well?" said Frank as Paloma pulled him into her embrace. "Well?"

"Well, bravo, bravo, bravo, darling. I was transported. Wasn't I transported, Serach?"

"Transported," said Serach. She gently shooed Paloma away, reached up for the back of Frank's neck and brought his face down to plant her own kiss on his cheek. "You were just perfect, Frank. Everything you did was perfect. We were so proud of you."

"And so?" said Paloma, standing back and staring pointedly at Kae-Dang. "Are you going to introduce me to the man you accompanied in the Brahms, or do I have to do it myself?"

Kae-Dang—almost as tall as Frank and even thinner—beamed down at her and lifted her hand to his lips.

"So this is the fabulous Paloma," he murmured, giving the palm a kiss that was considerably nicer than the one she'd received from Victor Bianchi.

Embouchure, thought Paloma, and grinned.

"You were totally amazing too, Kae-Dang," she said as she carefully appraised his face. "In all your pieces. I've never heard a clarinet sound so beautiful."

Kae-Dang's hair provided a thick, jet-black contrast to Frank's greying chestnut locks. His skin was as velvety as Frank's was paper-dry. His eyes threw out such blinding beams that Paloma had to look away after a second or two. Clearly, he was scrutinizing her as thoroughly as she was scrutinizing him. Altogether a formidable man.

She had initially been worried about the age difference—Kae-Dang couldn't have been more than thirty-five years old to Frank's fifty-eight—but then again, Frank was looking a lot younger than he had in a long time, salt-and-pepper hair and papery-white skin notwithstanding. Plus, he was an adult after all, capable of looking after himself with this fiery new young beau.

And most important of all, Kae-Dang seemed appropriately smitten as he turned his glance up to Frank's face and placed his arm possessively around his shoulders.

"Well, I must say you two make a fetching couple," Paloma finally remarked. "I approve."

She then stepped back to allow Serach to come forward and extend her hand to Kae-Dang.

"I'm Serach," she said. "And I'm also very pleased to meet you. I totally agree with Paloma. You played beautifully."

Kae-Dang disengaged his arm, bowed deeply to Serach and enclosed her hand in a clasp that was firm, warm and dry. Frank—temporarily freed from Kae-Dang's embrace—turned around to the bar, picked up two glasses of champagne and presented them with a small bow of his own.

"A toast," said Kae-Dang, taking over and lifting his glass toward them. "A toast to love."

"To love and to music," said Serach, and they all drank.

"So, Frank," said Paloma, putting down her glass. "Is there any way you can introduce us to the distinguished Musical Director of the Reykjavik Symphony Orchestra? Serach is dying to meet her, aren't you, my darling?"

Serach smiled enigmatically.

"Well, that depends," said Frank. "Did you like the Pörirsson?"

"Not… that much," said Paloma, and then quickly added: "Except for Kae-Dang's solo, of course. But Frank," she continued, "Serach and I aren't going to embarrass you in front of the Maestra. We'll be totally complimentary about her performance and show appropriate interest in her native country—ask her about how they make energy from all those underground geysers or something. Or maybe we'll just ask her what she thinks about New York. Foreigners love that."

In the end, they never did get to chat with Maestra Magnúsdóttir. Frank's attempt to lead them to her was thwarted by three tall blond brass players anxious to ask him about the way he had interpreted the Prokofiev. And when Serach decided they should head over to her on their own, she took one look at the depth of the crowd gathered around her and spun back around.

"The Maestra has evidently invited every last member of New York's Icelandic community to this concert," she said as she steered Paloma back to the bar. "And each one of them is desperate to congratulate her. You and I don't stand a chance. But it's okay. I can live without it."

Frank meanwhile moved from his animated talk with the three brass players into an equally heated conversation with Alyosha and one of the cellists from the Reykjavik orchestra—while Kae-Dang was quickly encircled by a three-person-deep crowd of his own fans.

Ultimately, the two women remained standing alone. They each had a second (and then a third) glass of champagne while nibbling on hors d'oeuvres and whispering to one another about what the different musicians looked like. And by the time the Café staff began clearing away the detritus of the evening and shooing everyone out, they were both leaning firmly against the bar for support.

"Serach, I am as tipsy as I've ever been," said Paloma, wrapping her arm around her partner's shoulders. "And you are even worse. Let's get out of here before we both totally keel over."

She located Frank in the thinning crowd and waved vigorously in his direction.

"Ciao, ciao, I love you!" he called out to her once she finally caught his eye. "I'll call you tomorrow!" He blew her a kiss.

"Love you, too!" she mouthed back at him. "You're the best! Enjoy the rest of your soirée!"

Serach somehow managed to slip out from under Paloma's arm, make her way to Kae-Dang and tap him on the back.

"Take good care of Frank," she declared in a tone whose atypical imperiousness was clearly fueled by the champagne. "Appreciate him. And send him home to us safe and sound when you're done with him."

"I will coddle him properly, I promise you," he said, turning gracefully toward her and lightly kissing each of her cheeks. "Plus, there is no 'done' in sight. I'll be as true to him as you two lovely ladies are to one another."

Serach walked back to Paloma, and they carefully made their way to the cloakroom to gather their raincoats and umbrella and tip the attendant. Holding hands, they negotiated the last flight of stairs to the front entrance and out the door. Paloma then stepped forward into the still lightly falling rain, flagged down a cab and told the driver to use whatever route made the most sense to get them back to their house in Prospect Park South.

The two women were soundly dozing in the back seat with their arms around one another by the time they reached the FDR Drive. They didn't fully wake up again until the driver—perhaps the last old Jewish cab driver in New York—pulled up in front of 98 Marlborough Road, slid open the door of the glass partition that separated him from his passengers, and proclaimed: "Ladies! You're home! Rise and shine! Let's get going."

"Good God," said Paloma, pulling herself out of the cab while Serach paid. "That's never happened to me before."

She straightened herself up and looked toward the porch. "And what the hell is that?"

"What is what?" asked Serach, catching up to her and taking her arm.

"That! That apparition in the sloppy green raincoat in front of our door."

Serach peered forward to better discern the shape.

"It's—good heavens, it's my friend Frayda!"

She ran up the steps of the porch, abruptly emerging from her own little fog to greet the one member of her old Boro Park community with whom she stayed in regular touch.

"Frayda! It's *Shabbos*—you're not supposed to be out and about. How did you get here? Did you come all this way on foot? And how long have you been standing there? Are you all right?"

"Serach," said Frayda—rain-soaked and stone sober. "Your mother's dead."

5.

"Okay, team," said Paloma, once she had released Serach from an immediate and near-crushing embrace. "We all need to get inside, dry off and warm up. Especially you, Frayda. You look like a drowned rat."

She reached into her bag to find the right key, unlocked and opened the front door, put her arm back around Serach's shoulders and bustled them all into the hallway.

"Did you walk all the way from your house to ours?" she asked, while Frayda planted herself just inside the entranceway and looked slowly and methodically around her.

Frayda swiveled back toward Paloma and gave a little shrug. "It's *Shabbos*. You walk."

"And… you went that whole distance in this downpour without an umbrella?"

"It is not permissible to open an umbrella on the *Shabbos*. It's comparable to pitching a tent."

Frayda and Paloma stared bluntly at one another for a moment while Paloma wondered what she could possibly reply to a statement such as that.

"And…" Paloma finally responded, "and I take it that even in a case of emergency such as this you couldn't have just picked up a phone and called?"

Frayda said nothing, just continued staring at her blankly.

"Got it. No phoning either. Though I guess news like this *is* probably best conveyed in person."

Except, of course, when it's conveyed with such total lack of empathy or tact.

"Well, never mind all that. Let's not just stand around in our raincoats. Give me yours and then let's all go upstairs."

Frayda didn't move.

"Frayda—shake a leg! Give me your raincoat. You're spending the night with us. I'm not letting you slog all the way back to Boro Park in that muck. There's a whole guest suite just waiting for you—bedroom and bathroom—on the third floor. I'll draw you a hot bath and lend you one of Serach's winter nightgowns—they're nice and long. Plus, some warm socks, if you want. You need to get some sleep."

Frayda continued to stare at her stolidly without saying a word.

"Frayda, for God's sake, get with the program. You're staying here tonight!"

"No need for the bath," said Frayda, handing Paloma her raincoat. "Or the socks." And then, without another word, she began moving robotically toward the staircase.

Serach finally found her voice and ran after her friend.

"Wait a minute, Frayda. Please wait."

"What?"

"I'm sorry—it took me a minute to pull myself together. I need to thank you."

"Don't mention it," Frayda replied, turning away again.

Paloma looked down at the ground and shook her head. Serach, however, was undeterred.

"No, Frayda," she continued, reaching out to catch Frayda's arm. "Of course, I'm going to mention it. You came all that distance on foot, in the rain on a *Shabbos* to give me news that no one else would have shared with me. You stood on my porch for what must have been hours till I returned. That took… fortitude. It took lovingkindness. I'm very grateful to you."

Frayda shrugged and began turning away again. But Serach, her hand firmly but gently in place, held her back.

"Please. Please accept my thanks. And also, please…" She took a breath and let go of Frayda's arm. "May I just… ask you a couple of things before we all go to sleep?"

Frayda took a half-step back to face her.

"What?"

"Well… this is all so very… abrupt. It's hard for me to absorb. But could you… possibly tell me how you heard the news? And… how it was that my mother died?"

She paused and swallowed before continuing.

"And what's going to happen now that she's dead?"

Frayda continued looking at her impassively for a long moment before answering.

"It was your sister Beile who called me. Just before candle-lighting time. I once gave her some guidance on a dental issue, so she sometimes remembers me. Your mother died as she was closing down her shop for *Shabbos*. Heart attack. No warning. Bang. All over. Her assistant was with her. Fortunately. And what's going to happen, now? The funeral will take place on Sunday at 11:00 at the *Beis Shel Kavod* Funeral Home. You know, the one right off of 12th Avenue? With the big parking lot? The one where—if I'm not mistaken—your father's funeral was also held? It will be a big deal. Everyone will be there. Your sisters, all your mother's clients, all her friends from the *shul*. And everyone's husbands and kids."

Frayda gave one final shrug.

"And now I have to go upstairs. I'm cold. I'm tired. Like your girlfriend said."

She looked meaningfully at Paloma before heading for the staircase again.

"Serach—don't you worry for a single minute about Frayda," Paloma cautioned her partner as she flung the three raincoats over a chair back. "I'll get her properly set up and you can finish asking her the details in the morning, when she's more rested."

Serach breathed out, slowly. "Oh, I doubt she'll have much to add, even then. In fact, I'm surprised she knows as much as she does. People generally just leave her in the dark. Beile was very kind to have thought to call her."

She paused.

"Of course, Beile was always the kindest of my sisters."

She shook her head and gave the barest hint of a sigh.

"I wish I could thank her for having done it," she said, smiling sadly. "I'm sure the gesture meant a lot to Frayda."

She sighed again.

"But, at the very least, I can thank *you* for having been so kind to my old friend. Inviting her to stay over and everything."

Paloma grunted. "Good heavens, Serach. I'm not totally socially clueless, even if Frayda is. Now please—let's stop talking and get ourselves upstairs as well. I'll finish settling Frayda into her room while you get dried off and get into bed. And then I'll join you."

"Well… I didn't actually get very wet, you know, between the taxi and your expert use of our umbrella," Serach said, suddenly standing up very straight. "So I don't need to dry out. And I couldn't possibly go to sleep quite yet. Couldn't I—just stay downstairs for a while and couldn't you maybe come back when you're done with Frayda and help me put my thoughts in order while we're both still vertical?"

Paloma gave Serach a quizzical look. Still, it was clear that her partner meant it, so she held her tongue, turned toward the stairs and sprinted upwards just in time to spy Frayda laboriously rounding the last corner to the top landing and peering around in her turtle-y way.

"Hold on, Frayda!" she called out. "Let me get you that warm nightgown. And a towel. And we must have an unopened toothbrush and tube of toothpaste somewhere."

Frayda paused in mid-stride as Paloma headed off to scout out what was needed.

"Follow me," said Paloma when she returned, "and I'll show you where everything is."

She led Frayda to the first door on the landing and opened it. "Here's where you'll be sleeping," she said, motioning to the bedroom within. "The room to the far left is Serach's study—you can just ignore that. But this one right here…" and she opened the middle door and turned on the light, "will be your bathroom. Here's your towel and toothbrush and toothpaste and nightgown, and…"

Frayda turned away from all the objects Paloma was offering, stuck her head into the bathroom and made a few clucking noises. She then whirled back toward Paloma, grabbed everything out of her hands, strode in and shut the door firmly behind her.

When Paloma re-descended the staircase, she found Serach standing in exactly the same spot in which she'd left her—still ramrod straight but looking very small.

"Let me say one thing before we go any farther," Serach announced—quietly but definitively, as she raised one hand to prevent Paloma from entrapping her in yet another bearlike embrace. "I really need to say it and you really need to hear it. So please just give me some breathing space."

Paloma slowly stepped back.

"Paloma, I'm going to be okay. Really. Truly. You don't have to worry. I'm strong."

"I know you're strong, it's just that..."

"Hush, Paloma. Please. Let me continue." She swallowed briefly. "I have to tell you the decision that I've reached."

"Of course, of course. But can't we talk it over in bed? We're both dead on our feet."

"Yes, and that's the whole point. I want to be completely awake and aware when I say what I need to say. In fact, could you… possibly make me a cup of tea?"

"Tea? You want tea? Now? After midnight? Well, sure. Of course. Whatever you want. Do you want a shot of cognac in it?"

"No, no. I want to be fully in possession of my senses. That's the whole point."

They walked into the kitchen and Paloma put the kettle on.

"Well, as for me," she said, "I need a shot of cognac. Straight up. I seem to be totally sober again and I don't like it."

Serach smiled. "You've always held your liquor better than I have."

She made her way to the table and sat down. She looked formidably pale and serious—like someone in an old-fashioned portrait—in her very white shirt and very black pants.

She also looked like someone completely in control of herself.

In fact, it was clear to Paloma that Serach was in much better shape than she was. That it was she—not Serach—who desperately needed to take off her fancy clothes and curl up under the covers in her partner's arms.

She knew, however, that when Serach set her mind on something it was impossible to budge her, so she contented herself with taking off her high heels and finding the bottle of cognac in the cupboard. She waited for the kettle to whistle, made Serach a cup of tea and added the right amount of milk and sugar. She poured the cognac straight from the bottle into her own cup, took one gulp and waited for Serach to speak.

"Here's what I've decided," Serach finally began in a preternaturally calm tone. "I'm going to go to my mother's funeral."

She put up one hand again before Paloma could leap toward her.

"Please, Paloma. Don't say anything yet."

"But I *have* to say something!"

"No, Paloma. You don't. I know what you're thinking. You're thinking I'm setting myself up to be hurt. To have one of what you like to call my 'damned sisters' tell me that I'm dead as far as the family is concerned and have no right to be there."

"Well, yes. Something like that."

"Well, I don't actually plan to go *into* the funeral home with my sisters. I plan to just stand in the big parking lot that Frayda mentioned with my face down so no one will recognize me."

"I don't get it. What's the point if you don't go inside?"

"Well then please let me explain. What I want is simply… the chance to take it all in."

She paused.

"And … to be there when they bring out my mother's coffin and put it in the hearse."

She looked down and took a large sip of her tea.

"And as the hearse drives away, I want to wave farewell. I never got to do that you know. I just up and left Mama—and everything she stood for—without a word of explanation. Snuck away like a thief when no one was home."

She inspected Paloma's face for a moment to take in the mixture of pity and apprehension that was constricting her partner's features.

"Don't worry," she added, kindly. "I don't regret doing it. But please try to understand that I need to feel some sort of closure, now. Best as I can."

Paloma uncharacteristically found that she had nothing to reply.

"You should also know that I'm planning to send Frayda back to her own house, first thing in the morning," Serach continued. "The rain will have ended by then and it isn't really such a long distance—at least, not when the sun is out. I cover that route regularly myself when Frayda and I lunch together in Kensington. On the way there, I take the bus. But on the way back, I walk. It's my little ritual. Perhaps because the first time I came here, I did it on foot."

Paloma nodded.

"I'm sure Frayda will be glad to get going as early as possible. Return in time for *Shabbos* morning services. She goes every Saturday. Without fail."

She seemed to have finished what she needed to say, so Paloma leaned toward her to ask the question that had suddenly and unexpectedly begun to plague her.

"But then…" she said, and then paused. It was surprisingly hard for her to pose it. "Are you going to ask Frayda to come back and stand with you in that parking lot on Sunday?"

Serach looked startled. "No, of course not. First of all, she's going to want to be where the action is. Inside. I doubt she's missed a single major funeral in our community in decades. And you heard her. This will definitely be a funeral not to be missed."

Serach smiled unexpectedly.

"But also, if I'm trying to go unnoticed, the last thing I should do is stand next to Frayda. Every woman in our busy-body community will run right up to her and say: 'What's the matter, Frayda? What are you waiting for? Come inside!' Then they'll take one look at me and ask: 'So who's this that you're with?'"

She paused to gaze down briefly into her teacup.

"But most importantly, the only person I want standing beside me at that… difficult moment is *you*, Paloma. No one will recognize you or give you a second glance. They'll think you're there for someone else's funeral—and me along with you. There are always several funerals going on at the same time at our funeral homes. I hate to ask you, knowing what you think about my community. But could you possibly see your way to doing it? Please?"

She slowly lifted her gaze, and Paloma—relieved in ways that she couldn't begin to explain—was once again struck by the fact that her partner had the most beautiful grey eyes in the world.

"Yes of course, Serach. How could you possibly doubt it?"

Jerusalem

6.

The crowd that arrived for the first formal Shabbos dinner in Shmuely and Ruchel's new house was relatively small. Just those who could easily stroll home again once the meal was over. Ruchel's parents, Yehuda and Binkel—who lived up the street in the ample duplex in which Ruchel and Shmuely had stayed as newlyweds. And Shmuely's cousin Reuven (and his wife Batya and four sons)—whose apartment was just a few short blocks to the east.

Ruchel was nonetheless as proud as if she were entertaining a roomful of heads of state.

And why shouldn't she be? Here she was at the tender age of nineteen juggling so many responsibilities so very well. Meeting all the needs of her rising-star-scholar husband. Taking on full supervision of a magnificent nine-room house (with its own garden and terrace) in *Sha'arei Hesed*—Jerusalem's most prestigious area for English-speaking Haredi Jews. Finessing the many challenges of being Associate Floor Manager in her father's flagship jewelry store.

And now flawlessly orchestrating a full Friday-night celebration for ten people, barely four hours after arriving home from that relentlessly-taxing job.

How elegant her table looked! How smart she'd been to register for those simple white table linens and that top-of-the-line blue-and-white-patterned china (just modern enough to be eye-catching, but not in any way showy). How clever to ask her good friend Esther to recommend a wine for Shmuely's first big *Kiddush* as the head of his own household.

"*Bijoux de Judea, 2016*," Esther had swiftly counseled. "Everyone in our circle is drinking it. Made right in the Judean Hills. Simply exquisite. Your guests will love it."

Esther had been right. Even Batya had remarked on how delicious it was.

And—perhaps most of all—how wise she'd been to snatch up little Dalisay when Esther and her family had moved to Tel Aviv and Esther no longer needed Dalisay's housekeeping services.

She could never have managed everything without her. Not only had Dalisay taken care of all the cooking preliminaries and produced a sparkling-clean house, she'd also somehow managed to pick up the *challahs* and cookies before hanging up her apron for the day.

"Who ever heard of a Filipina maid?" Binkel had asked when Ruchel first told her about her hiring decision. "I thought those people just provided elder care."

"She does that too," Ruchel had replied with a smile. "But the lady she takes care of only needs her at night. So during the day she works here. Lucky for me."

She smiled and nodded slightly to herself.

"She's a true gem. Speaks English—no muddled Hebrew, like so many other immigrants. Knows all there is to know about keeping a kosher kitchen. Esther trained her very well."

The first stages of the evening had rolled out beautifully.

The silverware had gleamed. The serving plates had been emptied almost as quickly as she'd placed them on the table. Reuven's oldest son (the one who blushed so charmingly every time she spoke to him) had even asked for a third helping of the brisket, while everyone else had happily accepted seconds.

And how proud she'd felt of her Shmuely! How easily he'd assumed the role of master of the house this evening. How effortlessly he'd held Reuven's four boys in rapt attention with his probing questions about their studies.

Perhaps most gratifyingly of all, snooty little Batya had not as much as hinted at the matter that continued to mar Ruchel's otherwise perfect life.

At the point at which the women retired to the kitchen to fix dessert, however, all the brakes came off. Batya picked up a cookie from the plate that Ruchel had just finished arranging, took a large bite and said: "So. Ruchel. I have a question. What do you do when Shmuely is finished with his business? Do you turn over immediately or do you lie there quietly? Because if you turn over too quickly everything can just pour right out of you, and you're left with nothing. *Bupkes*!"

Ruchel looked down.

"And…" Batya continued, "are you letting him know that you're ready at any time that it is permitted? And are you making yourself attractive enough to ensure that he wants it?"

"Sha-sha-sha," interjected Binkel. "She's a perfectly attractive girl, as anyone with eyes can see."

But Ruchel had heard more than enough. She hung her head briefly before muttering: "The men must be ready for their dessert, don't you think?" and began heading to the dining room with the cookie platter.

"Almost a year and nothing's happened," remarked Batya. "After a year, I had one son already and was on my way to the second."

"Enough, Batya. Now that she's finally in her own home, I'm sure things will change."

Shmuely, in the meantime, was having a very good time.

"So," he was saying, looking from one of Reuven's sons to the other, "so… after you four fine young men have been so thoroughly immersed in that new yeshiva that my cousin is so impressed by—and after we, ourselves, have been exploring so many important Talmudic questions tonight—I'm curious to know something."

He stroked his chin and gave a small smile that none of them caught before it evaporated.

"Tell me. In one word. How would each of you characterize the Talmud's teachings?"

"Sacred," said the eldest boy, almost immediately.

"Holy," said the third-to-eldest.

"Sacred," echoed the youngest. He always followed his oldest brother's lead.

But Nussen, the second-to-eldest son (just fifteen and already forging a reputation for his command of Talmudic rhetoric), remained momentarily silent. While he was more than eager to present his views to his impressive cousin, he wanted to do so as persuasively as possible. It required some thought.

"The word I would use is: 'perplexing,'" he finally said, closely scrutinizing his cousin's face.

Shmuely said nothing. He nodded briefly while arranging his features into a suitably stern expression. He had watched Nussen testing the borders of the permissible at several other points during the evening. And using such big words! Was that how they taught Talmud at Reuven's fancy yeshiva? Or was Nussen—*chas v'cholileh*—just showing off? He needed to dig a little deeper to assess what was what.

"Go on," he said.

"Yes, Cousin Shmuely," Nussen was continuing, a bit breathlessly. "My teachers of course, always strive to reconcile the different viewpoints presented. But to me, things often remain unresolved."

He paused.

"And therefore… perplexing."

He looked up slantwise at his cousin. Did he dare to push any further? Well, Shmuely hadn't stopped him yet. He would keep going.

"And even… at times…."

He swallowed.

"A bit… humorous. Humorously perplexing."

Shmuely attempted to make himself look even sterner, but his mouth betrayed him. He quickly turned his face away to hide his pleasure at hearing words that so vividly recalled the way his sister Serach had always approached the texts. The way she would sit with him on the floor of his bedroom, teasing him with paradoxes and wit while he squirmed and protested—and begged for more. He tented his hands and regarded Nussen over the tips of his delicate fingers.

"So, Nussen," he said. "I must say that your observations stir my curiosity. So why don't you cite a Talmudic passage for us that strikes you as… 'humorously perplexing,' as you put it?"

Nussen didn't hesitate.

"Well for example, right now we are studying *Tractate Pesachim*," he said, eagerly. He turned briefly to the youngest brother to add: "That's the tractate that covers the mandates of Passover."

His youngest brother made a face because he already knew all about that.

"And…" he continued, "in that tractate there is a famous passage in which the sages debate what should be done if someone sees a mouse carrying a piece of bread into a house that has been cleaned of all leavened products, and then sees a mouse leave—also carrying a piece of bread. Can we be certain that the mouse is carrying the same piece of bread with which it entered? Or might the mouse have eaten that first piece and then snatched a second piece from someplace that the housewife overlooked? And—given that possibility—does the housewife need to clean the house all over again, since who knows what else she missed?"

He took a breath, studied Shmuely's face again to detect any trace of reprimand and—finding none—continued.

"The sages then ask what should be done if someone sees a white mouse entering the house with a piece of bread and then a black mouse exiting with a piece of bread. Did the black mouse perhaps attack the white one and take away the piece of bread that the white mouse brought in? Or could it be that there was a second piece of bread hidden somewhere in the house that was taken away by that black mouse? So, once again, does the housewife need to go back and re-clean everything?"

He took another breath.

"Finally, the sages ask…" and at this point Nussen's eyes lit up, "what should be done if the animals in question are… first a mouse and *then a weasel?*"

He paused, saw that Shmuely was still not protesting, and continued.

"And after asking all those perplexing questions, the entire issue is never even settled."

He paused again.

"So how can we not think that the sages are somehow… having a little fun with us?"

Shmuely regarded his young cousin for a long moment while everyone else fidgeted. What would Rav Gottesman say to all this impudence? To this near blasphemy?

"Hmmnnn," Shmuely finally responded. "So. If we can agree that the sages are, in some way, 'having fun with us,' as you put it—to what deeper purpose do you think they are doing such a thing? For I'm sure you would not go so far as to say that they are… teasing to no good purpose. After all, nothing contained in the holy texts is incidental or without purpose…"

Nussen looked back at Shmuely without fear.

"No, of course not, Cousin Shmuely. I would never say such a thing. On the contrary. The sages are trying to perplex us—to tease us—so as to keep us interested. Curious. Attentive. For, in the end, is it not even more important to be attentive than to be solemn?"

Shmuely clapped his hands.

"Yes!" he crowed. "Yes, exactly. What you are saying is true. I might even go so far as to say that what you are saying is wise. For the chief thing is to stay perpetually engaged. To realize that we can learn from everyone and everything. From the perplexing and the humorous as well as from the solemn. Does not our Talmud include long discussions of bathroom activities as well as of business ethics and ritual observance? Is not each and every one of those matters a part of the life that *Ha-Shem* has given us—blessed be He—and therefore deserving of our close consideration?"

He sat back in his chair and smiled again, and the whole table relaxed.

"Gentlemen," he said, looking around and waving affectionately at Nussen. "I would contend that we have in our midst the makings of a Talmud scholar."

At which point Yehuda could not restrain himself either. He clapped his hands. How wise he had been to snag this marvelous *illui* for his youngest (and, if he was to be honest, most beloved) daughter! How wise to supplement Shmuely's income each month—and to buy him and Ruchel this house. To make sure, in short, that his exceptional son-in-law could continue pursuing his learning and teaching without any worldly worries.

Beaming from one side of his beard to the other—his chubby face bright pink from both wine and pride—he regarded Shmuely with joy.

"And I would say," he said, raising his glass, "that we also have… a true master teacher."

But before they could continue with all that pleasant *kvelling*—and before Ruchel (still paused in the doorway, awaiting just the right moment to bring in the cookies) could enter the room—they were interrupted by a loud rattling from the study.

"What is that?" asked Shmuely.

"It's your fax machine, Shmuely," answered Reuven who had, in fact, been the one to install the device in his technologically challenged cousin's new home—and whose heart was now sinking precipitously at the racket.

"And what is it doing?"

"It's telling you that someone is trying to get in touch, Shmuely. That's why you have it. It's there so… should there be an emergency back in Brooklyn, *chas v' cholileh*, the family can contact you."

"But it's *Shabbos*! I didn't think they could do so on a *Shabbos*."

"It's not yet *Shabbos* in New York, Shmuely. It is still permissible for them to use machines. They would not use a phone because they know it's already *Shabbos* here and we wouldn't answer it. They can, however, send us a fax because we are permitted to retrieve faxes—even on the Shabbos—if we've left our own machines running from before candle-lighting time."

"But…"

"No 'buts', Shmuely. It is permitted."

Reuven paused for a moment and then added, softly: "Shmuely! Go see what's up."

Shmuely, however, remained paralyzed. What terrible news was being processed by the unholy machine in the next room?

"Shmuely!" said Yehuda—and Yehuda almost never spoke sharply. But he, too, was scared. "If you have to do this thing, go do it already!"

Shmuely shook himself out of his stupor, stood up, and spied his wife hovering in the doorway.

"Ruchel!" he cried out. "Why do you just stand there? Go get that fax!"

7.

The following evening, sixty-two minutes after sundown—*Shabbos*' official end point plus a few extra minutes for celebrating that end point, plus a few extra minutes just to be safe—Reuven bolted out of his living room and into his little silver Hyundai. He sped down the street, screeched to a stop at Shmuely and Ruchel's house, got out and rang the bell at the gate.

It seemed like an eternity before anything happened. Eventually however, Shmuely pried open his front door, stumbled across the garden, halted mid-way to the gate and peered out through the iron slats at his cousin as if he'd never seen him before.

Ruchel followed close on Shmuely's heels, slamming the door behind her and nearly running into him as she barreled forward, baggage in hand. She stared at her husband's rigid back, debated what to do and concluded that—since they weren't really in public view—she was permitted to touch him. She gave him one short, determined poke. Nothing. She did it again and he edged slowly forward to unlock the gate and step out onto the sidewalk. She slipped around him, closed the gate and began lugging their suitcases toward the trunk of Reuven's car.

"Huh-uh, Ruchel," said Reuven, waving his hand briskly at her. "Don't put anything in the trunk. If they flag us for inspection at the perimeter, it will be easier to have the bags on the back seat. There should be more than enough room for both them and you."

He cast a glance back to Shmuely, still standing on the sidewalk looking bewildered, and yelled: "Shmuely—wake up! The car door is unlocked. Get in already!"

He then quickly bit his lip in remorse. One doesn't yell at an *onen*—at a person in the first fragile stages of mourning. One treats them with the utmost gentleness. Especially if they are as totally *farmisht* as his poor cousin appeared to be.

Still, they were about to face the uniquely daunting task of getting into Ben Gurion International Airport. If they wanted to make that flight, they needed to head out immediately.

"Shmuely!" he shouted again—he couldn't stop himself with his cousin just standing there like a pillar of salt. "*Eyl zikh tsu*! El Al waits for no one!"

Shmuely gave a tiny nod before moving tentatively toward the car. He stood beside it for a moment looking blankly around him before finally bending down, tugging the passenger door open and making his way inside as slowly and laboriously as an old man.

Reuven shook his head, ran around the front of the car to push the door shut for his cousin and then headed back for the driver's seat.

Ruchel meanwhile managed to wrench the back door wide open, push the two suitcases onto the seat, angle them in such a way as to make space for herself and scramble in. She needed no prodding from Reuven, *Baruch Ha-Shem*. She'd traveled often enough to know the drill. And she wasn't foggy headed with mourning over a mother-in-law whom she'd never even met.

Ruchel's parents had graciously invited Gittel to stay with them for the fortnight before the wedding—and Gittel had initially agreed. But somehow when it came time to buy the plane tickets, she'd developed a case of nerves serious enough to prevent the journey. She never even made it to Israel for the wedding itself.

For a few months thereafter, Gittel's *machatunim* had continued to invite her over and she'd continued to make excuses. Eventually, they'd given up.

"My mother gets like that," Shmuely had explained to his in-laws with a shrug. "She has her moods. You shouldn't worry. You've done what you had to."

"Seat belts on?" asked Reuven, turning the key in the ignition.

"Seat belts on," answered Ruchel.

"Okay. Twenty minutes to the airport if we're lucky. It all depends on the traffic. And then three hours of official *meshugas* before you're allowed to board your plane."

Even under the best of circumstances, driving with Shmuely wasn't easy. He would claim that he could smell gasoline as they drove (Reuven could smell no such thing) and that it made him nauseous. He would say that Reuven's air conditioning "chilled him to the bone" and make Reuven turn it off, even on the hottest of days. He would urge his cousin to slow down and be more careful—and then ask why it was taking so long.

He was like that. He had his ways as well.

On this evening, however, Shmuely wasn't saying a thing and somehow his silence was even more nerve-wracking than his complaints. He kept tapping his foot on the floor in a jittery staccato pulse. He kept moving his head around in large dramatic gestures—sometimes whipping it off to the right to peer out the window, sometimes tilting it back to glare at the car ceiling and sometimes lowering it forward to bury it in his hands. And he kept sighing!

Reuven sighed a few times, himself. He knew this was to be expected, but that didn't make it any easier. Shmuely's behavior had been disastrous ever since they'd received that terrible fax.

His first reaction upon reading it had been to crumple it up and throw it to the ground. His second had been to retreat to the side of the dining room and stand flat up against the wall.

"Shmuely—*Vos s aroyf?* What's up? What did the fax say?"

When Shmuely remained silent, Reuven had picked up the balled-up paper, smoothed it open and read it out loud. And when Reuven finished, Shmuely had proclaimed (in a voice a good half-octave higher than usual) that he wasn't going to New York for his mother's funeral.

It was all too hard—the packing, the mad rush to the airport when *Shabbos* ended. They would never make the plane. He didn't want to stay in Brooklyn for the entire week of *shiva.* His sister Mierle's husband, Yaakov, had essentially wasted his money on the tickets. He and Ruchel would just remain in Jerusalem and do whatever was necessary right there.

Reuven had walked back to his cousin and put his arm around his shoulders. He had spoken softly and soothingly but with just enough volume that the others could make out what he was saying and provide him back-up, as necessary.

Didn't Shmuely know that it was only right and appropriate for a son to personally bury a parent, no matter how far he had to travel? Didn't the Torah recount how Yitzhak and Ishmael had both journeyed great distances to bury their father Avraham?

And didn't Shmuely appreciate the miracles that his brother-in-law Yaakov had wrought in the tiny window of time between hearing about

Gittel's passing and the start of *Shabbos*, back in New York? Not only had Ya-akov managed to fax Shmuely as soon as he heard the news—he'd also managed to purchase airline tickets (for some huge sum of money, no doubt) and arranged for those tickets to be waiting at the El Al desk at whatever time Shmuely arrived.

And didn't Shmuely know that he—Reuven—would take personal responsibility for driving them to the airport once *Shabbos* was over to make sure they caught that plane?

That there was, in short, nothing to worry about. *A bi gezunt*!

Reuven had then gently steered Shmuely over toward Ruchel. And Ruchel (the woman was truly a marvel) had somehow managed to coax Shmuely upstairs, leaving her *Shabbos* guests to depart with the heart-heaviness that inevitably comes with the announcement of any death. And particularly when the death is so totally unexpected.

On *Shabbos* morning—after what Ruchel later described as a terrible night—Shmuely had evidently managed to get himself up and dressed and walk the five short blocks to *shul* for services. He had raised a polite hand of acknowledgement to the men who gathered silently around him. He had *davened* mechanically alongside them and stood in the Social Hall while they ate. Once that was finished, however, he had waved them firmly aside, shuffled home and buried himself in his study while Ruchel and her mother packed their bags for the trip.

Well, mused Reuven as he masterfully maneuvered his car past a convoy of armored jeeps and a line of lumbering trucks, was Shmuely's state of mind really so surprising? Hearing about a parent's death has to be one of life's greatest blows, no matter when or how it takes place. Living through the limbo period between receiving the news and laying the parent to rest is inevitably rough—and even rougher when a parent dies on or near the *Shabbos* and the cathartic first step of burial has to be delayed for a full additional day.

And when one has to fly 5,700 miles to attend the funeral in a place that one has pointedly avoided for nearly six years—it has to add yet another layer of disorientation to the mix.

And when the parent who has died was as difficult as Reuven's Aunt Gittel....

But at that point, Reuven clamped down violently on his runaway thoughts. His aunt hadn't even been lowered into her grave and here he was ruminating on how exasperating she'd been. On the way, she'd veered between insufferable bossiness and bottomless melancholy, making it impossible for anyone to be sure how to act with her. On the particularly taxing challenges—the pendulum swings between smothering attention, sharp reprimands and sudden withdrawals—that Shmuely (her youngest child and only son) must inevitably have suffered at her hands.

No, he certainly should not be thinking those things about someone newly dead. Better to just concentrate on the road.

Ruchel, meanwhile, was anxiously counting the minutes till they reached the outer perimeter of the airport. In the past, whenever her father had driven her and her mother there for a flight to New York or Antwerp, they had just sailed right through that potential bottleneck. But these days, things were different. There had been so much rancor in recent months between Israel's official establishment and a Haredi community that (so reasonably) was refusing to take up arms for a state they didn't acknowledge. Who knows how those smooth-shaven, showily muscular security screeners might treat her Brooklyn-bred, black-hatted husband?

And who knew how Shmuely might react to even the mildest of interrogations?

Snugly ensconced in his *yeshiva* world, Shmuely was—of course—a man to be reckoned with. Anyone who was anybody said so. But outside that space, not so much. How much easier tasks like this would be if her husband had ever acquired the social skills that now came to her so easily after two years of working at her father's jewelry store!

And how much easier it would be to handle the upcoming journey if he had ever openly talked with her about his relationship with the mother whom she'd never met—or with anyone else back in Brooklyn, for that matter.

And then, of course, how much easier everything would be if their conjugal relations were a source of comfort instead of an increasingly bitter reminder of their troubles in that area. If she could be the Biblical Rivka to his Yitzchak after the death of Yitzchak's mother, Sarah.

But—feh! This was no time to fret over all that. The only thing that mattered right now was getting through the checkpoints that loomed immediately ahead.

For, in fact, Reuven's car had finally arrived at the perimeter of the airport, and it was clear that they were going to be singled out for preliminary inspection. They were being waved to the side of the road and a grimly serious pair of screeners—a dark-haired woman and a very tan, very blond young man—were purposefully approaching Reuven's window.

"I'm just the driver," Reuven said in Hebrew to the male screener, hurriedly rolling his window down. "It's the man on my right and the woman in the back seat with all the suitcases who are doing the actual air travel."

The female screener, meanwhile, walked briskly to the back of the car, waited till Ruchel leaned over to unlock the door and slipped in on the other side of the piled-up suitcases. And Reuven hurriedly rolled down the passenger window as the male screener marched around the front of the car to talk to his cousin.

But then, as Reuven later told his wife Batya, everything turned upside down.

"Your name?" the male screener had asked Shmuely, also in Hebrew.

"My name is Shmuel Gottesman," Shmuely had responded, surprising his cousin both by his willingness to use the holy tongue for secular business and by his firm and friendly tone.

"And where are you from?"

"Brooklyn," said Shmuely, surprising his cousin yet again.

"He doesn't live in Brooklyn. He lives in Jerusalem," Reuven had rushed in to say.

"I am speaking with Mr. Gottesman," said the screener, seamlessly switching into English. "Please be quiet. So, where is it that you claim citizenship, Mr. Gottesman? Is this a visit to America for you, or are you flying back home?"

"No, no. Reuven is right—and thank you, Reuven, for making the correction. Brooklyn is where I'm originally from, but it is not my home now. I moved to Jerusalem nearly six years ago. After I married my wife, I filled out all the paperwork and became a citizen here."

"Your passport?"

"Ruchel—my passport!"

There was no need for the prompt. Ruchel had kept part of her attention firmly fixed on what was transpiring in the front seat, even as she smoothly negotiated her own screener's demands—and was already reaching forward to hand Shmuely the document he needed.

Shmuely plucked it from her hand and passed it to the male screener and the male screener began paging through it.

"Yes, I see. And did you pack your own bags?"

"No, my wife did. Ruchel?"

"Fine, okay, no need to interrupt her. She's doing exactly what she needs to do."

Shmuely took a peek behind him. And in fact, yes, there Ruchel was, helping the female screener sort through the piles of black clothes and white clothes—the underwear and accessories—that she and her mother had so carefully placed in the suitcases earlier that day.

"And is this your first trip out of the country, Mr. Gottesman? That is, your first trip out of Israel since you moved here?"

Along with everything else, Reuven was concerned about how his cousin might react to being so pointedly addressed as: "Mr. Gottesman" instead of "Rav Gottesman." Yet once again Reuven's apprehensions proved unwarranted. Shmuely seemed blessedly unaware of the slight.

"Yes," he was answering the screener with a rueful smile. "This will be the first trip that I have made since arriving here. My wife and her mother occasionally go to New York to visit family members. They also occasionally go to Belgium—to Antwerp—where my wife's mother also has family members. But I have always been perfectly happy to stay put."

"You've never been back to New York for a visit? Not even once? Has there been no one there whom you wanted to see?"

"No."

"No places from your childhood that you wanted to revisit?"

"No."

Shmuely waited a beat.

"Nothing but losses there," he mumbled.

And then he fell silent.

Reuven gave his cousin an astonished look. What was Shmuely talking about? What losses? Yes, Shmuely's father, of course. But he had never even known that father—he had died several months before Shmuely's birth. And what else did his cousin feel he had lost?

"So why the visit now?"

"Because I've just sustained yet another loss," said Shmuely, in full voice again. "One that I cannot flee from, evidently. My mother died yesterday. I'm going home to bury her."

"I'm sorry."

"Thank you."

"What was your mother's name?"

"Gittel Gottesman."

"What was your father's name?"

"Asher Gottesman."

"Where were your parents originally from?"

"My mother was born in Brooklyn, like me. And my father was born in Cleveland."

"The woman in the back seat is your wife?"

"That is correct. My wife, Ruchel Seligson Gottesman."

"Also, from New York?"

"Originally. Her family has been in Jerusalem for eleven years. Five more than I have."

"Your wife's parents are originally from…?"

"Her father—also from Brooklyn. Her mother—from Antwerp, as I mentioned."

"Your father-in-law's business?"

"My father-in-law owns two jewelry stores—one in Jerusalem, one in Tel Aviv. You've maybe heard of his company? *Keter Zahav*? No? My mother-in-law—Binkel Seligson—manages the flagship store in Jerusalem. My wife is an associate manager."

"And you? What do you do?"

"I am a teacher."

Reuven shook his head. He had never heard Shmuely so cogent, so straightforward—so forthcoming—in all the years that he'd known him.

But at that point, the female screener tapped the male screener on his shoulder.

"I'm done," she said, slapping a sticker on their bags. "And they're getting a 'Number One'."

"Fine," her partner replied. "All clear on my side as well."

He'd looked at Shmuely sharply but courteously. "Safe trip," he'd said.

"Thank you."

Then he'd waved brusquely at Reuven. "Get going."

"So you see, Batya," Reuven continued, once he was safely home and he and his wife were each re-settled in their own twin bed after a very pleasant session together. "The journey to the airport was completely *mitn kop arop.*"

He turned on his back, interlaced his hands behind his head and stared at the ceiling.

"I was really worried how Shmuely would react to that airport official. He wasn't exactly rude to us. But he wasn't as… respectful as Shmuely likes."

Batya snorted.

"And yet, Shmuely was fine with him. Answered all his questions. And later, when I asked him why those questions hadn't bothered him, he said: 'Everything he asked had an answer, Reuven. I've been struggling with questions that don't, of late. This was better.'"

Batya snorted again.

"And—evidently—Shmuely stayed cooperative the whole way to New York. Ya-akov texted me about an hour ago to say that they got through all the other check points without problems, made their plane with time to spare and arrived in New York safe and sound."

He shrugged.

"Who understands the mysterious ways of *Ha-Shem*?"

"Hmmmph," said Batya after a moment. "Not so mysterious. The way I look at it, your cousin could use a little more of being treated the way that official treated him and a little less of being treated like he's the Messiah. Which reminds me. Could you believe the house that Yehuda bought for him and Ruchel? That kitchen with every possible modern convenience? That study larger than our entire living room? Those three enormous bedrooms for children who may not even ever arrive—"

"This is becoming inappropriate, Batya," said Reuven. "It's becoming gossip—*lashon hara.*"

But he said it without any real anger.
Because, after all, it was he who had started it.
And because, in fact, he knew what she meant.

Brooklyn

8.

On the journey from JFK International Airport to their house in Boro Park, Ya-akov kept his foot on the pedal and his eyes on the Belt Parkway, while Mierle lectured Ruchel on how she could have better managed the stresses of the eleven-hour-and-fifty-five-minute El Al flight. Shmuely, meanwhile, remained plastered down in the passenger seat with his head lowered and his eyes squeezed shut in an effort to block out everything around him.

His strategy had been working just fine until the moment that Mierle switched from pronouncements on in-flight survival tactics to instructions on the day ahead and noticed that he wasn't paying attention. She rapped him sharply on the shoulder. "Have you heard a single word that I said, Shmuely?"

Shmuely shrugged.

"I was saying that once we arrive—I'm giving you the boys' room for the week, by the way, they can sleep on the couches in the living room—you should go upstairs and wash up a bit before we set out for the service. Nothing major, of course. A little swish of mouthwash, maybe. You can get so *shmutzik* sitting on a plane."

Shmuely was on the verge of shrugging again when he thought better of it and nodded. He knew that the less he acknowledged his sister, the worse she would become. Mierle had always been the bossiest female in a childhood home of bossy females. She clearly hadn't changed.

But there was no more time to dwell on all that. Ya-akov was pulling into the driveway and pushing the button to unlock the car doors. Mierle immediately popped out and Ruchel ran to the trunk to pull out their two suitcases. Shmuely opened his eyes, sighed audibly, and began maneuvering himself out of his seat and onto the sidewalk.

"Everyone has been waiting so we can all walk to the funeral together," Mierle was explaining as she led them all in. "If you freshen up quickly, you can maybe have a cup of tea—maybe a few *kichel*—and then off we go. What, Shmuely? No tea? No *kichel*? Are you sure? You're allowed to eat a little something, you know, to keep from fainting away during the funeral service. Still the shaking of the head? All right, all right. Don't say I didn't offer."

Ruchel kept silent. She would have loved a cup of tea. It was too late now.

They made their way through the hallway and Shmuely craned his head to take in his surroundings. Sure enough, there they all were—crammed into Mierle's living room.

There were Mierle and Ya-akov's five children. There were his other sisters—Beile, Chava and Shayna and their husbands and all their many children. There were his mother's two sisters and two brothers and their spouses, plus several of their grown children.

Conversation halted the moment that Shmuely and Ruchel entered the room.

Mierle told everyone to give them some breathing space and most of the group obeyed without protest. Only the two youngest sisters—Chava and Shayna—pointedly ignored her orders. They ran right up to their brother, burst into tears and hugged him tightly while Ruchel stood mutely off to the side, her two big suitcases at her feet.

It was not often that Ruchel Gottesman—youngest and most pampered daughter of one of Jerusalem's finest English-speaking Haredi families—felt so totally uncounted and unmoored.

No wonder Shmuely had fled this terrible group!

But even at a time like this, Ruchel was not without resources. She spied Shayna's two-year-old, Toibe, hovering near her mother's legs and bent down eagerly to talk with her.

Shmuely heaved another loud sigh. Why did his wife have to get so *nebechdik* whenever she saw a child? It was bad enough when it happened back in Jerusalem. Here—in the midst of his eagle-eyed, relentlessly reproducing sisters—her behavior was like some great big bulging accusatory finger pointing straight in his direction.

Mierle finally managed to pry Shmuely's two youngest sisters away from their brother and Ruchel away from little Toibe. She nodded to Yaakov, and he picked up the suitcases and ushered them upstairs. When they came back down, looking no less rumpled than before, she gave her two younger sisters a look so stern that they kept their distance.

"It's time to set out," she trumpeted. "We can't be late. Let's go."

One by one or two by two, the men and boys lined up to leave while the women and girls gathered up all the toddlers and babies and filed in behind them. And once on the street, their procession quickly began acquiring additional marchers.

A steady stream of black-hatted men—neighbors, synagogue leaders and local merchants—approached from all sides, nodded respectfully to Shmuely and fell in with the men at the head of the line. A robust group of Gittel's friends and female neighbors, the clients of her wig store and the members of her synagogue sisterhood—formed temporary wings around the women, offering small embraces as appropriate before inserting themselves seamlessly into their midst.

It was a beautiful May day and the sun sharply illuminated the familiar sights of Shmuely's early years. There they all were—the butcher shop, the bakery, the shoe store, the hosiery store. The *yeshiva* that he had attended and the one that his family had spurned. The store that sold the plaid skirts that his sisters wore to their own schools. The hat shop in which his mother had proudly bought him his first big black hat.

The wig shop.

Not Gittel's own wig shop, *Baruch Ha-Shem.* That was located on the next avenue over. Shmuely didn't know what he would have done had he been forced to confront the shuttered windows of the domain in which his mother had reigned so absolutely and for so long. But even the sight of Gittel's biggest competitor was enough to drive him into despair.

Two blocks from the funeral home, Shmuely's sister Beile—peering around her to take a tally of who was there and who was not—noticed that Ruchel was walking all by herself on the very outskirts of the marchers. Where was that overbearing Mierle when she was truly needed? Beile quickly stepped in to fill the breach. She told her eleven-year-old to keep an eye on her younger siblings and made her way forcefully through the mass of women until she reached her Israeli sister-in-law.

"How are you doing, my dear?" she said, linking her elbow firmly around Ruchel's upper arm. "Such a rude shock, such a long flight. So sudden, so difficult. I can't believe you made it here—that you were able to detach Shmuely from his life in Jerusalem and get him on a plane. Almost six years since he left, and he's never once come back to see his family."

"Please don't be peeved at Shmuely, Beile," Ruchel answered, looking away from her sister-in-law's steady gaze. "He's been busy. He's been very busy."

"It's not for me that I'm upset. We were never so close, Shmuely and I. But Mama…"

Ruchel said nothing for a moment but took Beile's hand in hers and stroked it lightly. Beile, however, wasn't going to let go of something that had been bothering her for so long.

"Shmuely was Mama's only son, you know. She was heart-broken when he left. Kept saying she was going to visit him but never seemed to find the will to do it. I wrote Shmuely that he should come back to see her. Or call her. Or at least write! But all she ever got was that Rosh Hashana card that I assume came from you. It doesn't seem right. Don't you agree?"

Ruchel had no answers. How could she explain something she understood so poorly herself?

"I'm sorry. Shmuely never… Shmuely doesn't… I can't…."

"Sha-sha-sha, it's all right, it's fine—never mind," said Beile, as Ruchel's speech faded into gibberish. "I just had to mention it. I couldn't ignore it any longer."

She leaned an inch closer.

"We all have to cope with what *Ha-Shem* sends us, best as we can, don't we?"

They walked on in silence while Beile extended her neck forward to catch a glimpse of her brother as he marched along within the throng of his fellow black hats. Finally, she spotted him, nodded and changed tone once again.

"He's so tall, I hardly recognized him," she said, with a touch of pride that she couldn't hide. "Is it true he's the youngest, most up-and-coming *maggid shiur* at *Yeshiva Derekh ha-Emeth*?"

Ruchel nodded her head with pleasure. "*Baruch Ha-Shem.*"

"And how is he taking all this? He seems in shock. But then he's always looked a bit *farmisht* except when he was studying Torah. Was it really terrible for him when he first got the news?"

"Not so good, to tell you the truth. But what can you expect?"

"When it comes to Shmuely, you never know what to expect."

Ruchel smiled and looked at Beile full face for the first time. She realized that she'd never given this sister-in-law a single thought prior to that day. And even now, in Beile's time of bereavement, she wasn't being particularly attentive. For shame!

It wasn't the first time they'd met. Ruchel had vague memories of being introduced to Beile at her own wedding. But it hadn't gone much further than that. Well, how could anyone blame her, given everything else she'd had to juggle during that momentous time in her life?

But even when Beile, her husband and her two oldest children had returned to Israel for an extended sight-seeing tour that winter—and the whole Gottesman-Seligson clan had gathered for lunch at Reuven's house—Ruchel had barely registered Beile's soft, unpresumptuous presence.

And, of course, she'd never had reason to think about Beile based on anything that Shmuely had ever said. To the extent that he'd ever mentioned her, he'd just lumped her in with everyone else in his family—a group of indistinguishable women that he'd gladly left behind him.

Now with everyone gathered in one place, however, Ruchel could see that the four sisters were all very different. Yes, Shayna and Chava were a bit hard to tell apart at first—equally short and blond and equally sloppily dressed. But even in their case, it was possible to make some distinctions. Shayna was a bit blonder, a bit prettier and considerably stouter.

Mierle and Beile, moreover, were not only completely different from one another, they were completely distinct from the two youngest sisters. Mierle was dark-haired, skinny and sharp-featured and clearly picked her clothes with care. Beile was the plainest of all, oddly tall and—yes—substantially nicer than any of the others. As she was now proving by catering so kindly to Ruchel when it really should have been the other way around. Who was the *onenet*, after all?

Well, maybe she could make up for that now. Beile was clearly open to the idea of a friendly chat, despite her *onenet* status. And who knows what could be gleaned from such an exchange?

"So now it's my turn to ask some things," she said, giving Beile's arm a warm squeeze.

Beile nodded cautiously back. What on earth had she been thinking, opening the door to prying questions when there were so many dangerous topics in her family?

"Yes?"

"What was Shmuely like when he was a little boy? Was he the same as he is now?"

"Hard to know," Beile replied after a brief pause. "Since I can't really tell what he's currently like—besides being really upset. He hasn't spoken a word to me since you arrived."

"Hmnnnn. All right—then let's just leave it at: 'what was he like as a little boy?'"

"Well," said Beile, cautiously, "first of all, he was always buried in his books. Which I assume is still true or he wouldn't have come so far so fast."

"Yes, still true. All day long, he reads with his students. And as soon as dinner is over, he goes into his study and continues on his own. Sometimes he's up all night, it seems."

"So. I'm right. Anyway, my clearest memory of my brother is also of him shutting himself up in his bedroom with his texts. There were these two big bookcases that came together in one of the room's corners. He'd drape his prayer shawl between them—calling it his *sukkat sh'lomecha*, his canopy of peace—and sit underneath it with his back to the shelves and a book on his lap. And none of us was allowed to disturb him, except for…"

"Except for…?"

Beile pinched her lips together.

Well, there it was. She hadn't meant to slip up, but perhaps it was bound to happen. Serach was never very far from her mind. From any of their minds, really.

Of course, none of the sisters had as much as breathed Serach's name once their mother had declared her dead. They had never questioned Gittel's actions or demanded to know what had happened. They had refrained from murmuring a word about losing the sister who had always been there for them—seamlessly soothing quarrels, wiping noses, helping with homework, and taking over entirely when Gittel fell into one of her darker moods.

And—most of all—they had remained in scrupulous collective denial about what Serach's supposed demise had done to their baby brother. About how Shmuely had evolved from private but affectionate little boy into a near recluse within his own home, endlessly mourning the one soul whom he had permitted to enter his room.

But despite the enforced silence, all that *tsuris* had—inevitably—remained in the air around them. And never more strongly than today, when emotions were so raw and the holes in their family so glaringly apparent.

So now the question became: Just how much did Ruchel know about all that? Was she being coy when she posed her question, or did she really have no idea about the oldest sister who had broken all the rules—and broken Shmuely's heart?

"And none of us was allowed to disturb him," Beile concluded, all the while meticulously scrutinizing her sister-in-law's face for reactions.

"So he just kept to himself and his books?" Ruchel was reprising. "Even as a young boy?"

No, that sealed it. Ruchel's expression had remained utterly guileless as she spoke. She was clearly clueless as to the *shanda* that had shadowed the Gottesman family for so many years. And Beile certainly wasn't going to enlighten her. Devoted as Ruchel might be to her husband and her marriage, there was no way to know how she would react to the truth.

"I don't know exactly how to say this," Beile responded at last. "But I guess straight out is best. Shmuely always had his books and his faith—and that's all that he ever seemed to need."

Then she took Ruchel firmly by the arm again and determinedly nudged her forward.

"Look, we're almost there."

For, in fact, the first members of a procession that was now nearly a hundred strong had reached the parking lot of the funeral home. The men were turning steadily to the men's entrance on the left and the women were peeling off toward the women's entrance on the right.

Beile continued steering Ruchel gently along. When they reached the door, Ruchel turned around briefly to check on her husband. And when she finally picked out his profile among all those identically garbed and identically solemn fellow marchers, it brought her up short.

He looked so drawn, so weak, so pale—so totally alone, despite the presence of all the other men—that it hurt her heart to see him. He looked as if he were about to faint away. And what would happen then? It would be a total catastrophe.

She had to make sure he was all right.

Instinctively, impulsively, and against all her better judgment, she broke rank, ran right up to Shmuely's side and gently reached out to him as if she were going to touch his shoulder. She didn't complete the act, *Baruch Ha-Shem.* She stopped herself before violating the tradition that wives do not ever touch their husbands in public. She did, however, clearly violate the practice that women do not barge into the men's line during a religious event.

"Ruchel—this is entirely inappropriate," Shmuely stuttered, waving his arm back and forth at her as if brushing off a fly. "Go back to the women's line. Go inside. We'll speak later."

Ruchel hung her head and withdrew. Shmuely slowly brought his breathing back to normal as he carefully monitored his wife's progress back toward the women's entrance.

But just at the point that he had finally calmed his pounding heart, he caught sight of something that pitched him right back into chaos.

It couldn't be. It just couldn't be. And yet there it was. Unmistakably.

That *Spanish Woman* was standing just to the left of the door, plain as day. That wanton *Spanish Woman* who had lured Serach out of the fold. Whose home contained all those forbidden pictures. Who'd roamed around her living room right in front of him—in such revealing garments—on the occasions when he'd garnered enough strength to sneak out of his mother's house to seek comfort and help from his exiled sister. Whose name he had excised bitterly from his mind the moment he had broken contact with Serach.

She wasn't wearing those offensive garments now, *Baruch Ha-Shem.* She was appropriately dressed. Long skirt, flat shoes, stockings with seams so no one should think that her legs were bare. She'd even thought to put on a headscarf over that obscenely abundant head of hair. But the impression that her body had made on him during all those memorably disturbing visits remained so indelibly etched in his mind that its image flashed right out at him even through all those modest clothes.

What on earth was that *Spanish Woman* doing at his mother's funeral? What was she doing in a place that was totally forbidden to her—in a place in which she had no business?

But then his eyes slowly drifted from the *Spanish Woman* to the little figure standing right beside her, dressed entirely in black with her head bowed and her hands clasped. And the sheer intensity of his regard made Serach lift her head until their gaze met—grey eyes to blue eyes—in an electric mega-second of mutual recognition.

Serach's face lit up at the sight of the brother who nobody thought would ever return home. Her arms reached instinctively forward. She looked totally—blissfully—angelic.

"Shmuely!" she mouthed. "Shmuely! Tatteleh!"

The expression, the words—the gesture—were all soundless. But their impact was explosive.

If anyone were to recognize his outlawed sister standing there, *chas v'cholileh*—if anyone were to notice her trying to communicate with him or (even worse) catch him responding to her advances—it would shatter the whole world that he had so carefully constructed for himself. All the effort of renouncing her—all his wrapping himself up in the impermeable protection of Jerusalem and Torah and marriage—would have been for naught.

For what seemed to be an endless moment, Shmuely stared in shock at his sister's cherished silhouette, physically unable to move. But then he somehow finally managed to turn his back on the terrible, terrible temptation—the terrible, terrible danger—that she represented. To slip back into the column of his fellow black hats as they swept inexorably into the building to take in the first raw view of his mother's coffin.

Serach's mother's coffin.

9.

Paloma returned to the master bedroom at top speed after a quickly gulped cup of espresso, to replace her hand on the thin shoulder on which it had been resting—nearly permanently—since she'd dragged Serach home from the funeral.

She knew, logically, that Serach would still be breathing. No one dies from grief. At least not so quickly. Still, the sliver of profile just visible between tightly wrapped comforter and rumpled curls remained so deathly pale and motionless that she couldn't be sure.

For four days, Paloma had relentlessly boomeranged between fear, concern and exasperation. And exasperation was beginning to win out. Nothing that she'd done had worked. No tender caress, no Prince Charming kiss—no proffered cup of tea—had penetrated the rock-solid despair that had engulfed Serach from the moment that Shmuely had turned his back on the most meltingly yearning smile that Paloma had ever seen on her partner's lovely lips.

And today, even those ineffectual gestures were out of reach.

"Serach—we need to talk."

Serach gave an involuntary head-to-toe shiver before returning to stillness.

"Help me out here, Serach. I have a big problem. *We* have a big problem."

Serach remained inert. Paloma sighed and forged ahead.

"Baby, I can't stay with you again today. I managed to get coverage for my Sunday, Monday and Tuesday shifts—and yesterday was my day off. But there's no one else left to ask. And my patients need me back."

Serach made a small noise. "So, go," she managed to say into her pillow. "Just go."

"Serach," Paloma said in as calm a tone as she could muster. "I can't leave you alone in this state. You don't eat. You don't drink. You go pee from time to time, but other than that…."

"I've drunk some water," murmured Serach. "Every time I go to the bathroom, I drink some water from the sink. So please just go do what you have to do."

"Serach, I'm a nurse. I know what dehydration does to a person. You need to take more than a couple of sips from the sink a few times a day. You need to eat something. And you certainly aren't going to do any of that if I leave you here on your own."

Serach shook her head.

"Serach, can't you please at least just sit up for a moment so I can look you in the face? Get some minimal reassurance that you'll be all right if I go into Manhattan?"

"But I'm not all right, Paloma," replied Serach. She began to shiver visibly, forcing Paloma to make fists and silently curse Shmuely yet again.

"Serach, what can I do? Frank has taken off for Amsterdam with Kae-Dang. Etha—who had originally agreed to spell me today—was unexpectedly called in to work. Should I arrange for a home health aide?"

"Call Frayda."

10.

As soon as the Q train pulled into her stop at Church Avenue, Paloma sprang from her seat. She pushed through the doors, sprinted down the platform and ran up the stairs to the street, where she expertly dodged the crowds to round the corner onto Marlborough Road.

After passing the sturdy stone columns that separate Prospect Park South from the area's most bustling commercial strip, she typically slowed her pace. The Neighborhood Beautification Committee kept the tree-lined single-family blocks of that community in pristine splendor, and she loved to savor the moment of transition from Church Avenue's nerve-jangling movement, colors, and noise into all that loveliness.

This evening, however, she didn't pause to dwell on the beauty of a single flower. She'd somehow gotten through the day and was desperate to get back home to see how Serach had fared in her absence.

Yet when she finally bolted up the short path from pavement to front porch—red-faced from the unnatural May heat—she found herself abruptly changing course. Instead of taking the stairs two at a time and heading directly for their second-floor bedroom, she ducked under the heavily leafed trees guarding the house's right side and headed for the kitchen door at the back.

I think I should cool down a bit before attempting anything else, she reflected, as she rooted through her bag for her big ring of keys. Catch my breath. Have a tall glass of the iced tea that I prepared last night. Steel myself for what awaits upstairs.

The deep breathing strategy never stood a chance, however. Nor did the iced tea. For when Paloma finally located the key ring, found the right key, turned it in the lock and pushed inward, she found her entry blocked by something massive and unyielding.

What the hell is this?

She gave one last huge shove and managed to ram her way through.

And was blind-sided by what she encountered.

The obstruction behind the door turned out to be two bulging black garbage bags stacked sloppily one on top of the other. And her efforts to muscle her way through them had done more than just move them aside.

They had slashed open the bottom bag and something very unpleasant was leaking out.

Several other large puddles of liquid stretched across the wooden floor from sink to stove—dealing a mortal blow to the patina that had taken Manny two full days of sanding, varnishing and polishing to achieve.

All but one of the teak wall cabinets had been sealed shut with thick layers of grey electrical tape. The doors and drawers of the single unsullied cabinet were splayed disrespectfully open, revealing near-empty innards.

Her two prized copper pans, her two cast-iron skillets and her entire collection of All-Clad-Stainless-Steel cookware had been removed from the wall and stacked haphazardly on the counter to the right of the stove—while two monstrous pots that she'd never seen before sprawled authoritatively across the four burners.

All the fabulous glassware she'd inherited from Judith—the beautifully-proportioned juice and water tumblers, the French wine goblets and the champagne flutes—had been filled to the brim with water and placed rim-to-rim across her kitchen table. One particularly lovely rose-pink goblet balanced so dangerously near the table edge that the slightest movement in its vicinity would send it crashing to the floor.

Her oven had been inexplicably turned to "broil" and had clearly been blasting away for hours—transforming her reliably cool, tree-shaded oasis of a room into an inferno.

And there, amidst all the bedlam, stood Frayda with her back to the door, sweating profusely as she vigorously slammed Paloma's brand-new Steamforce Rowenta iron back and forth across the marble surface of the main kitchen counter.

"Frayda! What are you doing? And what the hell have you done to my kitchen?"

"I'm cleansing away all the *trayf*. Burning away all the *trayf*."

Frayda neither turned to face Paloma nor missed a beat with the iron, but her voice was loud, and her words rang clear.

"Everything—every single thing—in this kitchen was *trayf*," she proclaimed. "Everything had to be *kashered*. The oven, the counters, the refrigerator, the shelves, the pots, the glassware, the silverware, the sink. The works."

"What are you talking about?"

Paloma knew what "trayf" was. Serach had told her about it early on in their relationship when she'd shyly requested that Paloma warn her when anything she'd cooked contained pork or shellfish. She'd explained that those things are called "trayf" and observant Jews don't eat them. That even Jews who had left the fold—Jews like herself—might balk at the idea of eating them. That old habits tend to die hard.

Okay, fine. No unannounced shrimp. But how did that relate to the current catastrophe?

Frayda peered over her shoulder at Paloma for a moment with an expression that hovered between belligerence and satisfaction. She then turned back to her ironing and her lecture.

"With a few things—like your drinking glasses," she intoned, "*kashering* is fairly simple. You don't have a dishwasher. Makes things easier. Since your glasses never contained hot liquids and were never in a dishwasher, you just need to scrub them, fill them with cold water and let them sit for 24 hours. For other things, however," and here she drew a breath, "it's more complicated. So, for example, when it comes to silverware and pots and pans—things made of metal—first you have to scrub them…."

Scrub my copper pans? You didn't! You couldn't! Don't you know that you need to treat copper with kid gloves?

"… and then you have to set them out to wait for the allotted period. Then you must submerge them completely in boiling water. I brought over some equipment from my house to do all the boiling in,"—and here she gestured with one thumb at the huge foreign pots usurping all the burner spots. "But I can't start that part of the process till the twenty-four prescribed waiting hours have elapsed."

Paloma glanced briefly in the direction Frayda had indicated before looking quickly away.

"And then there are the things," and here Frayda raised her voice a notch further, lifted Paloma's iron into the air and waved it around several times, "for which the only solution is *fire*. The counters, for example. The oven."

She brought the iron down on the marble surface with such force that Paloma flinched.

Paloma felt both completely paralyzed and unable to take her eyes away from Frayda's gesticulations—like some bystander at a five-car pile-up on the highway.

Why am I finding it so difficult to respond to all this lunacy? Why can't I figure out how to stop this woman?

"There are some rabbis who say that *kashering* a kitchen counter requires a blowtorch," Frayda said, almost musingly. "But my own rabbi," and here she picked up the iron and contemplated it with appreciation, "says that ironing is enough."

She returned to her task.

"When it comes to the oven, however," she continued, nodding vehemently to herself as she diligently dragged the iron back and forth, "there is no cutting corners. You must put it on the highest setting and leave it there for eight hours straight. I turned it on at eleven this morning, so we've only got an hour to go, *Baruch Ha-Shem*."

She paused for a moment before adding in a tone that Paloma later swore contained more than a trace of glee, "Of course there are some things that are totally hopeless. Even a blow torch won't do it. Your porcelain dishware, for example? All those porous surfaces? Who knows what kind of *trayf* they've absorbed over all the years? They have to be given away, thrown away or…"

Paloma blanched.

"But not to worry. I noticed how fancy-shmancy they all are—" Frayda unexpectedly snorted—"so I just sealed them up in those cabinets over there with some tape, so no one uses them by mistake. Plus, I sealed off all your *trayf* non-perishables.

"And in the meantime," she added, "I brought in some dishware from my own house—a few for meat, a few for dairy. The ones for dairy are on the bottom shelf of that cabinet—you can see them where I've left the door open. The ones for meat are on the second shelf, so you shouldn't mix them up. I also bought some plastic silverware for tonight, and some new sponges, different colors. White for dairy and pink for meat. Can't get confused with *that* for a system, can you?"

She paused momentarily while she caught her breath.

"Meanwhile, the one piece of good news is that your sink has two sides and they're both made of metal, so all I had to do was to scrub them. And tomorrow—when the waiting period is over—I'll dowse them with boiling water, and we can use one side for washing the dairy dishes and the other for the meat. Also, you seem to have two different sets of silverware so we can easily keep them apart."

Paloma shook out her head and finally found her voice.

"Frayda, will you kindly shut up? And will you stop ironing my counter like a crazy person?"

Frayda sniffed loudly and reached over to pull out the plug. "I was just finishing up," she said. But she kept her hand wrapped around the iron's handle.

Then she looked Paloma straight in the eye and added: "I also got rid of everything in your refrigerator and scrubbed out the shelves and walls with my special detergent. Also, the freezer."

It was still taking Paloma a moment to register each of Frayda's pronouncements—what the hell was wrong with her reflexes?—but this last remark grabbed her attention in real time.

"Got rid of everything in the refrigerator?"

She strode over to it, opened the door and peered in. One lone bag of food sat on the side of the top shelf and a second one on the shelf below it. But apart from that, the appliance was as pristine as when it was first delivered.

"Jesus Christ—what have you done with all my food?"

"It's all in there," said Frayda, gesturing to the garbage bags by the door. "It can go out tomorrow morning when the garbage collectors make their pick-up."

"Holy crap, woman! Do you have any idea what a waste…?"

"Not a waste. It was all *trayf*."

What could Paloma possibly say to that? One again she found herself speechless.

"But what are we going to eat in the meantime?" she finally spluttered.

"No worries, I brought in some kosher take-out. Serach ate a couple of bites of tuna salad on a Ritz cracker for lunch—*Baruch Ha-Shem* I finally persuaded her. The bag on the bottom shelf has a kosher rotisserie chicken that I'll serve cold tonight. And after everything is properly *kashered*, I'll start making everything fresh for *Shabbos* and for the next couple of weeks and…"

Making everything fresh for *Shabbos* and for the next couple of weeks? What is this woman talking about? How much longer does she think she's going to be here?

Paloma took a breath. "Frayda, you're talking sheer nonsense. This isn't going to last more than a couple of days. Serach will snap out of it and you'll be on your way."

"If she's anything like her mother, it'll take more than a couple of days…"

"What do you mean, 'if she's anything like her mother'? Serach is nothing like her mother!"

"So you say. In this matter, I don't see all that much difference. You didn't know Gittel. I did. Same thing, same thing. Into her bed with her face to the wall and the covers pulled up to her ears when she was having one of her fits. Or days and days of sitting in the living room with the lights off, not speaking and practically not eating. This is Gittel Gottesman all over again."

"From what Serach has told me, Gittel went off the deep end pretty regularly. But nothing like this has ever happened to Serach before. This is highly out of the ordinary."

"So is losing a mother."

"This has nothing to do with Serach's mother!"

"Of course it does. It's all over between them now. *Geyn kaput.* No hope for reconciliation. So Serach is in mourning. Maybe not 'sitting *shiva.*' More like 'lying *shiva.*' But it's definitely some kind of *shiva.* Fact is, she's actually doing it just like her mother might have done."

Paloma shook her head hard.

"Serach was coping with her mother's death just fine, Frayda," she said. "As you know. And no thanks to the totally clueless manner that you broke the news to her, by the way. But never mind all that. The point is, she was managing. She only fell apart when Shmuely behaved the way he did in that parking lot. If this is 'sitting *shiva*' like you say it is, then it's for the death of her relationship with Shmuely, not with her mother. God help her. She survived her mother's death. It's Shmuely the schmuck who's shattered her."

"Maybe yes, maybe no," said Frayda pointedly ignoring Paloma's colorful language. "Who's to say? But I wouldn't call her shattered. Deflated, maybe."

"Jesus, Frayda. What's the difference?"

"The difference is, she'll re-inflate. Like her mother always did. Gittel was a rock when she wasn't falling apart. Raised six children all by herself after her husband died. Ran her business. Paid her bills. Kept her house spotless—you could have eaten off those floors. You saw her in her shop, you'd never guess how she behaved when she was in one of her states. You saw her lying in bed, you'd never guess how tough she was when she was running her shop. She was up, she was down—there was no predicting. Eventually, she always recovered. So Serach will, too."

Paloma winced.

"And in the meantime, no worries. I'll stay here till Serach feels better. Make sure she's alive and breathing. You can go off to work, do whatever it is you have to do."

Paloma closed her eyes for a moment before nodding.

"I know," she finally said, turning away from the new mistress of her domain. "And… I'm grateful to you for all that. Don't think that I'm not."

She walked wearily away out of the kitchen to reach the back staircase. She rested her hand briefly on the wooden newel-post. It felt cool and smooth against her palm, as it always did, and she allowed herself to take some comfort from that. And then she began the slow climb up to the master bedroom to see what was happening with her partner.

Manhattan

11.

It had long bothered Etha that her friendship with Paloma was so lopsided.

For all the years they'd worked together at Maimonides Hospital, they'd essentially functioned as a seamless tag team. Exchanging shifts. Helping one another with difficult procedures. Trading tension-relieving wise cracks when the doctors barked orders at them or the Haredi patients balked visibly at their touch.

That equality swiftly shifted, however, once they were outside the hospital's walls.

Sure, on the rare occasions when their days off coincided, Paloma liked to buzz into Manhattan for a home-cooked lunch and catch-up chat at Etha's house. But it was only Paloma who—early on in their friendship—could blithely hand Etha a spare set of keys and say: "When you're stuck working late, just hop a cab to our house, let yourself in and camp out. It takes no time to get to us by car. You'll be tucked into bed within minutes instead of hanging out on a subway platform at some ghastly pre-dawn hour, waiting for a train back to the city."

And it was only Paloma who could furnish all the extras that went along with a "camp out" in Prospect Park South.

Etha would invariably find a fresh toothbrush and tube of toothpaste laid out on the table in the guest room when she climbed to the third floor of that impressive house. The comforter on the bed would be turned down just enough to reveal the soft sheets below. And when Paloma couldn't be there to personally make breakfast, Etha would wake to find a note explaining that there was a "nice pastry" for her in the microwave, a pitcher of fresh orange juice in the fridge and an espresso maker waiting for her use.

Etha therefore felt a jolt of real pleasure when Paloma announced that she was taking a position at Memorial Sloane Kettering on Manhattan's Upper East Side. The loss of her friend's presence at Maimonides was a small price to pay for the ability to finally say: "Come spend the night in my Stuyvesant Town apartment any time they keep you working into the wee hours."

Any chances for that pleasant reciprocity soon faded, however, as Paloma quickly mastered the art of avoiding MSK's graveyard shifts. And they evaporated entirely when Paloma was so fiercely courted by Manhattan East's new Cancer Research and Care Center that she was able to make "no late nights" a condition of that hiring.

She had never, in short, needed to take up Etha's kind offer of a sleepover in the city.

Until now.

"Of course you can stay with me, Paloma. You don't even have to ask."

"But what if it turns out to be more than just a night? Or two nights? What if it takes a whole week for things to, um, work themselves out?"

"Paloma! It's okay! *Mi casa es su casa*—or however you guys say it. How many times have you and Serach welcomed me into your house like a sister?"

"You know I wouldn't ask if I didn't really need it."

"Paloma, shut up already!"

Which is why Paloma landed on Etha's doorstep right after work on the second Saturday following Frayda's takeover of her kitchen.

"Boy, it sure is nice to just hop the Second Avenue bus from work and arrive here in a flash," she proclaimed as soon as Etha opened the door to her three short buzzes. "What a fool I was not to move in with you as soon as I took a job in Manhattan."

Etha smiled.

"What's more, I can't tell you how much I'm looking forward to some of your heavenly mac-and-cheese. Can I help you with something in the kitchen?"

"Huh-uh. Just make yourself at home. Supper will be ready in a jiff.'"

Etha ducked back to mind the stove while Paloma sat down on the couch, shed her nurses' Crocs, stretched out her pedicured toes and basked in a flow of relaxed energy.

The bus ride had been only the first step in the process of her decompression. The stroll through Stuyvesant Town's verdant paths under an unexpected spring breeze took her deeper. And the sight of Etha's cozily appointed living room offered the last critical bit of balm.

The supple brown leather sofa-bed on which she now relaxed promised a blissfully restful night of sleep. The thickly piled brown, black and white geometric rug felt marvelous under the soles of her bare feet. The painting of tropical mountains that took up most of the wall behind her—a gift from a cousin on the Jamaican side of Etha's family—reminded her of the landscape stretching out beyond her own grandmother's home, back in Colombia. The glistening-smooth surfaces of the Shona sculptures that Etha had arranged across the top of her bookshelf called out to her fingertips to be stroked.

Paloma took it all in gratefully for a minute. She then tucked her bags neatly into the space between the sofa-bed and one of the end tables, walked toward the kitchen and peered in.

"Are you sure I can't do anything for you?"

"Yes, I'm sure. Go sit down. I've prepared your favorite menu. Broiled shrimp, mac-and-cheese, greens with smoked turkey and some chilled Chardonnay."

Etha entered the living room five minutes later with silverware, napkins, placemats and plates and laid everything down on the neat square table under the window. She returned to the kitchen to retrieve two glasses and a cut-glass decanter of the wine. She then made a third and final trip to bring in a tray with the shrimp, the greens and the mac-and-cheese, all bubbling away in their Corning Ware dishes.

Paloma moved to the table with a sigh of pleasure.

"Oh, Etha, you are the best friend a girl could ever have," she said, pouring them each a glass of wine.

And then she took a good look at the food.

"Etha? What's with this mac-and-cheese?"

"Well, why don't you just taste it and see?"

"Etha, this is not the pillowy-soft, sinfully rich dish that has given me so much joy over the years. This looks like something appallingly 'good for me.' What the heck is this?"

"It's called 'Macaroni & Yeez'. It's a low-fat, no-dairy, non-refined-flour version. Artichoke noodles, nutritional yeast, mustard and unsweetened almond milk. No cream, no cheddar cheese, no white-flour macaroni. A whiff of margarine and some shredded carrots for color. Some salt and pepper and a little nutmeg for taste. That much I kept the same as always."

"And you've committed this travesty because…"

"Because… Paloma—how can we not follow the regimen that we preach to our patients day in and day out? I've been revising the way I cook. Less sugar, less wheat, less salt, less dairy. More nutrients."

"I'm going to cry, Etha. Neither of us is pre-diabetic! Or hypertensive. Or gluten intolerant. Or lactose intolerant. All that stuff isn't for us!"

Etha shook her headful of goddess braids.

"Just taste it, girlfriend, before you say anything."

They sat in silence for a moment as Paloma took a small bite, looked away and then took another. Etha smiled.

"So. Now that we've crossed that hurdle, do you want to tell me what's happening? Or do you want to wait till we're done with supper?"

Paloma sighed. "Perhaps it would be best for me to polish off what's on my plate first. This imitation mac-and-cheese isn't so bad, after all."

"Hmmph."

They finished up and Paloma spent more time than necessary bringing everything back to the kitchen, rinsing everything off and putting it in Etha's dishwasher. It was finally all done, however, and she returned to the table, looked down for a moment and began to speak.

"All right, Etha."

"I'm here."

"Well, as you know, I've been pretty bent out of shape about Serach's depression. But I could have gone on coping if it had just remained at that. I was—I was even resigned to Frayda being there all the time. And to all her *kashering* nonsense."

Etha nodded.

"After all," Paloma continued, "what could I do? I needed her. What's more, it turns out she's a pretty good cook. One night, she made this roast chicken and this dish of noodles with poppy seeds, cabbage shreds and something that she called 'schmaltz.' Really delicious. Who knew? She and I—God help us—began eating dinner together every night, as soon as Serach finished her four bites of soup on a bed tray upstairs. And it wasn't unpleasant. I would tell her about my day at the hospital and she would listen. Turns out, she used to be a receptionist in a dental office. She likes talking about medical procedures. Who knew that either?"

"So, if you were making peace with Serach's depression and Frayda's such a great chef and such good company…"

Paloma laughed.

"…then what drove you out of your house? Why are you here? Not that I mind, but…"

Paloma got up, sat down again, sighed a few times and then stopped sighing.

"Okay. So yesterday, I arrive home at 7:00, really looking forward to one of Frayda's meals. But instead of ushering me right in to eat, she's standing at the door with two candlesticks and some prayer books and announcing that I'm just in time to 'welcome in the *Shabbos*'. That we're going to go upstairs to Serach's bedside and light the candles and do the service that's permitted when it's just three women."

She paused.

"Are you familiar with that particular idiocy?"

"Yes, Paloma. You need ten Jewish men to conduct a full prayer service. A 'minyan,' it's called."

"You never cease to amaze me, Etha."

"Twelve years at Maimonides Hospital, Paloma."

"Ah, yes. Anyway, so Frayda leads me upstairs to where Serach is lying on our bed like a used tissue. She puts the candles in the candlesticks, places them on our dresser, lights them and starts chanting. And Serach manages to get up on one elbow and start chanting along with her. A minor miracle, you might say."

Etha nodded.

"So okay, fine. Good for Serach. Good for Frayda. Good for Jewish ritual. Catholics also light candles and say blessings. And—in my grandmother's day—they did it in Latin. Which is nearly as unintelligible as Hebrew."

"Go on."

"But then Frayda passes out the prayer books and we launch into the service. And suddenly Serach isn't just kind of 'chanting along,' propped up on one elbow. She's sitting fully upright and beginning to look happy. Happy!"

Paloma pressed her lips together and Etha reached over to put two well-groomed, deep-brown fingers lightly on her wrist.

"But I think: 'Okay, Paloma. This is helping Serach feel better. Cope!' I let everything wash over me nice and easy and just wait for it to be over."

She looked at Etha hard.

"Until all of a sudden, I glance down at the English translation on the other side of the prayer-book page, and what do I see? I see that what Frayda is mouthing is that women will die in childbirth if they don't do three things the way they're supposed to."

She threw Etha a blazing look.

"Do you want to hear what those three things are, Etha?"

Etha knew better than to say "no." She nodded.

"Okay. The first thing is lighting the Sabbath candles. Failure to light those candles and you're destined for death."

Paloma glowered even more. Etha ignored it.

"The second thing is baking this special bread—*challah* it's called—in some particular way."

"I know what *challah* is," Etha said, very softly.

"Okay, fine. Make a mistake with that bread and you're a goner. And the third thing—and I kid you not—is failing to observe this practice called 'niddah' which sets the schedule when women are allowed to have sex with their husbands, based on their menstrual cycles. Serach once told me about it. Flaunt that practice and you die. And not just any death. Death during childbirth."

Etha had the good sense to look horrified.

"So okay, I'm reading all this indecent stuff and I look over at Serach to see how she's taking it, and instead of being as appalled as I am, she's nodding along like it's the Gospel truth."

Paloma's voice leapt into a more strident register.

"Etha, what the hell has happened to my strong, modern, logical, feminist Serach? How could she be reveling in the same male-chauvinist-pig crap that made her suffer all those years?"

Paloma pulled her wrist away from Etha's fingers, stood up and began to pace.

"I'm not going to say anything until you've calmed down," said Etha, still very softly. She'd never seen Paloma this agitated, and it was frightening her. "And in the meantime, are you asking me to respond, or do you just need to vent?"

Paloma sighed and sat down.

"I'm asking you to respond. Please. And sorry."

"Okay. I'll tell you what I hear. I hear that your profoundly depressed partner is seeking comfort in her religion. Which is what religion is all about, you know."

"Not this religion. This religion is all about making people miserable."

"C'mon girl! Stop being so dumb."

Paloma shook her head, but she offered no retort.

"I also hear that…. Paloma, I hear that you're *jealous*. Of that prayer book. Of its power to do what… you couldn't. Of its power to reach Serach and cheer her up."

"It's not jealousy!"

"No need to shout, girl."

"Well, hell. Maybe it is jealousy. But even more than that, it's… impotence! Goddammit! I'm a healer. It's what I do. I help people heal from cancer for God's sake. And here is the love of my life—the woman I've always been able to take care of—so depressed that she can't even get out of bed. And nothing I do helps."

Paloma paused and swallowed.

"In fact, it's almost been as if she doesn't *want* my help. And what is it that she does want? The same damned stuff that plunged her into the pit in the first place. The stuff that made her brother behave like such a… such a…"

"Look, Paloma," said Etha in a voice that she might have used to soothe a miserable child. "First of all, there's no reason to feel bad that you couldn't help Serach when she was in the depths of despair. No one really understands depression or how to deal with it. All those TV ads about: 'Is your anti-depressant not working? Try adding Medication Q'. There's never been an easy solution. So… cut yourself some slack on that front."

Paloma looked away toward the darkening lawn.

"There's also no reason to feel bad that Serach is taking refuge in her old prayer book. That's what people do in times of trouble. It doesn't mean that she's on track to becoming a religious fanatic. She's just seeking out a bit of solace. You don't go to Mass every week, but you still pray to the Virgin Mary when you're in trouble, don't you?"

"That's different. The Virgin Mary is a woman! She understands things."

Etha shook her head. She reached over to take Paloma's hand. And Paloma let her.

"So my advice to you—and you said you wanted me to respond, so please let me finish—my advice to you is to stop focusing on Serach and start focusing on Paloma. Serach is in good hands, it seems. You can let go for a bit. You can take all the TLC you wish you could give her and give it to yourself. Coming to stay with me was a good beginning. I'll pamper you best as I can. But you also need to find something to remind yourself of your inner mojo. Which is still there, I guarantee you. It's just bruised up a bit."

"What kind of a something?"

"Well… maybe something you've never done before? Something new that you can discover you're really good at? Can you think of anything like that?"

Paloma closed her eyes, put one hand up to her forehead and rubbed. Then she stopped, opened her eyes and gave the ghost of a smile.

"Well… I recently heard about this place in the South Bronx that might be just the ticket. This girls' organization that… I'm not sure exactly what it does… Helps Latina juvenile delinquents do art projects? Something like that…"

"Paloma, be serious!"

Paloma chuckled, and it suddenly felt very good to do so.

"No, really. Funny how things work out. Remember that fundraising lunch I told you about at Manhattan East? Well, one of the donors was this snooty Argentinian man with this even snootier Salvadoran wife.

They came up to me after I spoke, and the wife began talking about that organization. She runs it, evidently. She told me I should come help with it. That I could be a role model for those girls."

Paloma made a face.

"I brushed her off because, well—shit. She annoyed the heck out of me. And besides, why should I go back to the South Bronx? I left that whole scene a long time ago. Thank God!"

She paused.

"But I did keep her card. Just in case."

"Paloma! It could be just what the doctor ordered. Take your mind off your troubles while also… uh… helping you to re-connect with your roots."

"I'm totally connected with my roots, thank you very much."

Etha smiled. "Didn't I just hear you gloating that you escaped all that a long time ago? Don't you live in Prospect Park South with a lily-white woman and an even lily-whiter concert pianist? Don't you dine on Limoges china every night—and make sure everyone knows it?"

"You're the one to talk!" said Paloma before she could help herself. "Since when did Stuyvesant Town become a center of Black culture?"

Etha carefully smoothed out the sleeve of her perfectly pressed striped cotton shirt with her long fingers.

"We're not talking about me. We're talking about you."

They both looked out the window for a bit.

"The point is," Etha finally reprised, "that besides distracting you, this could… help you balance things out a bit while Seṛach burrows back into her prayer book."

"Jesus, Etha!"

"So," said Etha, smiling sweetly. "My advice is that you call up that donor, pronto. And in the meanwhile, it's time for dessert. Some fruit salad?"

"You're breaking my heart, Etha. All day long I've been fantasizing about your famous coconut cream cake. Light as a feather, filled with airy custard, covered in vanilla frosting and with all those shreds of fresh coconut and divinely sweet maraschino cherries on the top…."

"Well, what we've got is fruit salad. Do you want some?"

"Sure."

12.

By going into Manhattan East both Sundays and staying late for a few nights, Paloma managed to repay her colleagues for all the shifts they'd covered while she was at home with Serach, to clear her desk of its backlog of paperwork and to put in for her normal Wednesday off.

She woke up at ten o'clock to find Etha long gone and turned her thoughts to the pressing question of what she should wear to the meeting she'd arranged.

As she rummaged through her little carry-all, it quickly become clear that she hadn't packed what she needed. Her scrubs would never do, and neither would her gym shorts. The pair of white jeans she'd thrown in at the last minute held some promise—they never seemed to wrinkle, and they fit like a glove. And, of course, her signature high-heeled red sandals were always right. Nonetheless, she definitely needed to cap it all off with something other than the stretched-out tank tops that she'd brought for exercise and sleep.

She quickly donned the jeans, the sandals and the least grungy of the tank tops, re-assembled the sofa-bed and placed the bedding back in the front hall linen closet.

She smiled at the box of whole-grain cereal, bottle of almond milk and canister of fair-trade decaffeinated coffee that awaited her on Etha's kitchen counter and carefully returned them to where they belonged. She then grabbed her bag and headed out to First Avenue where she picked up a chocolate croissant and a full-caffeine double espresso at the first Starbucks that she encountered before heading southward to the shop whose name had popped right up when she'd Googled "clothing stores near Stuyvesant Town" the previous evening.

The shop turned out to be everything that its website claimed and more—chock-full of gorgeously colored dresses, flowing pants, scarves and jewelry. Paloma steered clear of the most alluring of those temptations and chose just two things—a dusky-rose-pink, subtly-beaded sleeveless top and a pair of dangly gold earrings—that perfectly answered her needs.

Once they were paid for, she ducked back into the dressing room to trade her tank top for the new shirt and her simple silver "nurse's studs" for the new earrings. She gave herself a glance in the full-length mirror. It added up to a nicely eye-catching look—and the appreciative gazes she garnered on the bus ride uptown solidly confirmed that self-appraisal.

At the point that she dismounted at 48th Street and found her way to Carlota's building, however, she felt a small, uncharacteristic twinge of self-doubt. The dazzling bronze-colored glass of its façade brought back vivid memories of the bank-breaking, white-on-white knit suit that Carlota had worn to the lunch at Manhattan East.

And as if that flashback weren't bad enough, she began hearing Frank's voice bouncing around in her head—Kentucky cadence in full force:

Really, Paloma! Carlota Bianchi invites you to lunch at an apartment house that practically screams "corporate wealth", and this is how you dress? Are you never going to learn to "match the clothes to the occasion"? You couldn't find yourself a little Jackie Onassis shift and some Capezio flats instead of squeezing yourself into your old white jeans and your "come hither" red sandals and then adding in a pair of earrings and shirt that should never have left Nepal?

Oh, shut up, Frank, she barked back to her thoughts. *This isn't a business meeting at some fancy restaurant—it's a little lunch in a private home to talk about a South Bronx nonprofit. I'm clean, I'm pretty and I absolutely refuse to be cowed by wealth.*

She then shook out her shoulders, walked up the long, curved drive to the building's entrance, smiled as the heavy glass doors slid obediently apart at her approach and stepped into the vast, red-carpeted double-height lobby.

Two doormen sat at full attention behind the massive rectangular desk in front of the floor-to-ceiling windows at the back of that expansive space. They wore identical black jackets, red vests and natty black bowties that—in tandem with the men's impeccably straight spines—conveyed a clear double-edged message of vigilance and welcome.

The doorman seated to the left had pale skin, silver hair and mustache, and a smile that—given how he deployed it—someone must have told him looked "virile." The brass nameplate perched strategically in front of him on the desk announced that his name was: "Anatolie Balescu."

The doorman on the right sported a similarly trim mustache and the same properly puffed-up chest, but his hair was black and his smile more winsome than manly. He couldn't have been more than thirty years old, and his name plate said: "Ricardo Peña."

Paloma made a beeline for Ricardo.

"Hi there," she said, instinctively placing her hands down on the desk in front of him in such a way that her thumbs and forefingers surrounded his name plate cozily. "My name is Paloma Rodriguez and I'm here to see Carlota Bianchi in apartment 32 B."

Ricardo's smile became a few shades more winsome.

"Is Ms. Bianchi expecting you?"

"Oh yes. Definitely." said Paloma. "She's invited me to lunch."

"Just give me one moment, Ms. Rodriguez, and I'll call and send you right up to see her."

"Thank you," said Paloma and was rewarded with a blush.

The more she smiled at him, the more he blushed and fumbled. He bit his lower lip as he punched the numbers into the phone.

"Ms. Bianchi?"

There was a pause.

"Oh, sorry. Sorry. I thought I… oh…"

He looked up briefly at Paloma. "I punched in the wrong… one moment…"

"It's okay, Ricardo. Take your time."

Ricardo straightened up, stopped smiling and aimed his white-gloved index finger more carefully at the phone. This time it worked.

"Ms. Bianchi? Oh yes, Consuelo? Yes, of course. I have a Ms. Rodriguez here downstairs to see Ms. Bianchi. Yes, I'll wait."

Paloma smiled at him encouragingly.

"Wonderful," he finally said into the phone. "Thank you." And then he straightened up in his seat and gave Paloma a serious nod.

"She's waiting for you," he said. "Just take the elevator to the left up to the 32nd floor. It will be the only apartment to your right as you exit the elevator."

"Thank you, Ricardo," said Paloma, meeting his serious expression with her own before breaking into her most dazzling grin. "And I guess I'll be seeing you again after lunch."

She walked slowly toward the elevator bank that led to the East Tower. Just before getting there, she pivoted on one high-heeled sandal and looked back at him. And sure enough, he was still gazing at her. She gave him a little wave. And why not? Poor guy. Brighten his day.

Ricardo beamed sheepishly and then turned around quickly to greet the next visitor.

The interior of the elevator to the East Tower was lined in mirrors, providing Paloma with some reassurance that her outfit could (with a little flexibility) be deemed appropriate for a lunch date in a midtown apartment house at 1:00 p.m., on a weekday. She immediately suffered another setback however, when she traversed the five steps to the apartment door, rang the bell and was greeted by a small dark-skinned Latina in authentic maid's gear and caught a glimpse of the rooms stretching on beyond the maid's right shoulder.

"Please come in," said the maid in strongly accented English, instinctively lowering her face away from Paloma's keen stare. She led Paloma through a marble-floored foyer dominated by a pedestaled statue of a large naked man and into the living room.

"Please sit down, Ms. Rodriguez. Ms. Bianchi will be with you in a moment."

Not only was this the single largest room that Paloma had ever seen in any private home—twice the size of her own not-inconsiderable-sized living room—it was also so overwhelmingly, blindingly white that she blinked.

A long, low, L-shaped white couch stretched languidly across a large white rug embroidered with an intricate design in an even whiter white. A glass coffee table topped with two enormous vases overflowing with white dahlias reflected the flood of daylight emanating from the floor-to-ceiling windows. A glance cast through those windows revealed unobstructed views of the afternoon-white cloudy sky, the shimmering grey-white East River, and the glitteringly silver inverted arches of the Queensborough Bridge.

The single wall free from windows showcased a ten-foot-long painting on which nine silvery figures of indeterminate gender and race cavorted on a whiter-than-white background.

And in front of that splendidly art-enhanced, non-windowed wall stood the *pièce de résistance*—a gleaming white, nine-foot-long, Steinway D-274 concert grand piano with its magnificent lid propped up and its keyboard on full display.

Paloma—finding it impossible to contemplate doing anything that might mess up that perfectly white couch—ignored the maid's suggestion that she take a seat and instead walked up to the piano and carefully and soundlessly pressed down a few of the keys.

"Do you play, Paloma?"

Paloma spun around to see Carlota advancing toward her with both arms extended.

"No," Paloma answered carefully. "I don't. But my housemate does. He's a concert pianist. He's in Amsterdam on tour right now but when he's at home, he practices on our Bösendorfer."

Good heavens, Paloma, whom are you trying to impress? What is it about this situation that makes you need to do that? Why should Carlota care about Frank or the Bösendorfer—or whether he practices at home or not?

But Carlota simply glowed back at Paloma, walked close, and clasped her hands in her own.

"How nice for you," she said in her husky-soft voice. "And how nice that you finally decided to come meet us. We're in the dining room. Come on in!"

Carlota's blond hair lay heavily on the shoulders of the white silk tunic that she wore over wide white pants. Her feet were bare and the pearly white of her painted toenails shone translucently against the olive-brown of her thin toes.

"Oh!" said Paloma, after she glanced down and realized what the bareness of those feet might indicate. "Should I have taken off my shoes?"

"Bamboo floors," Carlota murmured, "do tend to scratch. But it's not your fault. Consuelo clearly didn't tell you. I'm surprised, frankly. I'll have to talk to her."

Paloma bent down to undo the buckles of her sandals and hopped along awkwardly as she tried to yank them off while also keeping pace with her host's gracefully long strides.

"What should I… what should I do with them?" she asked when they were finally off her feet and dangling by their straps from her fingers.

"Excuse me?"

"My sandals? What… where should I put them?"

"Consuelo!"

Consuelo appeared soundlessly within seconds.

"Yes, Ma'am."

"Please take Ms. Rodriguez's shoes and place them on the mat by the front door. And next time…" She arched an eyebrow.

Paloma handed the maid her shoes with an apologetic look that Consuelo pointedly ignored, and then scrambled off again to catch up with Carlota's onward march.

"Marta!" said Carlota as they rounded the bend to enter a dining room that was no less spacious and white than the living room—but whose windows provided a panoramic view of Midtown rather than of the East River. "Look who's arrived! Our honored guest."

Paloma scanned the room to see a woman standing at one end of the long glass dining room table, leaning forward slightly with two hammy palms pressed down on the glass—the better to give Paloma a stare of frank appraisal. The woman's face was broad and pock-marked, her hair was mouse-brown and messy, and her wide but small-busted chest was clad in a hot-pink tee-shirt that proclaimed: *¡Adelantamos-El Bronx!* in large black letters over what appeared to be a forest of alternating black raised fists and clasped hands.

"Paloma, this is Marta Figueroa, co-founder and Executive Director of *¡Adelantamos-El Bronx!*" Carlota announced, her voice drifting down to the deepest part of her vocal register. "And Marta, this is Paloma Rodriguez—whom I've told you so much about."

Paloma walked around the table to where Marta stood and extended her hand.

"*Mucho gusto*," she said and then quickly regretted it.

Jesus, Paloma, what is the matter with you? First you try to impress Carlota with your worldliness and now you try to make yourself more Latin for this woman? Since when do you have to prove yourself to anyone?

"I'm from the Bronx." Marta's accent was pure New York. "So… I speak English."

Paloma grinned awkwardly.

"So am I," she said. "From the Bronx, I mean. And… my English is probably as good as yours. It's… my Spanish that's kind of… inventive."

Marta gave her the preliminaries of a smile.

"Where in the Bronx?"

"Essex Hill. I started out on Featherbed Lane, but I don't remember much about that."

"Essex Hill…" Marta sniffed. "The gated complex? Carlota told me you were 'salt of the earth made good.' Essex Hill is hardly 'salt of the earth.' It's for Bronx residents who… want to pretend they don't live in the Bronx. Is it not?"

"I… well, we weren't owners there or anything. My mother was… we were, she was…her—Jesus, I never know how to put this—her boyfriend was the super."

Marta grinned.

"Ah. All right. I get it."

"Creds okay now?" said Paloma finally finding her sea legs.

"Creds okay."

"Make no mistake," said Carlota, smiling sleekly as Marta resumed her seat and Paloma found a chair directly opposite her. "Paloma is the real thing. A self-made woman—rising from humble beginnings to become a remarkable nurse, healer and ambassador for her hospital. And she's very interested in helping *¡Adelantamos-El Bronx!* Aren't you, Paloma?"

"In what way are you interested in helping us?" asked Marta. "Our three areas of focus are music, culinary arts and community organizing. Besides being a nurse, are you a musician? A chef? A community organizer?"

"Afraid not. I cook very well, but only within my own home. I'm pretty much tone deaf—or so my brother Manny says. And I've never… organized a community."

"I want Paloma to join our board, Marta—not teach our participants to play the guitar or chiffonade a bunch of basil. She could draw money from a stone. Persuaded my Victor to triple his annual donation to

Manhattan East's Cancer Research and Care Unit with a speech that was… what was it, Paloma? Five minutes long? Six?"

She gave Marta a brief private smile.

"How's that for persuasive, Marta?"

Marta suddenly looked intensely interested.

"Paloma could be an excellent spokesperson for us. Not to mention a wonderful role model for our girls. Show them the sky's the limit. That a Latinx girl growing up in a super's apartment can move on to conquer the world if she just puts her mind to it…"

Paloma looked down.

"I've hardly conquered the world yet…"

Carlota ignored her.

"And I can also see her being a fabulous mentor for some of our individual girls," she was continuing. "Some of our really… special girls. Can't you just see her taking someone like Melissa Fernandez under her wing?"

Marta snorted. "Well, I don't know about that. Melissa's pretty tough. I suspect she could teach Paloma a thing or two. Actually."

"I try to learn from everyone," said Paloma. "But I'm pretty tough, myself. Actually."

Marta leaned back in her chair.

"But not as rough around the edges as Melissa. I don't know how much Carlota told you, but we work with some of New York's most traumatized girls. They all have histories of violence—violence they've endured and violence they've inflicted. Melissa is someone who—if you saw her walking down the block—you'd probably duck into a doorway. Big as a tank and just as heavily armed. She cycled between foster families for years and now lives in a group home."

"Not a very pleasant place, I'm afraid," murmured Carlota.

"No place Melissa has ever lived has been very pleasant. Anyway, thanks to an anonymous donor, we were able to take her and a couple of other girls to Puerto Rico a few weeks after Hurricane Maria to help out in one of the Red Cross's recovery efforts. And when Melissa—who has been through things you can't even imagine but who never, ever cries—saw that devastation, she burst into tears. Pitched in as if her life depended on it. Ended by leading the project. Now that she's back, she keeps asking for other projects. It's like she'd been waiting all her life for the chance to make a difference."

"Wow," said Paloma.

"Exactly. Wow," said Carlota.

"Nonetheless, you probably wouldn't want to take Melissa under your wing," Marta reprised. "She'll eat you for breakfast if you rub her the wrong way. Still, if you managed to get Victor Bianchi to part with a considerable sum of money, you must definitely possess some… powerful skills."

She paused.

"I don't think even Carlota is able to do that as often as she'd like."

Carlota cast Marta a look that Paloma would not have liked to receive. It vanished quickly however, and she gave Marta a big smile. "Oh, I have my ways as well," she said.

Marta shook out her head for a small second and then smiled pleasantly back.

"So," she said, sitting back in her chair and cracking her knuckles. "Have you told Paloma about our Gala yet? Is she going to play a role?"

Carlota threw Marta another look. "I think it best to hold off talking about the Gala till after lunch. It's rather a… dessert topic… wouldn't you agree?"

She then walked to the sideboard, pulled a little silver bell off one of the shelves and rang it.

Consuelo appeared almost immediately. "Yes, Ma'am."

"You can begin preparing lunch. We'll be coming in shortly."

"Yes, Ma'am."

"While Consuelo sets up, let's retire to the living room. And Marta, I was thinking you could share some of your tango music with Paloma."

"That would also probably be better after lunch."

"No." Carlota smiled again with all her teeth. "I think it would be best right now."

Then she led them back into the living room.

Paloma, trailing three steps behind Marta, did her best to ignore the amazing size of the Executive Director's bare feet, and the fact that they had probably never—in all their forty-some-odd years—seen the inside of a nail salon. She also tried to steer her gaze away from Marta's vast rear end and the way that her super-sized jeans strained against all that bulk.

Well, that's that. Clearly no reason to worry about how I'm dressed.

"Paloma adores the piano, don't you Paloma?" Carlota was saying as they entered the living room. "She has a Bösendorfer in her living room and she lives with a concert pianist."

She waved Paloma over to the couch, gestured for her to sit down and then sat down right beside her. "And do tell us, Paloma," she added, as she lowered her voice dramatically, "is that concert pianist-house-mate of yours also your 'special friend'?"

"He's a very good friend," said Paloma, cautiously. "But his 'special friend' is a Korean clarinetist named Kae-Dang. They're off in Europe on a six-month tour right now."

"Ah. Well, Victor is abroad right now as well. In Toronto. On business. As usual."

Marta purposefully ignored their conversation and walked briskly up to the piano.

"I'll give you a bit of history before I begin, Paloma," she said, turning around. "I've always played piano. Went to La Guardia High School. Considered making it a career. But then my life took a turn and I began working in a domestic violence prevention program in East Harlem. I stayed till someone told me about this amazing anti-violence collective in Buenos Aires. I was due for another change. So I made my way there, remained a few years, and learned a great deal."

She paused to let one hand drift lazily over the keyboard.

"I also fell in love with the tango."

"And you also met me."

"Yes, and I also met Carlota. At a tango bar, as it turns out. Music had basically saved my life when I was a growing up as a tough Bronx Newyorican, aching for a fight. But I never fully grasped its power till I heard *La Cumparsita* played in a smoky bar. Are you familiar with the tango, Paloma?"

"No," said Paloma.

"Well then, let me show you what it's all about."

Marta pulled out the piano bench and slid onto it in a single fluid movement. She then launched into a piece that was so keenly haunting—

yet so insistently rhythmic—that Paloma was swept right out of Carlota's coolly sanitized white living room into a place that was dark, foreign, and urgently seductive.

"There," said Marta when she had finished—leaving Paloma feeling momentarily bereft. "That is the tango. How could I ever turn back from it? I knew it had to become the center of my life. But at the same time, how could I abandon all the girls and women who needed me? It was Carlota who whispered that I might be able to do both. That I could marry my two passions—music and social justice—by bringing the tango back home and using it to change girls' lives."

"And so…" said Carlota, "*¡Adelantamos!* was born."

"Eventually I realized that tango might not be the answer for every Latinx girl. That for some it might be salsa. For others it might be culinary arts. For some—like Melissa—it might be community action. I saw the point was simply giving girls something other than a life defined by the abuse of their fathers, stepfathers, boyfriends, johns and pimps. To help them channel their talents, passions and energies into something wonderful and satisfying. And all theirs."

"So…" Carlota interjected, "I bankrolled Marta's dream and have been doing so ever since—watching her vision grow from weekly tango classes into a full-blown music and culinary arts and community service organization. Giving nearly a hundred disadvantaged Latinx girls a year the chance to change their fates. And to change the world."

She paused, reached over to Paloma and squeezed her hand.

"And when you come to our Gala," she added, her voice going into its thrilling lower register, "you'll see exactly what we are talking about."

Paloma said nothing so Carlota squeezed her hand again.

"It will take place two weeks from this Tuesday at the Bronx County Courthouse. Six o'clock till ten. Food, music and… Latinx solidarity. And you will be our honored guest."

She stood and made a grand gesture with her arms. "And now, I'm sure that lunch is ready. Let's go eat."

"I knew she couldn't wait till dessert to talk about the Gala," Marta said, *sotto voce*, as she and Paloma rushed forward to catch up with Carlota's swift glide.

The table was set with thick white placemats, enormous square white dishes, silverware heavy enough to require muscle power, and outsized crystal goblets. Carlota waited till Marta and Paloma were seated, then reached for the silver bell that now sat to the right of her place setting. Seconds later, Consuelo materialized, bearing a silver tray aloft on one hand.

"We're ready, Consuelo," she said. "Please serve our new guest first."

Consuelo lowered the tray to Paloma's eye level to display a large white dish covered with triangular, crustless white-bread sandwiches and a few strategically placed sprigs of watercress. She waited a moment and then asked: "Roas' beef or smoke salmon?"

"Smok*ed* salmon, Consuelo," said Carlota. "It ends in a 'D'. And the 'roast' of 'roast beef' ends in a 'T.' 'D's and 'T's are the key to everything in English. As I'm sure I've said before."

Consuelo looked down and nodded.

"How about a few of each?" said Paloma, amiably.

Consuelo used a pair of silver tongs to transfer four thin sandwiches to the perimeters of Paloma's plate and arrange a few sprigs of watercress artistically around them.

"Thank you, Consuelo," said Paloma, trying to catch Consuelo's eye—with little success. "That looks… very nice."

Consuelo moved on to stand beside each of the other two women in turn and carry out the same procedure. She then hoisted the tray back up to shoulder level and exited.

Neither Carlota nor Marta made a move to pick up their sandwiches, so Paloma waited as well. She supposed that drinking was permitted however, reached for her goblet and downed half its contents, while Carlota tapped one finger against the table in a rhythm that only she perceived.

Finally, Consuelo came back into the room—this time with a large crystal bowl on her tray. Once again, she approached Paloma first.

"Po*t*a*t*o sala*d*?" she asked.

"Sure."

She placed a perfect scoop of what appeared to be extremely lumpy pink mayonnaise studded with canned peas and shreds of pimento pepper into the empty space at the center of Paloma's plate. She then provided the same service for the other two women.

"That will do, Consuelo," said Carlota once she had received her portion. "But perhaps you could bring in the water pitcher and refresh Ms. Rodriguez' glass?"

She shook her head as Consuelo departed and sighed, just under her breath: "Hopeless. Unteachable. Dumb as an ox. *Pura chusma.*"

Pure trash.

Consuelo returned almost immediately with a large silver pitcher beaded with water and neatly swathed in a big white napkin. She carefully tipped the pitcher forward to pour a perfect stream of water into Paloma's glass.

"Thank you, Consuelo, that's very kind," Paloma began. But once again, Consuelo was well ahead of her—making it halfway out the room before she'd even finished her sentence.

Paloma crossed her arms and leaned back in her chair as she contemplated Consuelo's rapidly retreating figure. Marta smiled into her napkin. Carlota raised one of her sandwiches in a manicured hand.

"*Buen provecho*," she said, taking a small bite. She surveyed the table with a smile of satisfaction that faded as fast as it appeared once she caught sight of Paloma's posture.

"Aren't you hungry, Paloma?"

"Oh. Yeah. Sure," Paloma answered, reaching forward slowly to pick up one of the triangles. She bit into it with great care to avoid spurting mayonnaise on her new shirt.

"Mnnn," she said, as soon as she could manage it.

Am I ever going to eat a decent meal again? Etha's new health regimen is bad enough, but this is even worse.

She had just taken another mini bite when a phone began ringing in the next room. Marta quickly consumed what was in her hand, but Paloma and Carlota returned their triangles to their plates and Carlota rose to her feet.

"It's Victor, of course," she said. "His timing is flawless. He only calls when I'm just about to eat or just about to pee. Please excuse me."

She glided out.

As soon as she left, Marta swept the three remaining sandwiches from her plate to her mouth with a practiced movement, chewed vigorously, swallowed hard, and then made equally short shrift of her scoop of potato salad. She then sat back, belched and patted her belly.

"So, Paloma," she said, smiling pleasantly and waving one thick hand at Paloma's practically untouched plate. "What do you really think of our little lunch?"

Paloma sighed. "It's…. "

"Unsatisfying?"

"Well, yes. And also… kind of puzzling. I mean if Carlota's trying to promote 'Latinx solidarity' why would she serve us stuff like this? We don't eat this way."

Marta grinned. "Well, you're right that most of us don't. But then Porteños—people from Buenos Aires—are not like the rest of us. They're their own thing. And while Carlota wasn't born a Porteño, she quickly adapted to the lifestyle. She eats practically nothing all day. A croissant. A bite of sandwich. Swigs of *maté*. And then, late in the evening—and the later the better—several pounds of steak and an entire bottle of wine."

"Okay. Thanks. That explains that one particular thing about her."

Marta looked at her hard.

"But not everything?"

"No," Paloma answered. "Not everything. Carlota is confusing in so many ways."

"Oh?" Marta said. "Just what about Carlota puzzles you?" she asked, carefully watching Paloma's face. "I mean, besides her peculiar eating habits."

Could Marta be proposing a gossip session? Might be fun. But was this a good moment?

"Um…" Paloma glanced toward the door. "Are we really free to talk like this? I mean, won't Carlota be back any minute?"

"Carlota complains bitterly about Victor's calls," Marta replied, continuing to take the measure of Paloma's interest. "But don't let that fool you. She'll be on the phone until she learns exactly where he is and what he's doing."

"All right, then." Paloma began. "Let me ask the most obvious question."

She swept the room with one arm.

"I've been in other fancy homes before. In fact, my own home is pretty fancy. But this goes way beyond anything I've ever seen. This is serious wealth. Where does it all come from?"

"Victor's an investor," Marta said, after a pause. "A very smart one."

"Investor into what?"

Marta chuckled.

"No one's ever let me in on that," she said. "They must know I'm a socialist at heart. Still, as long as those investments keep supporting *¡Adelantamos!* I'll keep my scruples to myself."

Paloma chuckled back.

"So… everything Carlota enjoys is just thanks to Victor's business deals? The super-fancy apartment? The super-fancy clothes? The *¡Adelantamos!* budget? Carlota is just… a girl with an indulgent husband? I've met Victor, you know. He didn't seem the over-indulgent type."

"Well, it's not exactly like that," Marta replied, slowly. "It's a bit more complicated."

Paloma waited for more information and—when none was offered—gave a small shrug.

Oh, well. Fun while it lasted.

Marta fiddled with her fork. Discretion competed with curiosity about Paloma's motivations. She finally couldn't resist.

"How familiar are you with the history of El Salvador, Paloma?"

"Not particularly," Paloma said, picking up her sandwich again, sniffing at it and then returning it to her plate. "They tried to teach me Latin American history when I was living in Colombia. It never took."

"So… you don't know about *Las Catorce*?"

"Huh-uh."

"*Las Catorce*," said Marta, leaning back in her seat, "are the fourteen families that have controlled everything in that country since the beginning of time. Agriculture, banks, government—the works. They appeared to fall from power a few decades back following some, uh, national trouble. But they just went underground."

She waited for a response, got none, and kept going.

"Well," she said with a flourish. "Carlota Quiñonez Regalado de Bianchi is a *bona fide* member of *Las Catorce*. On both sides of her family. And it's the family wealth that funds Victor's enterprises."

Paloma nodded vaguely and then looked away. Okay. Got it.

"Carlota has always had the best of everything," Marta continued—determined to recapture Paloma's full attention. "But she's also always had to… ask for it. It's the men who control the money. And just about everything else."

Well, that did it. Paloma looked right up, eyes glinting.

"Boy," she said. "Isn't it always like that?"

"When Carlota first met Victor," Marta continued, pleased at that small victory, "she saw his great promise as a rainmaker. All he needed was some steady capital behind him. She asked Papito to provide the necessary flow of support and—eventually—Papito agreed."

She paused.

"Over the years, that arrangement has proven highly profitable for both Victor and Papito. And Carlota has, of course, benefited as well. Nonetheless, she still has to ask for everything she gets. It's Victor she asks, now—not Papito. But it amounts to the same thing."

Paloma nodded briefly and then looked away once more—her brow constricted.

"You seem perplexed again," said Marta. "What about Latino machismo don't you get?"

Paloma waited a moment before replying.

"Oh, I totally get the machismo part," she finally said. "What I don't get is why Carlota chooses to use up so many chits on…*¡Adelantamos!*? Why not ask Victor to get her onto the board of something more in line with her background and tastes? Some fancy arts organization? The Women's Republican Club?"

She gazed at Marta, straight on.

"I mean, look. It's clear why you're involved with *¡Adelantamos!* It's your world."

She paused as she looked down at her hands.

"And as far as my involvement… that is, my potential involvement…"

Marta looked up sharply.

"I'll admit that this all kind of started as a lark."

Marta waited.

"But it seems that Carlota isn't entirely wrong about me and my background. I could easily have ended up like one of the girls you work with, except that I got lucky. Melissa's story really got to me. Turns out I'd really like to… be part of helping other girls get lucky, too."

She looked up to see Marta gazing at her with open approval.

"So that's why you're here and why I'm here. But why would someone like Carlota want anything to do with…."

She grinned.

"… with Da Bronx?"

Marta paused for a moment to scrape up the last bit of mayonnaise with the side of her fork and then lick the prongs. Paloma had the momentary vision of her picking up the plate and running her tongue over its surface. Fortunately, she didn't.

"When I first caught sight of Carlota in that smoky little club in Buenos Aires," Marta eventually answered, "she had just married Victor. Papito's backing was firmly in place. The glow from her society page wedding was beginning to fade. She was about to move to New York. And realizing that she'd probably be spending the rest of her life throwing little dinner parties for Victor's business associates. She found the prospect depressing."

"Yeah," said Paloma. "Sounds real tough."

Marta smiled.

"The point is that when we began spinning out ideas for *¡Adelantamos!* she pounced. It was the opportunity she'd been waiting for. The chance to finally have something all her own."

"Okay," said Paloma, nodding several times. "It all comes clear. Carlota provides the money and gets a purpose in life. You contribute the vision (and most of the legwork, I suspect) and get to realize your dreams. Everyone wins."

"Well," said Marta, smiling a bit less sweetly, "to be perfectly fair, Carlota provides a lot more than just money. She has killer instincts about what *¡Adelantamos!* needs. And she knows just how to reel it in."

She watched Paloma color and her smile deepened.

"Which is why—though I've never seen you in action—I'm sure Carlota is right about you. That once you're at her beck and call, you'll be a superb new asset for us."

Paloma colored further.

"Well, I definitely intend to make myself useful to you," she said slowly. "Not as a board member—Carlota's silly to even suggest it. Not my thing. But as something."

She watched relief spread across Marta's face.

"Still," she added, "I can assure you that whatever I end up doing, I will never be at Carlota's 'beck and call'."

"Touché," said Marta, with a look of out-and-out admiration. She was just about to say more when Carlota slid noiselessly back into the room on her slender bare feet.

"Well, *muchachas,*" she said. "Lunch is officially over. Victor is speeding back from Canada with three business partners in tow. He'll expect a formal dinner and appropriate entertainment. We'll reconvene soon, but right now I need to get to work. *Inmediatamente*!"

And with that, she rang the silver bell and told Consuelo to clear the plates.

"So I never got the chance to finish my 'smoke salmon' sandwich," Paloma later recounted as she dug into the smothered pork chops, black eyed peas and super-rich sweet potato pudding that Etha had finally (and kindly) made for their supper. "But then, I'm no fan of cold fish."

"Nor am I," said Etha. "The main question, however, is not the sandwich but whether you're now going to be spending all your evenings at Carlota's house, planning for that Gala."

"Well…some of my evenings," Paloma replied, musingly. "But not all. Carlota's a piranha. And Marta's a Mack truck. They'll eat me alive if I let them. Still," she added, "I'm definitely going to do my best for them. I really want to be part of this, Etha. They're doing God's work."

Etha smiled.

"Plus," Paloma added, smiling back, "I'd give a lot just to hear Marta play her tango music again. Plus…" and here she grinned broadly. "I'd love the chance to keep making Carlota's doorman blush. He did it so prettily."

"Jesus, girlfriend. You have no shame whatsoever."

"No," said Paloma, spooning up some more of the sweet potato pudding. "I don't."

Brooklyn

13.

It was 6:39 a.m. on the Friday following Paloma's abrupt departure. Frayda was standing at the foot of Serach's bed, prayer book in hand, as she'd done every morning for the past six days.

"Serach," she said, waving the book at her. "It's time for morning prayers."

As had been the case on each of those previous mornings, it took time for Serach to haul her mind out of the terrible place in which it had been stuck all night. To begin focusing on the task at hand while Frayda stood sentinel with an impatient expression on her face.

Well, what did Frayda expect? Really bad things were still swirling through her head.

If it had just been the matter of her mother's death, surely that would have been hard enough. Or just the matter of Shmuely's rejection. But then that last unspeakable thing with Paloma? That final catastrophe that detonated like a terrorist bomb tossed into an unsuspecting crowd?

That was surely too much to bear.

Just before it happened, Serach had felt herself finally emerging from her stupor. She was following the *Shabbos* service as Frayda led it. She was beginning to experience what is known as the "*Shabbos* canopy of peace." She was even feeling the first pangs of real hunger as she sniffed the air and anticipated the taste of Frayda's soup.

But then those terrible lines in the prayer book—those lines that had slipped right by her throughout her entire youth—had suddenly popped right off the page to sabotage everything.

For, as luck would have it, that was the precise moment when Paloma chose to zoom in on what they were reading. Before then, she had seemed blessedly tuned out. But in the presence of those lines, she had blown up into a creature several times her normal size.

If Serach were to be totally honest, Paloma's behavior even before that terrible moment hadn't been all that easy to take. For much of the first two weeks following the funeral, she'd kept swooping in and out of their bedroom with so much smothering concern that it had made things even worse. She'd pestered Serach with questions and suggestions and wrapped herself around her like some huge, winged creature when all Serach wanted was to be left alone.

Why didn't she get it that if Serach moved too suddenly—or was touched too intimately—her very soul might start seeping out of her pores and onto the pillow?

Yet, Serach mused, she might even have been able to cope with Paloma's hot and heavy approach to depression management if that prayer book passage hadn't turned her partner into a Category-Five hurricane, yelling about the "idiot sexism" of Serach's religion.

The ironic part was that—normally—Serach would have seconded Paloma's views. But not right then. Not when the familiar cadences of the Friday night service were bringing her the first waves of sweet relief that she'd felt in weeks.

But then (and Serach buried her face in her hands at the memory) why had *she*—Serach Gottesman—reacted as *she* did? How could she have told the person she loved best in the world: "Get out of my room, get out of my life—you don't understand a thing about me!"

Where did Paloma go after that terrible outburst? Where did she sleep that night? On the couch in the living room? On the bed in Frank's room? Where did she go the following morning without so much as a word of goodbye? And where had she been ever since?

Serach had been too terrified to try to track her partner down. What if Paloma had taken her terrible words to heart? What if she was planning to end their relationship and kick Serach out?

For, in fact, didn't she have every right to do that?

Hadn't Judith left their wonderful house to Paloma alone (with certain rights accorded to Frank)? She and Paloma hadn't been married at the time (they hadn't even met, actually). Nor had they bothered to take that formal step at any point since. *No need*, they'd agreed, when same-sex marriage was finally approved in New York. And too painful—at least on Serach's side—since no member of her family would have attended their wedding.

When you came right down to it, Serach despairingly concluded, her entire lovely life hinged on nothing more than Paloma's ongoing good graces.

And—crushed by that sudden insight—she'd crawled back under their comforter and stayed tightly wrapped up for another six days, emerging only long enough to take a sip of the soup that Frayda kept bringing her. Or to take part in the abbreviated bedside prayer services that Frayda insisted they conduct together, three times a day. As she was doing now. Intractable. Unmovable. Prayer books in hand.

Serach managed to make her way up into a sitting position, find her place in the book that Frayda handed her and begin responding in all the appropriate places. It was all progressing in its usual placid way till they reached the part in which women thank *Ha-Shem* for "making us who we are" and men thank Him for "not making us women"—when Frayda suddenly (and inexplicably) dissolved into giggles.

"I wonder what Paloma would make of those lines?" she'd said once she regained some composure. "I never really paid them much notice, myself. But I bet she'd pounce right down on them and throw another gigantic tantrum. I'll have to call her up tonight and read them to her. See what she says."

And upon hearing those words, Serach's mind had suddenly cleared.

There was certainly more to Frayda than met the eye, wasn't there? Imagine finding humor in this whole *ferkakte* situation! And… what was she saying about "calling up Paloma?"

"Frayda! Talk to me! What do you mean 'calling up Paloma?' Are you two in touch?"

"Yes, of course we are. We speak every day to discuss how you are."

"And you didn't tell me this because…?"

"Hard to tell you anything these days, Serach. I say three words to you, and you put your face in your hands and turn your whole little self to the wall."

"So tell me! What have you two have been saying to one another?"

"First things first. No—stop *kvetching.* We're going to finish the morning service. Then you're going to come downstairs and eat a good breakfast. Then we'll talk. I have some other things to tell you, as a matter of fact."

"Paloma is just fine," Frayda announced once she was satisfied that Serach had reached the bottom of her bowl of corn flakes and sliced banana. "No worries. She's with some friend of hers. Etta? Ella? Edna? Something like that. She's anxious to come home, as far as I can tell."

Serach gave her a look of such utter joy that Frayda was embarrassed for her.

"And it's time for me to go home, too. We've eaten through almost everything I *shlepped* here from Boro Park last week. It's *Shabbos* tonight. I want to be home for that. You can come with me if you don't want to be alone. Or I can call Paloma and tell her to come back to look after you."

"Oh, Frayda! I'm not ready to face Paloma yet. I'm still far too shaky...."

"Then come with me. Your *shiva* is over. It's been over for a while. Do you some good to get out of this house. Go get yourself dressed."

14.

Frayda strode briskly toward the middle of the bus, installed herself in one of the window seats on the right-hand side and waited impatiently for Serach to take her place beside her.

Serach arrived, sat down and grimly assessed the situation.

Frayda had arranged herself in such a way that her oversized head, wig and hat—together with the two overflowing canvas bags of kitchen implements that she'd stacked on her lap—made it next-to-impossible for Serach to see anything outside. Periodically, Frayda would shift around enough to grant a momentary glimpse of a passing storefront. But then almost immediately, she would shove everything back into its totally vista-obscuring position.

"Oh, well," thought Serach, looking down meekly at her hands.

Ever since she'd started making trips to the borders of Boro Park for her monthly lunches with her old friend, Serach had made it her business to snag a seat by one of the bus's right-side windows so she could gaze out at Church Avenue as she rode.

She loved to watch the scramble of establishments along that major commercial strip. The Caribbean food markets and Spanish evangelical churches wedged between Russian drug stores, Albanian mosques and Pakistani bodegas. The 99-cent stores with their outsized-boxes of overstock cereal planted side-by-side with health food stores touting wheat grass juice. The one astonishing meat store that contained both a *carniceria* specializing in pork sausage and a Halal butcher whose clients were forbidden to consume swine.

On one of those early trips, however, she'd made the mistake of noticing that little blue-and-white sign for *Pintlech's Limousine Service* tucked away in the upper window of a building whose ground floor housed the *Clouds-Over-the-Andes* Peruvian diner. And the sight of that distinctive blue, slightly Hebraicized font—not to mention the six-pointed star crowning the Pintlech name—had made her shiver.

For what it conveyed was a clear warning that the richly diverse parade of commercial establishments was about to yield to an impregnable wall of *yeshivas* and hat stores, Judaica shops and dairy restaurants. That she was inexorably heading back into a world that allowed for no deviation, no mixing and no escape.

And once she'd had that unfortunate insight, all was lost. Somewhere in her normally impeccably logical brain, the conviction took root that if she caught a glimpse of the Pintlech logo, she would be shielded from the dangers of her childhood stomping ground.

And if she didn't, she wouldn't.

And what had begun as a pleasant pastime morphed into a rigid ritual.

She'd tried valiantly to rid herself of that unbidden, unwelcome superstition. She'd reminded herself of how much she'd hated it when her mother tossed salt over her left shoulder or spat three times to avert the evil eye. She'd chided herself for discarding all those *meshugge* beliefs only to create her own—equally *meshugge*—new practice.

But it was of no use. Once the idea had taken hold, she couldn't shake it.

Nor did it help that the one time she'd neglected to look out for the *Pintlech Limousine* sign was on that soul-numbing bus ride to her mother's funeral. And just look how that had turned out!

So here she was. The bus that she and Frayda had mounted was inexorably heading toward the *Clouds-Over-the Andes* diner. Frayda had taken possession of the seat that Serach regarded as her own. And Frayda's enormous head, headgear and packages were all arranged at just the right angle to completely obscure any sight of that magically protective blue-and-white logo.

"Frayda, I'm going to sneeze," Serach gasped. "Do you have a tissue for me?"

Frayda gave her companion a brief weary look before bending her head to rummage through her purse for a package of Kleenex.

And in that tiny, vital interval, Serach spied the Pintlech sign as it sailed by.

She heaved a huge sigh of relief, closed her eyes, and sank back into her seat.

"Aren't you going to sneeze?" asked Frayda as she dangled the tissue before Serach's nose.

"What? Oh, the sneeze? Seems to have gone away. So frustrating! You know what it's like."

Frayda grunted loudly. And then neither woman said another word until Frayda reached a long arm in front of Serach to poke the buzzer on the pole to her left.

"We're here!" she announced.

15.

Frayda propelled herself from bus to sidewalk with surprising grace—two of her canvas bags swinging heavily from her shoulders and the third one dangling from one hand. She sped off for the corner of 13th Avenue, turned sharp right and began striding forward with Serach trailing at a carefully measured distance.

They had concluded it was safe for them to sit together on the bus back from Prospect Park South—just as they freely ate together every month in that kosher coffee shop in Kensington. There was no chance they would come under inquisitorial gazes in either situation. Boro Park matrons never ventured beyond their tightly defined turf.

Upon entering Boro Park itself, however, it was best to take precautions. Who knew who might spot them and begin asking unfortunate questions?

It took ten minutes of their disjointed march to reach the door of a three-story building tucked between Greenberg's *Glatt Kosher* Bakery and the *Eitz Chaim* Walk-in Medical Center. Frayda came to an abrupt halt, glanced furtively in both directions and motioned for Serach to catch up.

"Stand right behind me. Keep your eyes peeled. And be prepared to duck away," she commanded over her shoulder as she put down her bags, fiddled with the lock till it gave and pulled it open.

She then reclaimed the bags, strode across the vestibule, put them down again while she unlocked and yanked at the inner door, picked them up a second time and bustled through to the rear staircase with Serach close on her heels.

"I'm at the top—three flights up," she remarked, and began climbing.

"Mind your feet," she'd added as she reached the top of the first landing. "The fifth step between the second and third floors is loose."

The stairwell smelled strongly of cabbage. Serach sniffed with unexpected pleasure. While her own home had never smelled like that—her mother had hated cooking and they'd survived almost entirely on microwaved frozen dinners—scents of home-cooked meals had drifted out of other people's doorways throughout her entire childhood.

"Right here, right here," said Frayda once they reached the top floor. She put her bags down for the last time in front of a dull green door marked with a small black painted "3-B". Three locks were prominently stacked above the doorknob and a modest silver *mezuzah* was affixed to the right of the doorframe. Frayda used two fingers to give the *mezuzah* an absentminded brush before turning her attention to the locks.

Impressively, she was breathing normally as she did all that. Negotiating three long flights of stairs carrying bags jammed with books, candlesticks, and pots apparently didn't faze her. Serach's own thin chest, on the other hand, was heaving violently up and down.

Serach reminded herself that she had barely eaten a thing or moved more than a few feet for three long weeks and thus had every right to be winded. Still, she felt a sudden twinge of shame at seeing how much weaker she was than her much-older friend. And with that twinge came a burst of joy.

If I'm feeling competitive with Frayda that's a very good thing, she thought, with a small grin. I must finally be on my way to recovery.

Frayda meanwhile finished up with the locks, re-grabbed her bags and pushed into the apartment. Serach tenderly touched the *mezuzah* and then kissed her fingertips before following.

It would be odd—unseemly, even—to find fancy decorative touches in an apartment in one of Boro Park's walk-up apartment houses. The residents of those buildings tended to count every penny and to be far too distracted by relentless religious, wage-earning, and child-rearing obligations to indulge their aesthetic tastes in any elaborate way.

Nonetheless, even the humblest of those apartments inevitably contains some hint of life beyond the grind. A well-stocked bookcase. A few paintings displaying *shtetl* scenes. The silver Kiddush cup received as a wedding gift. Piles of balls, dolls, scooters and board games.

Frayda's home contained none of that.

Serach gazed around what seemed to be a combined foyer, living room, dining room and kitchen. There was a stained brown couch, a well-worn tan loveseat, and two wooden chairs bracketing a wooden table. One wall housed a small stove, a loudly humming refrigerator and two beaten-up cabinets over a large double sink.

A few squares of scuffed green linoleum covered the floor directly in front of the kitchen appliances and a grey braided rug lay under the table and chairs. Yellowing shades obscured the sunlight straining to enter the room through two small windows behind the couch. The single overhead light bulb made almost no difference when Frayda flicked it on.

"You'll be sleeping through there," said Frayda, putting her bags down on the table with a grunt and waving toward an arch on the far wall. "First room on the right. It has a cot in it. I used to sleep in there myself when I was in *niddah* and my husband worried that even twin beds weren't enough to protect us from our evil urges."

She gave a small—almost imperceptible—chuckle.

"It was… sort of my private hideaway. The sheets on the cot are fresh, by the way."

Serach nodded vaguely.

"As soon as I put down my things, I'm going out food shopping," Frayda concluded. Then she marched through the archway, made a small commotion in one of the rooms, came back into the living room and left the apartment without another word.

I wonder if I'm the first house guest she's ever had, thought Serach as she put down her own bag of pots and dishes and began making her way under the arch to inspect what she presumed would be the meagre comforts of the room she'd been assigned.

What she saw once she entered, however, made her swiftly reassess.

The room was small, it was true, but the cot in question looked sturdy and neat. Its top sheet was turned down over what appeared to be a faded but unstained yellow bedspread. And what she could see of that sheet and its matching white pillow did, in fact, seem perfectly clean.

The floor was well-swept and bathed in sunshine from two unshaded windows. A tall, off-white folding screen stood to the side of one of those windows, obscuring whatever lay behind it. A small chair and a bookcase jammed with volumes stood sentry along the single free wall.

It was sort of my private hideaway. Interesting!

Serach tossed her overnight bag onto the cot and approached the bookcase.

The top four shelves were stacked with a range of weighty tomes, all in German. Serach had never studied that language, but her Yiddish stood her in good enough stead to make out the gist of most of the titles and authors. There were history books and books on philosophy. There were works by Goethe and Rilke and Thomas Mann. There were three separate books on Sigmund Freud, one on Albert Einstein and one on Albert Schweitzer. There were even a few art books—as well as one on Ludwig Van Beethoven and another on Johann Sebastian Bach.

The books on the bottom two shelves were of a very different ilk—though equally intriguing. The first twelve volumes of the *ArtScroll* edition of the *Talmud Bavli* and a copy of the *ArtScroll* complete prayer book—mate to the ones Frayda had brought to Prospect Park South—held pride of place. There were copies of Rabbi Hayim Halevy Donin's *To Be a Jew* and *To Pray as a Jew* and Volumes I-III of Susie Fishbein's *Kosher by Design* cookbook series.

The entire collection of secular tomes was minor, of course, compared to the riches to be found in the wall-to-wall bookshelves of the library of Judith's house—a library that continued to serve as a major source of learning for both her and Paloma. And the circumscribed group of Jewish-themed books was similarly limited compared to the hundreds of scholarly tomes that Shmuely had always had at his disposal.

Nonetheless, it was impressive—not to mention thought-provoking in the extreme—given who owned all those books. Serach ran an appreciative finger across the spines of the volumes on each of the shelves in turn, nodding to herself as she recognized titles.

She then turned with great anticipation from the bookcase to the other corner of the room. To that innocent off-white folding screen.

I can't even begin to imagine what lurks behind this thing, she mused. But I doubt that anything about Frayda can surprise me at this point. Who knew that she spoke German? Or read philosophy? Or studied Talmud? Or was interested in Bach?

She reached out to grasp the two sides of the screen, folded it together with considerable difficulty, hauled it over to lean against the adjacent wall and turned back to the corner to inspect what it had been hiding. She blinked twice at what she saw. And then she clapped her hands.

What a complete marvel her friend Frayda was turning out to be!

For what stood in that corner was an enormous, elaborate dolls' house. Its outer walls were painted pure, stark white. Grey stone quoins trailed up the seams of those outer walls, leading the eye directly to a beautifully proportioned, dark-red mansard roof.

The wall to Serach's right was dominated by a portico whose slender columns framed a door of the same dark-red color as the roof. The door itself was topped by an elegant fan-shaped window and sported a brass knocker in the shape of a tiny hand.

The wall to her left contained six windows set with diamond-patterned glass panes. Some of those windows were half-open and some were tightly shut.

And the wall directly facing her was more of a frame than a wall—providing an almost unimpeded view of the three floors of rooms contained within.

A wave of wonder—as palpably pleasurable as it was unexpected—surged through Serach's body. She placed her hands reverently on the house's slanted roof and sank down to her knees to examine those intriguing rooms.

The ground-floor kitchen contained a large, old-fashioned stove flanked by a wall of neatly hung copper pots and a graceful single sink. There were wooden cabinets that opened and shut (Serach immediately tried them out) to reveal miniature canisters of flour and sugar, jars of fruits and vegetables and bottles of sauce. Its table was set for breakfast, with cups and saucers and a full coffee service and plates heaped with tiny plastic fried eggs and potatoes. A basket of ceramic toast sat next to a plate with a stick of butter and a miniature butter knife.

To the kitchen's left was a dining room. A long table covered with an embroidered tablecloth and twelve full place-settings and surrounded by twelve matching chairs stood at its center on a sumptuous wine-red rug. The breakfront that took up most of one wall displayed dozens of tiny plates and cups and saucers in all colors and patterns.

Stretching from the end of the dining room to the left wall of the house was a beautifully appointed living room. Its floor was covered by a nearly wall-to-wall rug in a richly hued mix of copper, forest green and dusky rose. There was a long couch covered in dull green velvet with a half-dozen deep red pillows strewn across the back. Several elaborately inlaid end-tables and a single pink marble coffee table were placed strategically about, as were eight upholstered chairs of slightly different vintages—an armchair, a wing chair, and six small side chairs with carved backs and arms. One wall was lined in bookshelves. The others were adorned with miniature copies of paintings—Impressionist by the look of them.

And, right at the point where the rug ended to reveal polished herringbone floors beneath, there stood—could it be? Yes, it was!—a tiny replica of a big, black Bösendorfer grand piano. The name was clearly displayed just above the keyboard in that iconic gold script. And perched on its music rack was a tiny book of music, open to what looked like a Chopin *Étude.*

Carefully raising the lid of the keyboard, Serach marveled at keys that went up and down when she touched them. The eighty-eight standard ones—plus the nine jet-black ones at the bass end of the keyboard that are the Bösendorfer's trademark feature.

She was happily ensconced on her knees exploring the bedrooms and bathrooms at the top of the grand staircase—examining tiny chests of drawers and night tables and opening wardrobes to inspect rows of clothes hung on tiny hangers and perfect stacks of linens and towels—when she heard a loud "harrumph!" behind her.

She discreetly replaced the little brass lamp that she had just picked up from a night table in one of the bedrooms and slowly turned her head. And yes, there was Frayda in all her glory, hovering in the doorway in the hat and coat that she hadn't yet taken off (and which she had been wearing outside, despite the late-spring heat)—a big shopping bag tightly gripped in each hand.

Serach couldn't figure out whether the look on Frayda's face was any more annoyed than usual, but it certainly didn't appear any too pleased.

"Oh," she said, getting quickly to her feet. "I'm so sorry! I should never have touched anything without permission! But how could I resist? I've never seen anything so lovely in all my life! How… how on earth… what… where did this beautiful little house come from?"

The lines on the sides of Frayda's mouth softened almost imperceptibly. There was a moment's pause during which Serach held her breath and Frayda swung one of the shopping bags back and forth in a dangerously large arc.

"Let me put this away," she finally said. "And I'll come back and tell you all about it."

There was a lot of clomping and sighing and sounds of opening and slamming doors and drawers, but eventually Frayda reappeared. She strode over to the bookcase and carefully replaced the three prayer books that she'd brought to Serach's house on the bottom shelf. She then marched toward Serach and lowered herself down to the floor in front of the dolls' house with unexpected agility, her legs crossing neatly under her voluminous black skirt as she sank.

"This was my mother's dolls' house," she said, as she reached up into one of the bedrooms, took out a miniature double bed with four posters and a snow-white canopy and began turning it round and round in her hands.

Serach waited, but Frayda said nothing for a long moment more.

"From when she was a child?"

"No. From when she was an adult. My father built it for her. He said it was the house that he would have liked them to have lived in," Frayda said, her normally monotone voice growing slightly husky. "And this—" and she held the canopied bed up toward Serach so she could see it more clearly. "This was supposed to be their bed."

Serach held her breath and waited for Frayda to say more.

"She and I played with it every day," Frayda finally resumed. "Till I was seven years old."

"And then?"

"And then she died."

Serach suppressed the strong urge to put her arm around Frayda's shoulders, but there was no telling how Frayda might react to such a gesture. So, instead, she reached into one of the smaller bedrooms and pulled out a different bed—also with tall posts and a canopy but much narrower than the one that Frayda held. It was covered in a flowery lavender comforter.

She held it out to Frayda timidly.

"And was this supposed to be your bed?" she ventured.

Frayda took it from her and sat there quietly for a small time with a bed in each hand.

"How could you tell?"

"I don't know. I guessed. Frayda—"

She rested her fingers lightly on Frayda's upper arm before beginning to speak again.

"Tell me about it," she said. "Tell me about your mother. Who died when you were… so very young."

"She had terrible nightmares," said Frayda. "Often. I heard her."

She paused for a few long seconds.

"And one day, after a very bad night, she walked outside and into oncoming traffic."

She paused a second time.

"She was properly buried in a Jewish cemetery since they couldn't prove it was a suicide. See, she left no note."

She paused yet again.

"But I knew."

Serach respected Frayda's ensuing silence for a long moment and then, once again, couldn't help herself. She touched Frayda's arm again and this time she left her hand there.

"Tell me about the house."

"Like I said. My father built it for her. The whole thing. Top to bottom. It's a replica—" and here Frayda sat straight upright and shook off Serach's hand. "It's an exact replica of the house he grew up in, in Grunewald."

"In Grunewald?"

"In Berlin. That's where he and his family lived. Before *Kristallnacht.* Before the War."

"Was your mother from there, too?"

"Yes. They went to the same *shul*, the two families. They didn't really know one another, but each one knew who the other one was."

"So they didn't leave Germany together—your parents?"

"No."

Frayda looked briefly down at the two beds that she held and then put them back carefully.

"My father came first. His family was very smart about him—sent him here almost immediately after the Germans started… smashing things. My mother's family not so much. They never believed anything bad would happen to them."

She paused for a minute and made a harsh noise.

"The Germans captured my father's whole family *en route* when they finally tried to flee. My mother's family was seized in their home."

She paused again.

"My mother was the only one to survive internment. When her camp was liberated, she came here and found my father through a Jewish agency. Their wedding was on June 4, 1950."

Serach said nothing. Hot waves of empathy enveloped her, and she welcomed them. How long had it been since she'd felt anything for anyone beside herself?

Finally, she cleared her throat.

"It's a lovely house, Frayda. Your father was a real artist. Is that how he earned a living?"

"As an artist? Of course not! He was a dentist." Frayda sat up even straighter. "He began his studies in Germany and finished them here. Top of his class. NYU School of Dentistry."

She paused.

"But dentists can be artists too, you know. All those perfect bridges and crowns."

Once again, Serach couldn't think of a thing to say. Her views about dentists were different. But she was saved from embarrassment by Frayda's oddly emerging enthusiasm.

"He was always modest about how hard he worked on this house, but my mother told me it took him months," she continued, nodding a bit to herself. "He made every piece by hand. Well, not every piece. He couldn't have made the clothes… the cups… the rugs… the food. There used to be places to buy those sorts of things. I don't know if they're still there. It was all long before I was born. Took a while for me to arrive, too. My mother was… 'Damaged in the War,' she liked to say."

She took a breath.

"They always spoke English with me—they had both studied it in Berlin. But they spoke German with each other. My father used to call my mother: 'Meine Kaiserin.' 'My Empress'."

She smiled.

"My mother was very distinguished-looking. Very tall, like me. My father was shorter."

She waved a hand at the bookshelf behind her.

"Those are all his books. The ones he managed to bring with him when he came to America."

Another fleeting smile of pride.

"Except for ones on the bottom shelf. Those I bought myself. So I could catch up to where my husband was. Or to where I thought he was. Turns out he wasn't much of a Torah scholar, though he was strictly observant."

"Who raised you, Frayda?" Serach asked after considering what she'd just learned. She found that she had a thousand questions, but this one seemed to be the most pressing. "Who raised you, if your mother… died when you were so young?"

"Maids. Spanish maids." Frayda gave an unexpected and very loud grunt. "Like your girlfriend. There were lots of Spanish people in Washington Heights by the time I was seven."

"Washington Heights? You didn't grow up in Boro Park?"

Frayda snorted.

"No. Not in Boro Park. In Washington Heights. German Jews started moving there in large numbers before the War. And for a while after." She flashed a small grin. "Was a time, you could get a lot of *mandelbrot* in Washington Heights."

"So how did you get to Boro Park, if you started out in Washington Heights?"

Serach's curiosity was truly getting the better of her. She began worrying that she was prying too deeply but Frayda answered promptly and—seemingly—very willingly.

"My husband brought me."

She spread her hands and looked down at the wedding ring that she still wore.

"Tell me about your husband," said Serach, after a moment. It had been her second-most-pressing question. "I never met him that I can remember. Nor did anyone ever talk about him"

Frayda shrugged.

"He died just two years after we were married. We never managed to have children. Of course, he didn't have children with his first wife, either."

Serach said nothing and in a moment Frayda began to speak again.

"He worked at Yeshiva University. In the bursar's office. He wasn't a full CPA, like you. No fancy degrees or anything. He was just a clerk."

"And you two met…?"

Frayda turned her head toward Serach and gave her a long look.

"When I graduated high school, my father said: 'No need for a girl like you to study any further. You can be my dental receptionist.' So I stopped my schooling to take care of my father's office needs. Along with his housekeeping needs."

She looked briefly toward the ceiling.

"And my husband—my husband-to-be—was one of my father's patients."

She gave a tiny, almost imperceptible grin.

"He was always having some tooth problem or other, my husband-to-be. Or so he said. But eventually he stopped complaining about his teeth and just started coming over to visit us at home. For twelve years, every Wednesday evening—right after dinner—he would come play chess with my father. They didn't have so much in common besides the chess. That and the fact that they were both widowers. My father always said he didn't need to remarry. He had me to take care of him. And my husband-to-be would always answer that he was just waiting for the right girl."

"You, again. Clearly."

Was that a smile? Serach couldn't be sure. It sure looked like a smile.

"I would serve them tea as they played. My father took his tea with milk and sugar in one of my mother's porcelain cups. And my husband-to-be took his tea without milk or sugar in a special glass cup."

She looked up sharply at Serach and Serach took the cue.

"And why was that? Why no porcelain cup for your suitor? Why no sugar or milk?"

"My home wasn't *frum*. We were 'German Reform.' Not that we ate pork or anything. But my father was known to work on a *Shabbos* if a patient had a dental emergency. And he read all those forbidden books. My mother's china, therefore, couldn't be trusted. Nor could our milk."

She looked down and seemed to smile again.

"But from a glass cup without milk or sugar—and from the hand of his dentist's daughter—Yascha would accept a cup of tea."

"That was your husband's name? Yascha?"

"Yes. Like the great violinist. But without the violin."

Frayda unexpectedly chortled at her own joke.

"He was much older than me. Not so old as my father. But old. And when I was thirty and my father passed away, Yascha proposed to me."

Serach grinned.

"How did he do it, Frayda?"

"I don't remember."

"Of course, you do."

Frayda grunted.

"He said: 'It's time, don't you think?'"

Serach smiled. "And it was."

"And it was."

"So how did you end up in Boro Park?"

"It's where Yascha wanted to live. Even though it was a huge *shlep* for him to get to and from his job—an hour and a half on the train going and an hour and a half coming back—he insisted that we move."

She spread her hands again, studied her wedding ring and then looked away.

"It can't have been easy for him, all that traveling..." Serach volunteered.

Frayda shrugged.

"For him, anything was better than staying in Washington Heights."

"If he hated Washington Heights so much, why did he stay so long to begin with?"

Frayda sat up and this time her small, swift grin was unmistakable.

"He stayed so he could keep seeing his dentist." Another smile. "And his dentist's daughter."

"And why did he hate it? Why did he leave as soon as he married the dentist's daughter?"

"He said it had become 'too full of spic—'"

Frayda put the brakes on so forcefully that Serach could actually see her doing it.

"Frayda!"

Frayda sniffed.

"His word. Not mine. *I* never minded the Spanish people." She grunted. "Like I said. Spanish women raised me. I liked them."

She looked up briefly toward the ceiling again.

"But they frightened him, all those Spanish people. All those *goyim*"

She looked down again."

"And he was the one in charge of us."

"And so he moved you here."

"And so he moved us here. I was hoping to get a dental receptionist's position in Boro Park, same as I'd had in Washington Heights. I liked my work. But Yascha said no. That we could manage on his salary. That my job was to be the *Akeres Ha-Bayis*—the foundation of his home. So that's what I did. I took care of his home. And of him. I became *frum*. I adjusted to that life. After he died, I stayed unemployed. And I stayed *frum*."

Frayda waited a moment before giving Serach another one of her fleeting grins.

"Turns out it suits me—being *frum*."

Serach grinned back.

"Yes, it does."

But then Serach turned serious.

"Yet.... the fact that you didn't start out life being *frum* explains a lot."

Frayda looked startled.

"Well, yes. Frayda. It explains why you refused to just sit behind the curtains in *shul* like a docile little Haredi lady. You wanted to see what it was all about—this thing you were now a part of. To see what all the men were doing. Same as I always have. Don't you remember how we both would peer around or above or between those curtains during services?"

Frayda was silent and for a moment Serach feared she had overstepped her bounds. But then Frayda emitted something between a chortle and a bray.

"I do," she replied.

"And it also explains why you bought your own copies of the *ArtScroll Talmud Bavli*—and why you spent time studying them. *Frum* ladies don't generally do that. That's for the boys and the men. Not to mention that you chose to buy and read something by a Modern Orthodox Jew. I'll bet Yascha was none too pleased with you reading Rabbi Donin. But you were right to do so. He's very good at explaining things. I've read him myself."

Frayda said nothing.

"It also explains why you know who Yascha Heifetz is. I can't imagine a Haredi lady knowing that."

No comment from Frayda. But no contradicting either.

"And it explains… about the dolls' house. About what it is. About why you kept it. I mean aside from it being your mother's."

Frayda suddenly stared hard at Serach, but she still didn't say a word.

"That dolls' house was most definitely not designed for a *frum* family, Frayda. A single matrimonial bed? A single kitchen sink? All that plastic food without a kosher certification symbol in sight?"

Frayda kept staring.

"You may have become *frum*. You may have given up your profession to become the *Akeres Ha-Bayis* for your husband. You may have relegated your father's books and mother's dolls' house to your private lair—with the dolls' house behind a screen, yet. But you couldn't give them up entirely. They were too much a part of who you were. And still are."

Something unreadable crossed Frayda's face. Defiance? Triumph? Hard to tell.

"And ultimately," Serach hesitated a moment and then plunged ahead. "Ultimately, the fact that you weren't '*frum* from birth' explains why you have accepted me. And accepted Paloma, for goodness' sake. Who else from this community would have done that?"

Frayda shrugged.

"Frayda! You and I have been meeting secretly for years. You were willing to walk all the way to my house on a *Shabbos* evening in the rain to tell me about my mother dying. You were willing to stay in my house so you could take care of me. What other Boro Park lady would even set foot on my porch?"

Frayda looked pointedly away.

"I like your house," she finally said. "I liked staying there."

She reached into the living room of the doll's house and pulled out the little piano.

"Some days," she said, in a tone that Serach could swear was almost dreamy, "some days I would just sit in your living room for a while and look at your piano. Sometimes I would open the lid and count the keys. Ninety-seven. Just like this one."

Serach couldn't sit still any longer. She reached over to put her hand firmly on Frayda's arm.

"Frayda," she said. "I will never be able to repay you for all your kindness. You have been the best friend—the best supporter—that I could ever have wanted during a truly rough period of my life. I'm really looking forward to celebrating *Shabbos* with you tonight. But I think that tomorrow morning, right after breakfast, I'm going to head back home. I seem to be okay now. I'm sure I can manage on my own from here on out."

Frayda got briskly to her feet.

"'Bout time," she said.

Then she strode out of the room to begin making *Shabbos* dinner.

16.

Serach was determined to make it all the way back to Prospect Park South on foot. She wasn't in any hurry, after all. She often did her best thinking while she was moving—and she had a lot to think about.

She had dutifully fortified herself that morning. Eaten the entire bagel and cream cheese that Frayda fixed for her, together with a large mug-full of tea with lots of milk and sugar. The unseasonable heat that had enveloped the city at the start of the month had broken. How hard could it be to walk the twenty-six blocks back to Marlborough Road?

She made it as far as Church Avenue without too much trouble. But as she continued wending her way down that avenue, she began to perspire profusely and to pant ever-so-slightly.

Serach, get a hold of yourself. This is ridiculous. Onward!

She pushed herself until she reached the Russian drug store at Church Avenue and Fifth Street—the midpoint of the journey—when she finally gave in to her exhaustion.

Okay. Be realistic. Take a break.

She entered the drug store, bought herself a bottle of water and stood drinking it in the shade of the store's dark green awning while she contemplated how best to proceed. She decided that the main barrier to progress was the heavily protective outfit she'd concocted to re-enter her old neighborhood. She couldn't ditch the long wool skirt or the thick panty hose right there in the middle of the street. But she could at least roll up her sleeves, remove her kerchief and shake out her sweat-drenched curls.

She did so, and then carefully inspected her reflection in the store's big front window.

Well, that's better. A little *shvach*—a little *farmisht*—but considerably better than what you must have looked like when you were lying in bed with the covers drawn up to your ears. Hurry up and get yourself home so you can complete the transformation.

It took her a full forty-five minutes longer to reach the front door of her house at the seriously compromised pace she was forced to maintain. She headed upstairs—tightly grabbing the banister—and steered herself forcibly away from the bed that had suddenly begun beckoning to her. She took a long cool shower and changed into a tee shirt, running shorts and sports sandals. Then she headed determinedly back down the stairs.

You'll be fine once you're fully re-hydrated, she reassured herself as she avoided thinking about the softness of her comforter. Pour yourself some ice water and stop being such a baby.

When she reached the doorway of the kitchen, however, all thoughts of rehydration raced out of her head and her hands flew up to her face.

Oh, my poor Paloma! What on earth did Frayda do in here? And how did I let it happen?

She walked over to the nearest cabinet, took hold of one of the strips of electrical tape and tried to pull it off the door. A major chunk of varnish came off as well.

"Oh, dear, oh dear," she murmured out loud this time as she hurriedly abandoned that task.

Perhaps Manny will know how to remedy this?

She looked down at the floor and saw the parade of stains marring the wood's finish from sink to stove. She stared at the copper pans tarnished by a thousand scratches.

Oh, my poor Paloma! Everything that was your pride and joy!

She approached the refrigerator and hesitantly opened it. A single plastic container of defunct tuna salad and part of a chicken carcass in a red and white checked cardboard box stood dead center on the second shelf. Not a single additional item in sight.

Where were all the condiments that Paloma kept on the inside of the refrigerator door? Where were all the tubes of chili paste, the jars of capers and anchovies, the Dijon Mustard and bottles of sesame oil and mirin that made Paloma's cooking so extraordinary?

She peeked into the freezer. Not a single zip-lock bag of the slow-cooked, farmers'- market-tomato sauce that Paloma prepared in huge batches at the end of every September. None of the frozen pork tamales or shrimp shumai that she enjoyed when Serach wasn't around. No half-eaten container of the Chocolate Cherry Chunk ice cream that was her secret late-at-night treat.

Nothing left of her partner's culinary achievements, habits or delights. *Bupkes.*

How will I ever make this up to you? Well, I have to begin someplace.

She reached for her smartphone. She closed her eyes for a short moment. She punched in the familiar number and begged her partner to come home.

PART TWO: Court Dates

The balance and scales of justice are the Lord's; all the weights of the bag are His work.

Proverbs, 16:11

March 2000: The Bronx

1.

Back when Paloma was an eighth grader at St. Gertrude's School for Girls in the Bronx, most of the faculty members were Carmelite nuns. They wore the brown wool habits that have been the hallmark of that order since the days of St. Teresa of Avila. They scrupulously observed all the prescribed religious rites. They lived communally in a convent behind the school.

Two teachers, however—Miss Edna Gallagher and Miss Evelyn Porter—decisively broke the mold. They wore stubbornly secular skirts and blouses. They skipped the three-times-a-day Masses (Miss Porter was, in fact, rumored to be an Episcopalian). And they lived in a pretty little green-and-white house on Valentine Avenue with their two calico cats, Paisley and Argyle.

Miss Gallagher was a large-boned woman with short brown hair and a big voice. She taught science and gym to the seventh and eighth graders. She kept a portrait of Paisley and Argyle as kittens in a prominent spot on her desk, and her fondness for recounting their antics—together with her inventive lab assignments and tendency to yell: "just whack it, dearie" during volleyball practice—deeply endeared her to her students.

Miss Porter, a small grey-haired woman with an unextinguishable patrician accent, was notorious for her tough grading practices and her bone-headed cane. Besides proctoring lunch and Study Halls, she split teaching duties for seventh-grade Social Studies and eighth-grade Civics with soft-hearted Sister Elinor—invariably taking the Honors Civics section for herself.

While most of the school regarded her with terror, Miss Porter's Honors Civics students tempered their fear with near-cult devotion. Every year, she invited that select fifteen-member group to high tea in the parlor of her Valentine Avenue house on the Sunday following Easter. Every year, those privileged few were pressed to reveal the details of the visit. Every year—as if bound by a strict blood pledge—they all replied: "Oh, it was very nice."

Throughout seventh and eighth grades, Paloma spent a great deal of time with Miss Gallagher—three classes a week of gym and two classes (plus a lab) of science. For the most part, she was fine with that. She discovered that she had a real talent for whacking the volleyball exactly where it needed to be. And that the traits that invariably got her into trouble elsewhere—relentless curiosity, super-sharp senses, adept hands and an itch to mix things together to see what might happen—were unexpectedly strong assets during labs.

Miss Porter was a different matter. Paloma assiduously restricted her dealings with a woman whose reputation for decorum went deeply against her grain. She kept a low profile in Study Hall and lunch and was deeply relieved to be assigned to Sister Elinor for both seventh-grade Social Studies and eighth-grade Civics.

Nonetheless, on the March afternoon that Miss Porter announced that she would be taking the first thirty non-Honors students to bring in a parental consent form on a "special field trip to the Bronx County Courthouse" the following Wednesday, Paloma made sure she was at the head of the line with her signed permission slip.

It wasn't that the Courthouse—that big old government building atop of one of the Grand Concourse's highest hills—held any real attraction for her. It was the prospect of escaping St. Gertrude's walls for an entire morning.

The day of the trip dawned frigid and windy on the heels of a freak early spring snowstorm. Thirty girls in identical navy-blue wool jackets, too-short plaid skirts and sagging knee socks disembarked from the bus and headed at top speed toward the granite steps that would take them out of that bitter cold and into the building. Mary Elizabeth Donahue was going so fast that she slipped and (in her dramatic recounting) "nearly broke my neck."

Miss Porter however—impervious to both the weather conditions and the discomfort of her young charges—had a different idea of the proper pace for a class outing.

"Haste makes waste, Mary Elizabeth!" was the extent of comfort she extended to the chubby, red-faced girl as she clambered back to her feet. "And as for the rest of you," she'd added, swirling her cane in a decisive little circle, "you also need to slow down and look around. This is your borough, girls. The building we are approaching is that borough's primary court of law. Pay attention! You can't just let life whizz right by you while you worry about your cold knees."

She then launched into a lecture about the architecture of a landmark that they'd all passed dozens (if not hundreds) of times without a moment's thought. She went on endlessly about how it had been built at the height of the Great Depression and had cost far more than the City could afford. How it combined Roman-inspired classic design with Art Deco details.

And then—as if that weren't bad enough—she proceeded to lead the girls all the way around the building to the southern portico, motioning for them to gather beneath one of the two massive rose-pink marble statuary groups flanking the Court's rear entrance.

"Come here, girls," she said, gesturing up at the marble figures with her cane. "Come take a look."

A few members of the group groaned audibly.

"The architects of the Courthouse," Miss Porter continued, implacably, "envisioned it not just as a monument to justice but also as a showplace for great masterworks of art."

She waved her cane around some more.

"And this piece right here," she pronounced, "is one of those masterworks. Come close. Tell me what you think it depicts. And what it says to you on a personal level."

The girls fidgeted in dismayed silence. Not only were they too bone-chilled to stand still for a single moment longer, the statuary looming in front of them was most definitely not something they wanted to discuss with their starchy teacher. What on earth was Miss Porter thinking?

Finally, Frances Kirkpatrick—a red-headed student whose reputation for bravado had much to do with the fact that her uncle was a Monsignor—piped up:

"It depicts some almost-naked men and women hugging some big, fancy block of stone. There's another—like—totally naked young woman kneeling on the ground at their feet, holding something weird in her arms. And I have no idea what it all 'says' to me. It's just—like—totally crazy. Now can we please go inside? Please?"

"Excellent powers of observation, Frances," said the unflappable Miss Porter. "It is, indeed, just as you describe. Except that—if you look very carefully—the nearly naked people aren't hugging some 'big, fancy block of stone'. They're embracing a classically proportioned government building. A building very much like the one that we are about to enter. A building dedicated to the ideals of civic government. Justice. Valor. Progress. This work of art—like all the works adorning the building—pays tribute to those ideals."

She looked around her once again with something that a group of young people less intent on escaping the cold might have interpreted as mischief on her thin lips.

"But why do you think the artist who created this piece would choose to make all the figures in it naked?" she continued. "Or practically naked?"

Even Frances Kirkpatrick didn't dare venture an answer to that one.

"Hmnnn? No one wants to take a chance? Well then, I suppose I'll have to spell it out for you. It's because the ideals of civic government are so beautiful. Just like the naked human body. Particularly the naked female body. The artist was expressing those parallels in… very concrete terms."

And with that, she'd lifted her cane one last time and pointed definitively to the entrance. Some of the girls shook their heads as they went, some giggled, some silently wondered whether and what they should tell their parents about their teacher's unusual remarks. A couple asked themselves why they hadn't tried harder to make it into Honors Civics.

Those tea parties were probably quite something.

Paloma, however, remained stock-still, gazing up at the statue, pondering Miss Porter's words. Not the stuff about civic government, of course. The stuff about the naked female body.

For, in fact, the rosy-pink marble women embracing the miniature Courthouse with their succulent backs and buttocks on ripe display were among the most beautiful sights she'd ever seen. And the single young woman kneeling in front with those perfectly round breasts and that insouciant expression on her face was the most beautiful sight of all.

She stood very still and considered. What must that young model have felt while posing for the artist? How would it feel for her—Paloma—to pose like that? To know that every day for years ever after, hosts of strangers would see exactly what she looked like under her white cotton parochial school blouse?

She remained there for a long minute, thinking and trembling, before scurrying up the stairs to join her classmates in a huge room to the right of the entranceway.

"This monumental room," Miss Porter was declaiming, "is called the 'Veterans' Memorial Hall'. Quite naturally, given that name, it is mostly devoted to honoring 'war' and 'warriors' and the after-effects of war. Make note of the large metal plaques in each of the four corners. They quote the presidents who led the country during various periods of major conflict."

She gave them a moment to take in the plaques.

"But while war holds the place of honor here," she continued, "this room also celebrates other things."

She began pointing to the murals displayed on each of the four walls.

"These murals, for example, depict pivotal moments in the history of the Bronx. Some are military, of course. But not all."

She gestured to the first mural.

"Here you see a man named Jonas Bronck supervising the workers carrying out various jobs on his farm—a farm that eventually became the heartland of the Bronx. Jonas Bronck? The Bronx? Yes, girls, that's where the name comes from."

She paused and surveyed her charges to see whether they were impressed. They weren't.

"Jonas Bronck was an immigrant from Sweden. He landed in New York—at that point it was still called New Amsterdam—in the year 1639. He promptly bought 500 acres of land from the Indians and began settling it."

She paused.

"So, girls. Dutch. Swedish. And British, of course. What do you notice? Anything special?"

No one answered.

"Girls! Think! The 'special thing' is that immigrants from across the globe have been seeking a foothold here for centuries. Not just your Irish and Italian precedents. It started long before any of your ancestors packed their trunks."

She gave a small smile.

"And it continues until this day. Different casts of characters. But the same basic intent."

She smiled again.

"So," she reprised. "Come take a good look. Notice Farmer Bronck's face as he supervises all that tree-cutting and land-clearing and housebuilding. What does his expression say to you?"

Jessica DeAngelo, a mousy-haired student who had never quite recovered from missing the cut for Honors Civics began waving her hand wildly.

"Yes, Jessica?"

"His expression tells me that he's very proud of himself, Miss Porter."

"Yes, that's right. And why not, after all? All those workers. All that land."

Miss Porter then motioned the girls toward the second mural.

"Here we have a depiction of the first convening of the Westchester County Court—the judicial body that preceded the current Bronx County Court. The Bronx was once a part of Westchester, did you know that? No? Well, all right. Now you do."

They approached the third mural.

"Here we have George Washington departing from Van Cortlandt House for the very last battle of the Revolution. A battle that the colonists decisively won. That house is still standing, you know. Have any of you ever been up there? Yes? No? Brenda has? Maureen has? No one else? Well then perhaps we need to plan another trip."

She shooed the girls forward toward the last mural.

"And this, girls, is the mural that best exemplifies the war-time theme of this room. It's a scene from the Battle of Pell's Point in what is now Pelham Bay Park. Look how the American soldiers are surrounding that one British soldier sitting on his horse. The British soldier is very tall and impressive, isn't he? But his horse is…"

"Terrified," said Mary Elizabeth, before Jessica could venture a response.

"Yes indeed, Mary Elizabeth. That's right. Terrified. He knows his time is up."

She moved to the center of the group.

"Well, girls. There you have it. And now you need to tell me what this collection of murals says to you. Don't think too hard. Just say whatever springs right into your mind."

Paloma, standing behind Miss Porter but several girls back, muttered very softly: "It's all about a bunch of guys. White guys, except for that one over there who was probably a slave."

"What, Paloma?" said Miss Porter, spinning around to fix Paloma with her small blue eyes.

How could someone so old have such sharp ears? Aren't old ladies supposed to be half-deaf? And how the hell did someone who's never even had me in her class know me by name?

"Nothing," said Paloma.

"No, Paloma. Definitely not 'nothing.' Please repeat it in a voice that everyone can hear."

Paloma wondered what to do. Except during certain science labs, she almost never spoke up in class. And wasn't her point perfectly obvious? Why repeat it?"

Still, there was Miss Porter, leaning on her cane and looking right at her with what might actually be called an encouraging expression on her leathery old face.

Paloma flicked the hair out of her eyes.

"Everything in this whole entire room is about men. Only about men."

She paused, took a breath, and then continued.

"I mean, you've got Mrs. Bronck over there in that picture where her husband is ordering everyone around. There are some ladies and one little girl in the picture with Washington, but they're not really doing anything. They aren't even fully drawn. They're just—barely sketched."

She held herself back from repeating the second part of her observation. The part about them all being white. As one of only three Latin or Black girls on the field trip (and only one of twelve in the entire grade) she figured it might not be a such a good idea. Anyway, she'd clearly said what Miss Porter wanted to hear. Why add anything else?

For, in fact, Miss Porter was continuing to say some very nice things about her.

"I want you all to think long and hard about what Paloma just pointed out," she was saying. "Because she is absolutely right. To look at these murals, you'd think that the entire founding of the Bronx had absolutely nothing to do with girls and women. That we were barely even there."

She rapped the marble floor three times with her cane.

"But of course, we were there!" she said. Her voice was no louder, but it somehow seemed to fill the room. "Just the same as all those men. Bearing up under horrible wartime conditions. Just the same as those men. Tending the fields and creating the homes. Just the same as those men. Bearing and raising all the children—unlike any of those men. We were right there, dedicating our lives and our energies and—*yes*—our sacred honor to the ideals of freedom and justice. Just the same as all those men."

She looked piercingly around the group.

"And getting absolutely none of the credit."

She paused for a moment and saw that every eye in the flock was finally fixed upon her.

"So here is the lesson at the heart of this whole expedition, girls. You need to go out and make your mark! To claim all the credit that you deserve. To take your rightful places in this room!"

June 2018: Brooklyn

2.

"You look more beautiful than I've ever seen you," Serach exclaimed as Paloma descended the staircase to stand before her, all decked out for the Gala.

"Don't be silly. I looked basically the same on the night of Frank's Carnegie Hall debut."

Serach didn't blink, even though Paloma was forcing her to recall an evening that she would much prefer to delete entirely from her memory.

"You looked beautiful then too, Paloma," she said gently. "But tonight, you look like… a shooting star. The crowds will be dazzled. I wish…"

Paloma held her breath. Was a miracle in the offing? Was her partner finally going to change her mind, change her clothes and come with her?

The changing-the-clothes thing was clearly too much to ask. Still, what Serach next volunteered was a good deal better than the unadorned refusals that she'd been offering up till then.

"I really wish I could accompany you," she murmured, looking down. "But the idea of all those people and commotion and loud music… I can't deal with it yet. I'd just sit at your table looking like a used teabag."

She paused.

"Look, Paloma. I know how hard it's been to have me still be so… absent… with you. When I was a girl, and my mother would be like that—when she'd act as if only her pain counted—it was devastating for me. For all of us."

She paused again.

"Depression… can make a person horribly selfish."

Paloma nodded briefly. What could she possibly add? Serach had just said it all.

"But," Serach continued, "I'm getting better, am I not? Bit by bit?"

Paloma nodded unwillingly.

"And by the time your next big triumph arrives, I should be completely recovered and able to decorate your arm in grand style. I promise."

She presented Paloma with one of her small, enchanting smiles.

"Nevertheless," she concluded, "for now… I'm still… emerging. So what you need to do is just put me and my problems completely out of your thoughts and go enjoy yourself. Show Marta and Carlota that you're a great deal more than just a work horse. That you're a superstar—as well as the most stunning woman in any room."

Paloma permitted herself to pirouette around a single time in front of Serach's openly appreciative gaze. To flare the long-fringed white satin shawl that she'd spotted in a Housing Works thrift shop and couldn't resist adding to her slinky dress, flashing CZs and stiletto heels.

"It all goes together pretty well, doesn't it?"

"Yes, Paloma. It does."

Paloma's cell phone suddenly rang, and she pulled it out of her purse.

"Well, Baby, my Lyft is here. I'm off."

"I'll be waiting up for your return," said Serach, leaning in to brush Paloma's lips with a barely-there, almost-childish kiss. "I'll bring out the cognac—along with two of those beautiful crystal glasses Judith left you. We'll toast your success. And then we'll go upstairs and celebrate… in other ways. I know I've been particularly… unresponsive… on that front. I know that it's been hard…."

Paloma felt the buzz raised by the unexpected mouth-to-mouth contact, brief as it had been. Not to mention the most explicit sexual invitation that her partner had offered in what felt like forever. Still, she wasn't about to let down her guard entirely till Serach finally delivered.

"Have a wonderful, wonderful time," Serach added, taking in Paloma's coolness.

"Thanks, Baby," Paloma answered. "I will."

Then she flared her shawl one last time and sashayed out the door.

The Bronx

3.

Paloma paused for a long moment in the doorway of the Veterans' Memorial Hall, contemplating the results of the Gala Planning Committee's many weeks of work.

Huge clusters of black and hot-pink balloons, two hot-pink-and-black banners proclaiming: *¡ADELANTAMOS-EL BRONX!*, and two rainbow-hued banners proclaiming: *¡WE ARE ALL PRECIOUS!* exuberantly obscured three of the murals of the founding of the Bronx. A temporary stage—on which the nine members of the *Las Marianas* Drum Corps were ecstatically pounding, rattling and clinking away on their congas, bongos, *batás* and cowbells—obscured the fourth.

A long table had been placed right under the big bronze plaques on the far wall and was straining under the weight of several massive stainless-steel chafing dishes of yellow rice, red beans, fried ripe *platanos* and *picadillo de carne*, plus four cut-glass bowls of diced pineapple and mango and two big platters of *queque de tres leches* and *flan de caramelo.*

Twenty-five round tables covered in hot-pink tablecloths with centerpieces of pink-and-white flowers were arranged artistically across the floor of the hall. And in every corner, vividly-dressed women and girls—donors, board members, guests and program participants—sat, stood or strode around, making their presence felt.

Well, Miss Porter, this may not be exactly what you had in mind on that long-ago March day, but we have definitely arrived!

Paloma's reverie was suddenly interrupted by a 100-decibel voice.

"Looking pretty good in there, huh?"

She spun around to see Marta looming behind her in a voluminous tomato-red pant suit.

"'Good' *es poco*," said Paloma, taking Marta's hand in both of her own. "It looks fabulous!"

"And just wait till all those girls get on that stage! Thunder and lightning!"

"I can't wait."

"And the food…"

"I know—the smells coming off of those tables are making me faint with hunger."

Marta patted Paloma's bottom almost imperceptibly before strutting into the room. Paloma took in the scene for one admiring moment longer and then trailed in happily behind her.

Paloma's table mates included two board members, three donors and two nervous-looking program participants. They were leaning across the table shouting introductions over the din of the drums as she approached.

Paloma sat down and smiled briefly at everyone before turning her attention to the goody bag that awaited on her seat. She sniffed at the face cream from the *Tu Belleza* cosmetics company. She sampled one of the chocolates from the box donated by the *Las Delicias de Hunts Point* sweet shop. She contemplated the 20%-off coupon from *Ideas Libres, Palabras Libres—The Only Independent Book Store in the Bronx.*

She was just about to pour herself some water when one of the board members sprang up.

"*Ay Dios Mio*, just look at the length of the food line—and we've barely sat down! *Vamos*, ladies—let's grab our meals while we can."

All Paloma's tablemates bolted from their seats but—before she could do the same—a slim white hand landed on her shoulder with a surprising degree of weight. She looked up to see Carlota, luminously clad in a diaphanous white silk pant suit standing over her.

"We have a problem," Carlota was now bending down to murmur.

"Yes?"

"Yes, Paloma. We do. As you know, the Deputy Borough President was supposed to fill in for the Borough President tonight, since the BP's schedule was so overbooked. And I was going to handle the Deputy BP's introduction. But at the last minute—and as a special favor to Victor—the BP found a way to squeeze us in between his meeting at the Mayor's

Office of Immigrant Affairs and his speech at the Riverdale Yacht Club. It's a big deal for us."

Paloma gave Carlota a blank look. "And so… the problem is…?"

Carlota sighed.

"The problem is that—seeing as the BP changed his whole schedule around because of Victor—he's going to expect Victor to introduce him."

"Carlota, you're not making any sense. Let Victor go do it."

"I'm making perfect sense, Paloma. Victor can't. He was called off to Miami this morning."

"Well…" said Paloma slowly. "You're Victor's wife. You make apologies for your husband and then you stand in for him. What am I not getting?"

Carlota ran her finger across Paloma's back, hooked one finger under one of her spaghetti straps and snapped it.

"Paloma," she said in a strained voice. "It's not so simple. Serious ego issues are at stake. I will, of course, publicly thank the BP at some point. But someone else needs to make the introduction."

She reached for Paloma's strap again. Paloma said nothing.

"I'm not to the BP's taste, Paloma," Carlota finally sighed. "He's a man's man. If he's forced to share a stage with a woman, she'd better be curvy, adoring and… preferably dressed in a very short skirt. Being a lustrous brunette wouldn't hurt. You'll do very nicely."

"What? You want *me* to introduce the BP? Just like that? But he doesn't even know me..."

"*Carajo*, Paloma, haven't you been listening? It doesn't matter that he doesn't know you. You're quite the eyeful, and that's all that counts. You'll make him feel very, very special."

She smiled a little cat's smile.

"I won't bring him to the stage quite yet. He wouldn't want to compete with the food." She assessed the food table with a practiced eye. "I'll make some opening remarks and by the time I'm done, everyone will have been served. And then… you're on!"

She released Paloma's spaghetti strap and handed her a scrap of paper.

"I've jotted down some notes for you. About how much the BP has done for our youth and how wonderful that he's arranged this marvelous space for us and how much we look forward to continuing to build a strong Bronx with him. You read the notes aloud. You give him a little smile—send a little wiggle in his direction. Then you're done. Got it? Got it. Follow me."

Paloma, still seated but with her heart suddenly pumping hard, took the paper out of Carlota's hand and began to peruse what Carlota had written.

"Paloma—let's go! I'm moving you to my table down front so you can just pop right up onto the stage. *¡Muevete!*"

Paloma stood.

"I'll be signaling Marta to get the drum corps back to their seats in about sixty seconds," Carlota announced over her shoulder as they scuttled forward. "And then watch out. Things will move very fast."

Carlota turned and waved a hand at Marta. Marta gave the drum corps their own high sign. The drummers obediently wrapped up their last set, gathered up their congas, bongos, *batás* and cowbells and headed for their seats.

Paloma took her place at her new table. Carlota glided up the stairs and onto center stage where she removed the microphone from its stand with one hand and used the other to trace a graceful arc through the air.

"Welcome, welcome, welcome," she purred into the mic. "Welcome to you all. Please finish filling your plates and return to your seats—we're about to begin!"

The line began to move a bit faster.

"I am Carlota Bianchi—founder and President of *¡Adelantamos-El Bronx!*—and I'm absolutely thrilled to see you all gathered here tonight to celebrate our wonderful girls."

The crowd began talking less and more people began moving back to their tables.

"Tell me—isn't this venue magnificent?"

A few scattered claps from those already seated.

"Haven't our girls done a magnificent job of decorating it?"

More claps.

"Wasn't the *Las Marianas* Drum Corps absolutely superb—and isn't this the most fabulous food you've ever eaten?"

Strong applause.

"And," she concluded, "could we possibly ask for a more gracious host than our beloved Borough President, Bernardo Suarez?"

She threw a rapturous look toward the BP's table, and he bounded to his feet. He was a chunky little man in a dark blue suit with a neat mustache and receding hair.

"We will hear from President Suarez himself in just a little moment," Carlota continued, raising her hand in an unmistakable stop-sign motion in case he mistook her words for an invitation to begin moving forward prematurely. "But before we have that pleasure, I need to say a few thank-yous to all the people who have helped make this evening such a success."

Carlota then rattled off the names of her Gala Committee members, her board members and her corporate sponsors—adding in a few choice details about each. She gave a shout-out to "our amazing chefs," and "our brilliant performers" and to the *¡Adelantamos-El Bronx!* staff. And just as she had planned, the conclusion of her thank-yous coincided perfectly with the departure of the last guests from the food table.

"And now," Carlota was wrapping up, "I'm delighted to invite one of the newest members of the *¡Adelantamos!* family to the podium. Please welcome Paloma Rodriguez—brilliant oncological nurse, proud daughter of the magnificent nation of Colombia, and worker-bee *extraordinaria*—who will introduce our illustrious Borough President."

Paloma's heart began beating so hard that she could barely get to her feet. She carefully climbed the stairs to receive Carlota's two dramatic air kisses. She took the mic that Carlota extended and watched Carlota slip off the stage while the BP took her place.

She then sent a brief, desperate plea to Frank and the Virgin Mary. The Virgin remained frustratingly silent, but Frank's voice immediately filled her brain.

For goodness' sake, darling—relax. You look fabulous. Hold out your hand to the Borough President. Now smile. That's right. You've been told what he likes—and what he likes is <u>you</u>. And now a big smile to the crowd. They're going to love you, too. They already do!

Paloma tossed back her hair and beamed all around. She remained gracefully upright as the Borough President parlayed her extended hand into a close embrace and a wet kiss on the cheek. She deftly slipped out of his grasp with three small sideways steps in her very high heels. She glanced down for a second at Carlota's notes and seamlessly reeled off the four introductory sentences that were scribbled there.

She was just about to give the audience one last smile, hand Suarez the mic and return to her seat when a second voice—prim, fluting and wholly unexpected—barged into her head.

Miss Porter!

Paloma, you are standing center stage in the Veteran's Memorial Room of the Bronx County Courthouse and a few hundred people are hanging on your every word. Don't just mouth the comments that Carlota provided. You have ideas of your own! This is your moment! Speak up!

And so she did.

"But before I turn over the mic to our wonderful Borough President," Paloma found herself saying, smiling sweetly at Suarez while she adeptly kept that mic just beyond his grasping hand. "I'd like to share just a couple of small… personal thoughts with all of you."

The voltage in the room rose to meet her. Yes indeed, this audience was all hers! And—in fact—so was Borough President Suarez. He seemed perfectly fine with postponing his remarks if it meant her staying by his side a moment longer. He reached for her waist and pulled her close again. And this time, she allowed it. What the hell?

"Like so many of you," she said, and actually leaned slightly up against him as she spoke, "I grew up in this beautiful borough—on Sedgewick Avenue, just off Fordham Road."

She paused, smiled a bit as if to herself and continued.

"If you grow up in that part of town, you're bound to pass by this Courthouse a lot. And wonder about it. Perched up so high on its very own hill. Crown jewel of our borough's most impressive boulevard. All decked out in wonderful columns and rosy marble statues."

She let the Borough President give her a little squeeze.

"As a girl, I had no idea exactly what went on in here." She turned and beamed at Suarez. "But it was clear that it was important. That history was being made. And being honored."

She smiled again, and more than a few people smiled right along with her.

"This room, for example," she said, almost dreamily, as she cast a brief glance at the murals lurking behind all those black and hot-pink balloons. "This room honors the heroes who built our borough and defended our nation and created the system of justice that supports our society."

She gave a visible little shiver that captured more than one heart.

"So it is only fitting that we should be here tonight honoring a new group of 'heroes-in-the-making'—heroes preparing themselves to shape the future of our city. It is only fitting that we should be celebrating… the magnificent young women of *¡Adelantamos-El Bronx!*"

There were loud bursts of applause from the floor.

"I can promise you," she concluded, "that these young women will do this magnificent courthouse full justice. You are in for a real treat. *¡Adelantamos!*"

She handed the mic to Suarez, said "Mr. Borough President?" in her best Marilyn Monroe voice, tossed him a parting smile he would never forget and returned to her seat.

"Brava!" murmured Carlota, as the applause died down and the Borough President launched happily into his prepared remarks. "How terribly clever you've turned out to be."

"Well," said Paloma, her heart still galloping away inside her. "I don't know about that. But I definitely meant every word that I said."

Flushed and happy, she grinned to herself. What a lot I'll have to tell Serach!

The Borough President's speech was blessedly brief. Once he finished speaking and headed back to his table, Carlota leapt after him to give him an appropriately gratitude-laced farewell. And while she was doing so, Paloma slipped out of her chair to finally fill her plate.

She had just begun contentedly eating her rice and beans when Marta began clambering heavily up the stairs to take center stage. She pushed the mic stand ostentatiously aside.

"I hardly need this thing, do I?" she said in her booming, unamplified voice and grinned at the laughs that her question provoked.

"I am Marta Figueroa, Executive Director of *¡Adelantamos-El Bronx!*" she continued, as the laughter dissipated. "And I'm thrilled to tell you that we've reached the point we've all been waiting for. Our girls are now going to perform."

The first girl played three of Enrique Granados' *Valses Poeticos y Sentimentales* on the piano to tumultuous applause, despite faltering several times during the second waltz. The second sang two upbeat Mexican ballads, accompanying herself on the guitar. The third performed an acapella version of "Seasons of Love" that had half the audience singing along.

Marta disappeared into the sidelines till they were done and then strode back to center stage.

"Marvelous, right?" she asked. "Simply marvelous." She then leaned forward and said in her deepest voice yet: "And now, all of us old-timers are in for a special treat."

She paused as she happily surveyed the house.

"Our next performer, Magdalena Torres, is one of *¡Adelantamos!*'s superstars. She's headed for the big time, no mistake. She has a voice that spans three full octaves. Like Björk."

She nodded to herself and then beamed again at the audience.

"She can go from an Audra McDonald—or a Luciano Pavarotti—to a pitch-perfect kd lang. She does a Lady Gaga so convincing that you'd swear she was wearing a meat suit."

The audience chuckled.

"Tonight, however, she'll be indulging those of us who have… more old-fashioned souls. She'll be paying tribute to that greatest of Puerto Rican singers—the magnificent Bobby Capó."

Several people in the audience made appreciative noises. One person whistled.

"She'll be accompanied by two of our supremely talented trumpet players…" she spoke their names too quickly for Paloma to catch, "and four members of the *Las Marianas* Drum Corps. And I…"—and here Marta gave a little bow of self-appreciation— "will be her pianist."

Magdalena's back-up band—all identically clad in hot-pink tops and tight black pants—stood up from their tables, instruments in hand, and headed toward the stage to steady applause.

Marta waited for a moment and then pointed to a table in the back of the room.

"And now let's bring our hands together for Magdalena, herself."

A tall young woman in a pink ruffled tuxedo jacket and sleek black pants—her short black hair pomaded back and her eyebrows sharply enhanced—stood up and began making her way toward the stage. Her shoulders pumped back and forth like an athlete in time to the clapping.

She found her place in the spotlight, plucked the mic from its holder with a flourish and leaned forward briefly in a gesture of such commanding intimacy that more than one aspiring fellow performer vowed to practice it till she'd mastered it herself.

"*Buenas tardes*—good evening to you all," she said, with a glance around the room that sized up every girl and woman present.

"I owe everything that I am to two great forces of nature," she went on. "To the grandmother who raised me. And to *¡Adelantamos!*—which rescued me when my grandmother died, and I landed in the foster care system and went a little crazy."

She gave a smile out of one side of her mouth.

"My grandmother was a big Bobby Capó fan," she continued. "And the song I'm going to sing tonight was my grandmother's favorite. It's called *Piel Canela.* Cinnamon Skin."

Paloma leaned forward suddenly in her seat.

"Bobby Capó was a cinnamon-skinned man himself," Magdalena added, almost musingly. "His first bandleader wouldn't use Bobby as a lead singer. Said it might make the nightclub crowd… uh… uncomfortable to have a brown-skinned man center stage."

She paused and briefly contemplated her own square brown hand, turning it up and down.

"'Bobby,' he would say, 'it's a pity you're so dark.'"

She paused again and tightened her lips.

"Finally, some stuff changed and Capó was allowed to come down front. And he wrote this song. To honor people who looked like him. And like my grandmother. And like me."

She relaxed her lips into a wide and handsome smile. She then spun around to cue her two trumpet players and they played eight lead-in measures that transformed the Veteran's Memorial Hall into a 1950's nightclub—complete with unmistakable hints of cocktail shakers and cigarette girls—for every audience member of a certain age.

And then she brought the mic back to her mouth.

"*Si se quede el infinito sin estrellas…*" she began, in a dead-on rendition of Capó's velvety tenor. *Let the infinity be without stars…as long as your black eyes, your cinnamon skin remain…*

And the audience went wild.

Paloma, however, suddenly found that she needed to put her head in her hands. Tears popped embarrassingly through her fingers and onto the half-eaten plate before her.

What the hell is wrong with me? Why are my emotions so completely out of control tonight?

And then a slim white hand found its way to her bare shoulder and a lightly whispering voice insinuated its way into her ear.

"*Querida*, why are you crying? *¿Querida, que te pasa?*"

Paloma shook her head and said nothing.

"That song was tailor made for you. It should make you happy."

"It is not tailor made for me," Paloma muttered as the chorus repeated and her eyes welled up once again despite all her best efforts. "It was tailor made for… oh hell!"

"Paloma—what are you trying to say?"

"It was tailor made for my mother."

"Your mother?"

"Yes. She looked like… like the woman in the song, too. Her boyfriend, Joe, used to sing it whenever she got into one of her moods. He'd sit in the tan Barcalounger in our living room with a beer in his hand and Capó on the phonograph and lip-synch the words. And my mother—a woman as tough as an old boot and just as likely to kick you—would totally melt."

Carlota's hand tightened on her shoulder.

"But that's a beautiful memory you're having, Paloma—not a sad one."

Paloma nodded miserably but found she had nothing to reply. She and Carlota remained in a silent tableau with Carlota's hand lightly on her shoulder until the trumpets spun out their last long note and Magdalena put the mic back in its stand, blew a very visible kiss to a girl at one of the back tables, took a group bow with her fellow musicians and led them back to their seats.

Paloma managed to sit up, shake off Carlota's hand, and brusquely re-wipe her eyes.

"Thanks, Carlota. I'm okay now," she muttered. "Really. It just kind of… took me by surprise. I guess I should have paid more attention when the Committee was discussing what music would be on the program. I would have been better prepared for it."

"Well, I think we actually finalized the list on a night when you weren't there."

Paloma took a large forkful of rice and beans, capped it off with a piece of *platano*, crammed everything into her mouth, washed it all down with a big gulp of water, and took a breath.

"So," she said, after swallowing hard. "What's next on the program?"

"Oh, the best is yet to come. Marta is going to lead us in a tango number to die for. And then all the girls are going to get on the stage to sing: 'When You're Good to Mama' from *Chicago*."

"And then the Gala will be over?"

"Not quite. We can't forget about coffee and dessert—all those *tres leches* cakes…"

Carlota made a face designed to convey delight.

"And as everyone is savoring those cakes," she continued, "Melissa Fernandez will bring down the house with the story of how she found redemption in Puerto Rico after Hurricane Maria. The *Las Marianas* will take to the stage for a final encore. And I'll step up to the mic, ask everyone for another contribution and send everyone home feeling very good."

Carlota returned her hand to Paloma's shoulder and gave it two short, authoritative taps.

"But hush, now. Here comes Marta, and what she is about to do is not to be missed."

Marta had, in fact, moved from the piano back to center stage and taken her place in the spotlight. She held both her hands out to the audience and closed her eyes.

"The tango," she began as she re-opened those eyes very, very slowly, "is an art form that evolved over time and across continents. Its rhythms and seductive movements are rooted in the *candombe* that the enslaved Africans brought to South America during colonization. Its fancy details are the contribution of the Europeans who came at the turn of the last century."

She stepped a foot closer to the edge of the stage.

"Tango first flourished in the Buenos Aires brothels," she added. "The women would dance with one another when they weren't… on call. It is the music of their longing… and their rage."

She gave the audience a smoldering look before turning back to the piano.

"I'm going to play you a tango called 'Youkali'," she continued in a dreamier tone. "It was written by a Jew named Kurt Weill. He lived in Germany in the 1930's—not a very nice place or time for Jews. He was undoubtedly acquainted with rage and longing, himself."

She sat down at the keyboard.

"I will be accompanied by Maria Fuente on cello, Maria José Solís on violin and Juliana Cortez on that supremely Argentinian instrument, the *bandoneón*," she said, returning to her normal resounding cadences. "Girls, come up on stage and let's make some music!"

When they had all assembled, Marta turned back one last time to address the audience.

"And now let me invite all of you to emulate the fine ladies of the Buenos Aires brothels. As I explained, this is a dance originally made by and for women. So take this opportunity to dance together! Don't be shy. You may not know the steps, but no one will be watching you—they will be too involved in their own dancing. Just do what comes naturally. The moves will evolve on their own for you, I promise you."

And with that, she nodded to the violinist and the Gala guests began getting to their feet.

Paloma assumed that she would just sit this one out, but it didn't turn out that way.

"What are you waiting for, Paloma?" asked a familiarly husky voice behind her. "Didn't you hear what Marta said? Come join me on the floor. I'm very good at this, as it turns out."

One of Carlota's hands lightly grasped Paloma's arm to lift her up out of her seat and move her into the proper position. The other hand found its way to the small of Paloma's back and began expertly moving her forward and bending her back again to the music.

A strand of blond hair caressed Paloma's cheek. A silkily firm leg pulsed rhythmically between her inner thighs. A kiss landed slyly and briefly on her mouth.

Oh. Oh. Oh my God.

4.

"Darling, when someone offers you three different excuses for something, none of them is ever the real story," Frank had once memorably explained to Paloma. "The real story is always something else entirely."

Stumbling back to her seat, dazedly watching Carlota drift off to court some important donor, Paloma pondered what single explanation might most convincingly justify an early departure from the remaining festivities. The dicey trains at this hour? An early morning shift at the hospital?

She finally decided that the best course was to remain as inexplicit as possible. She stood up, lifted her shawl, purse, and goody bag off the back of her chair and headed toward Carlota's side.

"Carlota, I'm off. It's time for me to go home."

Carlota looked up momentarily from her donor, murmuring an apology.

"A little shaken?" she said, giving Paloma a quick, cool, knowing grin. "Well, run along home then. We'll be in touch. We're hardly finished. There's lots of follow-up work to do."

And then she returned to her fundraising.

Outside, beyond the north portico of the Courthouse—on the moonlit stretch of granite between the two pink marble group statues at the building's front—Paloma took in deep breaths of the soft June evening air and considered her choices. She could call another Lyft. She could flag a gypsy cab. She could dash off to catch the subway back to Flatbush.

Heading for the train in her fancy tight dress and high heels was inarguably the most challenging option. But right now, it seemed like the best one. She wanted some solid commuting time to work out exactly what to tell Serach. How to begin, how to end—and how to lure her partner upstairs as efficiently as possible for the treats she'd finally been promised.

And which she needed more than ever after Carlota's expertly executed foreplay.

She carefully negotiated the steep downhill walk to the 161st Street stop, the further descent down the three staircases, the hearty shove required to get through the turnstile and the long walk along the platform to the spot where the B train would stop. She then stood there, occasionally peering down the tracks while shifting from foot to high-heeled foot.

Well, I can easily describe how the girls transformed that stuffy hall into a gorgeous party venue with all their banners and balloons, she decided. And how amazing the *Las Marianas* Drum Corps sounded in that huge and resonant space. I can give a glowing account of the food—and of my introduction of the Borough President.

The train finally arrived, she boarded it and she huddled in a seat by the window.

I may have to skip the whole Bobby Capó incident. I'll skip the tango interlude, for sure.

She wrapped her shawl around herself more tightly. The MTA always turned the damned air conditioning up way too high in warm weather.

And I can conclude it all nicely by… telling her how much I longed to come home. To her.

By the time she reached her stop, her talking points were all in place. She ambled down the three blocks to Marlborough Road, relishing the feel of the balmy air against her arms and legs after the unnatural refrigeration of the train car. She mounted the steps of her porch, unlocked the front door and walked toward the living room, eager to see what awaited within.

Serach's preparations were as lovely as she'd promised. She'd placed the bottle of cognac and the two crystal glasses prominently on one end table. She'd turned off all the lights except the single standing lamp that cast such a romantic glow. She'd donned the outfit that Paloma liked best—a tiny, almost transparent white camisole combined with a pair of striped boys' boxer shorts.

And then she'd evidently fallen sound asleep.

Paloma walked up close to take a good look at her partner—lying in a fetal position and breathing into the back of the couch in her peaceful Serach way. Her curls were mussed up, her camisole bunched up above her waist and her boxer shorts hanging so low on her hips that the whole bottom half of her spine was exposed. The individual vertebrae along that spine looked so protruding—the entire back looked so fragile—that Paloma found herself swallowing hard.

My poor Serach. You really did waste away to nothing during these tough past few weeks. And you must be so cold, exposed like that. You're always the coldest person in any room.

She retrieved Serach's favorite pink satin-covered down comforter from the linen closet and draped it tenderly over her partner's back.

She climbed back upstairs to their bedroom, peeled off her clothes and tossed them aside.

She opened the window a few inches to let in the June breeze.

And then she got into their bed and slipped her hand wearily under the bedsheet to appease the fire that Carlota had lit.

5.

Luigi's—up on Arthur Avenue in the Italian section of the Bronx—was Paloma's favorite restaurant.

Throughout her childhood, it had been the place reserved for the most special of occasions. Like when her mother's boyfriend Joe was promoted from porter to superintendent. Or when he'd made that unexpectedly big win on his weekly lottery ticket. And it remained the apex of luxury dining for her long after those faraway days. Even the fanciest of Frank's Manhattan bistros couldn't hold a candle to it.

She remained enchanted by its mirrors, chandeliers and powder pink walls. By the six murals in the dining room depicting scenes of old Napoli. By the red velvet curtains of its long narrow windows, tied back from their panes with big satin bows to let in the changing shafts of light from the street. By the impeccably attentive waiters in their somber black suits.

And, of course, by Luigi himself—the little bald owner who stopped by every table, every single meal, to compliment the women, shake hands with the men, kiss the babies and inquire whether everything was up to his guests' most exigent expectations.

I wonder what Manny needs from me, that he's invited me here today.

In the weeks following their disastrous Sunday brunch, Paloma and Manny had managed to avoid talking about anything that had come to pass that morning. Their phone calls were just as regular as ever. A bit more abbreviated, perhaps.

But then, out of the blue, Manny had called her up and—in the tone reserved for telling a customer that his once practically-defunct car was now ready to drive out of the shop—had asked Paloma to join him in a leisurely lunch on her next day off.

And not just any lunch. Lunch at *Luigi's*.

"He's feeling bad about how he wrecked your platter—and our brunch," Serach had declared when Paloma told her about his invitation. "He wants to make it up to you."

"I doubt it."

"Of course he does. And that gives you a chance to get back on track with him about Ramon's schooling. What do you say?"

"I say: 'Serach, I thought we were done with that subject.'"

"He'll be contrite, Paloma. You'll have an opening."

"Don't hold your breath. Manny doesn't do 'contrite.' He's taking me out because he wants to ask me some big favor. Trust me."

"Even better. If—besides feeling contrite—he needs that big favor from you, you'll have just that much extra leverage. Strike while the iron is hot, Paloma. If not now, when?"

Which is why—despite the palpable pleasure of sitting across the table from her beloved brother in her favorite restaurant—Paloma was having a hard time relaxing. Her mind kept reverting to the question of what Manny could possibly need from her. And of how she could steer the conversation through all the minefields lying ahead.

Still—*Luigi's* was *Luigi's*. Manny was Manny. She resolved to play it as it went and enjoy what she could.

"Order whatever you want, Hermanita," Manny was saying as they leafed through the ten-page red-leather-bound menus that were among the restaurant's signature features.

He was certainly looking dapper today. His hair was newly shorn, making him seem more like the boy he'd once been and less like the overworked man he'd become. He'd taken off his trademark blue *Los Milagros* coveralls to display a pair of clean jeans and a white button-down shirt whose partially rolled-up sleeves showcased the still-taut brown skin of his forearms. The muscles of those forearms kept flexing attractively as he flipped through the menu and his dimples kept flashing as he considered the options.

He knows how much I love it when he's just refreshed his crew cut. And when he decides to dress up a bit. And when he smiles like that. What the hell does he want from me?

"We'll start with *Antipasto Caldo*—with extra baked clams, of course," Manny was announcing. "And an order of garlic bread. And then, if you want *Veal Saltimbocca*, order *Saltimbocca*. And if what you want is *Aragosta Fra Diavolo*, go right ahead."

"No lobster for me, Manny," Paloma murmured, suppressing the alarm signals that were now going off full force in her head. "I've never been able to manage those creatures very gracefully. I'll be blissfully sucking away on a claw and not even notice that I've splattered orange grease all over my blouse."

"They can bring you a lobster bib if you want."

"I'm far too vain for a bib, Manny. I think I'll just stick to the linguine with shrimp, mussels and squid. I can stay presentable when the things on my plate can be easily lanced with a fork."

They smiled peaceably at one another as she poured them each some Chianti from the bottle that he'd ordered as soon as they'd sat down, and they tilted their glasses together.

"*Salud, amor y pesetas*," he said.

"*Y tiempo para gozarlos*," she added.

"*Y apetito*," he concluded, and they clinked.

Health, love and money. Time to enjoy them. And appetite.

And then Paloma couldn't take the suspense for a single moment longer.

"And now, Manny," she said. "Tell me what it is you need from me."

"My dear little sister. Always with the suspicions. Can't we just sit here and enjoy things before you start in on all that?"

"You know me, Manny. Patience is not my strong suit."

"And why are you so sure that I need something?"

"Why else would you be treating me to lunch in this bastion of fine dining instead of at the *Taco Bell* on Fordham Road? And telling me to order lobster at thirty-six dollars a pop instead of suggesting that I stick with the 'Lunch Special'? What's up?"

Manny took a long swig and then put down his glass.

"Well, Hermanita, it's like this. Beatriz's mother… she's not doing so well. And Beatriz thinks that her three sisters, her two sisters-in-law and her eighty-five female cousins can't possibly take care of her properly. So she's going down to the Dominican Republic to show those ignorant islanders how it's done."

Paloma grinned.

"She's leaving in a week," Manny continued. "And I'm going down for eight days with her. Give her some support."

"And sneak in some time on the beautiful beaches?"

"And sneak in some time on the beach."

Now Manny grinned.

"I even told her…" he added, tilting his head forward and back again in a mini-bow, "to leave her return ticket open—that I'll manage everything at home for her till she's back. She's between housekeeping jobs right now, so it's okay for her to take the time."

Paloma reached over and squeezed his hand.

"What a good husband you are."

Manny grunted.

"Well, at least now I know why you're wining and dining me," Paloma said, smiling indulgently at him. "I suppose that for the time that both you and Beatriz are away, you want me to come stay at your house and baby-sit your boys."

"No need, Hermana. The boys will be fine. They've got their jobs and their TV and computers. There's a McDonald's and a Domino's Pizza right down the block. Negrito and Gordito have their girlfriends—maybe they'll even come over to cook for everyone. The lady downstairs will do their laundry for a small fee. And mine too when I get back. We'll be fine."

Paloma shook her head.

Men! Can't they even find their own way to the laundry room? Oh, well.

"But what about Anteojitos?"

The question popped out before she could stop herself.

"What *about* Anteojitos?"

Almost a growl. Oh, dear. We seem to have gotten to the point that I can't even say my nephew's name without Manny having a fit. This is going to be every bit as hard as I feared.

"Well… won't he really miss having you and Beatriz around? He doesn't have a girlfriend to fall back on. And you can't expect Negrito and Gordito and their girlfriends to spend much time on him. Won't he be lonely with everyone out working all day—and then maybe even out all night? Wouldn't you like to drop him off with me and Serach for that week? Just him? Serach works from home most days, so she can look in on him from time to time. Come up with interesting things for him to do. Maybe teach him some more math."

Funny how I just assume that Serach would do all that. My bad. It's true though, isn't it? She would. And more. Without even being asked.

But Manny was firmly shaking his head.

"Anteojitos will feel far worse moving in with you than staying at home by himself. He likes staying at home. He doesn't need to do 'interesting things.' He can go to McDonald's himself if his brothers aren't there—I'm leaving him some cash and he knows how to order and pay. He'll be fine with his TV shows and his subway maps till it's time to go in and sweep my shop every day. It's… what he does…"

"Jesus, Manny!"

Manny had the decency to flush. But then he regrouped.

"Shit, Paloma. Don't start in with me. Anteojitos is happy. And how the hell will he get to work if he's stuck all the way out in Brooklyn with you? From our place it's just a bus ride that he's taken all his life. From your house… it's an hour on the subway. *Dios guarde.* He's never used the trains by himself. When he needs to go somewhere outside the neighborhood, I drive him. Or Negrito does."

Paloma snorted.

"Manny, it's practically a straight shot from our house to Fordham Road on the B train. And Anteojitos spends half his life studying subway maps. Don't you remember that time when he began reciting the names of all the stations on the 7 line from the Hudson Yards to Citi Field and back again until Negrito finally hit him on the head and made him shut up?"

Manny shrugged.

"And can't you see how great he'd feel if he could master a real train ride? You who are always so worried about his sense of self. Serach could go with him the first couple of times—show him the way—till he feels confident. He'll get it right after that."

"Look, Hermana," said Manny, a decided edge creeping into his voice. "Memorizing the subway map is one thing and taking the train by himself is another. It's a tough world out there. I don't want him getting in a car with a bunch of *malditos* and being beaten up because they think he's looking at them the wrong way."

"Manny, no one is going to pay him any mind. These days, the *malditos* on the subway are all imbedded in their smartphones."

Manny took a minute to reply. When he finally did, he used a tone that Paloma could never hear without a small frisson of fear.

"Look, Paloma. I know what I'm doing with Anteojitos. Just leave it alone, will you?"

He drained his glass of its wine, poured himself some more and sat very still for a moment.

"Much as I value your offer to babysit him," he added in a somewhat softer voice. "And much as Anteojitos loves seeing his Tías."

The waiter suddenly materialized at their table, antipasto platter and garlic bread basket in hand. Paloma and Manny watched him gratefully till he was done placing everything down—at which point Manny reached forcefully over to the platter, grabbed the serving spoon, and shoveled three of the five clams onto his plate.

"Go right ahead, Manny," said Paloma. "Take all the clams."

"Not all of them. Just most of them."

But the tension had dissipated as quickly as it had gathered, and Paloma was relieved.

She reached over to pry the serving spoon out of his grip and swiftly divvied up the rest of the platter. She then transferred what she calculated to be her fair share of the garlic bread from the basket to her plate. And finally, she looked across at her brother's face.

God, he looks tired. Haircut or no haircut, this is no fresh-faced boy sitting here with me. This is a man who spends his days taking care of everyone and everything besides himself.

"And so, Manny," she said gently. "If you don't need me to babysit the boys, what is it that you need from me?"

"Okay, it's like this. I need you to go up to my shop around 4:00 on the Saturday I'm away, stay till Anteojitos sweeps up and lock everything up."

She nodded. "And that's all?"

"Well, of course, you'll also need to make sure Negrito and Gordito put their tools away. And take the cash and checks out of the cash register to deposit them in the bank Monday morning. And see that Anteojitos gets on his bus after he's done sweeping."

Paloma nodded. She could certainly do all of that.

"One of the two new mechanics will handle all that during the week—he's great," Manny continued. "But I like to let both guys go home early on Saturdays. They treat me right. So I treat them right."

Paloma nodded again.

"I'm happy for you, Hermano. I'm glad the mechanics have been working out so well."

"Yeah, I can really count on them. Negrito and Gordito… well, they'll stay till closing time while you lock up and everything. But as far as the other stuff…."

"Say no more. I'll talk to my boss. I'm sure I can trade part of my Saturday shift with one of my colleagues and get up to the Bronx in time."

"Bless you, Palomita."

"Don't mention it. And I can't believe you thought you had to treat me to a fancy lunch at *Luigi*'s just to ask me to do that."

They then turned their attention to the antipasto and said not another word for several minutes. Eventually, however, Paloma found herself wiping her plate with the last piece of her garlic bread and looking up at her brother again.

"And now that you've asked me for what you need… there's something I need from you."

Her stomach constricted as soon as she'd said it. But the matter still hung right there in the air. And Serach would never let up if she didn't give it one last try. She took a breath.

"I still need to talk to you about… what happened at our brunch last month."

Manny's expression grew unreadable. But before he could respond, the waiter materialized again out of nowhere to clear away their antipasto plates and silverware and to refresh their wine and water. Manny focused intently on the details of that process and Paloma spent a few minutes taking a long drink from her wine glass, followed by an even longer one from her water glass.

Once the waiter withdrew again, however, she figured she had no choice but to proceed.

"Manny, you were really upset about Anteojitos that morning. About his…" she threw out a quick apologetic look, "disabilities. And Serach and I have some ideas about what you could…"

Manny banged his hand down on the table.

"Shit, Paloma, haven't you said enough about Anteojitos for one day? He's fine. I'm fine. Everything between us is fine. I'm not worried about him anymore. Okay?"

Paloma said nothing in response. She stared at him hard until he shrugged.

"All right. It's true I'd been wondering why he is… how he is. But I wasn't worried about, you know, about *him*. I was worried that… I mean… there are times when Beatriz—well, you know how women are—when she doesn't tell me where she's been or what she's been doing. I was thinking maybe that when she and I first got together…"

Sweet Jesus! Is the whole problem that Manny thinks Anteojitos may not really be his son? That Beatriz was having a side fling with some tall, geeky myopic lover early on in their marriage and nine months later, out popped baby Ramon? What an idiot my brother is!

"Manny!" she said. "You can't possibly think that… that Beatriz… That's crazy, Manny!"

"Yeah. Yeah, I know." Manny picked up the saltshaker and began passing it back and forth between his hands. "I know Beatriz would never dare cheat on me. I mean—shit! She knows that I'd kill her if she as much as looked at another man."

Manny, you are truly a Neanderthal. Oh, well. What do I care? I don't even like Beatriz.

"Although…" Manny picked up the shaker yet again and this time began absentmindedly shaking a not-insignificant pile of salt onto the tablecloth. "Although… maybe you could… explain why you're so absolutely sure that… she couldn't have…"

Paloma shook her head and grinned.

"Manny, I'm absolutely sure that Anteojitos is the fruit of your loins—and your loins alone—because he looks exactly like his grandfather."

"Are you nuts? Beatriz' father is an *enano*—he's five feet tall. And he's way darker than the rest of us. And he has this huge nose. And what the hell does Beatriz' father have to do with... what we're talking about?"

"His other grandfather, Manny."

Manny stared back at her with an expression that she couldn't quite place.

"Look, Manny. I've always hesitated to raise any of this with you because… well, because it never seemed relevant. But now it seems to be. So here goes."

Manny continued staring and she forged ahead.

"When Serach and I went down to see *Abuela* in that nursing home in Colombia a few years back—you remember when we did that, right?—*Abuela* told a story that led us to think that…"

She almost completed her sentence with: "your father was a son-of-a-bitch priest who sexually assaulted our mother," but she stopped herself just in time.

"…your father was the parish priest."

No reaction.

"The parish priest who looked just like an older version of what Anteojitos looks like now."

Manny raised his eyes with the expression that always made Paloma extremely nervous. She took in one slow breath, let it out even more slowly, and took in another.

"I actually met that priest when I was living with *Abuela.* His name was Father Domingo, and he was a real loser. His genes managed to skip you—thank God for your sake. But they came popping right out again in your son."

She swallowed.

"I'm so sorry not to have told you all this before, Manny. But it was only when Anteojitos started looking so much like Father Domingo that I was certain. And now with you being so… well, so worried about Beatriz' potential cheating … I wanted to reassure you."

Manny reached over the table and took her hand. He turned it over gently to study the palm. Then he turned it over again to look at her perfectly tended nails.

"Such nice hands you have, Hermanita."

He took a breath himself.

"Look, Paloma. I happen to know that my father was a priest. I just didn't know he was… so ugly. It's not what I would have expected from our mother."

"Joe was pretty ugly, too…" But then she suddenly stopped and yanked her hand away.

"Hey, wait a minute. What do you mean you 'already know your father was a priest'? How the—?"

Just at that moment, however, the waiter arrived yet again at their tableside, bearing a silver tray with their entrées—each one under its own silver dome. He put the tray down on the little stand that was parked against the wall behind Manny, transferred the dishes from the tray to the table and took the domes off with a flourish.

"Watch out please, these plates are very hot."

Paloma's order came with an extra bowl for the discarded mussel shells. And Manny's veal chops were accompanied by a sizable side dish of linguine marinara. So—efficient as the waiter was—it still took him a few moments to put everything down in its proper place, lay out a fresh set of silverware, offer his little bow and depart.

The food sat and steamed in front of them and neither Manny nor Paloma paid any attention.

"Manny?"

"Hermana?"

"Manny, how the hell do you know that your father was a priest?"

"How the hell do you think I know it? Mama told me."

"But Mama never told us anything about herself or us. She never told me who my father was, that's for sure. How did you make her tell you about yours?"

"I didn't make her, Hermana. She just told me."

Manny tilted back in his chair for a moment and nodded briefly to himself.

"It puzzled me, actually. I mean—why would she suddenly come out with all that? But now it all makes perfect sense."

"Manny, it's you who aren't making any sense. What do you mean?"

"Shut up and I'll tell you," Manny said. But pleasantly.

"Mama told me who my father was right after I showed her a picture of my boys. She wasn't interested in the picture at first—you wouldn't expect her to be, would you? But then she took another look and grabbed it and told me to go outside. When she called me back in, she began talking about my father. I thought she was just being crazy, like she always is—coming out with all that stuff for no reason at all. But now I see… she must have seen that priest in Anteojitos' face. And it got her going."

Paloma was still fixated—paralyzed, almost—by the revelation that Manny knew who his father was. That he knew all about the secret that she'd kept so long and so carefully from him. And that he was speaking about it so nonchalantly. Didn't he realize that he was the product of a rape? Well, perhaps their mother hadn't shared that particular detail with him.

"What did Mama actually say about your father? What did she tell you about that priest?"

"She told that me he was the 'love of her life.'"

"Bull shit!"

Manny looked offended.

"What do you mean, 'bull shit'? That's what she said. She told me that when she was a girl—a very young girl—she fell in love with the priest who heard her confessions. And he made her pregnant. But that seeing how he was a priest and everything, they couldn't make a go of it. So she was sent away. Actually, what she said was: 'your *hijueputa* of a grandmother sent me away to a convent in the goddamned Bronx.'"

He looked down at his plate, contemplated whether to begin digging in, and reached for his knife and fork. But then he put them down again and laughed.

"Well, at least now I know why she decided to tell me all that right then."

But Paloma was still stuck a few sentences back.

"She truly said that she loved him? She said that she loved that priest?"

"Yeah, that's what she said."

"Shit."

Paloma felt a wave of something approaching commiseration for her mother. How the hell could she have thought that she was in love with that pompous pedophile? What was that syndrome when you began emotionally bonding with your oppressor? She couldn't remember.

However, just as she'd almost re-captured the term, another thought came slamming into her brain to drive everything else out.

"But wait a minute, Manny! Wait a fucking minute! I just finished processing what you said. Mama told you about your father right after you 'showed her a photo of your boys'?"

"Yeah. That's what I said. Makes sense, doesn't it?"

"Which means that she told you about him recently."

"Well, not so recently. About a year and a half ago."

"Which means that you've been in touch with her! Recently. Maybe not 'totally-recently' but still 'pretty-damn-near-recently'."

"Yeah. What are you driving at?"

"I'm driving at the fact that—as you've always told it—Mama completely dropped off the face of the earth for both of us, ages ago. And yet now it turns out that..."

"Oh, Jesus, Hermanita. I'm sorry. I shouldn't have..."

"Shouldn't have what? Seen her? Told me? Left me behind when you went to see her?"

"*Cálmate*, Paloma. *Cálmate*. It's just that... well, maybe I shouldn't have, but I... promised her I wouldn't tell you that I'd seen her."

"She made you promise not to tell me?"

Manny nodded.

"Damn straight you shouldn't have promised. You should have told her to go right to hell! All these years that you've let me go on thinking that she didn't give a damn about—about either of us. That sure, maybe she never loved me, but that she didn't love you either. That she was just... incapable of loving her children. But now it turns out all that wasn't true. She did love you. She's been seeing you all this time. You've been betraying me all this time. I thought you were on my side, Manny! I thought we were a team. You and me. Not you and her."

Paloma stood up, pushed herself away from the table and sped off to the lady's room. When she came back—red-faced but composed—Manny was deeply involved in dissecting one of his veal chops and it fell to the waiter to rush to the table to push Paloma's chair back in for her.

Manny waited until the waiter had retreated before beginning to speak. And even then, he kept his hands busy sawing away at the meat and his eyes fixed on his hands.

"Listen, Paloma." He finally glanced up at her. And then looked down again quickly. "Jesus Christ, don't look at me that way."

"I'll look at you any goddamned way I choose, Manny."

"I don't know why she asked me not to tell you. Or why I agreed. But she did and I did. And my word is my word. When you come right down to it, that's all a man has."

"Well, you've sure as hell broken your word now, haven't you? And I don't see the ceiling falling down on you."

"Paloma, I don't know what to say. Maybe Mama was ashamed of how she treated you when you were a kid. Maybe she thought you wouldn't *want* to see her."

"Manny, shut up already. You're only making it worse. Mama wasn't ashamed of anything she did to me. She simply didn't want anything to do with me."

"Well, if it helps, she didn't get in touch with me either for… I don't know… fifteen years? Well, that's not true, either. Sometimes she'd call me up to ask me to send money. And yeah, maybe it was wrong not to tell you. But… she never asked to see me. She never asked me how I was. Not once, I swear it. The only reason I finally went to see her was that she was sick as a dog. And broke. And in-between men. You know how she gets when there's no man around. And I'm a man."

Paloma sniffed, blew her nose into her pink cloth napkin and then hurriedly balled the napkin up and put it to one side of the table, as far away from her plate as she could.

"She could have asked *me* to help her if she was so sick. I'd have gone if she'd only asked. I would have known what to do, too. I'm a nurse, you know."

"She wasn't all there, Hermana. Hadn't eaten in days. Hadn't washed. Burning up with fever. She probably wouldn't have wanted you to see her like that."

For a moment Paloma found it hard to draw a breath. Or to find a place to gaze at that didn't make her well up with tears. But when she finally decided to look back at her brother, he looked so totally stricken himself that she straightened up and wiped her eyes.

"What hurts the most," she said, "is that she probably didn't even know that I'd become a nurse. You've never told her, have you?"

"Yes, Hermanita. I did once."

Paloma paused for a moment.

"And she said…?"

"She didn't say anything."

"I would have liked her to say something."

She paused again.

"I would have liked her to be proud of me."

"Paloma." Manny spoke softly. Much more softly than he usually did. "Palomita. What good does it do, thinking all those terrible things?"

Paloma looked away as he continued.

"Anyway, as soon as I saw how bad-off Mama was—and she was in really, really bad shape, Hermanita—I drove her to the hospital. I stayed with her till her fever broke and then brought her back to her house. Bought her some food. Left her some money. I went back up to visit her once—once, that's all—after she got better, to make sure she was okay. That's when I showed her that picture of my boys. Thought it might—you know—cheer her up or something. And that's been all. I swear it. She must have found some other poor bastard to take care of her."

"So where did all these mother-son get-togethers take place? Where is she living?"

Paloma put her face in her hands, briefly.

"And why the hell do I still care?"

"She lives in East Bumblefuck, New York. See, I've made you laugh! That's better."

"What's it really called?"

"What does it matter, Hermana? You couldn't find it on the map, that's how small it is. She lives in a trailer. She bartends in some dive in town. Not all the time. She's like their spare help or something. But it's enough to allow her to survive."

He paused.

"And that's really all that I know."

Paloma finally spun some pasta around her fork and took a bite. It was excellent. *Luigi's* food always was. She sniffed again.

"So… do you think that she's really okay now? I mean…"

"Well, she's been okay enough not to have called me back again." He rubbed his hand over his head, back and forth. "But I wouldn't call her 'okay.' She's… old."

"How old could she be? She can't be more than fifty-five—fifty-six?"

"Well, she looks about a hundred. She's gone completely gray."

Paloma's hand flew up to her own hair without thinking.

"Yeah," he grinned. "You've always looked just like her, so you'll probably go gray early, too. Enjoy yourself while you can."

"Shut up."

"But it's not just that she's gray," Manny continued, a little more slowly now. "Some gray-haired ladies can still be pretty foxy. It's that she's all wrinkled. From all the smoking, I guess. Which you don't have to worry about, since you've never smoked. And she's all skin and bones. Which you definitely don't have to worry about."

Paloma stuck out her tongue.

"And she's got no teeth."

"No teeth!"

"No teeth. Well, they probably don't have all that many good dentists in East Bumblefuck."

Paloma laughed again.

"No, they probably don't. But it's probably more from… the drinking."

"What does drinking have to do with it?"

"Oh… Well, liver function is directly connected with tooth health. Don't ask me to explain, it's much too complicated. Bottom line, if you let alcohol totally destroy your liver—and I'm sure Mama's liver is shot to hell—your teeth are the next thing to go."

Manny shook his head. "Always the nurse."

"Well, shit, yes. And a damned good one, too. No thanks to her."

"Eat your pasta, Hermana. Let's talk about something else. All this stuff is taking away my appetite."

They cleaned their plates. They discussed how Negrito was thinking of buying a motorcycle. ("Over my dead body—he needs to save all the money that he's earning for school!") About Gordito's unexpected flare for computer programming. About the beaches that Manny was planning to lounge on when he got to the DR.

They ordered dessert—tiramisu for her, cheesecake for him. They doused their espressos with shots from the bottle of *Sambuca* that the waiter left discreetly on their table, and they split that little plate of biscotti that *Luigi's* provided to all its customers at the end of every meal.

When they were done, the waiter presented Manny with a red leather folder containing the bill, and Manny inserted his credit card in the appropriate place and handed it back to the waiter.

"You know that I love you, Hermanita," he said to Paloma when all the transactions were completed, and they were making their way to the door—Paloma in front and Manny behind her.

"I love you, too," she said, turning around to kiss him lightly on the cheek.

They headed outside, located the *Los Milagros* van that Manny had parked on a side street, and drove to the Grand Concourse where Paloma would catch the B train home.

"Beatriz and I leave for the DR on a late afternoon flight, just a week from today."

"So you said. Well, you don't have to worry. On the Saturday you're away, I'll take care of everything. And tell the boys they can call us if they need anything. Who knows if that lady downstairs will actually wash their socks the way they like?"

"*Que Dios te lo pague, Hermana.*" May God repay you. "And Serach too."

"Amen."

When they reached the subway stop, Paloma put one hand lightly on her brother's shoulder.

"But in the meantime, maybe you can also give a little thought to how you can give Anteojitos a better chance, Hermano? How you can stop treating him like such a *pobrecito* and help him develop some life skills? Send him back to school somewhere? We stand ready to help you do all that, you know. Serach and I."

"Yeah, Paloma," Manny replied, as he reached across her lap to open the van door on her side. "I know all that. We'll see."

6.

It was a gorgeous, sunny late Saturday afternoon. Fordham Road sparkled and pulsed as Paloma got out of the subway and navigated the ten blocks east from the Grand Concourse to the *Los Milagros* Auto Repair Shop.

The entire neighborhood was out on the street.

Teenage girls brushed past her as they swerved between storefronts or just barreled forward in impermeable groups. Women barely older than those girls shoved her aside with their king-sized baby strollers. Older women sitting by carts full of mangoes proffered her smoothly cut portions of that luminously yellow-orange fruit. Skinny middle-aged men in sleeveless undershirts and aprons casually flexed their triceps at her as they shaved heaps of ice into big white paper cones and then doused them with neon-colored syrups. Solemn ladies in white turbans guarding benches of religious pamphlets and candles cast stern looks in her direction. Young men in backward-facing baseball caps motioned her over to tables crammed with videotapes, designer handbag knockoffs, and elaborate hair ornaments.

Bone-deep muscle memory kicked in as she dodged the myriad forces competing for her attention. She moved forward as nimbly as she had as a girl.

She gave in to the call of one of the mango sellers—purchasing a large-sized plastic cup of slices, generously enhanced with lime, salt and hot sauce. She stopped to smile at the man who dashed out of the doorway of one of the 99-cent stores with a big blue megaphone to tell her that the lingerie for sale inside "will make your boyfriend sweat!".

"Another time, Papito!" She blew him a kiss.

The *Los Milagros* Auto Repair Shop was located on the south side of Fordham Road, between Bathgate Avenue and Lorillard Place. The garage in which Manny and his crew carried out their miraculous repairs was on the right, and the single-story office in which they recorded their customers' information and collected their money was on the left. Paloma grinned as she spotted the shop's familiar red, yellow, and black banner billowing gaily in a gust of wind and strode briskly toward Bathgate to reach the office door.

She stopped grinning, however, as her smartphone began buzzing insistently against her hip.

Oh, damn, not again. Please God, let it be Manny sending another tip on how to deal with the alarm system. Or Serach asking me to please pick up some Italian pastries in Belmont while I'm here, since I'll be so close by. Or some dethroned Nigerian prince asking me for the money to go home again. Let it be anybody but…

There was, however—and probably inevitably—no escaping who the texter was. It was the tenth one she'd received since the Gala.

How R U? (Two of those.)

Where R U? R U still at work? (Two of those.)

Lots of post-event cleanup still to do. What evening can U come by 2 help? (Two of those.)

Call. (Three of those—including the current one.)

And, of course, the one she'd received the previous evening—provoking a host of unpleasant little thumpings in her chest.

Victor away on business till Tuesday night. When can U come over?

She had responded to all of Carlota's messages with some variation of: *Catching up on all the stuff I didn't do while working on the Gala.* At some point, however, she was going to have to either block Carlota altogether or figure out how to manage her requests more adroitly.

She texted back quickly: *Helping out in my brother's shop today. Call U later.*

On the night after the Gala, Paloma had finally lured Serach to bed for something other than sleep. It was far from a passionate reunion. Serach was still troublingly fragile—more obliging than interested. Nonetheless (and tantalizing as that tango had been) Paloma was not about to risk their whole relationship for a brief electric fling with a Salvadoran Piranha.

A married Salvadoran Piranha.

A married Salvadoran Piranha who—by any measure—was not a very admirable character.

What was it that Frank had once let slip? Something to the effect that the zings of adultery are never worth the shit that inevitably follows? He hadn't elaborated (and he'd said it with a bit more couth—Kentucky altar-boy that he once was). That had, however, been the main gist.

So, no. No danger on that front.

Still, she didn't want to cut Carlota entirely off at the pass. She was, after all, the gateway to *¡Adelantamos-El Bronx!* To something that Paloma now very much wanted to keep in her life.

For, it seemed, something had shifted permanently inside her when she'd stood in the doorway of the redecorated Veteran's Memorial Hall and felt the ecstatic rhythms of the *Las Marianas* Drum Corps echoing in her rib cage. When she'd seen that line of proud young women in their chef's hats—and watched Magdalena Torres hold the audience in her sturdy brown hand.

The joy she'd felt in the presence of all that exuberant Bronx Latinness was too huge to discount. The ease with which she was now striding across Fordham Road—truly happy to be back—too marvelous to give up again.

Oh, the hell with it. She'd find a way to keep *La Piranha Salvadoreña* on the line without getting eaten alive herself. No need to ruin this lovely sunny walk with worry.

Negrito was standing half-in and half-out of the office door when she arrived. He had swapped out his coveralls and work boots for a pair of well-fitted black pants, an acid-green tee-shirt a couple of sizes too small for his pecs, and his beloved Air Jordan 11 Retro Concord sneakers. And he was topping off the whole look with one of his sharkish grins.

"Not a moment too soon, Tía. Gordito and I were just on our way out. Hot dates tonight!"

"What are you talking about, *Mijo*. Get back in there. You don't leave till I do."

She pushed him back bodily into the office. Those pecs were as firm as a plank. Nice.

Gordito was standing just inside, looking sheepish and not nearly as sharp as Negrito.

"We've got some coveralls for you, Tía, just especially," Negrito continued. "So you can tidy up after us without worrying about getting dirty."

"The hell I will! Get back in there, put on your own coveralls and do it yourselves!"

"But we—"

She surveyed them up and down and harrumphed.

"Have the two mechanics gone home already?"

"Long gone, Tía. Long gone. As is the receptionist. They've all got hot dates, too."

"So you're abandoning me to all the irate car owners who show up once you've left?"

"No worries, Tía. No one ever arrives after 4:00 on a Saturday. Hell, they're all home getting ready for their own hot dates. Come on—have a heart! Don't you remember what it was like to be… young and in love?"

"Jesus, Negrito. You really are a *pendejo*."

He gazed at her with his gorgeous black eyes. He may have even fluttered his eyelashes a bit.

"Okay, okay. Cut out all that flirtatious shit. You know it doesn't work with me. Show me how well you two idiots have cleaned up. Those are your father's orders. Let's go."

Negrito gave her a grin.

"We've actually done everything we needed to, Tía. I was only kidding you. But here—" he added, darting into the office, opening the metal locker just inside the door, and pulling out the coveralls in question. "Before we enter the garage, please do put these on for me. Hard as we slaved to clean up, we might have missed something. You don't want to get grease on those pretty white jeans of yours. Or on that sexy pink shirt."

She punched him in the shoulder. Not that lightly, either.

"Hey, I mean it! I wasn't being fresh. Don't think we don't appreciate how nicely put together our Tía always is. Don't we, Gordito? Here. Take the coveralls. Put them on. It's murder to get grease out of clothes. Or so I've heard…."

But by then, all traces of Paloma's irritability had vaporized. He did have his ways, Negrito. When he wanted to.

She took the coveralls from him, stepped into them gracefully, and zipped them up.

"And whose name do we have embroidered on the breast pocket here?" she asked, glancing down at her bosom. "Whose place am I taking today? Are these your coveralls, Gordito?"

Gordito blushed.

"No way, Tía. Mine would be way too big for you. These are Eduardo's. You know, one of the two mechanics? He's real little—I mean, for a guy. Real skinny. And not much taller than you. So you don't have to worry about tripping over your cuffs."

Negrito took the office keys down from their hook and handed them to his aunt so she could lock the door behind them. And then they all trooped out to the garage.

The sights and smells of that big, dirty, overcrowded space made Paloma suck in her breath. All those crazy huge objects! Vehicle lifts and strut compressors and air compressors and—what was that other thing called? The one Manny was always bragging about when they were young? An engine hoist? Yeah, an engine hoist. She remembered the day that Fernando's father had first purchased one, so many years ago. Manny had come home utterly jubilant. Couldn't stop talking about it. Joe finally had to tell him to shut up.

She made a big show of inspecting the length and breadth of the interior to see that everything was as clean as it should be and that all the tools had been put away when—in truth—all she wanted was the chance to reminisce.

She thought about the summer days when she would sit happily in a corner to observe Manny as he learned his trade. About the time she'd arrived at daybreak and Fernando had "borrowed" one of the cars and driven her off to the airport to go live with her grandmother in Colombia. About how—when she was newly back in the Bronx and subbing for Manny's receptionist—she would poke her head in at the end of the day to collect her brother and go home.

She could easily have gone on daydreaming for a while longer, but she caught the pained, impatient expression on Negrito's face and took pity on him.

She gave him and Gordito matching punches in the arm.

"Okay, boys. It all looks good except for the crud on the floor that I assume Anteojitos will take care of. Help me close this place down and you can leave. And for God's sake, don't be jerks with your girlfriends tonight. Don't rub without a glove! The world doesn't need any more 'little Rodriguezes.' You guys are enough of a pain in the ass."

They all exited the garage together, Negrito's arm thrown casually and affectionately around his aunt's shoulders and all three of them laughing. The two brothers pulled down the enormous metal gate with a great show of effort and secured it to the ground. They turned in tandem toward their aunt and leaned in to give her two large, simultaneous kisses—one on each cheek. They then spun around toward Bathgate Avenue and started sprinting down the sidewalk—Negrito in front and Gordito behind—till they both disappeared from sight.

"God, I hope those two idiots are right and no customer arrives at 4:45, desperate to get his brake shoes fixed," thought Paloma, as she let herself back into the office. She had no idea what brake shoes were, in fact, but she'd always thought the name was cool.

"I'll take care of the cash register first, since there will be no further transactions," she added, this time out loud, because—truth to tell—it spooked her a bit to be in that office all by herself. She left the door unlocked so Anteojitos could get in without problems and made her way to the green metal desk with the office phone and cash register.

"Hi, Manny!" she said waving up at the camera that was recording her every move. "I'm going to get everything out of the cash register and put it in my purse!"

She shook her head at her worries—at the sudden need to hear her own voice within that silent, empty space. She bent over the cash register to punch in the "No Sale" button just as she'd been taught to do, so many years ago. She typed in the new pass code that Manny had drummed into her head before leaving and the drawer popped open—much to her relief. She took everything out—cash, checks, credit card receipts—and stuffed it into the manila envelope she'd put in her purse that morning. She took out her phone and zipped the purse shut.

She could have stepped out of the coveralls at that point, but she was getting a kick out of wearing them. She snapped a selfie and sent it off to Serach. She then stuck the phone in one of the coverall's pockets and began making a slow circuit of the office, inspecting things.

"Well, Anteojitos certainly seems to keep the place nicely swept," she continued, out loud. "But the grime on all these shelves must be two inches deep, the calendar on the back wall shows that it is still October, and I don't think anyone has washed the windows in ten years."

She ran a finger along one windowsill. Atrocious.

"I bet there's some cleaning spray here somewhere. Let's see what I can do."

She walked back to the green metal locker, found a rag and a bottle of Lysol Bleach and began strolling around again, spraying and scrubbing as she saw fit.

The front door to the office opened behind her and a man walked in.

Paloma heard nothing at first, absorbed as she was in her scrubbing, as he crossed the floor toward her in his odd, loping pace. When he got within three feet of her, however, something electric surged through the air and the hair on the back of her neck rose of its own accord.

"Hello, Paloma."

She spun around to see a tall figure wearing a battered olive-green jacket despite the June heat and with a backward-facing baseball cap perched over a mass of stringy black hair. Her face must have shown horror as she reached for her phone, for he saw it and lunged for her arm. He pried the phone out of her hand and threw it across the room where it landed with a sickening thud.

"Is that any way to greet an old friend? Reaching for your phone like you were scared of me or something? Do you think I'd ever hurt you?"

She forced herself to look him full in the face. Crazed, glazed eyes, a scruffy beard and a broad grin with several missing teeth greeted her gaze.

"Don't you remember me, Palomita? Don't you remember your old pal, Fernando?"

She took a closer look.

"Fernando! Oh my God! Yes, of course, it's you! I didn't recognize you at first!"

"And don't I get a hug after so many years?"

"Sure, Fernando. Sure."

She reached out timidly toward him, and he grabbed her and pulled her close. He smelled as if he hadn't washed in a long time. He didn't let go of her for several seconds. Until he finally did.

Paloma stepped back a few cautious inches—it would not be a good thing to show exactly how appalled she was how at what she had just experienced.

"Fernando—how are you?"

"Well, how do I look, Paloma?"

Paloma managed a small smile. She picked up the cleaner from the shelf where she'd left it.

"Put that down, Paloma. You don't really think you need a weapon with me, do you? And besides, I could grab it from you in a minute—couldn't I—if you tried to get smart with me?"

She put it down.

"So how do I look? Not so good, eh?"

Paloma said nothing. What could she say?

"Well, wouldn't you like to hear why I look the way I do?"

She still couldn't utter a word.

"Don't you want to hear my sad story? Or has Manny already told it to you?"

She finally found her voice.

"He—I mean, I know you were in the army…"

"In the Marines, Paloma."

"And I know you've been deployed a few times."

"Six times, Paloma."

She paused. "But I didn't know anything else. Like, for example… that you'd come home."

"Yeah, Manny never wanted to let you know when I was back in town. Pity for me. But perhaps your dear brother was a little nervous about bringing us together."

He whistled a few bars of some unidentifiable tune.

"In fact, whenever I mentioned you, he'd quickly change the subject. And whenever I turned up here, he would just show me the door. Very inhospitable, wouldn't you say? Unreasonable, too, given that it's my father's shop."

He whistled one bar more.

"And clearly, he never told you of my interest in renewing our… friendship."

Fernando left Paloma's immediate vicinity and began walking around the office, looking here and there while keeping himself carefully positioned between her and the desk with the cash register and the phone.

"So… since Manny clearly hasn't told you my story, would you like me to fill you in?"

"Sure, Fernando. I'd love to hear it."

His eyes were perfectly empty. She'd never seen anything so terrifying in her life.

"Well, sometime in my last tour of duty in Af-gha-ni-stan, I had a little breakdown."

He looked off to a place she couldn't see.

"I've been doing some reading. Seems my experience isn't so rare. That it often happens after you've done so much killing. Been shot at yourself a whole lot. Woken up each morning wondering whether you're already dead."

He walked to the phone, picked up the receiver and listened to the dial tone for a moment.

Please, Mary, Mother of God, let him leave me that lifeline. Please, dear beloved Virgin!

He put the receiver down. He didn't even glance at the cash register. He did, however, toss his cap over the camera lens with impressively sharp aim before strolling back toward Paloma.

"Anyway, in the midst of that temporary insanity… I found myself just walking away from it all, into the… have you ever been to Afghanistan? In the sub-zero winter? Didn't think so."

Paloma moved her hand toward the cleaner. He rushed forward, grabbed it, and threw it aside.

"Naughty, naughty, Paloma. Still thinking of spraying that bad stuff at me? You always were a little fireball, weren't you? But I wouldn't try any fancy moves right now if I were you."

He gave her a smile that she wished she'd never seen.

"Don't you want to hear the rest of my story?"

"Yes, Fernando. Of course I do."

"When a Marine goes 'Absent-With-Out-Leave', it doesn't matter why he did it. Doesn't matter that he might have… hurt one of his fellow

Marines if he'd stuck around. I spent eighteen months in a military prison. They were not pleasant."

He looked at her and grinned his gap-toothed grin.

"And then they sent me home. Where I've been ever since. No medals for this Marine. No lifelong pension. I'd been shooting for that pension. Why go back into hell six times except for the chance of a lifetime of support from good old Uncle Sam? But I guess it wasn't in the cards. No, it's just a lifetime with my father now. Of watching him sit in his wheelchair wishing it was me who was dead instead of my mother whom he loved so much. But neither of us have much choice, do we? Where would I go if I left him, after all—a traitor like me? It's not like Uncle Sam will take care of me. Or as if I have any skills besides… killing. And where can my father go, half paralyzed? No, we're stuck together in our little joint hell."

He turned again suddenly and smiled broadly when he saw how it made Paloma jump.

"Turns out that there are some benefits to our situation, however. I have a place to stay. Which is more than many other veterans. My father has someone to do his shopping and cooking and help him get to the bathroom at night. I've become quite good at all that. Not as good as you, of course…. Yes, I remember what a whiz you were in the kitchen, Paloma. And I heard from your brother that you'd become a fine little home health aide to some rich old lady. Perhaps you could come over and help me and my Papito sometime? Wouldn't that be nice?"

He paused and stroked his scruffy chin.

"Then, of course, living with my father gives me the chance to listen in on his phone calls. Yes, he can still speak a bit, despite his other problems. Some of those phone calls have been very interesting. Like when Manny told him he'd be away this week in the DR with his wife and that you—little Paloma, my favorite girl—would be taking care of things this afternoon."

He smiled.

"When I came by a little earlier to see if you'd like to play, I didn't come in. After all, there were your two nephews standing right beside you, one on each side. The big fat one and the tall handsome one. They look very strong, those nephews of yours. And quite devoted. Wouldn't want to irritate them. I was just about to give up and go home when—what do you know? My luck changed. I watched them slip away down the street, while you went back inside."

He smiled.

"And… when I realized that my little Paloma was all alone now, it raised all sorts of lovely possibilities for me…."

Blessed Mary. Sweet Mother of God. Help me!

Fernando bent his head briefly, revealing that the hair hanging down around his ears framed a perfect bald spot. He began walking toward Paloma again, smiling his chilled, alien smile.

"Because, of course, I remembered something else about you, Paloma. I mean, something besides your fabulous cooking skills."

He suddenly looked up and smiled a little more.

"I remember how much you wanted me when we were young. And how much I wanted you. And how we couldn't get it together because of your stupid brother, Manny. Your stupid, stodgy, cowardly older brother, Manny. Who now owns the shop that my father built."

He frowned. There were deep lines between his eyebrows as well across his forehead.

"Well. He's not in the shop now—our dear Manny—is he? No, he's far, far away in another country. He can't stop us."

Fernando was now advancing relentlessly on Paloma—his arms raised as if to grab her, his head lowered as if to ram her. But as she focused on that inexorably approaching oval of pale, naked scalp, she was suddenly overwhelmed by an emotion that was—startlingly, inexplicably—far stronger than fear or disgust.

Compassion.

Well, bless you, my Virgin.

"Fernando, you still have that scar!"

She reached forward and ran her finger along it. Tenderly.

"You still have that scar where your father whacked you with a baseball bat."

He lifted his head with a jerk, but she reached out to tilt it down again, found the long white line of that old gash and stroked it a second time.

"You still have that scar where you were so wounded—so terribly wounded—by your father, so many years ago. And where I healed you.

Don't you remember that I did that, Fernando? Don't you remember how I healed you?"

He shook his head violently out of her grasp.

"You don't? Well, I certainly do. You were my first healing, you know. You set me on the path to becoming a nurse. It wasn't lust I felt for you, Fernando. It was caring. It was kindness. Kindness is the key to healing, you know. It's why my touch worked."

He raised his head to look straight at her and she saw the miracle take place. She saw his eyes fill slowly with something besides emptiness and pain. Something softer. More vulnerable.

His arms remained outstretched as he lurched forward. He remained six feet tall, deeply disheveled—totally appalling.

Nevertheless, she was certain that she had gotten to him. And that he wouldn't harm her, after all.

But then came what she later described as "the driest, sharpest sound I ever heard."

A small, sharp, dry explosion. And then a second one.

Fernando yelled, staggered, and fell heavily against her. The wall behind her supported them both—but just barely—as he grabbed at her.

Then he slipped down her body and landed on the floor.

"The bad man was going to hurt my Tía," was the next thing that Paloma heard.

The voice was so bellowing, so grating—so out of place in the silence that had followed the explosion—that she instinctively raised her hands to cover her ears.

"The bad man was going to hurt my Tía. And I shot him."

7.

Serach didn't recognize the number that was showing up on her smartphone. She barely recognized the voice.

"Paloma, calm down a minute. I can't understand a single word that you're saying. And—this isn't your number. Where are you calling from?"

"I'm calling from Manny's fucking office phone!"

"Why from his office phone? Why not from your own phone?"

Serach couldn't figure out what to focus on. She'd never heard Paloma sound this way.

"Dammit, Serach, never mind 'why not from my phone'! My phone is broken, my phone is smashed, it's dead, it's gone, it's never coming back again. He smashed my phone and he almost smashed me, but… but Anteojitos shot him and now he's lying on the floor bleeding and my idiot nephew won't shut up and oh my God, Serach!"

"Paloma, my darling Paloma, you aren't making any sense. Please start at the beginning. What happened?"

"Oh, Jesus, Serach. I just told you what happened!"

"No, you didn't. Trust me you didn't. But first things first. Are you all right? Is Ramon?"

Paloma took in a gasp of air. Serach sounded so sane. So serious. So Serach. Thank God.

"I'm fine," she said. "Just totally blood-spattered and going out of my mind, that's all. And Anteojitos is okay too, but he keeps ranting like a maniac and—Anteojitos, if you don't shut up about how the bad man was hurting me and how you shot him, I will personally take that gun from your hand and shoot *you* through the head!"

"Good heavens, Paloma. You're serious. Ramon did shoot someone."

"Fuck it, Serach, why the hell would I be saying he'd shot someone if he hadn't?"

"Is… is the man that he shot still alive?"

"He's alive. He's not moving, but he's breathing—and he's got a pulse. I've called an ambulance. I've called the cops. They're all on their way. And so now what I need is…"

She took a breath.

"Okay. I've finally got it all together. What I need is for you is to get us a criminal defense lawyer. Now. Fast. Like, yesterday. The cops will be here any minute and my idiot nephew keeps ranting about how he shot the man and won't shut up and—Anteojitos, I swear I'm going to kill you if you don't shut up! You're writing your own prison sentence."

But Serach was still stuck on the main point.

"So what you need is for me to get you a criminal defense lawyer?"

"Shit, Serach, what have I been saying? Anteojitos is hell-bent on sticking himself behind bars, so we need someone who can protect him from that. And if Fernando dies—I've called an ambulance, they're on the way—but if he should die…."

Paloma became totally incoherent again.

"Paloma? Paloma, are you there?"

There was a frightening moment of silence before Paloma got back on the phone.

"Yes. I'm here. I'm calm. No worries."

"Okay, I've got the picture. The police are coming. The ambulance is coming. You and Ramon are okay. The man that Ramon shot is still breathing. And… who is the man? Fernando, you say? The Fernando who was Manny's friend?"

"Yes, the Fernando who was Manny's friend."

"What was Fernando doing that Ramon shot him?"

"He was… he looked as if he was… going to attack me. He's—he's gone a bit crazy. Went AWOL while in the war. Served time in a military prison. Look, I don't think he actually would have raped me but that's what it must have looked like. To Anteojitos, I mean."

"Okay, I've got it," said Serach, after a moment. "And don't worry. I'll get you a lawyer."

How on earth am I going to get a criminal defense lawyer at 5:15 p.m. on a Saturday evening when I don't even know any criminal defense lawyers?

"I'll get you the best criminal defense lawyer in New York."

What am I saying? How can I promise such a thing?

Serach took a breath.

Never mind all that. I'll do it. I'll figure it out.

"But in the meantime, I have to be able to reach you. And you have to be able to reach me. You don't have your phone anymore?"

"Jesus fucking Christ, Serach! No, I don't have my fucking…"

Paloma caught her own breath.

"Oh Jesus, Serach."

She breathed again.

"I'm so sorry. I don't mean to curse at you. You're my rock. You're my home base. You're… Oh Jesus, God, I don't know what to do..."

"It's okay, Paloma. It's all okay. My goodness, Paloma. With what you've just been through, of course you're a bit *farmisht*! The main thing is that it's all going to be okay. I promise. You're going to be okay—you're the strongest person I know. And Ramon will be okay because we're going to make sure that he is. And Fernando will be okay because… well, I hope he'll be okay. He'll be okay if that's what you want."

She rubbed one hand briskly through her curls.

"But listen. Ramon has a phone, right?"

"Yes. No. I don't know."

"Of course he does. Everybody has a phone. Ask him for his phone. Take it from him if you have to. And…"

"Oh, shit, there's the ambulance."

"Okay, go. Get Fernando into the ambulance. Get Ramon to give you his phone so you can call me when you have more information. And in the meantime, I'll get a lawyer."

"Okay."

"And remember that we're in this together. I'll be there as soon as I can. And *Ha-Shem* will be with you in the meantime. Tell Ramon that I love him."

She paused.

"And remember that I love *you*."

"I love you, too," Paloma whispered.

But at that moment the two EMS workers barged in with their gurney. Paloma put the phone down, pushed Anteojitos out of their path and led them to where Fernando was lying on the floor, not moving, in a growing pool of his own blood.

They put him on the gurney and took him away.

8.

862 Grand Concourse is a six-story building occupying nearly half a block of prime real estate right across the Concourse from the Bronx County Courthouse.

Unlike so many of the structures along that boulevard, it emerged from the borough-spanning disinvestment of the 1970's with almost all its 1930's grandeur intact. Its creamy-white bricks and geometrically applied red ceramic details had all been lovingly restored. The concentric circles and interlocking triangles of grass-green, black and ochre marble of its lobby floor gleamed with the polish of ongoing maintenance. The lights on the lobby walls were either originals or exceptionally accurate copies of those originals. The doors of the two elevators still bore the signature stainless-steel zigzags and stripes of the Jazz Age.

Most wonderful of all—as apartment houses up and down the Concourse were cavalierly replacing their corner casement windows with single-panel, tilt-and-turn models—the building's Board of Directors had voted to use updated replicas of the distinctive two-door, crank-operated versions that so uniquely complemented an Art Deco façade. A few of the coop owners had squawked at the price of that installation, of course. But the Board had held out.

And New York City's preservation community had rejoiced.

When it came to the building's individual apartments, however, the drive to modernize had been unstoppable. Only a handful of units retained the brass railings separating their foyers from their sunken living rooms—or the banisters running along the three stairs descending to those living rooms. Only a scattering held on to their bathrooms' Miami Beach-Meets-the-Bronx lilac tiles—or the flamingos etched into the mirrors of their medicine cabinets.

Perhaps the most ruthless updating, however, had taken place in the eight units that lined the lobby. Converted to professional suites sometime in the early 1980's, all but one had been stripped not only of banisters and mirrors but also of arched doorways and recessed *tchotchke* hutches. If there had been some way to level up the sunken living rooms, that would undoubtedly have been done as well.

The eighth unit, however, had been spared all those indignities. Mendel Schachter, Esq. —born and raised on the building's fourth floor and still taking the elevator home every evening—had meticulously conserved everything he'd found when he first took over Suite 1-H from the lady who had lived there since the building opened.

He liked it that way.

Mendel's retro tastes, moreover, went considerably beyond décor. He also retained whatever old-fashioned methods he could in his legal dealings. He kept up with all the latest changes in the law, of course. But he still wrote everything out on big yellow lined pads before entering it on a computer screen. And he remained a firm believer in the power of face-to-face interactions.

Which is why—every year for the past nine years—Serach had been obliged to go all the way up to the Bronx to do Mendel's taxes.

"I'm far too busy to *shlep* out to Brooklyn and don't like entrusting private information to e-mail," he'd informed Serach the first time he'd inquired about her services—following a glowing recommendation from his old friend (and Serach's former accounting professor) Morton Stein. "Mort says you're just launching your tax prep business, so I assume you're not swamped with work yet. Can you make a house call?"

"Sure."

For, in fact, "not swamped" was an understatement. Mendel was Serach's very first client.

They had quickly settled into a yearly pattern of meeting at six o'clock on the last Friday in February, once Mendel shut down for the day. They convened at an enormous antique partners' desk in one of the suite's two former bedrooms. Mendel called it his "personal office", but what it mostly resembled was a boudoir. Serach invariably found herself sneaking furtive glances at its many interesting details in between perusing Mendel's earnings, expenditures and losses.

There were two glass-fronted bookcases brimful with books that clearly did not strictly pertain to the law. A daybed decked out in a turquoise satin bedspread was stationed near the window. Several unmatched Persian rugs lay helter-skelter on the floor. Two tall brass lamps—one with a stand shaped like a naked woman—framed a small round table whose glass-topped, scalloped-edged surface was covered in ash trays of every possible size, shape and vintage.

Because when Mendel took care of personal business, Mendel liked to smoke.

The first time that Serach had sat with him, he'd held his cigarette barely two feet from her face and periodically blown blasts of smoke in her direction. It had made her feel queasy, but she hadn't said a thing. After all, your client is always right, right?

Especially when he's your first client. And reminds you of your father's synagogue buddies so very much.

When they'd finished that first meeting, moreover, she was very glad she hadn't said a thing because Mendel had led her graciously out of that smoky room into the apartment's original kitchen to regale her with egg *kichels* and a glass of Manischewitz Concord Grape Wine ("I don't celebrate *Shabbos* anymore," he'd said to her with a shrug and a wink, "but I do miss the taste of this stuff") and they'd schmoozed pleasantly for a good half hour.

It soon became their tradition. And a very pleasant one, too.

Which is why Serach felt comfortable enough to call Mendel up at 5:30 on a Saturday afternoon and ask if she could come see him right away because she was "in deep trouble." And why Mendel was willing to get up from the most comfortable armchair in his apartment, pat his fat striped tabby cat peremptorily on the head, turn off all the lights and take the elevator back down to his office.

"So let me get this straight," he'd said as he sat back in his desk chair and lit up yet another Camel. "Your… 'friend's' nephew—who is sixteen years old and you don't know whether he has a gun permit but he's a brilliant shot—takes the gun out of the desk drawer in his father's place of business (and you're pretty sure that his father has a license for the gun, right?) and shoots a man he thinks is about to rape his aunt—your 'friend.'"

Serach nodded and Mendel took a deep drag of his cigarette.

"And the man he shoots is the son of the co-owner of that business concern. Served in the wars, went AWOL and is now crazy enough to attempt a rape."

Serach nodded again.

"And the nephew, the son of the other co-owner—the brother of your 'friend'—meanwhile, has some kind of condition, himself. Never been diagnosed—maybe he's retarded, maybe he's 'on the spectrum,'—something is up. Not, in short, entirely *compos mentis*, either."

"I guess you could say that."

"The guy he shoots doesn't die, but he's not in good shape. Your, uh, 'friend' calls an ambulance and the cops, and they show up and the cops are probably questioning her even as we speak—but you're not sure because you haven't heard anything further."

He looked at Serach and blew some smoke in her direction.

"Does that about sum it up?"

"Yes, Mendel. Now can you help me? Can you?"

Mendel looked down at his hands. He was a short, going-to-fat, 72-year-old man with a greying head of red hair plus many freckles and wrinkles in a face that Serach had always thought looked remarkably like that of a frog. He was still clad in the crumpled grey suit that he'd evidently worn all day, but he'd taken off his tie and loosened his shirt and there were sweat stains around his open collar.

He contemplated Serach's request for a long moment before making an ambiguous hand gesture that put Serach's heart in her mouth.

"Before we go any further," he said, "can you answer a couple more questions for me?"

"Sure, Mendel. But… I'm not sure there's anything more to say."

"Oh, there's always more to say."

He put out his cigarette, reached for the pack, thought better of it and put it down again.

"When you say 'friend'" he said, looking at Serach out of the corner of one eye, "do you just mean 'friend?' Or do you mean something else?"

They had never in all their years of acquaintance shared personal details. They'd talked weather, sports (Mendel was a passionate Yankees fan) and even (occasionally, cautiously) local politics. Serach knew he lived somewhere in the building (he'd often alluded to the "ease of my commute") but had no idea whether anyone was waiting for him when he went back upstairs. She hadn't a clue as to why someone with such a blatantly Jewish name—and, evidently, a past history of *Shabbos* observance—was now willing to smoke, take phone calls, and do who knows what else on a Saturday before sunset.

Nor had she ever said a word about her own life choices. Who knew how he might react?

But she now made the split-second decision that she needed to level with him.

"No, Mendel, she's not just a 'friend.' She's my girlfriend. My partner. The love of my life. We've been together for more than a decade. I care more about her—and the nephew in question—than about almost anyone else in the world."

Mendel nodded, self-satisfaction spreading across his freckly, froggy little face.

"But…" Serach asked, with care—and perhaps a degree of prickliness, "does any of that make any difference to you, Mendel?"

If Mendel picked up on the slight change in her tone, he didn't show it. He went ahead with his next cigarette. He lit it, inhaled, and blew out again.

"No. Just curious, is all."

They stared at each other for a moment.

"Let's just say," he added, "that it's something that I've… always had suspicions about."

"Why? Because I wear pants and cut my hair like a boy? Because I'm not married?"

"Nah, lots of girls take their time getting married these days. And lots of them wear pants and keep their hair short. And—in your case—it looks pretty cute."

He paused. He puffed. He put the cigarette out.

"Nah, I've always suspected it because…"

He looked down modestly at his little hands.

"Because generally… I have a pretty powerful effect on women. And yet here we were, year in and year out, drinking wine together and… *bupkes*! That's never happened before. What other explanation could there be? You had to be a dyke. I mean, a very nice dyke, of course…."

He shrugged and Serach put her face down in her hands. But it was because she was laughing.

"Okay, Mendel. I'm going to take all that as a compliment. But let's finish up here. Please. What's your second question?"

Was he or wasn't he going to help her? Had she come in vain?

"Serach, I'm a civil lawyer, not a criminal lawyer. It's different. Surely you know that. Why did you think I could help you?"

That was it. He wasn't going to do it. Serach pulled herself together with an effort.

"I know you're a civil lawyer, Mendel," she said slowly. "I do know the difference. But I turned to you because… I don't know any other lawyers. I mean, I have other lawyer clients. But no one else I could call on a Saturday evening and ask for personal help. And… well, we *have* drunk wine together. I feel comfortable with you. And you're right here up in the Bronx where it all happened. And I had no one else to turn to. Mendel—can you help me?"

"Let me tell you a little story," said Mendel, lighting up again.

Serach was ready to weep out of pure frustration but managed to hold back.

"I have a sister," Mendel began. "A sister, Esther, who was the smartest person you'd ever want to meet. Sparks used to fly out of her mouth when she spoke. She was a year ahead of me through high school and at City College and she never got anything less than an 'A'. She was, like, my role model. My hero. But then, when she's a senior in college and applying for law school—and she could have had her pick, I swear it—suddenly she just drops out."

He took a puff.

"She drops out to marry a Community Organizer. Negro fellow. Don't look at me like that—you're as bad as her. It's what I grew up calling them. Hey, my favorite judge is Black. Okay?"

He took a longer drag on the cigarette and Serach composed her face.

"So, she marries this *Black* Community Organizer who hadn't finished college himself. My sister, the smartest girl in the world, throws out all that education and all those brains and… well, never mind. It shook me up, I can tell you."

He puffed away for a minute and then looked back at Serach.

"So they get married and promptly have a kid. A baby girl. Whom my sister totally devotes herself to and there go all her professional aspirations."

He shrugged.

"Okay, okay. So, I go over to meet the baby as soon as she's born—and yes of course I do that, she's my sister's kid. And as far as the Community Organizer is concerned, well—whatever else I may think—he's always treated Esther right, so he's okay in my book, too."

He looked hard at Serach.

"So anyway, I go over—and the kid is two days old, mind you—and she fixes me with this look, like: 'who the hell are you?' Just born and brilliant already. I love her from that first moment. And ever after. I never had kids of my own, so she becomes… like my own kid."

He puffed again and then put the cigarette out.

"So she goes through Hunter Elementary School and Hunter High School. Where else? Then she gets into Harvard. Then into Harvard Law School. And she doesn't just 'get into' those places. She sails right through them. She's all 'A's', just like my sister. She's Phi Beta Kappa. She's Law Review. Whatever she does, she aces."

He took out another cigarette and rolled it back and forth between his stubby fingers.

"When she's done with all that, she goes on to become a famous criminal defense lawyer. She grows up to become…."

And he paused dramatically.

"Shulamit Robinson."

"Shulamit Robinson!"

"The very same."

"Shulamit Robinson who successfully defended that Arab man they thought had thrown a bomb into the Amazon warehouse? And who won the case for Cecil X the Rapper after he allegedly caused that riot in the bar? And who defended those three Rikers' Island guards who supposedly heisted the two paintings that the Museum of Modern Art had—for whatever reason—donated to the prison?"

"The very one."

"Shulamit Robinson whom even I have heard of, and I don't normally follow celebrity news except when I'm stuck in my dentist's office and the only thing to read is *People Magazine*?"

"The very same."

Mendel gave Serach a kindly smile.

"Yes, that's right, Serach. Shulamit Robinson is my niece. What's more, she happens to have her office right here in this building and works crazy hours like me. So now we're going to take a little stroll across the lobby and knock on her door and explain your situation. And after we tell her your story, she's going to take the case."

"How do you know that? She's got to be the most sought-after criminal lawyer in New York. Why would she take my 'small potatoes' case?"

"She'll not only take the case—she'll win it for you. And she'll do it for free."

"Mendel! How do you know that?"

"How do I know? She'll win it because she's the best. She'll do it for free because she's a *mensch*. Like you, by the way. And she'll take it if I ask her, because…"

And he smiled again.

"Who do you think paid for Harvard?"

9.

"It's open, Uncle Mendel."

"She even recognizes my knock. That's my Shulamit. No one sharper. Doesn't miss a trick."

Mendel pushed the door open to let Serach into a professional suite that was both the mirror image and the aesthetic opposite of his own. They traversed the small, stark, frosted-glass-walled waiting room and down the three steps into the living room that now served as the main office. Everything within sight was grey, rust red, silver or black—the couch, the leather-and-metal Wassily chairs, the carpet, the file cabinets, the abstract prints on the pale grey walls.

A tall lamp with three metal-shaded bulbs facing out at different angles stood at the back of the room next to a small gun-metal grey desk holding a laptop computer.

A single framed picture hung on the wall above the desk. In Hebrew calligraphy and in fancy-script English font, it proclaimed: "The balance and scales of justice are the Lord's; all the weights of the bag are His work. Proverbs, 16:11"

And sitting at that desk, directly under the framed picture and bathed in the harsh light of one of the metal-shaded bulbs, sat a slender, middle-aged woman whose small round head—perched on a long neck—just cleared the top of the laptop's screen.

The woman was wearing a dark-red turtleneck. A black jacket hung on the back of her desk chair. She kept typing as they entered. She was a very fast typist.

"Shuly, I want to introduce you to someone."

The woman looked up. The lamplight glinted on her glasses.

"Shuly—stand up so you can greet us properly!"

The woman turned back briefly to the computer, shut it down and got to her feet.

"Shuly, this is my old friend, Serach. Serach, this is my niece, Shulamit," Mendel continued as he trudged forward and motioned for Serach to do the same. "We have a very interesting story to tell you, Shuly. Where should we sit?"

Shulamit stepped out from behind her desk, flicked on the overhead lights and motioned them toward three chairs clustered around a small glass table on the right-hand side of the room.

She had a neatly trimmed, rusty-red Afro and a pretty face with skin that was nearly the same color as her hair but generously sprinkled with dark brown freckles. Her deep black eyes were magnified by a pair of large metallic aviator glasses. Her turtleneck was unadorned but clung nicely to a trim torso and her black pants draped in a similarly becoming manner around her long legs. Her waist looked startlingly small over her nicely rounded hips.

Had Serach been of an earlier generation (or had she been a keen student of the Black Power or Second-Wave Feminist movements) she might have thought: "Angela Davis." Or: "Gloria Steinem." Or some combination of the two. She wasn't any of those things, however, so the only image that came to mind as she surveyed Shulamit's sleek silhouette was: Tall Red Ant.

Grateful for the momentary distraction of that very silly thought, she stepped forward to offer Shulamit a warm handshake and a smile. Shulamit responded in kind.

They took their seats on the chairs to which Shulamit directed them and Mendel reprised his brisk summary of what Serach had told him. He described what had happened, clarified who everyone was and stressed that Ramon "couldn't stop repeating that he'd shot the guy." As soon as he finished, he said: "So, you'll help us, right?"

He and his niece exchanged a long look and Shulamit stood up.

"Well," she said to Serach, "if the cops were on their way at the time your girlfriend called and that was nearly two hours ago, they must all be at Central Booking by now. Let's go."

She grabbed her jacket off the back of the desk chair and turned off all the lights.

"Where's Central Booking?" asked Serach.

"Three blocks from here. No big deal. Come on!"

They traversed the lobby and exited, Shulamit ahead and Mendel and Serach behind.

Mendel put a hand on Serach's arm.

"Your boy is probably going to be in handcuffs, Serach," he said. "Prepare yourself."

Serach began to tremble and weep a bit. She couldn't help it.

"No time for that, sister," snapped Shulamit, spinning around. "Pull yourself together."

"He may even already have been taken to the holding pen," Mendel added gently.

"No!"

"Yes. Unless we're in time for Shuly to negotiate a Desk Appearance Ticket—a DAT—which will allow us to just fill out some paperwork, set a court date and take him home."

Serach grabbed Shulamit's arm.

"Do you think you can get us one of those?"

"There's a miniscule chance," Shulamit answered. "But it's doubtful. Armed assault is a serious offense. In any event, we're probably just plain too late."

By the time they crossed the Grand Concourse, Shulamit had picked up the pace several notches, leaving Serach and Mendel straining to keep up. But just as she turned the far corner, she heard Serach's phone ring, slammed to a stop and waited for them to reach her.

"Was that your girlfriend?" she asked as soon as Serach finished speaking.

"Yes."

"They're at Central Booking?"

"Yes. They arrived about an hour ago."

"You told her we were on our way?"

"Yes. I explained who you are and who Mendel is and…"

"Has one of the Assistant D.A.s shown up?"

"She didn't say. And I didn't ask."

"Well, if he hasn't, he'll be there soon. And he isn't going to waste any time getting the nephew into custody. The A.D.A.s in Bronx Homicide are super-tough and super-swift."

Serach shut her eyes.

"Serach, like Uncle Mendel says, you need to steel yourself. Your girlfriend is bound to be a basket case after nearly getting raped and seeing someone shot. That leaves you to handle things. Buck up and stay bucked."

Serach straightened her face, straightened her back, wiped the eyes that had started filling up again and nodded.

"Here's what I'm going to be doing, just so you know," Shulamit added, in a slightly milder tone. "Besides trying for the DAT—which, as I said, is highly unlikely—I'll be finding out when the nephew will be coming before the judge. And trying to keep your girlfriend (and the nephew, if he's still there) from spilling their guts. The cops will have read them their rights, but people can be really stupid in the aftermath of a shooting. Cops count on that. They're rarely disappointed."

She paused.

"The nephew sounds set on doing himself in, but what about your girlfriend? Will she play it the way I tell her?"

Serach swallowed hard.

"I think you can count on Paloma to be reasonable."

Her eyes began welling up again, but she caught herself and wiped them brusquely.

They arrived at the glass-and-steel Bronx Criminal Court and Shulamit slammed to a stop.

"Central Booking is right behind here," she said, pointing to the far side of the structure and turning to Serach one last time. She waited a moment, pushing her lips together before tapping Serach's shoulder hard with one finger. Her fingernails were painted a deep red.

"Okay, Serach," she said. "I've got it. If the nephew is hell-bent on confessing his guilt—and if his fingerprints are all over the gun—we're not going to waste any breath denying that he fired it. We'll acknowledge it up front as true. Sometimes truth is the best course."

Serach couldn't tell whether Shulamit was being frank or cynical, so she just nodded.

"We'll focus on the fact that he's a teenager, that he has stuff wrong with his head, that he was sure your girlfriend was in mortal danger, and that the guy he shot is a traitor and a thug."

The three of them pushed through the glass door, Shulamit and Mendel flashing their identification cards. Serach dumped her backpack, her belt, the contents of her pockets and the summer-weight blazer she'd donned to consult Mendel into the grey plastic bin that the guard handed her, pushed it through the X-ray machine and ducked through the body scanner. She then swiftly reassembled herself and posed the only question that truly mattered.

"And do you really think you can…?"

Shulamit gave a small flip to her head—which made her look more like a red ant than ever.

"What? Save my newest client's ass? Of course I can. I always do."

10.

The room that Shulamit, Serach and Mendel entered was jammed with people but neither Anteojitos nor Paloma appeared to be anywhere in the crowd. Shulamit left her companions standing against one wall, strode forward to speak briefly with the officer at the front desk and then strode back again.

"Well, it's definitely too late to rescue the nephew," she announced as she approached. "He's been taken into custody. And please," she added, catching Serach's stricken face. "No histrionics. Even if we'd gotten here an hour ago, it would have been a miracle if we'd snagged a DAT, given what he did."

She paused.

"Don't worry, Serach. They don't keep people longer than twenty-four hours."

Serach gasped. Twenty-four hours! But then she suddenly spotted Paloma, half-hidden behind a pillar, and everything else flew out of her thoughts. She sped to her partner's side.

Shulamit shook her head, marched after Serach, and took hold of her shoulder just as she brought Paloma into her arms.

"Save that for later, ladies," Shulamit said. "We have work to do."

Serach didn't immediately loosen her grip, but Paloma did. She pulled back sharply, stood up straight, shook the hair out of her eyes, and surveyed their new attorney.

"I'm Shulamit Robinson," Shulamit remarked, surveying Paloma back. "I'll be representing your nephew."

Paloma made no move to introduce herself (hell, she already knows who I am) and neither woman extended a hand in greeting.

"Too bad I couldn't meet with him," Shulamit added, after a beat. "But like I told your girlfriend, there's almost nothing I could have done for him, anyway."

Paloma continued to say nothing. Serach gave a couple of small but unmistakable shivers. Mendel—having slipped back into the room after briefly disappearing downstairs for a much-needed smoke—took a position right behind Serach.

"So," Shulamit continued. "I've already heard a lot about the crime itself. We'll get back to it later. Tell me about the cops. What did they do? What did they ask? What did you answer?"

"There were four of them," Paloma replied, after a pause. "I can't believe they sent four fucking cops to overpower a scrawny teenager and an unarmed young woman."

Shulamit said nothing.

"They come slamming down the street in two separate cop cars—lights flashing, sirens wailing—not ten minutes after I make my call. They burst into the shop, guns out, and two of them immediately pounce on my nephew, grab the gun from his hand, slap handcuffs on his wrists and hustle him into one of the two cars parked outside."

Serach leaned over to put a steadying hand on Paloma's shoulder. Paloma took a breath.

"Meanwhile, the other two cops start marching around the shop inspecting things, putting things in plastic bags, writing things down, taping things off. They read me my rights. They tell me to take off my bloody coveralls so they can pack them up. And then they stop talking to me altogether."

She paused.

"They probably thought their silence would rattle me. It didn't. It just made me mad."

Serach's hand tightened. Shulamit said nothing, so Paloma went back to her tale.

"They start going through everything in the office. Real thorough, real slow. More than an hour, it took them. And all that time my nephew is out there with those other damned cops, where I can't do anything to help him and it's making me sick. Finally, they gesture to the door. They don't grab at me, thank God, because—I swear—I would have fought back."

She stopped in case Shulamit wanted to say something. She didn't, so she continued.

"They escort me to the second cop car and, as soon as we get in, the car with my nephew takes off. Meanwhile, we dawdle. And by the time we get there, Anteojitos is in the far corner of the room and the cops are slapping him around and he's howling."

Paloma bit her lip, but she didn't permit herself to cry.

"The cops let me watch as they keep doing it. One even looks me straight in the eye to make sure I'm getting the picture. Until they finally get bored and begin hauling him away."

She swallowed.

"They drag him across that whole floor—handcuffed and yelling. They make sure to pass right in front of me so I can get a good, close look. Then they take him out through that door."

She paused and pointed.

"And that's the last I see of my nephew."

Her voice cracked. One glance at Shulamit's unmoved face however, and she rallied.

"So now you know what happened when the cops came," she concluded. "And I hope you also know that this criminal justice system of yours is a total piece of shit."

Serach used the hand on Paloma's shoulder to begin turning her gently away from the attorney's stony gaze. But Shulamit was having none of that.

"Just where do you think you're going?" she intoned. "We're not finished yet. I have to go talk with the A.D.A. and I need to know you'll be right here when I get back."

She then turned on her heel and sped out of the room.

"How are you holding up, my dear?"

Mendel—still perched directly behind Serach—leaned in close to murmur his question. Startled, she glanced back at him. She had totally forgotten he was there.

"I'm okay."

"And—uh—is that one all right?" he gestured toward Paloma with his thumb.

Paloma shook Serach's hand off her shoulder and pivoted to face Mendel directly. It was the first time she'd as much as acknowledged his presence.

"I'm okay, too," she said.

Mendel inclined his head toward her in a slight bow and extended his hand.

"Mendel Schacter. Serach's oldest client. Shulamit's uncle. The man who arranged this *shidduch* between your family and mine."

"Nice to meet you," didn't quite fit the circumstances, so Paloma hesitated a moment. But then—why not? She flashed him a small smile, shook his hand, and said something to that effect.

She waited a beat and added: "And thank you."

"Glad to be of service," he replied affably. "Serach and I go back a long time, you know."

He'd already absorbed much of Paloma's style from watching her interact with his niece. But he still took his time doing a full face-to-face assessment. And—despite the anguish that distorted Paloma's features, and the harshness of the fluorescent lighting and the blood smudges left on one of her cheeks—he registered that this was a woman to be reckoned with.

Not to mention drop-dead gorgeous.

Who would have thought little Serach with all her modest ways could land herself such a hot tomato? Just goes to show that what I don't know about dykes could fill a book.

But Mendel's train of thought was abruptly interrupted by Shulamit's brisk re-entrance. He moved back a few steps as she reached Serach's side.

"Okay," she said to Serach, ignoring Paloma entirely. "Monday morning. Probably around ten. I'll call you if it changes."

Serach gave her a dazed look.

"The nephew's appearance before the judge, Serach."

"But that means he'll be here two nights! I thought… I thought he couldn't be held more than twenty-four hours."

"Yeah, well, it's high-crime season in the Bronx—you saw all the people here ahead of us. Slows things down. Listen, I'll meet with the nephew tomorrow—and I'll get him out of here as fast as possible on Monday. That's all I can do."

She looked hard at Serach.

"Let me warn you: the bail will be set high. Maybe $50,000. You can put down just 10% if you work with a bail bondsman—they're all over the place in this neighborhood—but…."

Serach shook her head briskly.

"Whatever it is, I'll pay," she said quietly.

Shulamit nodded. She continued to look pointedly—and exclusively—toward Serach as she said the next thing.

"And you should plan on attending the hearing. It'll go much better for him if it's clear that someone presentable is waiting to collect him."

Serach felt Paloma begin to seethe and put a firm hand on her arm.

"Hush," she said.

She waited a small beat before nodding slowly at Shulamit—and another beat before asking: "So can Paloma and I go now?"

"No way." Shulamit gestured to Paloma with her thumb, like Mendel had. It seemed to be a family trait. "She and I need to talk some more. C'mon, Paloma. Let's get this over with."

She led Paloma to one side of the chamber and then—not five minutes later—out the far door.

Mendel, meanwhile, put a lightly protective arm around Serach's shoulders, and they remained in that position for several moments. She was grateful both for his gesture and for the silence he maintained. A single kind word might have completely undone her.

Mendel also instinctively seemed to know that he needed to retract that arm as soon as Shulamit and Paloma came charging back into the room—each looking angrier than the other. This was definitely not a time for Serach to be seen burrowing helplessly into a man's shoulder.

"Okay, we're done till Monday," Shulamit said as she zipped toward them. "Get here early," she added, pointing a finger at Serach. "Security's a zoo on a weekday."

And then she turned on her heel and sped toward the exit.

Serach glanced back at Mendel. "I was hoping to thank her for everything, but she didn't give me much of a chance, did she?"

"I wouldn't lose any sleep over it."

"I won't," said Serach. She then turned to face him fully. "But I can at least properly thank *you*, Mendel. You saved my life."

She gave him a small angelic look and he glanced down modestly.

"No, really," she continued. "And not just by connecting me to the best defense lawyer in New York. By … just being there for me. You seemed to know exactly what I needed."

She waited a minute for him to look back up at her, but he didn't. So she leaned forward herself to give him a short, shy hug before taking Paloma's arm and heading swiftly for the exit.

Which was a good thing for Mendel, since it would have deeply embarrassed him had Serach seen just how brightly he lit up in the wake of that small, friendly gesture.

"We'll take a gypsy cab," Serach announced to Paloma as they sailed through the door and headed toward the Grand Concourse. "Yes, yes, I know I've questioned their safety in the past. Their legality as well, no doubt. But I seem to be evolving in all sorts of ways today. Look—there's one right over there. Let's flag it and get ourselves home."

Bronx and Manhattan

11.

Shulamit Robinson may be the best defense attorney in New York City, but who gave her the right to talk to me like that? She's not the boss of me!

When Shulamit pulled Paloma aside at Central Booking, Paloma had immediately exploded.

"Why the hell should Serach be the only one at Anteojitos' hearing?" she spit out. "Why not me, too?"

"Because of your obvious contempt for our legal system," Shulamit had responded, crisply. "And your tendency to shoot off your mouth. You could throw the whole case."

Paloma kept silent with difficulty. Shulamit did have a point, however. Respect was a far cry from what she was feeling for the cops and the courts at that moment.

"If you want to help your nephew, you need to accept my judgement on this, Paloma," Shulamit was continuing. "And on other matters."

They exchanged glares—black eyes to black eyes.

"Meanwhile, let's get down to business. There's stuff I need to know."

Paloma nodded despite herself. There would be opportunities to talk back later. She'd make sure of it. Right now, there appeared to be no choice but to submit to Shulamit's questioning.

No, the weapon didn't belong to Anteojitos—it was her brother Manny's. No, Anteojitos hadn't brought it in with him—it lived in the top drawer of the desk of the auto repair shop's office. Yes, Manny had a license for it.

No, Manny couldn't possibly attend the hearing—he was in the D.R. with his wife and her dying mother.

Yes, Fernando had seemed crazy as a bedbug when he'd first swaggered into the office, but she'd been managing him just fine. He'd already begun backing off when her nephew pulled that damned trigger.

But at that point—instead of showing proper admiration for Paloma's strength under fire—Shulamit had yanked her out of the room altogether.

"Did you repeat any of that bullshit to the police?" she'd snarled as she marched Paloma into a secluded corner of the corridor, right next to the Ladies' Room.

"As I said, I told the police nothing," Paloma had replied stiffly, pulling her arm out from the attorney's grip. "I'm no fool. I know my rights."

"Well, I'm glad you didn't fuck *that* up. Still, it didn't take much encouragement for you to start blabbing all that garbage to me."

"You're Anteojitos' attorney," Paloma had said, rubbing her arm surreptitiously. "That puts you on our side, doesn't it? And you need to know the facts, don't you?"

"What I don't need are half-assed theories about how you were defusing the thug who was about to assault you without as much as mussing your mascara."

Paloma had attempted to turn away, but Shulamit grabbed her arm again and spun her around.

"I mean business, Paloma. If you ever again as much as whisper that you could have handled your would-be rapist, I'll quit this case. Leaving your nephew to spend the rest of his life in an upstate prison being sodomized by his cellmates every night."

Shulamit's face had turned red as fire as she spoke.

"Here's your story," she'd hissed. "Get it straight and keep it straight. 'I knew Fernando was going to assault me. I was terrified for my life. My nephew saved me.'"

She'd gestured for them to head back inside.

"And by the way, it's all true," she'd added as she continued shoeing Paloma forward. "Fernando would have raped you left, right and center if your nephew hadn't intervened. It wasn't the depth of your charm that stopped him. It was your nephew's well-aimed bullets."

She'd waited two beats before making her final point.

"You need to step back, Paloma. This isn't your show."

Who did that bitch think she was, anyway?

And—even worse—why was Serach so completely in her thrall?

"She's the very best, Paloma. She's going to win this thing for us. What else could possibly matter?"

Paloma had raged on and off all day Sunday, only letting the subject go when she was directly involved with a patient. By Monday morning, she had devised a plan of action.

For there were always two ways to approach a case, weren't there? The defense side and the prosecution side? And didn't she have a potentially solid "in" with the prosecution? Weren't the Bronx Borough President's office and the District Attorney's office linked somehow? Didn't they work together all the time? Couldn't she somehow persuade Carlota to ask Victor to use his influence on the BP and his buddy, the Bronx D.A.? Offer the BP the chance to help rescue the brunette who'd enchanted him so thoroughly at the *¡Adelantamos!* Gala?

She'd do it. She'd approach *La Piranha Salvadoreña* and make nice, just like Carlota had been suggesting so insistently. Drop in while Victor was still away and see what developed.

She'd tell Serach she had to stay a bit late at work, head for Carlota's apartment for a brief rendezvous and still be home in time for dinner. No sweat. And well worth it to save her nephew—and show that damned attorney who was who and what was what.

She rode up to the third-floor staff bathroom to change from her scrubs into the well-fitting red dress that she'd worn to the hospital that morning. She re-applied a slick of matching red lipstick and brushed out her hair. She surveyed the results in the full-length mirror and concluded that it would do. The circles under her eyes were barely visible. Her smile still worked.

And when she stepped out of the Second Avenue bus at 48th Street, marched into Carlota's building and used that smile on Ricardo, he'd more than confirmed her assessment.

"I'm going up to the Bianchis'!" she'd mouthed at him as she ran toward the elevators. "No need to call up—she's expecting me. See you on the way down!"

And he'd blushed and nodded and let her go.

Well Carlota—here I come, Paloma mused as the elevator sped upward. A fancy gift package unexpectedly landing on your doorstep, all tied up in a great big bow.

The elevator doors opened at the 32nd floor and she crossed the few feet of black-and-white marble-tiled floor. She shook out her hair and reminded herself to be properly deferential (but not too deferential) to Consuelo the housemaid.

But, as it turned out, the door wasn't opened by Consuelo. It was opened by Carlota herself—half-dressed in a hastily-tied white silk wrap and a pair of white satin mules with bunches of ostrich feathers at the toes that would have made Frank swoon.

Carlota leaned through the doorway and Paloma prepared herself for a warm mouth kiss.

"What the hell are you doing here?" Carlota hissed before stepping back again. "I've texted you six times since Saturday night and not a word of response!"

"I—"

"And then you just show up like this after my text this morning? My *urgent* text?"

"I—"

"Victor's back. Unexpectedly. We're getting ready to go out to dinner with friends."

Paloma brought her hand up to her mouth as a voice emerged from a farther room.

"Who's here, Carlota?"

Soft footsteps approached and Victor Bianchi suddenly materialized at his wife's side, wearing his own well-fastened silk bathrobe—royal blue—and mahogany-brown leather slippers. There was a small dot of shaving cream near his left sideburn. But his hair was perfectly in place, and he smelled of some lovely after-shave lotion.

If he recognized Paloma from the Manhattan East luncheon, he gave no indication. He looked her up and down with impassive curiosity.

"And who is this? And what is she doing here? And how did she get past the doormen? I didn't hear the intercom buzz before the doorbell rang."

"I have no idea," sighed Carlota.

He paused and pressed his lips together.

"Which doormen are on call this evening, anyway?"

"I don't know."

"Well, find out and get them fired."

Paloma gasped.

"And tell her to get lost, whoever the hell she is," he concluded, turning on his heel.

Carlota gave Paloma an acid smile.

"You heard my husband. Time to go 'bye-bye'."

"Carlota," Paloma said, registering only one thing from all of Victor's remarks. "Is he really going to fire Ricardo?"

Carlota took her time before giving Paloma a second, even tighter smile.

"I suspect he'll have forgotten all about it by the time the elevator reaches the lobby. He has a short fuse, as you can see. But he has an even shorter memory."

Paloma let out her breath while Carlota reached up her hand and carefully tucked a few stray hairs back into her chignon.

"Though you never know, of course," she added, bemusedly. "He was pretty angry. As am I, Paloma. I don't like it when people ignore my texts. Not one tiny bit."

"Carlota—please. I am so sorry. For everything. For not getting back to you—my phone has been broken, so I never even saw all your last messages. For not calling before coming over. For sneaking past Ricardo. I would never have done any of that except that I had an emergency. A terrible emergency."

Carlota raised an eyebrow. A Paloma emergency might just be amusing.

"Step in, Paloma. I'll give you one minute to tell me about it."

"My nephew—shot someone," Paloma stuttered as she moved past the doorway. "With a gun," she added, unnecessarily. "In... my brother's garage. Up on Fordham Road. Do you think Borough President Suarez might be willing to help him somehow? It was entirely self-defense, that shot. And…."

Carlota placed a slim hand on Paloma's shoulder and pulled her close.

Maybe it's going to be alright. Maybe she'll help me after all.

The blond wisp escaped its chignon again to graze Paloma's cheek, just like at the Gala.

Maybe! Please God! Maybe!

"And why exactly should I care about your nephew and his gun, Paloma?" Carlota murmured in Paloma's ear, tender as a lover. "Or about your brother's garage up there in the Bronx?"

She let go of Paloma's shoulder and regarded Paloma with perfect calm.

"And I'm sure that the BP has totally forgotten about you by now."

She flicked one finger at Paloma's chest. Paloma shrank back quickly from her touch and turned to leave. But Carlota began speaking again and she spun back.

"I'm not at all surprised to hear about your predicament, by the way," Carlota said with one last cool smile. "About all those guns and garages and other drivel." She paused and curled her lips back a bit further. "I always knew you were *pura chusma*."

I always knew you were pure trash.

And then she strode forward, pushed Paloma fully out the door and closed it firmly behind her.

Ricardo gazed wistfully at Paloma's shape as she dashed out of the elevator like a streak of mottled light without so much as a glance in his direction.

"Oh, well," he thought. "Maybe next time."

Brooklyn

12.

During the whole, long, tense stretch of time between coming home Saturday night and sitting down to Monday's dinner, Serach had taken charge of everything.

She'd coaxed Paloma into bed and surprised herself with the resurgence of her own tender desire. She'd prepared Paloma's favorite breakfast (a corn muffin from the Cortelyou Road Diner and a double shot of espresso) before sending her off to work with the stern command that she immerse herself in her usual routines and leave her troubles behind. She'd had supper waiting as soon as Paloma returned home (Campbell's Tomato Soup and buttered Ritz Crackers—the only menu she'd ever fully mastered).

She'd also handled everything related to the auto repair shop. Texted the two mechanics and receptionist to say that "something had come up" (all under control, not to worry) so they should take a couple more days off. Texted Negrito and Gordito with roughly the same message, plus the reassurance that "Ramon will be staying with us till it reopens." Prayed that the incident wouldn't make it to the local evening news or the next day's *New York Post.* It didn't.

And in between all that, she'd concocted a strategy to help mitigate the blatant (and potentially risky) antipathy that Paloma seemed to feel toward their wonder-working attorney.

"Doesn't Shulamit look like a red ant?" she'd ventured. "Should we start calling her that?"

Paloma had shown gratifying—if brief—pleasure at that last suggestion. Though she'd also quickly pointed out that if Serach wished to embrace the "Latin nickname thing," she'd have to do it in Spanish. "It should be '*La Hormiga Colorada*,' not 'The Red Ant,'" she'd declared, throwing Serach an amused smile. "Do you think you can manage that?"

Finally, first thing Monday morning, Serach had deposited the payments that Paloma had retrieved from the *Los Milagros* cash register, emptied her own money market account into her checking account, dashed off to the hearing and brought their nephew back home with her.

It had, in short, been an unspeakably exhausting two days.

Nonetheless, it all seemed to be paying off. When Paloma came down for breakfast on Monday, she'd showed promising signs of revival. She'd donned her prettiest dress. She'd eaten her muffin with an approximation of appetite. She'd taken off for work with something approaching her usual positive energy. And she was certain to be in even better shape after receiving Serach's later-afternoon text that Ramon was home and the case on a good track.

Yet, when she'd appeared at the back door that evening, she'd looked perfectly terrible.

"Paloma! What's the matter? Didn't you get my text? Did I get Ramon's number wrong?"

"Your text? Oh, yeah. I saw you'd sent me something, but I didn't…"

"We got Ramon out, Paloma! He's right up in our guest bedroom—sound asleep."

Paloma gave a small involuntary shiver.

"And Paloma—the Red Ant is well on her way to getting the whole case dismissed!"

Paloma looked down.

"For goodness' sake! Didn't you hear me?"

Paloma finally looked Serach straight in the eye.

"And can't you understand how miserable I feel about… my role in all of this?"

She looked away again.

"About the fact that… I've done nothing right since this whole nightmare began."

"Paloma, what are you saying? You acted like a hero. You called the police. And the ambulance. You took care of everything, despite…" Serach's voice cracked, "despite nearly getting raped. And witnessing a near-murder. What more could you have done?"

Paloma shook her head.

"Serach, I've been totally useless. And both Fernando and Anteojitos have gone through hell as a result. And God knows what more awaits them. How can you not get that?"

"Well, Paloma," Serach replied after a pause. "I can't say I know much about Fernando's situation. But I have a pretty good idea about what Ramon has faced. And what he still may face if we don't get this right."

Paloma looked up at Serach's tone.

"Who do you think was there to witness them bringing our nephew into the courtroom this morning, writhing and howling? Who was it who rocked him in her arms the whole cab ride home when he began sobbing anew? Who got him upstairs and persuaded him to take two Benadryl and rubbed his back and crooned nonsense syllables till he fell asleep? Who has remained on red alert all afternoon in case he woke up again? That would be me, Paloma."

She swallowed hard.

"I'm not saying any of that to pat myself on the back or make you feel bad. I know you feel bad enough. But you might… at least ask me how *I'm* doing after all that, instead of…."

Paloma blushed. She took a long drink of water.

"Oh, shit, Serach. Forgive me." She drank some more. "It's just that I'm… that I feel like… such a total piece of trash."

Serach felt her anger dissipate as she gazed at Paloma's crumpled face.

"Paloma, you must never say that. You aren't trash. You aren't anything of the sort."

She paused.

"Still, if you'd like to feel a bit more useful, I can suggest a few things you can do."

"Like what?"

"Like listening to everything that happened today."

Paloma looked down.

"Okay."

"Shulamit evidently met with Ramon on Sunday and somehow won his confidence," Serach began. She tried to stay matter of fact, but her excitement kept breaking through. "When they brought him into the courtroom—incoherent and hysterical—she took him in hand and calmed him right down. She told him to just tell the judge what had happened, same as he had with her. And in that voice of his—you know the voice—he began repeating: 'The bad man was going to hurt my Tía, and I shot him' over and over, till he finally ran out of steam. Shulamit turned to the judge, and said: 'Your Honor, I'd say it's clear who Ramon is. And why he did what he did.' And what could the judge do? He nodded."

Paloma reluctantly nodded as well.

"Shulamit then began talking all about Fernando. Describing this six-foot-tall ex-Marine—imprisoned for going AWOL—who returns home and promptly gets himself into trouble. Bad trouble. Yes, Paloma. Turns out you're not the only person he's attacked. He's in the middle of his own legal proceedings for having assaulted someone in a bar up near Kingsbridge Road. Shulamit does her homework."

Paloma flinched.

"And then she painted this irresistible picture of Manny. Of the hardworking husband and devoted father who would have been there today except he was in the Dominican Republic, helping his wife get through her mother's last days on earth."

Paloma shut her eyes.

"And then she described you—the lovely sister selflessly pitching in while her brother was away—putting herself at the mercy of a monster intent on raping her. And so traumatized by what happened that evening… that she couldn't even make it to the hearing…."

Paloma winced.

"And the whole time Shulamit was speaking, the judge kept nodding. And when she introduced me as Ramon's 'other' aunt and said I was willing to be fully responsible for him, the judge sent him home with me without another word."

Serach paused and permitted herself a small look of pride.

"Well… after I'd posted bail, of course. And after Ramon ran straight into my arms."

She paused again.

"The judge set the date for the arraignment. It will be on July 16th. Which gives the A.D.A. enough time to prepare the case for the Grand Jury in such a way that it gets dismissed."

"But that's crazy, Serach. Why on earth would the A.D.A do such a thing? Isn't it his job to get Anteojitos convicted?"

"Yes, sure, but he's also just gotten a taste of what it would be like to go head-to-head in a criminal trial against New York City's most brilliant defense lawyer."

Serach smiled.

"Trust me, Paloma—the A.D.A. didn't look any too happy when the judge started reacting so encouragingly to Shulamit's presentation. And when Shulamit announced that she won't plea bargain—that she's determined to take the case to trial—he visibly blanched. He knows that any group of Bronx jurors will include people who know—and deeply empathize with—kids like Ramon and families like yours. He knows whose side they'll take. And he knows that any trial featuring Shulamit will get lots of media coverage—everything she touches does. He's young. He's ambitious. He can't afford a big, well-publicized defeat at this point in his career. He'll come around."

She smiled yet again.

"Shulamit is a total master, Paloma."

Paloma looked away.

"Okay, Serach. I hear you. But that's more than enough about Shulamit's miraculous performance. It's time to talk about what *you've* done. I've been so damned preoccupied that…"

Serach waited.

"… I haven't as much as thanked you for all that. You've been so incredibly strong. So resourceful. So… generous. I mean… Jesus—I hadn't even thought of it till now—you probably lost a whole bunch of interest by raiding your money market before it was due…."

"Generosity had nothing to do with it," Serach interrupted, perhaps more sharply than she'd intended. "And the lost interest is *bupkes* in the overall scheme of things. I'm just glad I had it to use. I love Ramon."

She stopped to calm herself down.

"But never mind all that," she finally continued. "Let's get back to what else *you* need to do."

Paloma looked startled. Serach ignored it.

"First of all, you need to make sure that Ramon finally gets a formal diagnosis. And then you need to get him enrolled in one of those special schools. And you need to do all that before the Grand Jury meets. The whole case rides on the fact that Ramon has a recognized disability—and that his loving family is doing everything they can to help him."

"Jesus, Serach!"

"Well, Paloma, we can't have anyone thinking that Manny's just letting him sit at home fantasizing about what he'll do next time he has a gun in his hands. It would undermine everything."

"Manny will never let Anteojitos near a gun again, Serach. You know that."

"It doesn't matter what I know. It's all about appearances."

"But you also know how Manny is on the whole subject of… Anteojitos' disabilities! How am I going to budge him?"

"You're going to tell him that his son will go to prison if he doesn't. He'll budge."

Paloma shook her head.

"And how are we going to go about getting the diagnosis? And the right school? I bet it'll all cost a fortune. How will Manny ever pay for it?"

"Well, I would suggest you begin by asking your new friend, Marta, for advice."

Paloma cringed, but Serach didn't see it. Or chose not to.

"Why would I do that?"

"Well, aren't most of the girls she works with seriously traumatized? She must know all about diagnoses and schools and how to get kids in and how to pay."

"I can't ask Marta for help, Serach. I just can't"

"Why not?"

Paloma blushed deeply.

"Things have changed. I've broken with her organization. I can't go back."

Serach raised an eyebrow. This was the first she'd heard of it.

"Well, you're going to have to find a way to make amends. Ramon needs her help."

Paloma nodded grimly.

"Okay," she sighed. "I'll try."

"And then there is that one final matter," Serach said, somewhat more gently. "The matter that you've been dodging since Saturday…"

Paloma looked stricken.

"You need to call Manny."

"Oh, Jesus, Serach! Of course I've been dodging it. Everything's been so bleak… I wanted to wait till… things were a little…"

"Well, they're better now, aren't they? So pick up the phone and get him on the next plane back to New York. Before Shulamit does it for you."

"Oh, Jesus, my poor brother! I can't even begin to think…."

"Well then don't think. Just do it."

Paloma grimaced.

"It'll only get harder, Paloma."

Paloma nodded. She reached for the wall-phone and punched in the number she knew better than any other. She told Manny what had happened. She told him to come home.

PART THREE: Pilgrimages

"Am I not here, I who am your mother? Are you not under my shadow and protection?"

Our Lady, the Virgin of Guadalupe, as spoken to Saint Juan Diego and recorded in the *Nican Mopohua*

November 2018: Jerusalem

1.

"I have something to tell you, Mama!"

The clinic doctor had been very explicit. After waiting so long—and with everyone so worried—it was best not to raise any hopes. Best to wait till everything was well on its way before saying a word.

But that morning, just as Ruchel was fixing her first cup of tea, she'd felt something light and bubbly and (to be frank) kind of annoying moving around inside of her.

Like gas, it had been.

She was beginning to wonder what might have disagreed with her when she realized what was causing that feeling. Someone was in there! Someone was kicking! Someone was absolutely, definitely—irrefutably—'well on his way'!

She could finally tell the world. She could finally tell her mother.

She ran up the street to her parents' house and barged into the kitchen to blurt out the news. And Binkel had grabbed her daughter by the middle—right there, right in front of the maid—and spun her around and around. Two stout little women, whirling together in a mad dance of joy until they came to a sudden, dizzy stop.

"Wait, wait, Ruchele," Binkel had said, panting hard. She said "Kenehora" and spit three times. "There," she said. "Let's not tempt the evil eye."

But then she grabbed Ruchel again, hugged her tightly and started twirling her in the other direction. She couldn't help herself.

"Beile, I didn't want to call you before it was official, but… it's official! And Beile—it's a boy! I saw the proof, right there on the ultrasound screen. Large as life!"

"Ruchel, that's wonderful! I am so happy for you."

Ruchel swallowed.

"And Beile, I have to say it: it's all thanks to you. If we hadn't become so close during your mother's *shiva*… if I hadn't been able to confide in you… if you hadn't been so determined to help me that you came all the way to Jerusalem for ten long days to accompany me to all my clinic appointments… if you hadn't been able to persuade Shmuely to undergo his own tests and to agree to that treatment, which I still don't know how you did it…"

"It was easy. I told him that Mama was distraught that he hadn't produced an heir. That she saw him as the vessel for carrying on Tatteh's name. That she expected him to do whatever it took to fulfill that mitzvah. Shmuely could never ignore Mama's demands."

"Well, whatever you did, it was a miracle. I don't know what I would have done without you. You were like a sister to me. Better, even."

"Sha-sha-sha. It had to be this way."

She paused.

"So… what did he say when you told him, my brother? Was he happy?"

Ruchel had entered Shmuely's private study without so much as knocking—definitely a first in their marriage. She had stood in front of her husband with her hands on her belly—the tiny shoves against her palms giving her the confidence she needed to risk interrupting him when he was settled down in his scholar's seat.

What had Shmuely felt in the first moments of hearing her message? So hard to tell. His turquoise eyes had gone almost green—as they always did when he was holding himself together. But then they'd cleared again. He'd swallowed hard. And then he'd blushed.

"*Baruch Ha-Shem*," he'd said, so quietly she almost missed it.

"However," he'd added, after a pause—quickly burying his eyes back into the text that he'd been studying. "However, you should not be bragging about such a thing, Ruchel. For are we not instructed that boasting is wrong, for we know not what tomorrow will bring?"

"Shmuely—of course we don't know what tomorrow will bring. *Ha-Shem* has granted us free choice, but only *Ha-Shem* knows what is to come."

Shmuely looked up at her, startled. From whom had she learned that Talmudic concept? Not from him, certainly. They didn't talk Torah together. One didn't, with one's wife.

"And of course, we shouldn't boast," Ruchel had continued. "I would never think of boasting about such an important matter."

She had patted her stomach a few times more and then smiled into the distance.

"What I'm doing, Shmuely, is feeling grateful. Like our matriarch Ruchel when she finally became pregnant. What I'm saying—as she did as well, if I am not mistaken—is: '*Adonai* has finally taken away my disgrace.'"

She paused.

"Which is something that you might also consider saying. If I am not mistaken."

She gave him a look and he raised his eyes to meet it. And then he'd blushed some more.

He nodded. Once. And then a second time.

"He was very happy of course," Ruchel assured Beile.

Brooklyn

2.

"Darling, I can't take a single additional appalling detail," Frank drawled as he helped himself to more of Paloma's scrambled eggs with shallots, mushrooms and parsley. "You haven't let up on your litany of catastrophes since I first arrived, two long days ago. Must I remind you that I came here straight from the airport rather than accompanying Kae-Dang back to his place because I was so eager to have some nice, long, one-on-one catch-up chats with you?"

"And haven't I found us whole entire hours when Serach has been out so we could do that?"

Frank sniffed.

"I wouldn't describe any of our chatting sessions as 'nice,' Paloma," he said, looking off to one side. "They have been nothing but non-stop recitations of your grim adventures."

"I… has it really been all that grim?"

"No, dear. There was nothing grim about your blow-by-blow account of Serach's bout with clinical depression. Or the harrowing story of your near rape. Or the ego-crushed saga of how you had to play the helpless maiden instead of the heroic woman that you are. Don't snarl at me, Paloma! Really, it wasn't such a big deal. There are times one simply does what one has to do."

He took a sip of orange juice. Freshly squeezed. Just the way he liked it.

"And then there was the tale of the razor-toothed Salvadoran and her poor doorman. That little plot twist had some interesting possibilities, though ultimately it was a downer as well."

He drained the juice and put the glass back down on the table with care.

"And, of course, there's been nothing grim in all your talk about your nephew's PTSD. Or how hard it was to get him into that 'School for Traumatized Teens with Special Needs.'"

"Well, dammit, it really *was* difficult!"

"This morning," Frank said, picking up his fork and putting it down again, "this morning, I came downstairs thinking we could finally have our long-awaited talk about my concert tour. And what happens? You start right in again about the tragedy of your rapist and his father sitting side-by-side in their matching wheelchairs. Oh, God!"

Frank buried his face in his hands.

"And I haven't even properly recovered from my jet lag."

"Sorry."

"Paloma, don't you know not to dwell on the irredeemably ugly? That there's no future in it?"

Paloma nodded and looked down.

"Here's what you should focus on: Serach is her cheery old self again. You didn't get ravaged by that thug. Your Salvadoran would-be lover is history. Your nephew is safely ensconced in his new school, safe from the perils of the South Bronx."

He cast a longing glance at the orange juice pitcher and Paloma brought it over and poured him a second glass.

"And," Frank concluded, "for God's sake, the case was dismissed. The whole long nightmare is over! You need to be celebrating—not taking all the fun out of this otherwise exquisite breakfast."

"Well, I did celebrate, Frank," Paloma said primly, sitting down again and taking her own forkful of egg. "Several times, as a matter of fact. Serach and I drank a toast to Anteojitos' freedom as soon as everything was settled. Manny took me and the boys out to the Red Lobster on Fordham Road for a festive lunch the following Sunday. And Etha treated me to dinner at one of her fancy Union Square restaurants."

"Which one?"

"It's called 'The House.' Upscale New American. Fine wines. Exquisite service. The works."

"Lovely."

"Indeed. And Etha seemed even keener on celebrating than I was. She ordered us a full bottle of their best California champagne and promptly drank the lion's share herself."

"Well, she was probably overcome with gratitude that she wouldn't have to hear further tales of woe from you. I'm beginning to think I was very lucky to have been away all this time."

Paloma took a deep breath before speaking.

"Frank, that isn't fair. In fact, it's cruel. Yes, of course I talked to Etha about everything. And she was always more than happy to listen. Because she cares about me."

Frank had the decency to turn pink.

"And also, because... I don't really know how to put this, Frank, but I'll try. Because this whole sad adventure brought us—brought me and Etha, that is—a lot closer in certain ways."

She paused.

"Oh?" asked Frank, suddenly interested. "How so?"

New territory. Should she venture there? Could she? Would it achieve anything? Would it wreck anything? But she had to. Things had changed. She couldn't just let it ride.

"Okay, Frank."

She stopped again to consider, and Frank paused in his eating as well. It wasn't like Paloma to think before she spoke.

"Here's the deal," she finally said, softly. "The only reason Anteojitos came out of this mess in one piece—more or less—is because he had three advantages that boys in my community generally don't. Access to Serach's legal connections. Access to Serach's money market. Access to Serach herself—a 'presentable woman', as Shulamit called her—backing him in court. And by 'presentable' you know she meant 'white.' Shulamit knows the score."

She stopped once more to take a sip of coffee.

"Most Black and brown boys—most boys from my community—don't have anything like those kinds of advantages."

She stole a glance at Frank, who definitely looked a bit lost.

"Most boys from my community get sent upstate without a murmur for things a lot less terrible than shooting someone twice in the spine."

They sat for a moment in silence.

"And yes, Frank," she finally added, "I use the term 'my community' advisedly. As Etha always has. And my brother Manny always has. But which I've always tried to avoid doing."

She paused again and looked down.

"Look, Frank, it's hard to say this stuff. We never talk like this. But here's how it is: Regardless of what Etha and I do for a living or where we live—or how many Carnegie Hall concerts we attend—the first thing most white folks register when they see us is: 'Black woman. Brown woman.' It's not even conscious! And with that labeling comes… a lot of baggage. And when it's the justice system that's doing the labeling…."

She took a breath.

"I'd always thought I'd escaped all that. Until I had my little brush with the law."

She looked at Frank hard.

"Oh, Frank—the way those cops treated me! The way they treated Anteojitos! The things they get away with! The way they *see* us!"

Frank flinched.

"I… don't see you that way, Paloma."

"I know that, Frank. And I've always done everything I could to make sure you wouldn't."

The poor man looked miserable. Paloma took pity.

"But Frank, there's one last big reason why Etha never grew tired of hearing my accounts," she finally continued, skillfully wending her way back to him.

"Dare I ask?"

"That's why I'm bringing it up, Frank. Etha also stayed interested because those accounts put her within one degree of separation from the much-celebrated Shulamit Robinson. For Etha is as big a celebrity junkie as anyone else."

She took Frank's free hand in hers, smiled up at him, and began playing with his fingers.

"I'd never even heard of Shulamit before she became involved with us," she said musingly. "But she evidently has quite the reputation. Etha never said as much, but it was clear she was seriously impressed that I was consorting with such a superstar. I kept waiting for her to say: 'can I touch you?'"

Paloma took another sip of coffee before going on in a slightly stronger voice.

"But Frank, seriously. You mustn't disparage how hard this all was for me. Or how hard it is for me to live straddled between my two worlds."

Frank colored again.

"I'm sorry," he said, after a pause. "I guess I've been a pill."

They sat quietly for a moment as Frank helped himself to another spoonful of eggs.

"But here, let me redeem myself a bit," he said as he speared a mushroom. "As it turns out, I'm still desperately curious about one matter that you touched upon only very lightly in all your accounts. Something I would love to hear more about."

"Yes?"

"How did Serach take the fact that you nearly had an affair with another woman?"

Paloma stopped in her own mid-bite. She put down her fork.

"Serach doesn't know anything about that."

Frank raised an eyebrow.

"Well, Frank. What do you expect?"

"I don't know. I figured that you two shared absolutely everything. You know that I've never personally subscribed to that approach to relationship hygiene, but I always thought that…"

"I don't subscribe to it, either. Why cause pointless anguish? Especially since nothing really happened besides that one startling tango at the Gala."

She smoothed her napkin with one finger.

"In fact, you're the only person who knows anything about any of that. I mean, besides Carlota, of course."

"You mean you didn't tell Etha?"

"Good God, no. Etha can be so tediously moral. Whereas you… I've never known you to be judgmental on that front. Which is why you're also the only person who knows anything about my whole wild past."

"Hmmmph. Well, I'm honored. I guess."

"And I also feel free to share this stuff with you because I know you would never breathe a word of it to anyone else."

She paused.

"You wouldn't, would you? You'll never tell Serach, now that you...."

"Paloma, you cut me to the quick. I won't even tell Kae-Dang. Once a piece of juicy news drifts beyond the person who initially receives it, you never know where it will end up."

He took a bite of egg.

"Well, all's well that ends well, in any event. No more dances with the dangerous Salvadoran sea creature, I take it?"

Paloma sighed.

"No, I'm sure she won't be calling again."

She fiddled with her eggs and Frank leaned precipitously closer to her.

"Paloma, what am I hearing in your voice?"

"Huh?"

"Paloma, you're talking with your oldest and dearest friend. I thought I caught a trace of… shall we say 'disappointment' in your voice? Please tell me I'm wrong. Tell me you aren't pining away for future engagements with our Carlota."

Paloma smiled. He knew her so well. She loved him so much.

"Well, perhaps," she said. "But not for the reasons you might think. I have no further desire to be personally involved with her. But her organization really got to me. It's doing some really amazing work. I would have liked to have stayed connected to it."

"Well, all may not be lost. You had no problems with that other woman, did you?"

"You mean Marta?"

"Yes. Nothing bad happened with her, did it? In fact, didn't you say she was the one who helped your nephew get into that school?"

"Yes, she was. And she was surprisingly okay with my sudden departure from *¡Adelantamos!*. I told her there'd been a… misunderstanding with Carlota and she didn't even blink. I suspect it's happened before, given Carlota's ways. Or maybe she saw us dancing the tango and put two and two together."

Paloma sipped at her coffee, put the cup down again and sighed.

"But *¡Adelantamos!* doesn't belong to Marta, Frank. Carlota totally owns it. And there's no chance in hell she'll want me back."

"Oh, I wouldn't be so certain of that either," said Frank, absentmindedly turning over his empty coffee cup to inspect the Limoges insignia on the bottom. "People like Carlota rarely hold long-term grudges against people who might be useful to them. I wouldn't be surprised if one of these days she calls you up as if nothing happened and asks you to pitch in on their—uh—*Mid-Winter Festival of Salsa and Song*. Or whatever event they come up with next."

"I don't know how I'd handle that."

"You'll go with your gut, dear. As you do with everything. But this time, I hope, you'll make sure from the get-go that Carlota knows your Dance Card is filled."

He waited a few beats.

"Did they fire that doorman, by the way?"

"No, thank God. I snuck by Carlota's apartment building a few weeks after our… run-in… to see whether Ricardo was still at his post. I stood at the glass entrance and peered between the potted plants. And there he still was. I don't think I've ever felt so relieved."

"Of course you did, darling. You do have a conscience, despite your incorrigible need to seduce everyone and everything in sight."

Frank picked up a piece of toast from its basket and coated it lightly with marmalade.

"You might, however, finally begin reining that all in a bit, given what just happened. I never thought I'd find myself giving you that particular piece of advice. But clearly…."

Paloma laughed.

"I'll have to think about it. It's kind of second nature to me, as you know."

She finished off her own piece of toast and licked her fingers.

"But that's it for the difficult stuff, Frank. I promise. And meantime, I have one very cheery news morsel to share before we have our long-delayed chat about your European conquests."

She tilted her head to one side and smiled coyly at her friend.

"Well, praise the Lord," said Frank.

"The Oncological Nurse's Society is having its three-day biennial conference in late-February in Tel Aviv, this year. And guess who's going to be representing Manhattan East Medical Center's Cancer Research and Care Unit at that conference. All expenses paid!"

"Well, that *is* marvelous news, Paloma. What will you be doing for them?"

"I'll be leading a break-out session on the stress management program we offer nurses working in the Marrow Transplant Unit. Seems the cancer care industry has finally caught on that it's hard to carry out exquisitely painful procedures on terrified patients, day after day."

Frank looked down briefly at the table.

"I do tend to forget..." he said softly, "what you do out there in the real world."

He paused.

"And that it must be hard on you sometimes."

He paused again.

"And so perhaps I'm not as...."

"No worries, Frank. Enough penance. You do plenty of stuff to keep me sane and afloat."

Frank nodded and waved away Paloma's attempt to pour him more coffee.

"Is Serach going off to the Holy Land with you?"

Paloma shook her head.

"No. She's got one of those beastly re-certification exams that week. She's postponed it twice already—once because of the Anteojitos drama and once because she had a stomach flu. She claims she'll be left behind in the dust if she waits another minute."

"She's always been a bit of an all-work-and-no-play girl, hasn't she? Well, no matter. You can certainly find ways to enjoy yourself on your own. Unless, of course, you're planning to spend your entire trip discussing the stresses of the Marrow Transplant Unit."

"No, of course not! The conference is being held in the super-posh InterContinental David Hotel, and I intend to take full advantage of its spa, its gym, and all the luxury shopping opportunities in its lobby. Plus, Serach persuaded me to tack on three more nights after the conference to do some sight-seeing. So, in fact, I was hoping that my world-traveled best friend could make some suggestions about what I should see and do."

Frank tilted his head back, closed his eyes and smiled.

"Well, alas, it won't exactly be beach season in February. Tel Aviv is one of the most gay-friendly places in the world, you know. There is this one beach—the Hilton Beach—that…."

"A gay beach? Gay as in… 'gay men'?"

"Well, yes."

"And you think I would be interested in lounging around on that beach because…?"

"Oh, Paloma. Israeli men! There's nothing like them. It's the sun, I suppose. And the military training. All those push-ups…."

Paloma had a brief flash of her skinny, eternally pale older friend sitting in a beach chair gazing longingly at the glories around him. She brushed it away quickly. Frank did very well for himself after all, didn't he?

"It doesn't sound like my kind of scene, Frank," she said, grinning. "And, as you say, February isn't really beach weather. And as you also just said—it may be time for me to start curbing my inner party animal."

"Mnnnnn."

"So what… cultural sites… should I visit?"

"Let me think."

He pyramided his fingers.

"Hmmnn. Oh, my God—of course!"

He clapped his hands.

"The Basilica of the Annunciation. In Nazareth. How could I possibly forget?"

"Nazareth? Is that near Tel Aviv?"

"The whole country is barely bigger than New Jersey, dear. It's—I don't know—two hours by bus? Paloma, you absolutely must see it!"

"And why is it so special?"

"Because it contains the grotto where the Blessed Virgin Mary's house stood when she was visited by the Archangel Gabriel. Most of the house is in Loreto, of course, but its fourth wall and some stairs remain in Nazareth. It's been the site of miraculous healings for centuries. Like Lourdes."

Paloma smiled. The BVM and all her healings. The faith that was still at the heart of so much in her life. And so central to the bond she shared with Frank.

"The Basilica itself is… nothing to write home about," Frank was continuing. "It was designed by some Italian in the late 'sixties…that ghastliest of all architectural periods. The outside is utterly mundane. The inside is horrendous."

He paused.

"But it has the grotto. And it has these two galleries—one in an adjacent cloister and one upstairs—that are simply not to be believed. They contain dozens and dozens of portraits of the BVM at different points in her life, donated by artists from different countries."

He clasped his hands as he pictured them.

"Not all the portraits are spectacular. Some are pretty hokey, actually. But the cumulative effect of all those Madonnas, in all those different styles…"

He slammed his hands palms down on the table.

"Paloma, you absolutely cannot miss the Basilica. Promise me you'll go!"

"Okay, Frank. I promise."

Paloma stood up, shook out her shoulders, and began carrying the dirty dishes to the sink. She was about to turn the water on when she spun around to face her friend.

"And what about Jerusalem, Frank? Worth a day trip?"

"Oh my God, yes. Thousands of things to do. Not to mention how amazing it is to see all those little Shmuely's roaming through the streets, hither and yon."

Paloma suddenly got very quiet.

"What, Paloma?"

"You're reminding me of… Oh, God! Something that Etha has been nagging me to do. 'Suggesting,' she says. 'Just suggesting.' Baloney. Nagging."

"Paloma, you are making me crazy. What are you talking about?"

"Etha thinks that… while I'm in Israel, I should take a side trip to Jerusalem to give Shmuely a piece of my mind. That I should tell him to finally act like a man. To get back in touch with Serach. To make up for what he did to her. Etha's crazy, of course. He's not going to budge—he's a religious fanatic. And how would I possibly…? Totally nutty idea, right?"

Frank said nothing.

"Frank! Really! Can you blame me for thinking she's crazy?"

But instead of agreeing with her, Frank intertwined his fingers, turned the palms outward and languidly stretched out his arms. He yawned, brought his hands back again and folded them in front of him. He then gave Paloma what would have been a totally beguiling look, had he thrown it to a man. A look of pure mischievous intent.

"Paloma, it's a marvelous idea. Tailor-made for your powers of seduction and persuasion, not to mention your bone-deep desire to play Avenging Angel, Knight-in-Shining-Armor and Healer Supreme all rolled into one."

"I…"

"Paloma, when have you ever turned down a dare?"

"I…"

"Never. The answer is 'never'. So… go call up your new 'best friend.' What's her name? Freddy? Friedel? The one who wreaked havoc on this kitchen?"

"Frayda."

"Frayda. Ask her to get you Shmuely's address. And then head off to Jerusalem and drop in on the boy, first free moment that you get. Tell him what you think about the way he treated his sister. Tell him to atone. Don't Jews have this big 'thing' about atonement? Some whole big holiday dedicated to it?"

"Serach would kill me if I ever did anything like that."

"Serach need never know. Tell… uh… Friedel not to tell her. Etha won't tell her. I certainly won't tell her. And you can bet that Shmuely will never tell her. And it won't be the first thing that you yourself have kept from her… now, will it?"

"Frank!"

"And who better than you, Paloma, to carry out such an important errand? Practically a mission of mercy. And not just in terms of what it will mean for Serach. In terms of what it will mean for the brother. You might just save the poor boy from burning eternally in hell. Or whatever it is that those people think happens to sinners."

February 2019: Tel Aviv

3.

It had been an interminable trip made even longer by the security measures enforced by the El Al officials. Nonetheless, the comforts of the jitney that the hotel sent to collect her did a great deal toward reviving Paloma's spirits. And the first enticing glimpse of the suite she'd been given provided the perfect finishing touch.

She stood stock still in the doorway for several moments, taking in the view before striding in on a carpet so deep that her tread made no sound.

She perched her carry-on bag on the luggage rack and took out and hung up the things that needed hanging.

She pulled out her notes on "stress management for nurses," placed them on the desk that they'd provided and spent several tense seconds pondering the details of the presentation she'd be making.

She unpacked the Hermès scarf that Frank had brought back from his last European tour and dedicated four more seconds to considering her still-half-baked plans to infiltrate Shmuely-land with her hair all kerchiefed up like a properly religious Jewish lady.

Then she pushed away all those pesky thoughts and took a long, slow, pleased walk around the perimeters of the room.

She ran her hands across the length of the granite-topped dresser, taking in its smooth cool surface with her fingertips and palms.

She pulled down the bronze-hued bedspread and stroked the 1800-thread cotton sheets.

She prowled through the bathroom, inspecting the floor-to-ceiling mirrors, the blindingly shiny fixtures, the shower with its three separate shower heads and the tub so deep she could swim in it. She caressed the heavenly-thick bath towels.

She opened the medicine cabinet to note that it held a glorious range of shampoos and conditioners, bath salts, soaps in both liquid and bar form, a generously proportioned deodorant stick, a carefully packaged new toothbrush, a sizable bottle of golden-hued mouthwash and a fat tube of anise-flavored toothpaste. Everything jazzily branded with the InterContinental David Hotel logo. Everything beckoning to be sampled.

She returned to the bedroom, drew back the heavy silk curtains from the double-sized windows, and spent a good ten minutes gazing through the late afternoon mist as the waves of the Mediterranean lapped the edge of the long, empty, private beach stretching out below her.

Well, my dear, she mused, you have truly come into your own. A professional at the top of her game, representing New York City's most up-and-coming new cancer center at a prestigious international conference. A woman contemplating a glorious pre-dinner soak in the most luxurious tub in the world.

Your speech will be fine.

The trip to Jerusalem will sort itself out.

Put everything out of your mind besides the delights that await you!

Nazareth

4.

Damn good thing I'm a tough Bronx girl. It takes killer instincts to survive an Israeli bus ride in the morning rush hour.

The last leg of Paloma's rainstorm-encumbered, three-bus journey to the Basilica of the Annunciation in Nazareth was (fortunately) the shortest. She could not have stood a single minute longer of being shoe-horned into that mass of wet, shoving, fellow passengers.

She spied the station at which she needed to get off, steadied herself against the bus's lurching, and rammed her way out its back door—whereupon her umbrella flipped irrevocably inside-out, forcing her to brave the last three blocks with no protection whatsoever.

Well, that's that. If it's like this tomorrow, I'm not embarking on another monsoon-drenched expedition. I did Manhattan East more than proud this week. I deserve a luxurious morning at the hotel spa followed by a leisurely afternoon of touring Tel Aviv's modern art museums—not a wild goose chase into Ultra-Orthodox Jerusalem.

The Basilica suddenly loomed on her right. She contemplated its exterior and decided that Frank had been too harsh. Yes, its silhouette bore an unfortunate resemblance to a 1960's Catholic high school. But it was faced in very pretty rose-gold stone. The inscriptions on its outer walls were etched in an unusually lovely font. Its front doors were covered in eye-arresting bas reliefs.

He'd sure been right about the interior, however. Built entirely of grey concrete—lit only by the shafts of rainy daylight that managed to sift through its concrete-and-glass central dome—it looked like a cross between a crypt and an airplane hangar.

She descended the long circular path that led down to the grotto. She stepped through the ruins that surrounded that holy site and peered through the metal gate that kept it safe. She waited to be gripped by emotion. She felt nothing.

Perhaps it was all that concrete. Or the bleakness of those ruins. Or the chill that remained in her bones, thanks to all the rain. Whatever it was, she found herself thoroughly unmoved by the grotto, by the wall—by the little makeshift altar. By the whole thing.

Slowly and more sadly than she cared to admit, she began retracing her steps.

So. The question is: should I even bother looking at anything else? Or should I just head back to Tel Aviv for a nice hot shower? Still. I've come this far. And Frank will expect a full report. Come on, Paloma, steel yourself. Go look at all those Madonnas he was raving about.

She determinedly marched toward the open cloister to the right of the main hall. And then slammed to a stop at what she beheld within.

This was—most definitely—not the tedious collection of BVM images in the chapel of St. Gertrude's School for Girls in the Bronx. Nor the worn, morose statues and paintings in the Colombian Cathedral where Father Domingo held sway. Nor even the group of first-class Renaissance reproductions that Judith displayed so tastefully on her living room walls.

This was a riot of ingenious portraits of the Blessed Mother—each one trumpeting its own culture and color scheme and point of view.

Okay, Frank. You win. Totally cool.

The Annunciation from the Philippines featured a slender young Mary with glowingly golden skin and a head full of flowing black hair. No veil, no shoes, a fetchingly off-the-shoulder blouse and a festively striped skirt. The Archangel Gabriel delivering his historic message sported a set of traditional robes, but the body beneath was as lithe and attractive as the Virgin's.

In the Indonesian version of the Annunciation, Mary—sinuous and lovely—was surrounded by butterflies, flowers, birds and what looked like flexing tentacles. She wore an expression of utter dreaminess as she gazed upward at the dove hovering purposefully over her head. No dutifully chaperoning Angel was anywhere in sight.

In the mosaic donated by the Vatican, two tiny scenes of Mary's life—one, a rendering of the Annunciation and the other a depiction of her farewell to Jesus as he walked toward Golgotha—were totally eclipsed by a towering Pope Paul VI.

The Mary from Guatemala—the only Virgin visibly nursing her Divine son—looked utterly exhausted. And the face of the Mary from the Slovak Republic—the lone *Pietà* in the group—was twisted in agony as she gazed at the enormous, crucified Jesus in her lap.

For most of that long, damp, windy stroll, Paloma was too absorbed in what she was seeing to pay much mind to the rain that continued to pelt her. By the time she neared its end, however, she was very much aware of just how cold and wet she was and of how long the ride back to Tel Aviv was bound to be. She turned to depart.

But just then, one last Virgin seized her attention.

Clad in a red-and-gold robe—haloed in yet more gold and holding a tiny Jesus wearing a crown twice the size of his head—this BVM was a dead ringer for Paloma's Colombian grandmother, Doña Isabel Teresa Gonzales de Rodriguez.

Doña Isabel's eerily familiar gaze held Paloma motionless for a long moment. And then her unmistakable intonations began flooding into Paloma's mind.

Paloma! Mijita! Tomorrow is a day for action—not self-indulgence! You've been called to the Holy Land for a reason. Attend to it!

Paloma quickly spun around to confront a dark-skinned Mary perched astride a big blue globe and robed in a white gown as crisp as a Brooks Brothers blouse. Etha! Totally Etha!

Girlfriend, have you forgotten how miserable you were about Serach's bottomless depression last spring? Well, I haven't. Have you forgotten how much you wanted to wring the neck of the brother who pushed her into that depression? Well, I most certainly haven't. So here's your chance. Take yourself off to Jerusalem and make him pay for what he did!

She whirled back again to be stopped in her tracks by an Irish Madonna standing on a little island in the middle of undulating blue waves, flanked by a fierce-looking Archbishop and speaking in the unmistakable accents of her old sports coach, Edna Gallagher.

That's right, dearie. No excuses! Just whack it!

A big blue-and-white mosaic Czech Virgin looking out over an adoring crowd took up the chant in the cadence that emerged whenever Frank was exasperated:

For God's sake, Paloma. A mani-pedi and some art galleries? Please, darling. I'll treat you to all that and more when you get back to New York. Your job tomorrow is to go out and be the Knight-in-Shining-Armor you've always dreamed of being.

And from somewhere across the cloister, a single chilly voice emerged:

I knew you'd fail at this, Querida. Chusma through and through, aren't you?

Carlota!

Paloma covered her ears—which of course made no difference, since the voices were springing directly out of her own brain. Still, the cacophony slowly ebbed away.

All right! Enough! All of you! I'll go. But can anyone please give me some more specific guidance around what I should say when I finally confront Shmuely? It doesn't do much good to tell me to "just whack it!"

One last voice emerged—clear and sweet—from the mouth of a pretty little French BVM on the wall directly to Paloma's right. Serach's voice.

Call Frayda.

Tel Aviv

5.

"You should have asked me all that before you left for Israel instead of waiting to phone me now," Frayda had scolded Paloma when she received the call. "It would have saved you a lot of expense—and me a lot of trouble. But okay, fine, you didn't. I'll see what I can do. Call me back in two hours."

Paloma held few expectations for Frayda's investigations, but—in fact—Frayda had hit pay dirt when she'd phoned Beile to nose around. Beile had thought it perfectly natural that someone of Frayda's busy-body proclivities would want to hear all about Shmuely's latest foibles. And she was filled with information about Shmuely's situation and routines, thanks to the ten days she'd spent supporting Ruchel's fertility quest—and to the steady line of communication that she and Ruchel had maintained since that pivotal period.

"It seems that Shmuely's in-laws are currently in Cedarhurst, Long Island, staying with their oldest daughter while they oversee a long-planned, two-store American expansion of their jewelry business, *Keter Zahav* (that's 'Crown of Gold')", Frayda had begun. "And why not? New York is where they started out. They know the territory."

Paloma took a breath. Where the hell was this headed?

"They're putting one of the stores right there in Cedarhurst," Frayda had continued. "And the other in Great Neck. Both very nice places with good-sized Jewish populations."

Paloma had let out her breath very slowly. Annoyingly taciturn so much of the time, once you started Frayda talking, there was no way to stop her.

"Frayda! I appreciate all the wonderful sleuthing you've done. But I didn't call you all the way from Tel Aviv to hear about Shmuely's in-laws' business plans. What I need to know—as I first explained—is two things. Number one: Shmuely's daily routine, so I can plan when and where I should approach him. Number two: the texts I should quote to persuade him to repent. Can you please just focus on that instead of all these unnecessary details?"

"Not a single one of these details is unnecessary," Frayda had sniffed. "As you will see."

Paloma took another breath. Once again, she really needed this impossible woman.

"So. As I was saying. The in-laws originally planned to leave for Long Island in January, figuring they'd stay for six months to make sure everything is kosher with the launch of the new stores. Sounds reasonable, right? But as it turns out, that timing could not have been worse for Shmuely and his wife, Ruchel."

Frayda paused dramatically and Paloma obliged her.

"And that would be because?"

"And that would be because... Ruchel is due to give birth in early April. Ah hah! Now you're all interested, right?"

Paloma grunted.

"This is not going to be just any child, Paloma. This will be the baby of the century. The first son of the only son in that entire branch of the Gottesman family. They were all really worried it might never happen. Beile actually went all the way to Israel to take Ruchel to a specialist."

Frayda stopped and smacked her lips.

"And now—when everything finally works out—Ruchel's mother isn't going to be there to tend to her beloved daughter while she produces this miraculous being."

Paloma gave up. Frayda was going to go at her own pace and there was nothing she could do about it. The call was going to cost a small fortune. Naturally Frayda didn't have *WhatsApp*.

"Interesting, yes?" Frayda asked.

"Mnnn."

"Wake up, Paloma. Of course, it's interesting."

Frayda nodded to herself.

"So Ruchel decides that if her mother can't be in Jerusalem, she's going to go to Cedarhurst. She takes off, settles in with her Long Island family, and announces she's staying there all the way through the birth and the *bris*. And who can blame her? At such a time, wouldn't you want to be with your mother?"

Paloma remained silent. What did she know about pregnancies or births? About the potential helpfulness of mothers?

Frayda waited for a moment and then plunged back.

"The only question left was what should Shmuely do? Should he go, too? Join Ruchel for all those weeks? Of course not—not with his big teaching position. But can he miss out on the birth and *bris* of his own son? Also, of course not. So they decide he'll arrive a bit before the birth, stay through the *bris* and then go back to Israel with Ruchel and the baby."

Paloma wondered just how rude it would be to simply thank Frayda and get off the phone.

"But then," Frayda was continuing, "Ruchel decides she wants to stay on Long Island even longer. At least through the eight days of *Pesach*. And who can blame her for that, either? Why should she fly through the air with a baby barely eight days old? Why should she go through all the *tsuris* of Passover preparations by herself, with a newborn on her hands? Sure, of course, she'll have her maid. A nurse too, no doubt. But at a time like that, she figures there's nothing like a mother."

She waited for a comment and once again receiving none, continued.

"So Shmuely—who can't be away all that time—resigns himself to returning to Jerusalem all by himself right after the *bris* and celebrating *Pesach* with his cousin Reuven."

"Okay, Frayda. Thank you. I think I'm going to hang up now."

"No, you're not. You need to know this."

Frayda guffawed.

"So, Ruchel's been gone a few weeks and Shmuely's getting more and more *farmisht* without her there to make sure he doesn't put his salami sandwich on a dairy plate. According to Beile he's been calling Long Island every day, long distance, just to say… 'hello.' Which is totally new, since—also according to Beile—until now he's barely noticed when his wife was around and when she wasn't."

She paused.

"But, of course, it's not just the salami dilemma that's making him *meshugge*. He's worried about something else."

"What, Frayda?"

"About the fact that—with the arrival of his son—everything will change. He won't be the darling baby boy of the family anymore. All attention will be on the new Messiah."

Paloma sighed very loudly. Frayda kept going.

"And as he ponders how bad it might get, he may also be more interested in… renewing contact with Serach. Seeing as how he'll always be her cherished little brother. How no one could possibly unseat him. That might just give you an opening."

Paloma laughed out loud.

"Okay, Frayda. I finally get it. And you may well be right. But let's get back to my original questions! Tell me how and where to track Shmuely down tomorrow afternoon so I can remind him of just how *farmisht* he is and how much in need of Serach's devotion."

"Well, you're definitely in luck about that, Paloma. Shmuely is evidently a man of fixed habits. Since tomorrow is Friday, he'll be coming home early. 1:45? 2:00? The Filipina maid will have set everything up for his lunch and depart as soon as he appears. He'll stay home till it's time for the end-of-day prayer services, when he'll go off to *shul*. And when services are over, he'll go to his cousin Reuven's for dinner. Evidently, he eats there every night, now. *Chas v'cholileh* he should have to broil his own lamb chops."

"Okay, Frayda. I think I've got the picture now."

"No. Not quite."

Was Frayda laughing at her the way she'd been laughing at Shmuely?

"What, Frayda? What else?"

"There's one last problem. You won't be able to get near him while he's at *shul*. And he won't let you in once he's home. He can't be inside with a woman other than his wife or close relative without a chaperone."

"Don't worry, Frayda. I *am* a close relative. I'm, like, his sister-in-law."

Frayda made an unintelligible sound.

"And it won't be the first time I've managed to chat with him under… less than ideal circumstances. I'll find a way."

Paloma smiled to herself.

"Meanwhile, let's get down to my other question. What do I need to know about making amends, Jewish-style? Which big shots do I need to cite to persuade him to do what he needs to do? And what kind of gesture—what kind of atonement—would be both acceptable to him and meaningful for Serach?"

"Oh, I have plenty of ideas about that, too," Frayda replied.

Jerusalem

6.

The next morning dawned with no hint of the fog, drizzle or pouring rain that had marred the first days of Paloma's Israel sojourn. Pure blue skies, soft breezes and brilliant sunshine. One of those oddly perfect days that sometimes crop up in late winter on the Eastern Mediterranean.

A dozen intrepid bathers could be spotted on the beach below Paloma's window, dashing in and out of the waves. Paloma was sorely tempted to pop into one of the lobby boutiques, pick out a bikini and go join them. But she had places to go. Things to do.

She donned her midi-length, goes-with-everything black skirt, her white silk shell, her little black cardigan, her knee-high black stockings, her low black heels. She twisted the Hermès silk kerchief around her hair in the way she'd learned from Alicia Keys' "How to Knot a Headscarf" video. She then negotiated the three buses to her Jerusalem rendezvous, arriving at 1:20 sharp.

It's not always easy to judge income levels in the neighborhoods of a foreign city. Vast assets often hide behind ancient, shabby exteriors. But in some areas, the signs of wealth are unmistakable. And as Paloma approached *Sha'arei Hesed*, she registered them all.

The streets were broad and clean. The original houses had all been lovingly restored—their golden façades buffed to a shine and enhanced by well-placed Mediterranean greenery. The height of the newer homes had been thoughtfully matched to that of the older ones—as was the color of their building materials and the lushness of the gardens that surrounded them. Even the occasional modern apartment houses were designed to echo those visuals with their sunny hues, elegant terraces, sparkling glass windows and throngs of well-tended shrubbery.

Paloma let herself off the bus on what appeared to be the main commercial strip (yet more glass, steel and pink stone—and signage whose fonts and logos clearly proclaimed: "luxury goods") and walked across its length and down the next couple of blocks toward the address she'd typed into Google Maps earlier that morning. She found herself on a street of houses shielded behind thick stone walls. Hard to tell what lay within.

She reached the gate of Shmuely's house and peered beyond the ironwork and thickly hanging bougainvillea. And was seriously (and unwillingly) impressed by its dimensions.

So now what?

It was just 1:30. According to Frayda's estimates, the Filipina housekeeper would be inside, setting up Shmuely's lunch. Should she ring the gate bell, insinuate herself into the house somehow and stay till Shmuely arrived? Should she remain outside and try to engage him on the street? Should she wait till he was inside, ring the bell and push her way in?

Hard to decide. Each of those strategies had its dangers.

Oh, what the hell? Impatience won over calculation. She rang the bell.

The figure who came out to greet her was a short, stocky, brown-skinned Asian woman. She wore a knee-length sky-blue house dress over what appeared to be jeans and white sneakers. She opened the gate a half-foot, looked Paloma up and down and said something unintelligible.

That has to be Hebrew. She wouldn't be speaking Tagalog to someone she presumes to be Israeli, would she? The question is—does she also speak English? She must. Every Filipina I've ever known has spoken English.

"Hi!" Paloma said, with her biggest smile. "Do you by any chance…?"

She waved her hands around, hoping to convey a query about English language proficiency.

The housekeeper didn't wave back. Nor did she smile.

"Yes, I do," she finally offered. "How can I help you?"

Paloma did a quick assessment. She noted the seriousness of the housekeeper's demeanor, the discreet cross at her neck, the formal way in which she held herself.

Chances are this woman won't take too well to the truth about who I am and why I'm here. I'll have to pick and choose what I share very carefully.

"My name is Paloma," she said, brightly. "I'm from the South American side of Shmuely's family. May I come in?"

The housekeeper suddenly looked more perplexed—more curious—than stern.

"You're Rav Gottesman's….?"

"South American relative. It's complicated. May I please come in?"

"Rav Gottesman didn't tell me anything about…."

"Yes, this is a surprise visit. I'm in Tel Aviv for an international oncological nursing conference. I had some free time and being that I know that Shmuely—that Rav Gottesman—comes home early on Fridays, I thought I might surprise him. May I please come in?"

"But if he isn't…?"

"Expecting me? Don't worry. He'll be thrilled. I promise you. Please, may I?"

The housekeeper relaxed her grip on the gate but resumed her stern expression.

"But if he isn't expecting you and the Rebbetzin isn't here, he won't…."

"Won't want to be alone with me? So maybe you'll stick around? Be our chaperone?"

Paloma took on a conspiratorial tone.

"Shmuely and I were very close when he was a boy. He was always over at our house. But since he's moved to Israel, I haven't as much as seen him. Well, except when he came back for Gittel's funeral, of course. But you know how these things are—who gets to talk? I barely managed to speak with Ruchel, and I'd been hoping to get to know her a bit. Shmuely's sister Beile monopolized her the whole time. You met Beile, right? When she was here last spring? Lovely woman…."

And God bless you, Frayda, for all these details!

"So here's a chance for him and me to finally catch up. How can I not take advantage of it?"

Paloma smiled and this time the housekeeper almost smiled back.

"I know he'll be very glad to see me. Come, let's go in!"

She took the housekeeper gently but firmly by the arm, and—in one seamless movement—eased her away from the gate, slipped in behind her and headed for the still-ajar front door.

And what could the housekeeper do but close the gate and scurry after her? What would the Rebbetzin say if she heard there'd been a major scuffle in front of her house? Or that her housekeeper hadn't shown appropriate courtesy to a relative of the Rav? For this woman must be who she says she is or else how would she know so much about the family?

The two women entered the kitchen in tandem and the housekeeper stood sentry as Paloma gazed around the room with open curiosity. Two sinks, two stoves, two refrigerators, two microwaves, dozens of wall cabinets. An island in the center with additional cabinet space—plus shelves and drawers. A large table with four matching chairs. Everything stainless steel, bleached wood or pale granite. Everything spacious, top-of-the line and sparkling clean.

"Would you like some tea?" the housekeeper finally asked—gesturing to a large urn on one of the counters. She knew her employer would want her to show hospitality to a guest.

"Just some water would be fine."

The housekeeper produced a glass, pulled a pitcher from one of the refrigerators and poured.

"And so," continued Paloma, taking the glass while continuing to inspect her surroundings. "What's your name?"

"Dalisay."

"Well, Dalisay, I'm very glad to meet you."

Paloma put down her glass and extended her hand. Dalisay hesitated a barely perceptible instant before taking it in her own small, slightly damp one. They shook briefly.

"I didn't know Rav Gottesman had family in South America…"

"Oh, yes. Lots. Though… less than before. Many of us have… moved to the States. Or here. I was born in New York, myself. Like Shmuely."

Paloma picked up the glass again, took a gulp and gestured toward the table.

"Come, let's sit! Have ourselves a little chat."

Dalisay hesitated. No guest of the Gottesmans had ever suggested such a thing.

"Please. Don't offend me."

Well, I certainly can't offend a relative. And the two of them sat.

"So tell me," Paloma continued. "What's it like working for Ruchel? As I said, I've barely met her. She seems very nice, of course."

"The Rebbetzin *is* very nice," Dalisay finally responded. "I'm very lucky."

Paloma nodded encouragingly.

"Lucky how?"

Dalisay carefully considered. Could she tell this woman about her wonderful arrangement? It wasn't as if it were anything bad. In fact, it reflected very well on her employer's generosity.

"Tell me!"

"Well… on Wednesdays and Fridays, the Rav gets home early, and—of course—I can't be alone with him. So I set the table, put his lunch in the microwave and then leave for the day as soon as I let him in."

Dalisay gave a small smile of satisfaction.

"And even on those days, the Rebbetzin pays me for a full day of work!"

"That's wonderful, Dalisay."

"She says she pays for a job well done, not for the hours I put in. And I do my job very well."

Paloma found herself unexpectedly pleased that Ruchel was treating this plain-spoken, hard-working woman with fairness.

"So," she continued, with genuine interest. "What do you do on your afternoons off?"

"I rest," said Dalisay. "Before I go on to my other job."

"And what other job is that?"

"I'm the night-time home attendant for an old woman in *Ramot Alon*. There's a bus that goes almost directly between here and there."

She paused.

"It's what most Filipinas do in Israel—take care of old ladies. In fact…."

She gazed at Paloma, suddenly curious to see her reaction.

"… in fact, the Hebrew word for home attendant is actually: 'Filipina.'"

Paloma threw back her head and laughed.

"Back home, the word for any domestic worker is 'my girl.' What a world!"

Suddenly—reluctantly—Dalisay found herself liking this surprisingly empathic woman.

"Still, that's a lot of work," Paloma added, after a small pause. "Housekeeping all day and taking care of an old woman all night."

Dalisay shrugged.

"Oh," she responded. "It's not that bad. And it means I can send really good money back to Manila each month. My mother and three children live very well, thanks to me."

She looked straight at Paloma again.

"And that's a woman's job, isn't it? Doing whatever it takes for our mothers and children?"

Paloma colored.

"Yes," she said. "I guess."

But at that moment something caught Dalisay's eye from beyond the kitchen window and she blanched. Her hand flew to her neck, and she hurriedly tucked her cross into her shirt.

"Oh, no! Here comes the Rav! He's opened the front gate and is headed right in. And I haven't even prepared his lunch! And, oh Lord, now that I see him… are you sure it's okay that I let you in without permission? Will I get in trouble?"

There was a knock at the door.

"Oh, my goodness, will I lose my…?"

"Dalisay! Relax! He wouldn't dare fire you. Who's going to set out his lunch if you aren't here? Do you think he can manage alone? Or find someone to replace you, all on his own?"

For the very briefest of seconds, Dalisay's face relaxed. Paloma's confidence was dazzling.

"I'll tell him I came barreling in here and there was nothing you could do to stop me. He'll believe it—trust me. He knows how pushy we New Yorkers can be. Plus, it's the truth."

Jesus, Mary and Joseph, Paloma! How the hell could you have been so cavalier about this poor woman's livelihood after what you almost did to Ricardo?

"I'll take him to the mat for you, if I have to."

Dalisay gave Paloma an agonized look and Paloma winced at all that it implied.

"I've got this, Dalisay. I swear it. Here—watch!"

Paloma strode out of the kitchen to reach the front door and opened it herself.

"Hi, Shmuely!"

7.

Paloma regarded Shmuely's comically shocked face for a moment before reaching forward, grabbing his sleeve, dragging him into the hall and slamming the door behind him. Stunned and temporarily mute, Shmuely permitted it to happen.

"Yes, Shmuely. It's me—Paloma. Come on in. We have much to discuss."

He finally found his voice.

"I cannot—you cannot!"

"What are you going to do? Call in the military?"

Shmuely opened and shut his mouth a few times.

"Shmuely! We need to talk. It's about Serach."

"Why? What? Is she? I mean…."

"She'll survive," said Paloma ducking behind him and pushing an insistent finger into the middle of his back. He skidded ahead of her, desperate to get away from that sinful touch.

"I can't be alone with…."

"Yes, yes. I know all about that," Paloma said as she maneuvered him into the kitchen. "But no worries. We won't be alone. Dalisay will stay and stand guard over us. Won't you, Dalisay?"

Dalisay—horrified and fascinated by what she was witnessing—nodded.

"Now. It's time for your lunch, isn't it, Shmuely? Go sit!"

She was hovering determinedly right on top of him. He'd have to make physical contact to escape. She might fight back. He edged toward the table and sat down, while Dalisay stood in the far corner of the room looking almost as dazed as he did.

"Dalisay! Don't worry! He's not going to do anything to you. Are you, Shmuely?"

The Rav made a tiny move that might have been interpreted as a head shake.

Why do I feel so helpless? How do I stop this woman?

"See, Dalisay? No problem. Let's get him his lunch. How does it work? What does he eat?"

"The Rav eats…." Dalisay walked to the freezer, feeling a bit reassured, took out a package of Heimische's Frozen Mushroom Barley Soup and loosened the wrapping. "He eats this."

She walked over to the microwave.

"I put it in here and once the Rav gets to the front door, I let him in and leave. Like I said."

Dalisay opened the microwave door and placed the soup inside.

"And then he sets the timer for five minutes and turns it on himself."

She swiveled toward Paloma with a serious face.

"I can't do that part for him. Non-Jews are not allowed to light the flame that cooks a Jew's meal." She paused for a moment before adding—perhaps more boldly than she might have, had Paloma not been there: "Rav! Everything's all set up. Come warm up your lunch!"

But Shmuely remained inert. On this matter, at the very least, he could take a stance.

"I am not ready to eat yet. I will eat… after… after...."

"I won't be here long," Paloma said, smiling at Dalisay. "He won't starve."

Dalisay nodded.

"So," Paloma continued. "What do you do next?"

"I set the table," Dalisay said, quickly doing so. "And I put out his little bowties."

She pulled a box of egg *kichels* out of one of the cupboards, put four *kichels* on a plate, placed the plate on the table and put the box back again.

"He gets his own tea." She pointed at the urn. "Once I've set up his teacup and spoon."

This can't be happening! What is that *Spanish Woman* doing here?

"There, Rav," Dalisay said, as she had laid out those last things. "And maybe your… um…" she pointed, "maybe she can help with anything I've forgotten…?"

"I'm sure we can manage, Dalisay," said Paloma. "But can you possibly play bodyguard? Stay close and… visible?"

Dalisay's panic was ebbing and her curiosity growing. This South American relative was certainly something. And the Rav wasn't making a move to fire her. She should try to be helpful.

"Shall I go into the dining room, leave the door open, and vacuum very loudly? Be out of your way but… make enough noise that the Rav will know I'm still here?"

"Dalisay—you are one in a million. No wonder Ruchel loves you."

Dalisay disappeared. Paloma went to the refrigerator, refilled her glass, and sat down.

"Okay, Shmuely. Time to talk."

Shmuely looked as if he were going to sprint for the door. But his legs wouldn't cooperate.

I am sitting at the table with the *Spanish Woman*. I can't get away—she will block me. I can't call the police—what would I say? They'll think I'm… I don't know what they'll think, but I can't do it. Where is my wife? Where is Ruchel? She would know what to do!

He finally pulled himself together enough to get out three complete sentences.

"Why are you here? You have no right to be here! You have to leave!"

Paloma contemplated his fierce expression with amusement, waited till she heard the vacuum cleaner's first roar and then spoke confidently over the din.

"Oh," she said. "That's where you're mistaken, Shmuely. I do have a right to be here. More than a right. A duty. You have sins on your conscience. I need to help you deal with them."

"Sins on my…? What are you talking about?"

"Yes, Shmuely. Big sins. Sins for which you need to make personal atonement. I mean… now that the Temple's gone and you can't sacrifice a goat or an ox."

Shmuely shook out his head several times in quick succession.

What is this *Spanish Person* talking about? And how dare she quote Torah to me?

"I thought you were here to talk to me about Serach," he was finally able to mutter.

"Well, yes. I am. It's all related."

Paloma waited for him to ask something more specific about Serach's condition. He didn't.

"I'm here to tell you what happens when a man chooses religious rules over basic decency."

"I don't know what you're talking about," he said, putting some steel behind his voice.

Paloma sighed. This was going to be even harder than she'd feared.

"Shmuely," she reprised. "You have committed an injustice. It's time to atone."

Shmuely opened his mouth, but Paloma rode right over him.

"When you first stopped Skyping Serach—with no word of warning, I might add—she refused to believe it was intentional. Or permanent. For several months, she would sit down at her computer on the mornings you were scheduled to chat, eagerly waiting for the icon that never appeared." She paused. "It was heartbreaking to watch her do that." She paused again. "And even more heartbreaking to see her finally give up."

Shmuely colored. He had never considered what it had been like on Serach's end.

"An observant man marries," he finally said. "And marriage necessitates certain changes."

"Serach—poor soul—continued to trust you'd find a way to reconnect," Paloma resumed. "Until your mother's funeral fiasco. When you unambiguously turned your back on her."

"Serach forsook our law," Shmuely said, clearly and distinctly—but without looking in Paloma's direction. "I had no choice."

"Oh yes you did. You could have made some small gesture of acknowledgement to her. A nod. A smile. She wouldn't have expected more—she knows what your religion is like. But that tiny gesture would have been huge for her. And you couldn't even manage that much."

"We were in a public place. It would have been… unseemly."

"Yes, and so rather than risking something that I'm sure a clever man like yourself could have covered up, you humiliated her in that public place. Isn't humiliating a person in public a sin grievous enough for a man to lose his spot in the world to come?"

The *Spanish Woman* has no right to quote Talmud to me! I will not put up with it!

He started to stand up again.

"Sit down, Shmuely!"

She sounded just like his mother. How did she do that? He resumed his seat and fumbled briefly with his napkin.

"You hardened your heart against the person who has always cared for you. And taught you. And defended you. The person who essentially raised you. Isn't 'hardening the heart' top of the list of things for which you need to atone at Yom Kippur?"

"How do you know about…?" he finally whispered, staring down at his place mat.

"How do I know about Yom Kippur? About your laws? About the Temple sacrifices?"

Shmuely blinked.

"I know because I live with a Jew, Shmuely."

He blinked again.

"Yes, a Jew. And a very good one at that. A Jew who does justice. And loves mercy. And acts humbly—before God and everyone else. Where was *your* sense of justice on the day you turned away from her in that parking lot? Or your love of mercy? Or your humility?"

"You have no right to…."

"Yes, I do. I've had to live with the results of your cruelty. I've had to pick up the pieces. No—you must not stand up! You need to stay right where you are and hear me out!"

Shmuely couldn't help obeying. It was part of his DNA—obeying fierce women. Suddenly ten years old again, he sat back down. But by that time, Paloma had changed tactics.

"When Serach returned from your mother's funeral," she said, her voice dropping down a few portentous notes, "she crawled into bed and didn't come out for weeks."

Shmuely glanced up with a sudden look of recognition.

"Serach? In bed? For weeks?"

"Yes, Shmuely," Paloma continued, watching his face. "Serach. The strongest person I know. Probably the strongest person you know. Not eating. Barely speaking. Barely moving."

Shmuely flinched.

"Our mother used to do that," he murmured.

"Yes. I know all about that. But for your mother, it was a matter of… some untreated mental health condition. For Serach, it was… a response to your hard-heartedness."

She stared hard at him and Shmuely finally met her gaze.

God, he looks so much like Serach! Yes, sure, his eyes are turquoise rather than grey—but they contain that same dazzling intelligence. And he has those same sculpted cheekbones and shapely nose and exquisitely curved lips under all that scraggly facial hair. He even has those same golden curls framing that perfectly shaped forehead.

And Shmuely, looking back at Paloma's face, saw a woman so beautiful that it made him blink. A woman so beautiful and… so lucky! A woman who basked in Serach's full love and attention, every single day.

Paloma caught his profoundly bereft expression and dropped her own gaze. She put aside her anger. She put aside the complicated religious arguments that she'd spent half the night memorizing under Frayda's determined coaching. She veered in a new direction.

"Shmuely, here's the scoop," she said, as gently as she could. "Serach is better now. But the wound you caused her remains right under the surface, ready to begin bleeding again."

Shmuely remained passive with great effort.

"And the reason for that is because she still loves you so very, very much."

She saw Shmuely's lip tremble for the briefest of moments and went in for the kill.

"Yes, Shmuely. Loves you dearly. Even knowing all your weaknesses. And without demanding a single thing back."

He raised his eyes to meet hers. She counted it a small victory and continued.

"Serach is a person who needs—who loves—only a very few people in this world. And you and I are among the members of that incredibly small and fortunate group."

She paused.

"And sometimes I wonder whether either of us really deserves it."

Shmuely looked startled.

"Well, Shmuely, just look at how you've treated her. Hmmnn?"

She waited one last beat.

"And… I haven't exactly been an angel with her, either."

Shmuely couldn't help himself. He looked back at Paloma and wondered what she could have done. And felt—yes—a flash of protective anger on his sister's behalf.

Paloma caught that look and bit her lip. No way was she going to share any of *that* stuff with this self-important young man. To confess how regularly she'd berated the very Jewish tenets that she was now deploying to make her case. Or (God forbid) to describe what she'd almost done with Carlota.

She took a long drink of water, swallowed hard, and continued.

"I'm beginning to carry out my own atonement by being here today," she said, putting the glass down again. "By doing whatever I can to bring you and Serach back together again, like Aaron the peacemaker. But…."

Shmuely re-hardened his face.

There she goes again. How dare she keep quoting Torah at me like that?

"Serach forsook the *halacha*. I cannot be expected to condone what she has done."

"Oh, you condoned it just fine when it suited you, Shmuely. Seems like I remember you coming by our house a whole lot when you needed Serach's help. It's only now that you're a big cheese that you suddenly can't seem to do that sort of condoning anymore."

Shmuely colored.

"And what's more, Shmuely—as I'm sure you very well know—Serach isn't breaking any *halachic* rules by being with me. Men can't love one another because of the whole seed-spilling thing. But women can basically do what they want with each other. I have it on good authority."

And God bless you, Frayda for all of this! When I get back to New York, I'm going to treat you to dinner at the finest kosher restaurant in the city.

"Do I really need to tell you that… 'the balance and scales of justice are the Lord's—all the weights of the bag are His work?' Your job isn't to judge Serach. Your job is simply to figure out how you are going to stand before your Maker next Yom Kippur."

Shmuely almost nodded and then, with great effort, pulled himself back.

But Paloma had one more strategy at her disposal.

"Atoning for your behavior will, of course, help Serach," she said. "But it will also help *you.* I can't believe that you haven't also suffered from your painful break with your beloved sister. That your heart hasn't been in conflict. That you haven't had trouble feeling 'at one' with yourself. So, here's your golden chance, Shmuely. With a single act of lovingkindness, you can clear the path for your sister's healing. Even more importantly, you can begin to heal yourself."

Paloma saw the yearning in his face—there was no mistaking it. She had him now.

"But what…?" he finally began, looking up at her. "But how…? How can I possibly….?"

"I have just the solution for you. Very safe. No one will ever know but you, me and her."

And now what was she seeing? Could it be? Yes, it was. The same marvelous look of mischief that she sometimes caught on Serach's face. Well, Glory Hallelujah! That was a character trait she could easily work with.

"Look, Shmuely, I hear that your finally pregnant wife is currently on Long Island for your son's birth and *bris*. And that you'll soon be traveling to join her for those events."

Shmuely didn't question where she'd heard all that.

"Yes. Both events will take place in Cedarhurst if *Ha-Shem* grants us life."

He paused and straightened up, suddenly stern.

"And the *bris* will—the *bris* will be taking place in a *shul*, that is—well, yes, of course it's Orthodox. But lax. Very lax. Men and women will be eating together after the service!"

He shuddered.

"But there is nothing I can do about it. It's Ruchel's family. I can't help how they are."

Paloma took a deep breath.

For God's sake, don't waste a single drop of energy arguing with him about his idiotic gender beliefs! Keep your eye on the ball—you're just about to whack it right across the net.

"The main thing," she said, slowly and carefully, "is that it wouldn't be so hard to get to Cedarhurst from Brooklyn, would it? Not like having to *shlep* all the way to Israel. Serach could just zip right over to that *shul* on the Long Island Railroad, couldn't she?"

He looked back at her blankly. What was the Long Island Railroad?

"So let me suggest that you begin your atonement by inviting her to that *bris*."

Shmuely's face suddenly became smug.

"If you actually knew anything about Jewish practice," he said with pointed dignity, "you would know that you don't invite people to a *bris*. They just come."

"Yes. And if you actually knew anything about human nature, you'd know that you don't go to something when you don't think you'll be welcome."

Shmuely looked away.

"So what you need to do is let Serach know that she'll be welcome. And then…."

"Let her know that she's welcome? How?"

"You call Serach's old friend Frayda as soon as your son is born. You remember her, right? You say you're letting her know where and when your son's *bris* will be because you don't think anyone else will. Which is true. Then you say you really hope all your sisters will be there. Stress the 'all' part so she'll know you're including Serach without your having to specify that. She'll understand what you mean. And she'll know to tell Serach."

Slowly, slowly, Shmuely nodded. Then he thought better of it.

"But what if someone recognizes her? And thinks… I'm responsible for her being there!"

"No one will as much as notice her. She'll dress *frum* and keep her head down. As will I. Everyone will just assume that we're people from 'the other side of the family.'"

He arched an eyebrow.

"Yes, Shmuely. I'm going to be there too, since Serach is going to need my support. *Goyim* are allowed at these things. I checked that all out."

Shmuely finally looked back at her with something approaching respect.

"And one thing more, Shmuely," Paloma added, after a short pause. "When Serach comes to that *bris*, you need to let her know that you're glad she's there."

"You can't expect me to…"

"No one expects you to give your sister a big public hug, Shmuely."

She caught her breath. The vacuuming was beginning to let up in the next room. How many times could poor Dalisay go round and round, after all? She was going to have to wrap up.

"Just… find a way to catch her eye from across the room. Give her a little smile. Make that small, subtle, compassionate gesture that you were incapable of making at your mother's funeral. It will mean the world to her. And… just think how good you will feel when she smiles back."

She caught him flush and continued.

"Do you think you can do that much, Shmuely? That very, very small little something?"

Shmuely lifted his turquoise eyes to meet Paloma's spark-hurtling black ones and nodded.

The vacuuming stopped.

"And now," said Paloma, "it's time for me and Dalisay to leave—and for you to finally hit those microwave buttons and have your lunch."

She poked her head into the dining room where Dalisay stood motionless, vacuum cleaner in hand.

"Thanks, Dalisay. You saved my life. Shall we get out of here?"

Dalisay nodded. She peeled off her housecoat, put it in the hall closet along with the vacuum cleaner, and re-joined Paloma in the kitchen.

"We're off, Shmuely—Dalisay and me."

He didn't answer.

"And listen. No worries that anyone will learn what took place today. I won't say a word. And Dalisay… you're not going to say anything to anyone about my visit either, are you?"

"Not if I shouldn't," Dalisay replied. "I only want to do what is good for the Rav. And for the Rebbetzin. This job has been the answer to my prayers."

Paloma felt her eyes well up.

Jesus! Talk about walking humbly with one's God!

She took a moment to recover before turning to give Shmuely one last magnificent smile.

"So, I guess we're all set, aren't we? Bye-bye, Shmuely! See you!"

Then grasping Dalisay firmly by the elbow, she maneuvered them swiftly out the front door.

Shmuely gave them a minute to reach the sidewalk and then slipped out the door as well. He crossed the garden, planted himself discreetly behind the front gate, and began peering anxiously to the right and left.

The street was empty—and remained blessedly empty long after the two women had disappeared around the corner. No one could possibly have witnessed them exiting the Gottesman house at a time when the Rebbetzin was known to be away. No one would be in a position to start unfortunate rumors.

He was safe. Everything was going to be all right. Maybe even better than all right.

Baruch Ha-Shem.

Early April 2019: Piermont, New York

8.

Don't we make a great pair, Paloma sighed as she and Serach sat side-by-sullen-side on the bus to Piermont. Hard to know which one of us is more ticked off.

She pressed her lips together.

No, there's no contest: I am. With good reason. Here I am making this totally unnecessary visit, just to placate her. And what does she give me in return? *Bupkes.* As she likes to say.

Paloma had already visited Anteojitos' new school twice. Once with Manny, three weeks after Anteojitos first arrived. Once (also with Manny) just before Christmas. Plus, of course, she'd seen Anteojitos back in July when she'd joined her brother and nephews at the Red Lobster restaurant on Fordham Road to celebrate the dismissal of the case.

Surely that was enough.

But had it satisfied Serach? No. Just because she'd been *shlepping* off to Piermont once a month since Anteojitos arrived there, she'd decided Paloma should do likewise. Well, why the hell should she? She'd never had as easy a time with Anteojitos as Serach. And ever since the shooting incident, she'd found his nonsense more intolerable than ever.

Not to mention that Serach was being infuriatingly inflexible, herself. That—impossible as it was to believe—she was refusing to go to Shmuely's son's *bris.*

Everything—every tough detail—had worked out perfectly. Ruchel had given birth on schedule. Shmuely had called Frayda and said what he'd agreed to say. Even Frayda (always a wild card) had played her role to perfection—repeating Shmuely's words to Serach verbatim and pointing out what they so clearly implied.

But had little Serach appreciated all those Herculean efforts? No. She'd decided to screw the whole thing up instead.

"Paloma, how can you be sure that Shmuely wants me there based on that single elliptical remark?" she'd asked in her maddeningly calm way. "You can't, can you? So how can ask me to make myself so vulnerable? Goodness, Paloma! Aren't you the one who's always said that we can't trust Shmuely farther than we can throw him? I don't know what's gotten into you!"

Short of confessing all the particulars of her scheme, there had been nothing Paloma could do.

"Serach," she'd managed to sputter. "Your brother spends his life studying the meaning of words. If he says something in a particular way, it's because he means it in that way."

"Paloma, if you can't understand why I don't want to go," Serach had replied with irritating mildness, "then you don't understand anything about me at all."

So here they were—on the Sunday before the damned *bris*—barreling up to Piermont, just like Serach wanted. But when Paloma had very gently tried raising the subject one last time on that bus ride, Serach had pointedly turned away and mumbled something about: "I thought we were done with all that, Paloma. I thought I'd made myself clear."

After which, she'd continued to sit stiffly and primly, staring out the bus window as if Paloma were a big bully and this was the only way she could protect herself. She'd only turned around when the big red "Excelsior School" sign appeared on the side of the road to their left.

"We're here," she'd announced. "Let's go."

"Serach, I'm leaving it totally up to you to get us where we're going, since you know the way so well," said Paloma, sliding from her seat to let Serach out. "Go on. You're the expert."

Serach sighed. This was no way for them to be acting on a trip to see poor Ramon.

"Let's not fight," she finally said, very quietly.

"I'm not fighting. You are."

But Paloma unexpectedly found that she was ready to give in as well. Still, she maintained a few steps of distance between them so Serach shouldn't misinterpret her softening as weakness.

They walked up one path and down another, taking in the surroundings. Only a few students tended to stay on campus on Sundays, and the ones that were there were all huddled in one spot, perched on what appeared to be a picnic table outside the main campus hall. Some wore light jackets, some sweatshirts, and some shivered in shirtsleeves in the unexpectedly chilly April air.

All of them were smoking. All of them were on their smartphones, paying scant attention to one another—and even less to the two strangers entering their terrain.

"Every cottage has a 'house parent'," Serach was explaining, glancing back at Paloma every few feet. "Ramon's house parent is named André. Did you meet him when you were here?"

"Mnnnnn. Don't remember."

"Oh, you'd remember him if you'd met him. And here he is!"

A tall, very muscular, very dark-skinned Black man with enormous dimples and dreadlocks drawn up into a big, loose ponytail emerged from the house and bounded toward them. He must have been watching out the front window as they approached.

"Hello, hello and good afternoon to Ramon's wonderful Aunt Serach!" he intoned in his triple-deep, slightly West-Indian accented voice as he took Serach's two small, cold hands into his two very large warm ones. "Ramon has been waiting anxiously for you all morning. He's going to be really glad to see you."

"I'll be really glad to see him, too, André."

She pulled her hands gently out of his grasp and motioned to Paloma.

"This is Ramon's other aunt. Paloma Rodriguez. Come, Paloma. Come meet André."

Paloma slowly wended her way forward as André surveyed her with great interest.

"Paloma is Manny's sister," Serach added as Paloma extended her hand and André took it.

"Of course you are," André said. "You look just like your brother. Prettier, of course."

He paused for a moment before adding: "I know Ramon will be thrilled to see you, too. Shall we all go inside? Shall I go get him? He's up in his room."

"Yes, let's go in," said Paloma. "But before you bring him down, I'd love a few minutes of your time, if you don't mind. As you know, I haven't been around here that much. So I have a few questions. Would that be okay?"

"And in the meantime, I can go get Ramon," Serach added. "Which will give you the time you need."

"Of course," André replied, opening the front door and motioning them in. "Of course, to both things. You know the way, Serach. Just go on up. And you, Paloma—come sit."

He waved at a big, grey, much-used couch on the far side of the room with a little coffee table planted in front of it. "Can I get you something? Water? Coffee? Tea?"

"I'm okay just as I am," said Paloma. "But thanks anyway."

André approached the matching grey chair, catty-corner to the couch. It took a moment for him to fit his large frame within its confines. He ended by stretching his long legs at an angle in front of him and firmly embracing the arm rests with his two significant-looking hands.

"I think I caught sight of you when you were here with your brother in the fall."

"Mnnn. Don't know."

"Oh, I do. I never forget a face. Especially such a lovely one."

He grinned at her and then remembered himself.

"So. What is it you'd like to know?"

"Well, first of all, who besides Serach comes to visit Anteojitos—I mean Ramon?"

André observed her for a moment before saying anything.

"Go ahead and call him Anteojitos. His father calls him that, too."

Paloma smiled.

"Okay. Thanks. But what about my question? Does Anteojitos' mother come to see him?"

"She has," André replied slowly. "Though not as often as your brother. Or as Serach."

Paloma raised one lovely eyebrow.

"Interesting. Why do you think she's stayed away?"

"Well," André answered, "some parents have a hard time facing that their children are here."

Paloma nodded. Plus, Beatriz is a bitch.

"I think Ramon's father initially had some trouble, too," André added. "But he seems to have gotten over it. He's here almost every week."

"Yeah, well. My brother can be hard-headed but he's not totally *pig-*headed."

André grinned. He had a smile as killer attractive as Paloma's own.

"He also loves his son more than he shows," she said, glancing away from André's radiance.

"Oh, he shows it all right."

"Which is not to say," Paloma added with a trace of defiance, "that he wasn't totally devastated by what Anteojitos did. He was the one to teach him to shoot, you know."

Paloma looked up at André's handsome face and suddenly felt she could be frank.

"Fernando—the man that Anteojitos shot—used to be Manny's best friend," she began. "Manny goes to visit him regularly, too. On the Sundays when he doesn't come here, that's where he goes. It's killing him, what happened to Fernando."

André knew to hold his tongue. He hadn't spent six years as a House Parent for children with acute Post Traumatic Stress Disorder for nothing. He allowed Paloma to collect herself.

"And…" Paloma finally continued, slowly. "Fernando was my good friend, too. Once upon a time, before all those tours of duty in Afghanistan destroyed him. It wasn't his fault, what he became. He was a victim as much as… as Anteojitos…."

She visibly calmed herself.

"Do you know about him? About his time in the Marines? About what he nearly did to me?"

"Yes," said André. "It's all in Ramon's records."

"Well, he never would have done what he did—or almost did—if those tours of combat hadn't ripped out his soul. And now, his life is basically over. It's made it hard for me to forgive Anteojitos. Or to… want to come see him."

She looked up to see André nodding at her with so much kindness that it made her blush.

"Yeah," André ventured. "But you should stop beating yourself up about it."

He paused.

"Still, I get what you're saying. I did a tour in Iraq, myself. I managed to emerge in one piece, thank God. But some of my buddies weren't so lucky."

They sat in peculiarly comfortable silence for a moment.

"And his brothers?" Paloma finally asked.

"His brothers?"

"Yes. Anteojitos' two older brothers. Have they been to visit him?"

"Yes. They have. They've been here three times. With their father."

"Well… that's at least one more time than I have. I mean, before today."

"True. But now I'm hoping that will change."

Paloma blushed.

"Your nephew is well settled in now. He doesn't seem to like to go home. It really jarred him the first few times he did it—took him a long while to readjust when he got back. He does, however, most definitely like to receive visitors. So please do start coming more frequently."

They sat in silence again for a moment. It was peaceful.

"So, Paloma. Any other big questions before Serach and Ramon come down to join us?"

"Yes. One."

She looked down at her hands and then back at him.

"As you probably know, Anteojitos originally dropped out of high school because… well, because he was so horribly bullied. He's always been an easy target. I can't…."

"Yes?"

"I can't even let myself think about what must have happened to him when he was in that holding pen for more than thirty-six hours. They must have… had a field day with him…."

André somehow magically produced a box of tissues and handed it to her.

"I've been spending a lot of time with him on that incident," he said, cautiously. "And on… well… other incidents when he's felt at other people's mercy. We've been making progress."

Paloma nodded, blew her nose with a honk, balled up the tissue and tossed it easily into the wastepaper basket on the other side of the couch.

"Whoa! I can see where Ramon gets his flawless aim."

"Oh. Yeah. Well, we Rodriguezes are all pretty coordinated. But let's get back to what we were talking about. Like I said, Anteojitos has been bullied just about anywhere he's ever gone. So… tell me. How's it been for him here? Do the kids bully him? And if so—what have you been doing about it?"

André suddenly laughed. He had a big, deep gorgeous laugh.

"Ramon bullied by these kids? Are you kidding? Ramon is held in awe by these kids. Hell, he shot and nearly killed someone. As far as they're concerned, Ramon is… 'The Man.'"

"Holy shit—what a world!" Paloma shook her head. But before she could say anything further, she was diverted by a blur of awkward energy hurtling its way toward her.

"Tía Paloma! Tía Paloma! Tía Serach brought us chopped liver sandwiches! She went to her favorite deli and bought them. And she's brought pickles! And Coca Cola! And she got me a new *Sudoku* book! And five new sharpened pencils! Really pointy ones, like I like them."

"Hi there, Anteojitos," said Paloma, standing up to receive his clumsy embrace. "Nice to see you, too."

"Well," said André, casting an appraising eye at the situation to take in the attentive way in which Paloma suddenly looked up at Serach and the glowing way in which Serach returned her look. "I think I can leave Ramon to you two lovely ladies. Come get me when you're ready to go, so I can take Ramon back in hand."

Anteojitos plopped himself down next to Paloma on the couch and Serach sat down in the chair that André had vacated.

"Yes, Ramon, we have a feast in store for us," Serach said.

She reached into her bag, pulled out three beautifully wrapped sandwiches, three napkins, three straws and three small bottles of Coca Cola and spread them out on the coffee table. She unscrewed Anteojitos' bottle for him, took the straw out of its paper cover to place it near the bottle and unwrapped his sandwich.

For a good ten minutes, the only noise to be heard in that room was Anteojitos periodically smacking his lips and saying: "Mnnnnn-good!"

Serach waited till she was sure everyone had finished and then cleaned everything up again with a few small, efficient moves. She then reached back into her bag, produced the promised book of *Sudoku* puzzles and the five sharpened pencils and lay them down in front of Anteojitos.

"It's an intermediate-level book this time," she said with a broad smile.

He gave her a blank look.

"That means you're becoming really good."

Anteojitos beamed. He then grabbed one of the pencils, whipped the book open, and immediately immersed himself within it.

"So," said Serach, turning to Paloma after a moment of watching him with deep satisfaction. "Did you have a good chat with André?"

"Oh, most definitely. I'll tell you all about it on the bus ride home."

She paused.

"But right now, seeing as Anteojitos is… so thoroughly occupied… I thought we might talk a bit about something else."

Serach looked at her warily.

"Yes, that's right. You and I have some… important unfinished business to attend to."

Serach knew what was coming and couldn't believe that Paloma was being so underhanded. She gestured toward Anteojitos.

"Paloma, this really is not a good time or place to…."

"Anteojitos is fully engaged, Serach," said Paloma, with a smile. "You're so terribly wise about what you bring him when you come to visit. An earthquake could occur and he'd still be too focused on those beloved little puzzles to notice it."

Serach bit her lip.

"And," Paloma added, "as you like to say: 'if not now, when?'"

"Okay, Paloma. Go ahead. Speak your piece."

"Serach, on Thursday morning your newborn nephew is going to be circumcised in front of his family, his community… and God. And your idiot brother clearly wants you to be there. There is no other way to explain why he called Frayda out of the blue the way that he did. And why he phrased things in the way that he phrased them."

"I don't know, Paloma. What if…."

"Serach, there is no: 'What if?' There is only: 'Yes, I'll go.' There is only: 'Yes, I'll be there for my brother Shmuely, who has taken this enormously difficult step to reconcile with me.' There is only: 'Yes, I'll be there to bear witness to my newborn nephew's entry into the most sacred of Jewish covenants!' There is only: 'Yes, I'll be there to—'"

But Paloma was suddenly cut off in her lecture by a sharp snap on the table and a huge rumbling on the couch beside her. Anteojitos had slammed down his pencil and was making loud, unintelligible noises in his throat.

What was going on with him? What had set him off so violently?

His face was convulsing with the effort he was making.

"Tía Serach!" he finally said in his bellowing voice. "Tía Serach—you *have* to go!"

Serach looked at him in astonishment as he forced out the next three words—almost as if he were in pain.

"*Nephews. Are. Important.*"

EPILOGUE: An Unusual Bris

"May he live a life of Torah, of marriage and of acts of kindness."

Blessing for the baby boy at his bris

April 2019: Cedarhurst, Long Island

The congregation of *Tiferes Israel* of Cedarhurst met for morning services in a large grey private house that had been converted into a synagogue—complete with a spacious Social Hall, a sanctuary boasting a stately *bimah*, a magnificent mahogany Torah Ark (complete with five Torah scrolls) and a set of elegant pews for the men.

As often happened in early April, there had been a total switch in the weather. It was suddenly a perfectly beautiful day—cool fresh air and wonderfully warm sun—with the tree branches around the *shul* suddenly swathed in the first pale green leaf buds of the season.

As Serach, Paloma and Frayda—Paloma and Serach on one side of the street and Frayda on the other so they wouldn't be seen together and identified—approached the house from the LIRR train station, Paloma carefully probed into the upcoming proceedings in ways that she hoped might guide her seat-of-the-pants strategy.

"How long will the service last?"

"Forty minutes? Maybe forty-five? On a Thursday like today, there is a Torah reading, so it might be as long as fifty. And then there'll be the *bris*. So probably… an hour, all told?"

"And where will we be sitting? You said that we're kept separate from the men?"

"No doubt we'll be sitting on little chairs behind a curtain up in a special balcony."

"And how will we know what's going on if we're way up there, hidden behind a curtain?"

"Good question. We may miss some. But there's no way we'll miss the baby's scream. That part is guaranteed."

"Oh, sweet Jesus," Paloma shook her head. "I'll never understand your religion, Serach."

"Nor I yours," said Serach with a small smile.

"So… is it just cut and go? Does the *mohel* do anything else?"

Serach was suddenly speaking very softly and very fast.

"Yes. Yes, he does," she said, looking down. "Once he's made the cut, he… leans in further and sucks off the drop of blood before bandaging it all up."

"Holy Mary, Mother of God. You're kidding!"

"No, I'm not. The procedure is called *metzitzah b'peh*."

"Serach, that's the most perverted, most barbaric—most unhygienic—thing I've ever heard!"

"Paloma, please don't speak so loud."

"And this happens at every *bris*?"

"Well, in our particular community it does. I doubt if Reform Jews do it."

"And… that thing… happened to Shmuely?"

Serach put her head in her hands.

"Yes, Paloma," she said, after a long moment. "It happened to Shmuely. But like everything else in Shmuely's life, it didn't happen exactly according to plan."

Paloma considered. Did she really want to know any more about that? No, she did not.

"And after the… uh… sucking procedure, what happens?" she finally ventured.

"Someone—sometimes the *mohel*, sometimes someone else—announces the child's name and says a few words about it. It's been kept a secret until then."

She smiled.

"After that, everyone drinks some wine—even the baby gets a drop. Then the baby goes back to his mother, and everyone goes down to the Social Hall for bagels and lox."

She paused and looked at Paloma with a serious face.

"And once the eating starts, I hope you won't mind if we just slip out of there and go home."

Paloma sighed. It was going to be even harder to arrange eye-to-eye contact between Serach and Shmuely than she'd feared. Well, she'd figure it out somehow.

"Whatever you like, Serach. I've never been much of a fan of smoked fish."

"I assume Frayda will stay on," Serach lowered her voice. "She likes to eat, and she likes to *schmooze*. But I'm sure she can find her own way back to the train station."

Paloma glanced briefly across the street to check on Frayda's progress. She caught Frayda's eye—and Frayda may or may not have winked. You could never tell with Frayda.

"We're here," Paloma suddenly said. "Gird your loins, Baby."

Serach fumbled around in her purse, found a tissue and dabbed at her eyes. Her hands trembled visibly as she did it, but then she pulled herself straight and snapped the purse shut.

"We need to head for the rear of the balcony," she said. "Frayda will undoubtedly go down front to peer through the curtain. She always liked to do that. But we should stay out of sight."

They scurried to those seats, heads lowered and kerchiefs pulled forward to shield their faces.

"Oh, my goodness—look over there!" Serach abruptly grabbed Paloma's arm. "Those two women in navy blue? It's my sisters Chava and Shayna! Oh! They've gotten so big!"

They most certainly have, thought Paloma, as the two exceedingly fat blond women strutted in and took their places down near the front.

"And that's—oh good heavens, it's Mierle!"

Paloma reached over and took her partner's hand.

"Directing traffic as always!" added Serach, smiling despite herself. "But I don't see Beile anywhere..." she continued. And then she caught her breath. "Oh wait! I bet she'll be bringing the baby to the entrance of the sanctuary. It would be an appropriate honor. She's the oldest sister. I mean—after me, of course."

She blinked hard.

"I don't recognize anyone else. They must all be regular congregants—or else women from Ruchel's side of the family."

Paloma took a breath. Serach seemed to be surviving, thank God. Still, she kept a firm arm around her partner's shoulders, just in case. It didn't seem out of place. All the other women were being highly affectionate with one another. Not to mention talking non-stop—seemingly oblivious to the interminable, unintelligible male droning going on below them.

Well of course, Paloma mused. How could anyone possibly stay focused on all that gibberish? Serach, however, seemed to have no problem staying electrically attentive.

"Paloma!" she suddenly drew in her breath. "The *bris* is going to start!"

Paloma looked at her hard.

"And are we going to stay sitting back here like two dopes and miss out on the whole thing?"

Serach hesitated a moment and then grinned.

"No," she said. "We're not. Follow me."

She took Paloma's hand and led them down to the front, just opposite from where Frayda was perched. She moved the curtain aside and motioned for Paloma to join her in peeking down.

Paloma beheld a sea of bowing men in black. Most but not all had full beards. Most had big hats—though a few just wore *yarmulkes*. All were wrapped in big black and white shawls.

"There—look! That woman standing right in the doorway to the sanctuary must be Ruchel! She's handing the baby—oh my word, Shmuely's baby! —to that other woman over there. Oh, my goodness, it *is* Beile! She's handing the baby to Beile!"

"Angel—my poor sweet Angel—don't cry!"

"I can't help it! Oh, how I wish my father were here! Oh!"

"Serach, Serach, love of my life. He is here. Trust me. Watching over everything. And—what is it you call it? *Kvelling*? But shush, now. Here's a tissue. We can't afford to make a spectacle of ourselves."

Serach nodded and pulled herself together for what seemed like the hundredth time.

Beile only held the baby for a moment. She quickly handed him over to the man by her side and escorted Ruchel back out of the doorway. The man then set out, infant in arms, toward a big, fancy, blue-cushioned chair at the front of the sanctuary—while a chubby, jaunty middle-aged man and a skinny youth in a hat far too big for his head fell into line behind him.

"That must be Ruchel's father…" Serach said with an effort as she nodded to the middle-aged man. "They'll have given him the honor of holding the baby during… the procedure."

"Yes, my dear," said Paloma, keeping her hand firmly planted on Serach's shoulder. "And that little guy right next to him is undoubtedly your brother, Shmuely."

And—Shmuely, my boy—you'd better behave yourself! You'd better keep your word!

There was a flurry of choreography that ended with Ruchel's father sitting down on the special chair with the special pillow—and the baby—on his lap. He wrapped his short arms around the baby with the ease of someone who had held many children.

More mumbled prayers and scurrying around until finally one of the many bearded, black-hatted men stepped up to the chair, turned his back to the congregation and bent forward over the child. Half a moment later, a high-pitched shriek issued from behind the bent man's silhouette and the women in the balcony answered it with a swell of fierce chattering.

"Done," said Serach, who had kept her eyes fixed on Shmuely the whole time. "All done."

She then lifted her eyes from her brother to gaze over toward Frayda—poised at the other side of the balcony. And Paloma—witnessing that gaze and realizing that in all the years she'd loved Serach, she'd never received a look of such deep connection—determinedly pushed down the flood of jealous shivers that it triggered and resumed her inspection of the action below.

A new man stepped up to the chair.

"That's my cousin Reuven!" whispered Serach, turning back to Paloma. "Reuven's been given the honor of announcing the baby's name!"

Reuven immediately began spouting an effortless mixture of Hebrew prayers and English narrative. Serach listened motionless until the moment she gasped out loud.

"Oh! Shmuely's named his son Asher! Like my father! Like *our* father! Oh!"

She buried her face in Paloma's shoulder.

There were a few more prayers and pronouncements, the name "Asher Zelig" surfacing from time to time. Serach kept her face glued to Paloma's shoulder for most of that segment, but eventually she gathered herself together yet again and began tugging at Paloma's arm.

"Okay. Now it really is over. Beile and her husband will carry the baby back to Ruchel. And then everyone will march into the Social Hall to eat. And you and I will take advantage of their total focus on the food to fly away. Okay? Okay. Nod to Frayda, Paloma, and let's go!"

Paloma nodded as ordered and then she and Serach scuttled past everyone else and down the stairs to the Social Hall where the men had already begun heading for the bagels.

"Come on, Paloma! We need to leave the premises before anyone sees us!"

Okay, Shmuely, here comes your sister! In plain view. Turn around to catch her eye before she leaves. And then give her that smile you promised!

Shmuely however, was enmeshed in fervent conversation with a group of men at the far wall—his back firmly turned toward the food tables and the women.

Shmuely! Turn around! Over here!

Paloma and Serach were halfway to the door when Serach—blissfully oblivious to Shmuely's breach of promise—suddenly spun toward Paloma, threw her arms around her and gave her cheek the sweetest kiss it had ever received.

"Oh, Paloma! Thank you! Thank you for making me come. And thank you for orchestrating everything. I don't know exactly what you did—or how—but I do know that it's all because of you that things have worked out the way they have. May *Ha-Shem* bless you for it!"

It was at that point that Shmuely finally snuck a surreptitious look in their direction. And felt a cannon ball hit him right in the gut.

It was a bigger feeling—an even more overwhelming feeling—than he had experienced while watching his newborn son become a member of the covenant. He had never in all his life wanted anything more than to be that *Spanish Woman* at that particular moment. He had never, in all his life, wanted anything more than to feel Serach's warm embrace and that innocent, grateful kiss on his own cheek. Paralyzed, he watched as the two women turned away and began marching to the door, arm in arm.

Serach is going to walk out of the shul! And I'm going back to Jerusalem on Sunday and will never see her again.

His first instinct was to seek comfort within the reliable fortress of his fellow black hats. But then he felt a desire even stronger than that.

He wanted to hold his son.

In the week since Asher's birth, he had discovered a baby's near-magical power to bring things into perspective—to provide an ineffable sense of solace and fulfillment. He turned his back on the men and strode across the room to where Ruchel was holding court with little Asher clasped tightly to her breast.

"Ruchel, I'd like to take Asher for a moment."

Ruchel beamed. Shmuely had become so much more attentive in recent months. When she first left Jerusalem for her sister's house, he'd started calling her every day. And what a good father he was turning out to be—always wanting to cuddle with his son!

Pleased and triumphant, she handed the baby over to her husband and—with a remarkable degree of naturalness—Shmuely drew him close.

He peeked over to Serach one last time to note her making her way steadily forward, while Paloma remained riveted in place, staring directly at him with rage in her eyes. He lowered his face as she spun back again to Serach and began steering her briskly out the door.

"Paloma! Please stop pushing me! We don't have to go so fast—I'm getting a stitch in my side. And why do you look so murderous? It was a wonderful *bris*. Everything was just right."

Paloma said nothing. How could she explain how Shmuely had copped out yet again? And why on earth should she slow down? She wanted to put miles and miles between Serach and that shifty, shameless young man.

"Paloma—please stop for a moment! I want—I want to take one last look back at the *shul*."

Paloma finally relented but refused to turn around herself.

Which is why it was Serach who first caught sight of the wildly flapping figure approaching them at top speed—black coattails flying, clumsy shoes stumbling, one arm lifted to his hat and the other clutched firmly around a tiny blue and white wrapped bundle

"Wait! Serach! Wait! Wait for me! Wait!"

Serach held her breath.

"I only have a minute!" Shmuely panted as he slammed to a halt in front of the two women. "I told them that I would be right back. But… but…."

He finally looked Serach straight in the face.

"But I wanted… I needed…."

He gestured to the baby and Serach reached out and took him into her arms.

And Paloma stepped aside.

"His name is Asher," Shmuely concluded.

"I know," Serach whispered. "I know. And may *Ha-Shem* bless you for that."

Serach brought Asher to her shoulder and found that he fit exactly between that shoulder and her embracing arm. She brought her face down to his warm, soft head and felt the silkiness of his hair against her cheek.

"Tatteleh!" she murmured against his fragrant scalp. "Tatteleh!"

She then looked back at Shmuely. He was standing perfectly straight—like a real adult man—and a stream of tears was descending steadily into his scraggly beard.

But Serach wasn't crying. She was smiling.

She reached over and tugged at Shmuely's sleeve.

"Tatteleh," she said to him. "Tatteleh."

GLOSSARY

a bi gezunt .... everything is healthy, everything is okay
Abuela .... grandmother
¡Adelantamos-El Bronx! .... Onward—The Bronx!
Adonai... the Lord
Akeres Ha-Bayes .... the foundation of the home
Anteojitos .... little glasses. Literally: "little in front of the eyes"
apikoris, apikorsim .... apostate, apostates
Avraham .... Abraham
BVM .... Blessed Virgin Mary
bandoneón .... a concertina popular in Argentina and Uruguay
Baruch Ha-Shem......... Praised be God (literally: "praised be the name")
¡basta! .... enough!
batá .... a double-headed drum shaped like an hourglass with one end larger than the other
Beit Shel Kavod... House of Dignity
Bijoux de Judea... Jewels of Judea
bimah .... the podium or platform in a synagogue from which the Torah and Prophets are read.
b'nei mitzvah..................... plural of "bar mitzvah"—the celebration of a boy's entry into full religious observance.
Bösendorfer .... a make of grand piano
bris .... ritual circumcision
buen provecho......................... enjoy your meal (literally: "good benefit")
buenas tardes .... good afternoon, good evening (until nightfall)
bupkes .... nothing
¡cálmate! .... calm down!
Candombe .... a style of music and dance brought to Latin America by enslaved Africans.
¡carajo! .... damn it!
cannoli .... Italian pastries filled with ricotta cheese, chocolate and candied fruit.
carniceria .... butcher shop
challah .... the special—generally-braided—bread that is eaten on the *Shabbos.*

chas v'cholileh ....God forbid
cholent ....a stew made on Friday afternoon, kept warm and eaten the next day for lunch
chusma, pura chusma .... vulgar, trashy
compos mentis .... sane
daven, davening, daveners ....to pray, praying, those who pray.
Derekh ha-Emet.. the way of truth
¡Dios guarde!...God forbid!
¡Dios mio!... my God!
Eitz Chaim Walk-In Clinic ....Tree of Life Walk-In Clinic
El Al ....Israel's national airline
embouchure ....the way wind instrument players hold their lips around their instruments
"es poco" .... literally: "is little" generally used to convey: "that doesn't even begin to say it."
enano..dwarf
extraordinaria... extraordinary
eyl zikh tsu...hurry up!
farmisht.. befuddled
ferkakte .... idiotic
flan de caramel............popular Latin dessert (literally: "caramel custard")
frum..religiously observant
geyn kaput ....all over, all finished
glatt kosher....................processed under the strictest Jewish dietary laws
Gordito ....Little Fatty
goy, goyishe.. a non-Jew, non-Jewish
halacha, halachic............................... Jewish law, approved by Jewish law.
Haredi .... a fervently observant Orthodox Jew
Ha-Shem...God (literally: "The Name")
Hermana, Hermanita............ Sister, Little Sister—a term of endearment
Hermano...Brother
Ideas Libres, Palabras Libres Bookstore .... Free Ideas, Free Words Bookstore
illui .... a young Torah and Talmudic prodigy or genius
inmediatamente .... immediately

Kaddish (Mourners' Kaddish) .... central element of Jewish service (version said by mourners)
kasher, kashering.............................. the act of making something kosher.
kashrut ....the set of laws governing all aspects of food and eating
kenehora ....keep away the evil eye
Keter Zahav Jewelry... Crown of Gold Jewelry
kichel.. small egg pastry shaped like a bowtie
Kiddush ....blessing said over wine to sanctify the *Shabbos*/ small meal following a service
k'lal Yisroel...all of Israel, all Jews
kosher.................................food or premises in compliance with the laws of kashrut. Informally: "okay"
kreplach .... a Jewish filled dumpling
Kristallnacht...November 9, 1938, when Nazis torched Jewish synagogues and murdered Jews
kvell, kvelling ....taking pleasure in family or in an achievement
kvetch.. complain

La Cumparsita ....famous Uruguayan tango (literally: a group wearing costumes and masks)
La Hormiga Colorada...The Red Ant
La Piranha Salvadoreña...the Salvadoran Piranha
Las Catorce. ....the fourteen families that held control/still hold control of El Salvador.
Las Delicias de Hunts Point.............................The Delights of Hunts Point
Las Marianas "Stars of the Sea." (Mariana is also a plucky Latin cartoon character)
lashon hara ....gossip
locura... craziness
Los Milagros Auto Repair Shop................The Miracles Auto Repair Shop
machatunim........................."co-in-laws"—the parents of a child's spouse
malditos ....bad people (literally: cursed ones)
maggid (shiur)...teacher (of Talmud)
mandelbrot ....Jewish cookie made with almonds
maté...................hot caffeinated drink enjoyed in Argentina and Uruguay

meine Kaiserin .... my empress
mensch .... a person of integrity, a good person
meshugas .... nuttiness
meshugge .... nutty
metzitzah b'peh .... orally suctioning the blood in a ritual circumcision
mezuzah .... a parchment with specific Torah verses, encased and affixed the doorpost
mi casa es su casa. .... my home is your home
mijo, mijos .... my son, my sons (can be a term of affection)
mijita .... my little girl (definitely a term of affection)
minyan .... the ten Jews (ten men, in Orthodox Judaism) that must be present for certain prayers or certain parts of the service to be conducted.
Mishna .... the first major written collection of Jewish oral traditions
mitz kop arop .... upside down
mitzvah, mitzvoth. literally: commandment(s); informally: good deed(s)
mohel. .... the rabbi who performs a ritual circumcision
muchacha, muchachita .... girl, little girl
mucho gusto .... glad to meet you (literally: "great pleasure")
¡muevete! .... move it!
Mujeres en La Lucha .... Women in the Battle
nada .... nothing
narishkeit .... foolishness
nebechdik .... pathetic
Negrito .... Little Blackie
Nican Mopohua .... "Here it is Told," a tract written in 1649 in the Nahuatl language by Luis Laso de la Vega, describing the miracles performed by the Virgin of Guadalupe
niddah .... the monthly twelve days when married couples are forbidden to have sexual relations.
nu? .... so?
onen (onenet) .... man (woman) in the period between the death and the burial of a close relative
Papito .... Father, Little Father—a term of endearment
pendejo .... schmuck—literally: "pubic hair"
Pesach .... the Hebrew term for the holiday of Passover

picadillo de carne............................Latin dish of chopped beef with olives and raisins

pièce de résistance.. masterpiece, main event

piel canela ....cinnamon skin

ojos negros piel canela que me llegan a desesperar .... black eyes, cinnamon skin that drive me to desperation.

Pietà........... a depiction of the Virgin Mary cradling the dead body of Jesus

Pirkei Avoth...a compilation of ethical teachings from the Rabbinic Jewish tradition

platano(s) ....plantain(s) (a tropical fruit, like a banana but that requires cooking)

pobrecito .... a poor little thing

que Dios te lo pague.. may God repay you

¿que te pasa?..what's wrong?

queque de tres leches............. popular Latin dessert (literally "three milks cake")

querido/a.. dear

Ramot Alon....................................Oak Tree Heights, a neighborhood to the north of East Jerusalem

Rav ....Hebrew term for rabbi and the honorific used before that rabbi's name

Rebbetzin ....the wife of a rabbi

Rivka .... Rebecca

Rosh Hashanah ....Jewish New Year—the first of the High Holy Days

Ruchel .... Rachel

rugelach..small Jewish rolled pastry generally containing cinnamon, nuts, raisins or chocolate.

Sabra....................................... a Jew born in Israel (literally: a prickly pear)

salud, amor, pesetas, tiempo para gozarlos—y apetito........ health, love, money, time to enjoy them—and appetite

schmaltz..chicken fat (literally)

schmuck.. bad person (literally: "penis")

Shabbos ....the Jewish Sabbath: a day of strictly regulated rest and prayer

Sha'arei Hesed.................................... a neighborhood in Jerusalem (literally: "Gates of Mercy")

shanda .... shame
shidduch .... literally: Jewish arranged marriage; informally: other important matches
shiva, sitting shiva ....the Jewish seven-day mourning period for a close relative
shlep ....to lug oneself or something else.
shmutzik ....dirty, grimy
shtetl ....a small Jewish town in Eastern Europe
sukkat sh'lomecha .... canopy of peace
Shavuos...................................a major Jewish commemorating God's giving the Law (the Torah) to the Israelites
shul ....synagogue
shvach .... weak
si se quede el infinito sin estrellas.. if the infinite were left without stars
Talmud... a central text of Rabbinic Judaism
Talmud Bavli............ the Talmud compiled during the Babylonian Exile.
Tatteh..Father, Dad
Tatteleh.......................................Little father—a term of endearment
tchotchkes .... knickknacks
Tiferes Israel ....Beauty/Compassion of Israel
Torah.. the scrolls containing the first five books of the Jewish Bible
Torah Ark...................................... the ornamental chamber in which the Torah scrolls are housed
Tractate Pesachim.......................the volumes of the Talmud that concern the observance of Passover
trayf ....not kosher
tsuris .... heartache, problems
Tu Belleza... Your Beauty
vamos .... let's go
verklempt.. overcome with emotion
vos s aroyf?... what's with you?
Valses Poeticos y Sentimentales .... piano work by Enrique Granados
Ya-akov..Jacob
yarmulke .... Jewish skull cap

yahrzeit.. the anniversary of someone's death, especially of a parent
yeshiva.. Jewish school
Yeshiva Derekh ha-Emet .... Yeshiva Way of the Truth
yichus .... family reputation
Yitzchak.. Isaac
Yom Kippur.. the High Holy Day of Repentance
Yosef...Joseph

ACKNOWLEDGEMENTS

It takes many hands to produce a book.

My friends and family endured years of ruminations about character, plot and setting with admirable patience—while contributing an ongoing stream of pithy details, life-saving *caveats* and much-appreciated words of encouragement. Several read the evolving manuscript cover to cover—posing astute questions and suggesting vital changes and corrections. A few undertook a practically Talmudic line-by-line analysis and critique.

My love and gratitude to you all.

I relied on Rabbi Lewis Warshauer for his guidance (and wit) on matters of Jewish observance, wine, art, Jerusalem architecture and Yiddish. Andrew McDonough and Elba Montalvo kindly corrected my inventive Spanish. Gladys Carrión and Hector Soto provided knowledgeable, inspired counsel on the workings of the criminal justice system. A special shout out to Jim Holmes for introducing me to the Basilica of the Annunciation.

Any factual or conceptual errors regarding any of those matters are mine alone.

Joan, my publisher—your impeccable artistic stewardship brought the manuscript across the finish line.

Warm thanks to Javier Perez, my publicist, for helping me get the word out.

Tony—you were my rock from start to finish, providing the feedback of a superb fellow writer while sustaining me with unconditional support.

And Aguica—you bequeathed me the means, the fire and the grit. The final *gracias* goes to you.

About the Author

S.W. Leicher grew up in the Bronx in a bi-cultural (Latina and Jewish) home. She moved to Manhattan after graduate school and raised her family on the Upper West Side, where she still lives with her husband and two black cats. When not dreaming up fiction, she writes about social justice issues for nonprofit organizations.

www.swleicher.com